Northern Blood

Northern Wolf Series
Book Three

Daniel Greene

For my Mother - for showing us that hard work, dedication, and determination are the path to success, and that no one, not even the strongest among us, makes it alone. Thank you for the unending support.

Chapter One

April 29, 1864
Libby Prison, Richmond, Virginia

"Roll 'em!" Major Olmsted called out in the stinking night air.

With heavy sighs and disrupted snores, the imprisoned Union officers began the communal shift in sleeping positions like a herd of entrapped cattle.

The rotation of bodies was a labored one. The men would have to more or less all roll over at the same time, but it resembled more an old man tossing in his bed by the moonlight, achy and slow, trying to steal comfort wherever possible. Every man was wedged into the others like an enormous drawer filled with spoons all facing the same way, almost two hundred men moving at once.

Rats squeaked in the corners, sounding like tittering children, and a man awoke from a nightmare with a call for his mother. One man coughed and another cursed the men nearby for the stench.

Libby Prison was never meant to hold men. Early in the war, the Confederate government had a surplus of prisoners and nowhere to put them so they modified a chandlery on the embankments of the James River to store them. But there was a problem. Even if they wanted to stock the warehouse with them, it was never meant to keep this many.

The stink of two hundred unwashed men always seemed to hang in the air longer when they all moved at once; it smelled as if they lived inside an overflowing latrine and this was only one of six giant rooms.

Wolf tried to adjust onto his shoulder then scratched at his snarled beard with his index finger to avoid using his thumb. The weight of an arm draped over him from behind, stinging and rubbing the raw skin on his back, making him cringe.

"Back off, Roberts." He jerked his shoulder, and his friend's hand fell around Wolf's waist. He ignored it. This was the way they all slept every night. Together. In the winter, the only way to stay warm was by soaking in the scant body heat from the man beside you.

The back of the head in front of him was snowy white in the darkness. With a slap of his cheeks, the officer ahead of Wolf passed gas in his direction, forcing him to gulp down the fetid odor with a grit of his teeth and a wrinkle of his nose.

Using the remaining meat of his arm as a makeshift pillow, he tried to get comfortable. It was nearly impossible to sleep on his back with the freshly branded skin.

Although summer had come for Richmond, the nights were still cool despite the crowded men. Cold air would flow through the open windows in gusting breezes. It was a bittersweet feeling in the night: on one hand, it wiped away the stench but on the other chilled the men clothed in tatters. Wolf tightened his colonel's coat around his body, snuggling into the collar as much to escape Reynolds's flatulence as the cold.

Reynolds began to snore to the tune of an overworked sawmill. Despite the noise, Wolf found himself dozing back off into a dusky sleep until Major Olmsted was giving the call of reveille.

The thickly bearded major stood near a far wall next to the willowy Lieutenant Elm. The young Lieutenant from the 1st Maine cleared his throat, spit, and then began singing the bugle call in a loud baritone voice. "Ba-ba-bup-ba-da-bup-bup,bup-ba-da-bup-bup,bup-ba-da-bup-bup-baa-ba." They begrudgingly awakened as he continued to sing.

Discipline, duties, and routine kept the captured Union officers sane during their confinement to the second floor of the prison that they never could leave even for a breath of fresh air. A man didn't know the depth of his need for the outdoors until he was deprived of it. Then stick him in an overcrowded room with one latrine and no way out and watch him squirm as it slowly maddens him.

Inch by inch the confinement eats away at his soul until nothing remains but a husk of a man. Then one day he voluntarily steps out in front of one of the open windows, providing the bored as hell Confederate guards below some target practice. Wolf had seen it done.

A broken captain from the 34th Indiana just stood one day, basking in the fishy breeze from the James River docks. The sunlight shone on his face, making him glow, and despite the calls from his comrades to return to the safety of the interior, he basked in it.

His friends called to him. "Please, Joseph, come back."

"They'll do it, Joe. Don't give the rebs the satisfaction."

Wolf and Roberts could only watch. They knew the captain ushered in his own death at the hand of a rebel sharpshooter who would end in it all with lead and smoke. The men around him ducked, covering their heads, calling to him to lay down.

It only took one shot. The crack of a rifled musket boomed below, echoing off the walls of the warehouses. The bullet knocked the captain's head backward. He collapsed almost peacefully, a Minié ball rattling the insides of his skull.

Today, the men went about their morning routines. Those that had toothbrushes, a most lucrative luxury of only the luckiest, brushed their teeth. Others went to prepare food. Clusters of men sat in semicircles trading smudged newspapers that had already been read by hundreds of eager officers, grasping for any bit of information they could find.

A few played cards and others went about searching for rats to exterminate, or if the rodents were substantial enough, add them to whatever rations were available for the day.

Furniture was sparse and cherished among the men. The few stools and tables they used had been crafted from old crates.

Roberts scratched his head, picking at an infestation of lice that had taken residence upon his scalp. With no good way to bathe, the lice colonized the filthy prisoners with impunity. "How'd you sleep?"

"About as good as you could expect in this hellhole."

"I didn't sleep bad. Had a dream about Rosie last night." A roguish grin crossed Roberts's boyish cheeks.

"Not while you held me. Tell me it was when you were turned to the other side."

Roberts's grin didn't subside. "We're pals, right? Ain't no shame in it."

Wolf sighed, pushing himself to his feet. He shook his arms, trying to loosen the stiffness from them. "Better than Reynolds's farts." He locked hands with Roberts and helped him upright.

They weaved through the too-sick-and-tired-to-stand Union officers. The longer they'd been imprisoned, the worse off the captives were. Over seven weeks of quarter rations combined with his battered body and Wolf felt it too. He felt beaten. Not defeated, but ground down like a knife sharpened too many times. Colonel Dahlgren's slender coat was starting to fit better by the day over Wolf's once thick shoulders.

Wolf and Roberts waded through the sea of dirty blue prisoners toward a group of twenty waiting near the locked prison door. The sun hadn't crept through the windows casting the prisoners in dim shadows. They were all part of the first shift of prisoners to cook meals for their room and were known simply as the "mess squad."

Lieutenant Colonel James Sanderson was in charge of the kitchen operations for the entire prison and had organized the men into mess squads. Each squad was entrusted with the rations for their room. However, that didn't matter much when they had to scrape together whatever they could.

A winding crank was winched on the other side of the door. After the escape almost three months ago, a retractable staircase had been installed, thus preventing the prisoners from leaving the upper floors at night. With a loud thump, the stairs settled on the floor below.

Heavy footsteps echoed upwards like a man nailing boards with the heel of his boot. The door vibrated beneath a meaty fist. "Get back," Wolf said quietly. The mess squad took an uneasy rearward step. If they crowded the door too close, they risked a beating.

The jangle of keys sounded on the other side. Then the soft splat of tobacco juice hit the floorboards. The door jerked open. If a man was too close, it would have bopped his skull.

A mountainous tangle-bearded man stuck his head through the doorway. "Get back, rats. Get back." His yellow-toothed smile was as cruel as he was large. The guard opened the door wide, stepping inside. A thick hand held a long cudgel, and he tapped it in his other palm. He wore a soiled gray private's infantry jacket. It was open, revealing a brown shirt that masked its stains. Matted chest hair like a full-grown grizzly bear, crept from underneath. His trousers were brown, and a long dagger dangled from his belt.

The dagger was a heavy double-sided blade. Wolf recognized it instantly because it had once been his. He'd stolen it from a captain in Cobb's Legion. In turn it was stolen from Wolf during his capture. Now the cruel guard the prisoners only knew as Griff carried the fine weapon.

"Smells like a dung heap fell into a sewer," Griff said. His dark eyes held a crude intelligence. He knew enough to vary his abuse of the men.

"Stinkin' rats." He was joined by another hulking guard. His eyes held a diminished glow of even less intellect than his partner, but Hank was equally as ruthless and in every way Griff's equal in size and strength. Both men were large enough to make Wolf question his ability to take them down one on one. Yet he would relish a go with either of the guards.

"Nice and slow, stinkies," Hank said, waving them by with his baton.

The Union prisoner mess squad filed past the men one at a time. Hank touched each man with his club. It was a slight tap, more of a warning than anything else. Made the men feel like children in the schoolhouse. He supposed that was the point, ultimate emasculating control.

Roberts walked past with his head hunched and Wolf hurriedly followed, trying to not be noticed. The stick slapped Wolf's chest, pressing in the center and halting him.

"I see you, Colonel." Hank licked his blubbery lips. "You got something tricky in you." He cocked his head to the side.

Griff leaned in on Wolf's other side. His breath smelled like sour beer mixed with an old spittoon that hadn't been cleaned in twelve years. "No ideas out of you." His stick shifted beneath Wolf's chin, lifting it roughly upward. "You healed up pretty nice. Be a shame if we had to teach you another lesson."

"I ain't looking for trouble," Wolf grunted.

"No one looks for it," Griff said. "But somehow we find it." He shoved Wolf with a fist and banged him into the stairwell, but he managed to keep on his feet. His bad leg struggled under the assault. The lieutenant behind him took a step back and all of the officers cast their eyes down.

Wolf stood back up straight, keeping his eyes forward.

"I always remember a face. Especially an ugly one like yours," Griff said. "Let me see your hands."

Praying to God the man didn't take a swing at them, Wolf held out his hands in front of his chest. The nails atop his thumbs were cracked and yellow, having been drilled to relieve the pressure from where they'd been crushed by Captain Marshall Payne during his interrogation. Over the past seven weeks, they'd mostly healed, his itchy and broken fingers shrinking back down to a more normal if still swollen size.

"How's them thumbs?"

Wolf's hands shook a bit.

Griff rested his stick along the tops of Wolf's hands, letting him bear its weight. "Maybe Payne will come back? Ask a few more questions." He watched Wolf from the side, judging the fear and tension in his demeanor. He leaned closer to his ear, calmly speaking like he would to a calf before putting him under the knife. "Or maybe I can ask a few questions, huh? How would that be?"

"I don't got nothing to say."

Griff stood back. "I bet you don't. Nothing worth a damn." Wielding his stick, he pushed Wolf off balance again. "Get on out of here, you ugly son of a bitch."

Wolf propped himself along the stairwell down the steps. The officers ahead of him had already rounded the corner to the kitchen.

"Well, he ain't running nowhere," Hank said with a laugh.

Wolf ignored his captors, hurrying before they started after him again. To be beaten in the morning was rare but not unheard of. He wouldn't put it past the guards to go after a man. Nothing was off limits under the savage rule of the prison's commanding officer, Lieutenant Erasmus Ross. In fact, all of it seemed condoned if not encouraged.

Near the bottom of the stairs stood another couple of guards. Gray uniformed with white and blue shirts underneath, each wore a wide-brimmed hat. One smoked a cigar; the other had a huge bulge in his lower lip. The door to the city street hung open behind them, mocking Wolf's imprisonment.

A bird chirped. Men called out to one another. Horse-drawn carts clopped by. A group of slaves sang as they unloaded cargo on the docks. The guards were so confident that the prisoners wouldn't run, they left the door open to the outside.

Across the street sat the barracks for the other guards not on duty. Smoke drifted from campfires. Still more guards rested near street corners waiting for a captive to make an appearance by a window.

Wolf turned the corner passing more guards at desks, an area for sick prisoners, a few offices for the Confederate officers, and a communal kitchen.

As the first mess squad to enter the kitchen, the men lit fires in the four stoves. A box of daily rations was resting atop a stove and filled with bags of cornmeal and flour and maybe a sweet potato hidden in there. No meat. The meat rations had stopped before Wolf and Roberts had been captured.

The other officers were already starting the process of mixing the meal with water and baking dense flat breads.

Being in the kitchen while they cooked the bread was its own special type of torture. Every man had no choice but to indulge in the delicious smell while it became food for the others. It was a living nightmare of hunger-driven fantasies. The heat from the stoves was welcome now, but the other officers made sure to remind them that in the summer they would suffer.

Wolf and Roberts were at the end of the line, having been deemed too new to properly respect the actual cooking. As the bread was removed and stacked, dirty pots and pans came their way. They would scrub the scalding pans and rotate them back over for use or prep them for the next group, restocking them atop the stoves.

Roberts took charred and burnt bread, scraping the bottom of each pan with his blackened fingernails for a little extra to eat. Wolf did the same but was forced to scrub the pans with his knuckles to avoid using his damaged thumbs. The action left his knuckles chafed and raw.

Sanderson stuck his head inside the kitchen. His gray beard was streaked with black and he had cold brown eyes. "Next shift is a'clamoring up there. Are you men almost finished?"

"Yes, sir," Captain Harold Reynolds said. Their mess squad leader was the same man who had helped treat Wolf after his interrogation. The white-haired surgeon from the 5th Iowa Volunteer Infantry Regiment bent over, eyeing inside a stove. "Last one's just finishing."

"Very good. We shouldn't keep the men waiting. A hungry man is a desperate man."

"Aren't they," came a voice from the hall. The men peered over their shoulders. They knew that shrewd voice anywhere.

Sanderson bowed his head speaking in deference. "Lieutenant Ross, sir."

A short man in a gray uniform and glasses poked his head inside the kitchen with leisure. His eyes quickly counted the men, taking stock of their faces. He was the commanding officer and a former clerk of the prison. He was as cruel as he was calculating, always counting the prisoners. "I trust that today's rations will be enough?" he asked of Sanderson. Ross eyed him, almost daring him to say the truth about its inadequacies.

"Of course, Lieutenant. We won't complain," Sanderson said.

"I expect that you won't," Ross said. His eyes shifted back to the men in the kitchen. "Remember it can always get worse." He reached inside the room and broke off a piece of corn bread between his fingers.

The officers breathed heavily at this. Hungry eyes ate at the man in quiet rage, but they would never dare show it for fear of violent retribution. All they could do was watch in silence.

Ross smiled to himself, studying the yellowish crumbly bread. He shoved some in his mouth, tonguing it apart. He blinked and swallowed. Turning his head, he violently spat and tossed the rest of the bread to the side.

Every single man ogled the bread with wanton gluttonous greed. That was someone's morning ration, if not perhaps two men's, and this man flung it on the ground while the others starved around him.

"I would say stick to fighting because you men really are terrible cooks, but you're here, so perhaps something else entirely. Sanderson, you used to work for a hotel at one point?"

Sanderson's jaw tightened. "I did."

"Perhaps you'll have a future when the war is over."

"Perhaps, sir."

The prisoners seethed. Wolf clenched his jaw and shifted his eyes toward the floor to keep from killing the man.

Ross spit again. "Christ, that's terrible." He took the sole of his shoe and ground the bread into the grain of the wood. "A rat wouldn't touch the stuff. Plain awful."

He twisted his head to the side, and Wolf could feel Ross's eyes boring into him. "Colonel, do you have something to say?"

The only indication of his irritation was a blink. He had plenty to say to Ross, starting with a punch to the face and ending with a knife in the belly. This disgusting human reveled in the prisoners' torture and mistreatment like it was an everyday pastime. He deserved the most heinous of deaths, and if Wolf took a dozen bullets to the heart after he crushed the life from this evil little man, it would be worth every shot. Hell, if they wanted to put bullets in every single one of them, it would still be worth obliterating this man out of existence. He could think of no man on earth who deserved death more.

Wolf dipped his head and stared from beneath his brow. "No, sir."

"Do not mock me. You have something to say, don't you?"

The air grew tighter in his chest. *Oh, I have something to say to you. You pigheaded, gopher-brained, dickless, bloody stinkin' cunt.* But no such words rolled off his tongue. Only a simple. "No, sir."

Ross took a step closer, cocking his head to the side. "Suppose Captain Payne took all your fight. A pity." He turned and left the room. Roberts knelt on the floor, chipping at the crushed bread with his jagged black fingernails.

Sanderson observed him with indifference. "You men finish up."

Roberts stood with his flattened prize. "Ain't bad enough to eat." He shoved it in his pocket with a pat.

***

The Union officers ate their meager rations and spent the day confined to their floor. Before the escape a few months prior, the men could travel from room to room. Now they'd sealed the doorways. The prisoners would slip notes and papers underneath, but everything was harder than it had been.

In the afternoon, they repeated the process of cooking food. And with the encroaching darkness, the men all sat on the floor listening to the *Libby Chronicle*, a weekly rendition of the happenings outside and inside the prison. Everyone would stop what they were doing to hear what the newspaper said.

"You think anyone's coming for us? Like we did with Kill-Cavalry?" Roberts asked.

"No, I don't."

"Why not?"

Wolf gave his friend a curt glance. "'Cause it didn't work. Now be quiet. Beaudry's gonna talk."

"Hear ye, hear ye!" Beaudry shouted, holding a newspaper. He was a handsome man with a theatrical flair to him. He had a short mustache and a comb-over. His blue captain's jacket hung open. He waved a red handkerchief at the men. "Come hither and let me tell you a tale." He snapped the handkerchief at a man in the front. "Do not dither or you will miss out on the most privy of gossip." He threw the handkerchief over the top of his head like a woman's veil and his voice raised an octave. "Do I have your attention now, gentlemen?"

The men laughed. "Take it off!" said a voice in the back. More men chuckled and smiled. It was odd hearing merriment in a place like this, but it eased the men's souls as they grasped onto a fraction of their humanity.

Beaudry walked along the wall, shaking his behind with every step, batting his eyelashes at the crowd. He waved his hand with a limp wrist. Another officer jumped up from the congregation and took him by the hand, spinning him around like they were dancing a waltz.

The crowd roared with approval. After the officer dipped him and placed him upright, he planted a big kiss on his cheek and took his seat again to the laughter of prisoners. It was a tired mirth but still a lantern of joy in their cavern of despair.

"Very well, my brave men." He pointed a finger out at all of them. "Now, nobody get any ideas, okay? I'm a married man!"

More laughter echoed from weary throats.

Beaudry tucked the handkerchief into his coat pocket. "We have much news this week. I'm going to need all of you who haven't paid for this show to go on ahead and cough up the fee."

A fellow officer rose from the crowd, using his hat to panhandle the others. Boos pummeled him until he sat down.

"Not all bad. Not all good. But it's free." He shrugged his shoulders. "Who knows?" Holding a sheet of paper out, he added, "Maybe someday I'll get paid for this."

He licked his lips. "Let's see here. Captain Hitchcock is looking for any man alive that can beat him at a game of chess. He sits over in the east side river corner of the room." Beaudry pointed over. "Every day. Can one of you for the love of God beat him? Seriously, so I can stop making this announcement." He lifted his eyebrows then glanced at the paper again. "Ahh, let's see. Captain Reynolds and Major Olmsted will be doing their daily riddle contest over near the west end. And Lieutenant Hector is looking for someone to best him at a wrestling match. Be aware. He is quite hairy."

A once beastly man stood and removed his shirt in one movement, revealing a body covered with coarse black hair. "Give me your best shot." He pounded his chest with a fist.

"Enticing," Beaudry said with a twist of his head to the side. The men chuckled and Hector took a seat. The master of prison ceremony flipped his paper over. "Ahh, yes, Colonel Federico Cavada's Spanish course is full."

The officers sighed in disappointment.

"What we need Spanish for anyway?" Roberts asked quietly. "I can hardly speak English."

"Not everyone speaks English." Wolf had been attending. "You know if you stick with the Army, you never know where we might go. What if you got sent down to Old Mexico? Or Argentina? Cuba? Then what?"

"I suppose I'd shoot them like I shoot Southerners."

Wolf snorted, "I suppose you would."

"Suppose you would too."

"Suppose I would."

"So what you need to talk like 'em for then?"

"I dunno. To understand 'em."

"Hmm."

Beaudry continued speaking. "On the war front, Major General Ulysses S. Grant has been named as head of all Union Armies."

The officers smiled at one another. Backs were clapped. A few of the men shook their heads in dismay and disgust. Everyone had their favorite generals they'd served under.

"He is expected to shatter the Southern Cause by the year's end."

This led to a cheer from all the men and a round of applause.

"My brave men, that is all!" Beaudry gave them all a sweeping bow with arms extended, a true entertainer relishing his time in front of a crowd. The officers stood chatting excitedly with one another for this was the first time they'd had any true hope since Wolf's capture.

"You think this Grant is the one?" Roberts asked.

"I dunno. The officers seem to think he's got a shot."

"Maybe we'll be home by Christmas?"

Wolf gripped his friend by the shoulder. "We can only hope." They clapped hands with one another and hugged.

A rousing rendition of "Yankee Doodle" filled the room from wall to wall, ceiling to floor, every word fortified with battered patriotic spirit. The officers wrapped arms around one another's shoulders.

Wolf and Roberts sang with the rest. Their merrymaking would only last so long. Eventually Griff and Hank would pound up the stairs and beat them until the prisoners stopped.

Spirits and each other were all the men had, and once their spirits broke, they would soon succumb to the deadly elements and die.

A strong hand squeezed Wolf's shoulder. He turned to see Beaudry standing there. His uniform was relatively clean, and despite all the filthy men around them, Wolf could swear the man carried no odor, almost as if he had bathed, making him by far the best smelling man in the room.

The officers continued to sing, and the yells and threats of violence traveled from the guards below.

"The snow goose flies north before summer."

Wolf's brow creased. "Excuse me? You practicing for Reynolds's riddles?"

The flamboyant man flapped his arms. "When the weather warms, geese go north. Perhaps even tonight."

Roberts leaned in next to Wolf and yelled over the din. "Why's he talking about flying birds?"

Beaudry flashed a smile and Wolf gulped. Van Lew hadn't lied. She'd meant every word. "I bid you, birdies, Godspeed." Beaudry gave them a short bow and mingled through the crowd singing along.

"What's all that flying around talk?"

Wolf wanted to cry, but then again, he wanted to roar like a beast emerging from the depths of a jungle. Freedom rested on the mere midnight toll of the clock. He gave Roberts a wide grin and gripped his shoulders. "Tonight we escape."

Chapter Two

April 29, 1864
Richmond, Virginia

Seamus MacAllister drank the whiskey like it was the finest of liquors, knowing full well the rancid drink was probably made in the barkeep's basement despite the bottles expensive label. Either way, he loved the burn of the alcohol down his gullet.

Thumping the glass back on the bar, he flexed a gnarled hand that had been broken more times than he could count. Mostly from punching in another man's skull.

He was relatively short with broad shoulders and a bald head he kept silky smooth with regular shaves. One of his ears stuck out farther than its mate where it had been almost bitten off by a rabid Irishman over a game of cards. A knife across the belly calmed the wild man down.

Seamus bore no facial hair despite the custom of the time. Instead crisscrossing scars from blades decorated his broad-jawed face and body, tattoos of his countless fights.

Sawdust littered the floor along with the puke from last night's patrons and spilt liquor and a couple of questionable puddles that were probably piss. The Tavern as the locals called it had no other name. It sat near the row of tobacco warehouses and was popular with sailors and dockworkers alike. It was also frequented by other local working-class folk but not slaves or coloreds.

"Another," he breathed. His stomach wanted to reverse the alcohol's current trajectory, but he swallowed, keeping it down.

The barkeep stood expectantly, waiting for payment.

Seamus dipped his hand into his pocket and removed a greenback, slipping it over the counter. "Leave the bottle."

Snatching the bill, the keep eyed him for a moment. "That's not enough."

With a flash of his hand, Seamus snatched his coat, pulling the man closer. "For that?" he gestured with his head.

"For that, it's double," the keep said. His mustache fluttered in fear and anger.

Seamus licked his lips. "You mean for this shit you're cutting with water out back? We talkin' about the same thing?"

The keep's eyes enlarged, and his voice shook. "The prices went up. The war."

A typical and pathetic alibi that every shop owner wore like a badge of honor. The war. It was an opportunity to overcharge and underserve every resident of the city, something that irritated a working man like Seamus, but his work offered him a certain leverage. Seamus tongued his lower lip. "Listen here, Mr. Harris, we been turnin' a blind eye to the crates you bring in at night. You know, the ones you ain't paying taxes on on account of the war. The ones no one is supposed to know about."

The keep's cheeks quivered. "I don't know what you're talking about."

Seamus released the keep and used his other hand to slam his face into the bar top. He was rewarded with a nice little crunch. A drunk in the corner looked up, hiccuped, and laid a greasy head back on his table. Seamus's partner grinned in amusement.

"My nose," Harris cried.

A heavy arm kept Harris's face pinned on the bar, and he pushed down even harder. He could practically hear the grinding of cartilage and bone. "I didn't hear you. What'd you say?"

"I done it."

Seamus let him up. "I don't care how you get by, but let's not overcharge me and the Uglies."

Harris held his nose and nodded, trying to wipe away the blood. His eyes darted to a man hovering near the door.

The hulking patron stepped closer to Seamus. He knew the man already. His name was Richard Westingbrook, but everyone called him Little Dick. The problem with Little Dick was his dick probably was little, but his body was huge, weighing at least 260 pounds. He dwarfed Seamus and served as muscle for Harris when especially inebriated patrons needed to be tossed from the establishment. He was a stupid son of a bitch but a big one.

Seamus didn't bother to even glance at the big man. "Don't touch me, Little Dick."

There was a second of hesitation before a heavy paw landed on Seamus's shoulder. "You should leave. Stay out of Mr. Harris's business." Dick's hand squeezed tighter as a warning.

Little Dick's appearance should have surprised him, but it hadn't. Seamus didn't acknowledge the man. Dick's fingertips dug deeper. Never let a man know you're about to tussle with him. Only gives him a chance to fight back. With a drop of his shoulder, Seamus deflected Little Dick away and kicked him in the stomach. The big man doubled over like a book being snapped closed.

Seamus's partner, Jimmy English, leapt to his feet, tugging his top hat that was stuffed with wool low over his ears, acting as a layer of protection in a street fight. His chair went crashing to the ground, his hand touching the hilt of one of his six daggers. Seamus waved him off and Jimmy took a flanking step to the side.

"I told you to stand down, Dick," Seamus said.

Clutching his stomach, a knife appeared in Dick's hand. It was a wicked looking Bowie knife, big enough to put an adequate-sized hole in a man.

Seamus had been stabbed, cut, and sliced so many times in his life he'd lost count. Probably upwards of thirty. Whenever a man wielded a knife in your direction, if you didn't run, odds were you'd get cut. A stupid man never considered a run. He'd seen all manner of men die in a puddle of their own blood, some with even superficial wounds to the arms and legs. They just bled too much until they were dry. When men played with knives, everyone always ended up a bloody mess.

"Put the knife away," Seamus commanded. "Don't be stupid."

"Fuck you, Yank," Little Dick thundered.

Little Dick should have known better. He knew that Seamus and Jimmy were members of the notorious street gang, the Plug Uglies, a gang specifically recruited from Baltimore by Confederate General Winder who was in charge of martial law in Richmond, to help weed out and round up Northern sympathizers.

While north of Washington, D.C., Maryland was what the newspapers were calling a border state, a state that fell between the warring factions of the North and South. She gave units to both Union and Confederate armies, but she was a Southern belle through and through. No doubt where Maryland's loyalties lay.

Draft riots had been put down by Federal troops. Martial law ruled a town that was just too close to the Federal capital to allow anything different.

Seamus and his boys had been given a handsome bonus to incite those riots and an even handsomer bonus to come down and act as "detectives" for General Winder. Given some of his boys had a better knack of it than others, some had been shipped back home. Those that stayed were paid handsomely and given free reign as de facto secret police. Little Dick knew better. Mr. Harris knew better, yet here they stood with Little Dick waving around his Bowie knife like a battle axe.

Another thing that Little Dick didn't realize was that his heavy and wide Bowie was basically a butcher's knife. Great for the wilderness, a multi-use tool of a frontiersman. It was supposedly designed for knife fighting, but in the streets, in particular in a bar room, big knives were about as practical as a cane sword. Difficult to wield effectively even for the skilled. A knife didn't need power; it only needed to reach out and say hello.

"I don't have time for you today. Put the knife away."

"You shouldn't push on Mr. Harris like you do. The people here are tired of you pushing them around." The big man bounded forward. His attack was as predictable as he was big. Overarching, incredible force probably won the brute dozens of fights against smaller, drunken opponents. Hell, Little Dick was still alive in a short-lived profession, so his aggression had served him in all his fights. But not this fight.

Seamus looked past the fact he would be cut. The situation was beyond that. Then it began. Dick brandished his knife overhead in his direction. *Bastard trying to cut me in half* snapped in his mind, but he didn't have time to dwell on it.

Seamus stepped into the man's swing using both his hands to deflect the blow. He then ducked under his arm, twisting his hand in a flash, penetrating through the man's jacket through his shirt and into the flesh of his belly. As he slipped by, he hooked his four-inch bladed knife again through the man's gut. Kicking out the back of Little Dick's knee, the man crashed to the floor, sending airborne a cloud of dust.

Quickly, Seamus pressed his short blade to Little Dick's neck. A quick cut and the man would die here. "Now you're gonna be alright, but if you keep this up, I'll kill you."

Little Dick groaned. "I'm done." His knife clanked on the floor.

"Yes, you are."

Seamus sheathed his knife back into the sleeve of his frock coat and picked up the Bowie knife, flipping it to the hilt while avoiding the red on its tip. "Fine blade, a bit too heavy though." He tossed it to Jimmy.

Jimmy caught the knife by the hilt and wedged it through his belt. "Thanks, chap."

"You men need to leave," Harris said.

Seamus faced him. "We'll keep your little operation here between us. But on account of this *event* we're going to need a regular gift."

Harris shook his head in disgust. "What do you want?"

"Ten percent."

Harris's lip lifted, but the rules were clear. This was non-negotiable, compliance or shutdown. "Fine."

"We'll see you next week." Seamus looked down at Little Dick holding his hands on his belly. "I'll see you soon, Little Dick." Seamus donned his top hat and walked out the door.

The two Plug Uglies stepped into the daylight. The temperature was mild today, promising some afternoon heat. Horses pulled carts filled with rattling barrels. Wagon wheels rounded over cobblestone roadways. Negros unloaded a boat near the river. It was a regular day in wartime Richmond.

"You're bleeding," Jimmy said.

Seamus looked down at his sleeve. Blood seeped through his brown frock coat. He dipped his finger through the sliced fabric. You never don't get cut. His fingertip found the gash and he ran it along the wound. A few inches across. Not too deep. "It ain't bad. But I'll need Emma to fix my coat." For a little extra, he could find a girl to do just about anything.

"Seamus," Jimmy said. His partner gestured his head toward a woman walking across the street. She had a handsome face, a broad square jaw, and an aristocratic nose. But it wasn't these things that he recognized immediately. It was her clothes.

Her black dress was a finely made garment. Exquisite stitching and padding, not like any of the loose ill-fitting dresses of the women that resided in this part of town. Much too fine for this area near the docks. It reeked of someone with money and status. Someone, in particular, a woman who had no business traversing the streets alone.

The two men watched her walking up the street toward the center of Richmond like two hawks eyeing a rodent in distress.

"You think that's her?" Jimmy asked. He rubbed his thick mustache with his knuckle and thumb.

"Matches the description. Come on." Seamus burped and wiped his mouth on his sleeve, ignoring the warmth running down his arm.

The two men strolled alongside the cobblestone street casually trailing the woman. She fit the description of a woman they'd heard about. Either way, he'd find out.

There had been rumors since he'd arrived in Richmond about Union sympathizers. Most were only empty words and fictitious hearsay. But they'd rolled up almost twenty-seven since the Plug Uglies had started their work. A knife to the right throat, eyes in the right spot, or a broken limb or two had amazing results. His boys' specialty was intimidation.

They'd gotten a good taste of it in Baltimore. Everyone needed someone intimidated to make ends meet. The politicians needed voters swayed. The businessmen needed workers in line. Businesses needed protection from competitors. Everyone that had money needed something done. That's where his Uglies came in.

The Confederate government needed enemies rooted out and martial law maintained. Anything that was a bit more sensitive to the government was where his boys showed up. Everyone was well aware they were General Winder's thugs, and no one seemed to care about their "unofficial" activities as long as Northerners were weeded out.

They tailed her along Cary Street through the industrial district. Smoke hung in the air from the furnaces. Workers bustled around the shops in aprons with rolled up sleeves. Slaves unloaded lead ingots in crates from wagons to be cast into much-needed ammunition. It had been far too long since a shipment had been received. She made her way out of the industrial district and they followed.

When she stopped at a shop, he nodded to his partner. Jimmy tugged his top hat a little lower on his forehead, covering his eyes, and kept walking.

Tailing someone usually required more of his gang. It also helped to know where they were going, but in this case, since it was only him and Jimmy, it took a bit more tact.

Jimmy strolled past the shop, hands in his pockets. He would travel the street within eyeshot of the shop and wait. Then they would take turns following behind. They would do this all the way back to the woman's home, taking notes on who she met with and who she saw.

Seamus dipped inside the shop, removing his top hat and running a hand over the crown of his bald head. Baked goods lined the counter, and he could feel the stuffy heat coming from the oven in the back. Two negroes manned it, using a long stick with a flat end to remove bread.

A man with a wispy mustache and an apron stood behind the counter. White flour dusted his clothes. His eyes darted toward Seamus with nervous disdain. The woman in black pointed at a pile of scones, and the man smiled at her. She handed him money; Seamus noted it was a greenback. Northern tender and the only currency that held any real value. The shop owner placed the scones in the woman's bag.

Seamus slowly walked along the baked goods. The entire establishment wafted a fluffy and delicious aroma. His mouth began to water. The woman turned and he glanced away, leaning in to study loaves of golden bread.

"Excuse me, sir," the shop owner said. "If you aren't going to buy, you can leave." He'd pegged Seamus for a poor man and probably a thief.

"Bugger off, ya Yank lover."

The man's face reddened. "How dare you come into my shop and insult me."

"I do as I please."

The owner grabbed a stick and marched around the counter. "You can leave!"

Seamus licked his lips. His eyes darted at the woman as she stepped onto the street. He quickly flashed the owner a smile. "We can discuss your business operations later."

The owner waved a stick at him. "Who do you work for? Maxwell down the way? I would love to meet with him." He pointed his stick threateningly. "You come on behalf of them women?"

There had been plenty of unrest in the city as more people came for work. Prices on regular goods like food soared as the Union blockade got a little tighter. At one point, a riot of women had tried to burn down this bakery and others for price gouging the citizens of Richmond.

In reality, that was the cost of doing business during a war where supplies were short. In the end, the rampage was blamed on Negros and women with loose morals, but both working- and upper-class women filled the streets with war-time anger.

"Winder," Seamus spat.

The owner paled. And now for the first time, he realized he wasn't looking at some thug or sailor, but one of the Confederacy's detectives. His eyes shifted downward. "I meant no disrespect, sir. I thought you were someone else."

Seamus laughed. "You know who that woman is?"

"Of course. Everyone does. That's Crazy Bet."

"Elizabeth Van Lew?"

"Aye, that's it, Elizabeth. Has some money that one. You know, I hear that when her father died, she took all of her inheritance, marched down to the slave auction block, and bought three families. Signed their freedom papers on the spot."

"Sounds like an abolitionist to me."

"Sounds like the actions of a mad woman!" The store owner laughed nervously. "Waste of money." His eyes shifted at the colored men still working. "What I'd do with a few more."

"She come here often?"

The owner gulped. "Every now and again. Usually after she's visited the prison."

"She ever leave you anythin'?"

Beads of sweat formed on the shop owner's forehead. "Never. She only buys scones to eat," he said, shaking his head in nervous little jaunts.

"Well you see, I must be going. But I think you and I will speak again soon," Seamus said with a nod.

The owner's smile faded a touch. "I am a true patriot, secessionist to the core."

Seamus didn't respond and stepped outside. He immediately skimmed along the street in the direction of the wealthier citizens' homes. He vaguely could make out Jimmy's top hat in a sea of people.

Without being too conspicuous, he jogged until he closed on Jimmy. She turned a corner at a redbrick townhome and into an alley. Jimmy stole a glance behind him, made contact with Seamus, and kept walking. Seamus turned the same corner and followed her.

She stood motionless like a marble statue. He stopped, watching her. Pointing at the heavens, her voice grew louder filled with torment. "You have misled me, my Lord!"

He was taken aback. She spun around. "Oh, thank God, there you are." She speedily walked toward him. Her eyes were almost vacant like he was a ghost, nothing there at all.

A slight grin curved the left side of his face. "Ma'am." He pointed at her for a moment. "Say, I know you. You're Miss Van Lew, right?"

A pleasant smile settled on her lips. "Why, yes, I am. It is a pleasure to see you again, young man."

He let out a soft chuckle. "I'm hardly a young man." For Chrissake, he was thirty-two, at least that's what he thought.

"Say you wouldn't mind if I took a look inside your sack, do you?"

"Why of course, Mr. Lincoln."

Seamus snatched her bag and dug through the scones. Unsatisfied he upended it, letting the baked goods fall to the ground. Nothing else fell from the bag. No papers or notes. Just plain round biscuits that were now soiled with mud and piss and dirt.

"Oh, President Lincoln, why did you go and do that? Mary Todd is going to be so upset when I don't show with the scones. She just loves scones, Mr. President. You know that." She bent down scooping the scones back into her bag, and he glared at her with narrowed eyes. *Ain't no way she's this crazy. She's faking. She must be.*

He crouched down next to her while she gathered her scones. He studied her and she continued her task. "We be watching you, Crazy Bet. You think you got everyone fooled. Well, you don't."

A fierce glint overtook her eyes and they both watched one another as they stood. Her eyes held a shrewd intelligence. Then as quick as it'd come on, it faded. She grinned wildly. "Thank you, Mr. Lincoln."

"I ain't Mr. Lincoln. Just consider me a concerned citizen."

Her brows narrowed and she cocked her head. "You should burn for what you done to the South, Mr. Lincoln. You're no good."

"Don't try to fool with me."

"I do apologize. I must find something else to bring to dinner, Mr. President." She paused, cocking her head the other way. "You're not as tall as I thought you'd be."

He spat out a laugh and let her pass by as he shook his head. "Have a good dinner with Mr. Lincoln. And remember, we will be watching."

He moseyed on out of the alley and waited for Jimmy on a street corner. He returned roughly twenty minutes later. "She went home. No further stops. Mumbling to herself the whole time." He glanced around and his voice grew quieter. "She's got a big house, Seamus. You sure it's a good idea to follow her?"

"It's a perfectly fine idea. The rich are spies just as much as the poor."

"But the poor know less important people."

"Very true."

"She's crazy anyway. You should have heard her conversatin' to herself. You'd think she was in the middle of a group of ten people." Jimmy adjusted his top hat even higher on his head almost to the point where it might fall off. "People be crossing the street to avoid her, and others laughed at her. Maybe we should take another look at the prison guards. You know some of them are taking bribes."

Seamus eyed his partner. "Everyone takes bribes. We don't want no small fish guard taking money to buy a bottle of whiskey. I want the leader of this spy ring and Miss Van Lew knows who that is."

Jimmy sighed. "I'm hungry. Let's try that tavern near the foundry. Hear they have a good stew."

"Then we'll grab Leon and Harold. I want eyes on that house. She knows something."

***

Elizabeth Van Lew busied herself in her kitchen, dropping the sack of dirty scones on a table. A young colored girl appeared and began digging through the scones.

"They fell on the ground. Better crumble them up and feed the chickens in the back."

The young woman looked at her questioningly.

"One of Winder's thugs tailed me from the prison. Goddamn hooligans and strong arms."

"There's no note, ma'am."

Elizabeth shook her head in anger. "No, there's no note. I'm pretty sure another one of them followed me here, and I couldn't double back to the church." She spoke to herself for a moment. "Which means we will have to wait for the signal every night."

"Mr. Henry won't like that."

"I know, but he doesn't have a choice. You said yourself the orders came from Davis's mouth. He's sending all the prisoners south."

Mary eyed the scones. "He did, ma'am. Those were his words."

"Then we must help them escape while we can. As many as we can."

"Yes, ma'am."

"You go on out the back and find Mr. Henry and tell him to be ready tonight."

"Yes, ma'am," Mary said. Her servant left the kitchen. One could say that Mary Jane Bowser was the most vital spy in the whole network. She'd been put into place, directly into Jefferson Davis's very home, by Van Lew's skillful hand. Mary was extremely smart, capable of memorizing entire conversations verbatim.

Her words had given the Union the upper hand in many engagements, but Kilpatrick's raid was still giving her fits and starts at night. She gave every scrap of information she could get her hands on, but if they didn't use it, what more could she do? She had told them and Butler that they would need a force three or four times the number that had come with Kilpatrick. Butler hadn't even stirred from Fort Monroe. Hard to imagine, considering she was in Richmond. It all led to a wasted effort with many dead and captured boys to show for it.

Poor young Ulric Dahlgren's body sat on display near the center of town. His coatless body was wrapped in a dirty U.S. Army blanket. Birds and flies feasted on his rotting corpse. In his current state, he was hardly recognizable save for the sign.

A sign had been placed around his neck that read DAHLGREN THE HUN. It made her sick to pass that sunken-eyed corpse every day. She would change that too. Given the right time, she would undermine this abomination of the Confederate experiment. But first she would liberate the man. The man that saved the Union's pride. A mysterious young colonel named Wolf.

She took her custom-made Derringer pocket pistol from inside her dress. It was a single-shot pistol. She carried it loaded and would use it too if need be, on that prick Plug Ugly if he got too close. Then she'd play the "he tried to touch me" card. And they'd believe her too because that bigger prick Winder had hired a bunch of thugs to run his counterspy network and a crazy rich lady could never be a part of a Union spy ring. Ha! That didn't mean she wasn't careful. She'd hidden messages in hollowed-out eggs and written notes with invisible ink.

No, she was a careful woman. She had to be when she was treading such an openly fine line in a society at war. But if that man thought he was going to scare her, he needed to reevaluate how long he wanted to live in this life.

She'd considered attempting to assassinate the leader of the detectives earlier in the year, but that would only make the Uglies more vigilant. And she wanted them drunk and more interested in lining their own pockets than following any of her people. The tide was finally turning in the Union's favor, and soon they would win this war. Then she could relax, but now she must plan. Every man she filtered through her network north was a man that could help end this war.

Chapter Three

Evening, April 29, 1864
Libby Prison, Richmond, Virginia

The Union officers on the second floor of Libby Prison were bedding down in their usual spots for the night. Heavy footsteps thumped upward on the retractable staircase, causing many a man to stare expectantly at the door. Anything that wasn't a normal part of the routine caused immense stress.

The door creaked open to their room and two bulky men entered.

"Wolf!" Hank said. He scanned the huddled prisoners, squinting his eyes.

"Cripple man!" Griff added.

Wolf peered around for assurance against the obvious. These men could not be his saviors. *They can't be.* They were devils escaped from hell itself in an enemy uniform.

"If ya don't pipe up, we're going to beat ya worse!" Griff called at them.

Wolf slowly got to his feet. These men must know his plan. There was no other way. Reynolds stood alongside him, straightening his jacket. The white-haired surgeon's eyes clouded with worry. "Now, gentleman, this is no way to treat a man, especially one like the colonel."

The two brutes kicked their way through the crowd. A sharp thwack here and there hurried the prisoners crawling out of their path with yelps and curses.

Griff smiled as he reached the surgeon, blocking his path. His tongue massaged chewing tobacco in his mouth. He pointed his whipping stick at him. "Listen, old man, don't get in our way."

Someone must have lied. How could they have known? Was it all a ruse the whole time? A wicked and cruel way to torture my mind with hope.

Hank shoved the end of his stick into Reynolds's gut. The aged surgeon wheezed a cough, doubling over. Wolf rested a hand on his shoulder. "It's okay." With a grimace, Reynolds forced himself upright again.

"You say that now," Griff said with a smirk. He jabbed his cudgel into Wolf's belly, forcing the air from his lungs. The baton blurred as he struck Wolf's leg and shoved him to the ground. A sharp slap sounded out as Griff connected another blow to the meat of his raw back.

Roberts grabbed at his assailant's hand. Every eye in the room watched the hapless struggle. More prisoners got to their feet. Others shouldered in closer.

"What's this pup doing?" Hank said. With a thick hand and iron fingers, he cupped Roberts by the neck, restraining him. "Both of you go in the cellar now." He let out a laugh.

Griff hauled Wolf upright then pointed his truncheon out at the rest of the officers. "I saw you fellows standing up. Don't think for a second you would make it ten feet without this place going up in a ball of flames."

"But we could take you with us," Major Olmsted said. He was their unofficial leader, and there was anger in his eyes. The cramped officers inched closer like a phalanx of the imprisoned and the guards tensed, scanning the crowd. Griff spit on the floor. "You want to get killed over these two nobodies? You want all these innocent men to die?"

Olmsted raised his chin, resting a hand on Reynolds's shoulder. "You remember what we can do."

Griff laughed like a deep booming bass drum. "You remember where you are." He shoved his way through the crowd, both Roberts and Wolf at their mercy.

A cold sweat broke out over Wolf's body. They'd been found out. Horror must await them, and the men were saddened to see it. They turned away from them as if their bad luck could infect the others.

The steps creaked as they made their way to the first floor. When they reached the bottom, a guard wound a crank and the staircase mechanically clicked until back in place, inaccessible from above and effectively trapping the prisoners in the upper two floors.

Wolf slowed his gait in resistance, and Griff drove him onward as if he were a scolded child. "Hurry up." The two guards forced the prisoners down drab hallway past the kitchen and bringing them to a halt at the commander's office.

Griff knocked with hard knuckles.

"Enter," came a voice.

Griff opened the door and shoved Wolf inside closely followed by Roberts.

Lieutenant Ross sat behind his desk. Two candles illuminated the room, casting long shadows in the corners. His brow creased at the sight of the prisoners.

"I said only Colonel Wolf."

Hank scratched his head. "The little one tried to fight. I was going to take him to the cellar."

Ross shoed him away. "Get rid of him."

"Come," Hank said, manhandling Roberts by the collar. His boots squeaked over the floor. Wolf reached for him, and a sharp crack from Griff's stick kept Wolf in place.

"Close the door," Ross said. He glanced down at his papers again. His eyes scanned the document from behind his glasses.

Griff chuckled. "I'll be waiting for you." The door clicked closed.

Ross glared at the door. The nib of his pen aggressively dunked inside the inkwell. "Colonel Wolf. We keep meeting like this." He scribbled on a sheet of paper; his eyes locked in on his work.

Wolf stood silently, rubbing his hand. Cold sweat began to form on his brow. *Did they find me out? A mere corporal masquerading as an unknown colonel. Or is it worse? Is Payne back for another round?* The thought made his stomach roil. The melted skin on his back had only just begun to heal into a tight raw leather. "I already told you everything."

A deep sigh escaped from Ross's lips. "No, you didn't. I know you lied, Mr. Wolf." *Have they found the letter?*

He shook his head no. *Deny. Deny. Deny.* "I didn't."

"Have I ever told you about the books?"

"Yes, sir." Wolf gulped, the threat of the unknown looming like the shadow of death.

"I told you how strict they are about the numbers?"

"Yes, sir."

Ross inspected the paper in front of him again. "Everything is just a number. *You* are just a number. *We* are all just numbers." He paused, letting the truth of it all sink in. "All entrusted to me. It takes a meticulous mind to make sure they are always correct. Do you know what makes a number correct?" His eyes narrowed at Wolf as he tried to determine if he understood his meaning. "A man makes a number correct." He raised his eyebrows. "Or incorrect, but my numbers are never incorrect."

Candlelight flickered and melted wax dribbled from the flame down the sticks and on their bases, reminding Wolf of the skin on his back under Payne's tortuous brand. The flames reflected upon Ross's glasses, making it difficult to read the man's eyes. He would not meet Payne again a prisoner. He'd die before that. Revenge or death, but never on unlevel ground.

Ross stood, gesturing like he would at a dog. "Take off your clothes."

His ears must have betrayed him. Why on earth would a man want him to strip down? He gulped down a parched throat. What sick and depraved torture did Ross have in store for him? "Pardon?"

"Remove your uniform." Ross turned around and opened a wardrobe cabinet and began rummaging through. He held up Confederate gray uniforms judging the size. "Hurry now, off with it. We don't have time."

"I don't understand."

"There isn't much to understand, Colonel. You are being liberated from Libby."

Wolf's entire body was paralyzed in shock as if he'd grown roots and become a tree in a second. *It's a trick. He'll strip me naked and whip me or something even more devious.*

"This should do," Ross turned around and tossed him a jacket. Wolf caught the rebel coat in his arms, holding it out for inspection.

"Give me your overcoat and jacket," Ross said, ushering him to throw it over.

"You're going to get me shot."

"I assure you I am not. Now, hurry. After we take down the stairs for the night, the guards start drinking. Hell, most fall asleep or leave. The longer you tarry here, the less time you have to distance yourself from Richmond."

Hesitantly, Wolf took off his overcoat and frock coat, handing them to Ross. The prison commander took them and crumpled them in a bag.

Draping the plain wool rebel jacket over his shoulders as best he could, he gently pulled it tight. It fit him well. Yellow piping braided the cuffs.

"Off with you pants. Hurry," Ross said. Wolf gave him a questioning glance, but Ross paid him no heed. "Here try on these trousers," he said, handing them over. "No need to be total regulation."

Wolf still felt awkward like he was being duped into a false escape only to be humiliated. He hurriedly pulled the pants on and Ross approached, inspecting him.

He straightened Wolf's collar. "Try and comb your hair over."

Wolf wiped a hand over his head then smoothed his beard.

"This will have to do. I will send away Griffin. We will wait for a while, and you will simply walk out the front."

"Walk out? I'll be shot."

"Why would we shoot our own men? Take a look at your uniform, Colonel. You are now a rebel."

"But why are you doing this?"

Ross stared up at him. "We've been given orders to start sending the Union officers south. In the next few weeks, we will begin to transport the prisoners. Apparently, high command doesn't like sitting on 15,000 enemy combatants in their home capital all waiting to break free and ravage her. No, no." He grinned and Wolf wondered if he'd gone insane. Perhaps they'd be shot together. "Every mile further south you go diminishes your chances of escape." Ross grabbed the bag filled with Wolf's clothes and shoved it into a larger cloth satchel.

"But the beatings and you let Payne?" Wolf's eyes narrowed. "The Union men here hate you. How is it possible for you to be both a Union man and tormentor in one?"

Ross stopped what he was doing, dropping the bag. "How do you convince everyone you aren't a sympathizer? You act like the meanest, cruelest patriot there is. It allows me free reign all over this place. No one questions my orders because I rule with an iron fist." He sighed. "Your circumstances were regrettable, but I assure you that I am your ally." He snuck a nervous look out the window. "I had to be more careful when I was under Taylor, but when he got *sick*, everything became easier. Even now, everyone thinks I'm extracting information from you. Rumors run the mill. Now step aside."

Wolf took a few steps toward the corner of his office. Ross opened the door a crack, poking his head into the hallway. "Griff, you may go. I will put this one away when I'm done."

"Okay, boss. You sure?"

Ross shoved a hand in his pocket removing a greenback. "Why don't you grab a bottle of something for you and the boys?"

"Thanks, Ross! Everyone thinks you're a cold-hearted bastard, but y'all right by me."

"I'm sure they do, now goodnight." The prison commander closed the door and let out a deep breath. "Now, we wait."

"I ain't going."

Ross ignored him walking back to his desk.

"I said, I ain't going," Wolf said louder.

"What do you mean you're not going?" Ross said, anger encircling his eyes.

"I can't go without Roberts."

"Nonsense. I can only get you out."

Wolf gave him a terse shake of his head. "Not without Roberts."

"I don't have a uniform for him. Do you understand what it takes to get one of you out of here? You cannot even fathom the risks involved for everyone in our network. One slip and we all hang."

"I do. But I can't leave my pal. You can go on and take out Captain Reynolds. He's a surgeon and a good man."

Ross shook his head. "I don't pick." He rubbed his hands together like a guilty thief on trial. "I suppose I should be trying to get more of you out while

I can." He peeked through the window again. "Your chances of success will go up alone."

"Roberts or send me back upstairs."

With a dirty glare, Ross hurried for the door and disappeared into the hallway. He soon returned with Roberts. His short comrade squinted at Wolf as he walked in. "Wolf?"

"Yes."

"What in the hell you wearing that for?"

Ross stripped off his rebel jacket. "I don't have time to find you another one that might fit. You must take mine."

Roberts gawked at it. "You gotta be shittin' me. You're gonna shoot us, right?"

"We don't have time. Wolf will explain later."

"Put it on," Wolf said.

Ross went to his window, narrowing his eyes as he examined the street again. "We must go now. Out the front door. Continue along Cary Street. It's this one here." He pointed out. "Someone else will meet you a few blocks north." Ross hastily took a candle and set it on the windowsill. The flame flicked and rolled. He sat back down at his desk and rearranged his papers. "The signal is set. Good luck, gentleman."

Chapter Four

April 29, 1864
Libby Prison, Richmond, Virginia

The two prisoners stepped into the darkened musty hallway as free men. The door closed loudly behind them. The warped floorboards creaked beneath their feet.

"Is he bein' honest?" Roberts said softly.

"We're in it now."

"Don't matter, I suppose. You don't want to be in the cellars. Rats. Tons of rats. And them colored boys down there have it worse."

They passed empty desks and tables that normally held the guards during the day. The kitchen was dark, the stink of constant use seeping forth like an overflowing sewer.

The door to the prison that sat open during the daylight hours was now closed. Wolf placed his hand on the door. He looked to his friend for confirmation that he was ready to step into the unknown. Roberts gave him a determined nod. With a push, the door swung open with an angry groan.

Campfires in front of the guard barracks across the street blazed in the night. Shadowed guards huddled around them drinking, eating, and chatting with one another.

A couple of guards stood sentry on each corner of the warehouse. They lazily kept their eyes on the whitewashed walls for the dark silhouettes of prisoners scaling them in the night.

The former prisoners took a step onto the street lined with uneven cobbles. The stars above them shone like little pinpricks of light in the tapestry of night. Although it had been over seven weeks, it felt like a lifetime of imprisonment.

The faint smell of tobacco mixed with stagnant water blew from the nearby riverfront, and Wolf never smelled anything so pure and sweet.

"Nice and easy now. Just two officers out for a stroll," Wolf said. He tried to control his gait and make his limp less noticeable. Anything to normalize the appearance of the two escaping prisoners.

They made it to the corner. Two night sentries stood there. They leaned on their muskets like exhausted men on walking sticks. Neither wore rebel gray, but instead, butternut jackets and broad slouch hats. Without much concern, they glanced at the disguised prisoners and quickly dismissed them.

Wolf nodded in their direction and turned down Cary Street, making for the other side of the road away from the guard barracks.

They passed along a dark warehouse, each step giving them a burst of optimism that maybe they would escape.

"If they'd been trickin' us, Ross would have shot us by now," Roberts said.

"We can only hope. Just stay steady. A few blocks to the meeting point." He chanced a glance back at Libby Prison. The candle had disappeared from Ross's window. The guards on the corner still had their heads down. The two men continued away from the James River wharfs and warehouses. Three men passed by on the other side of the street, loud and drunk. Wolf kept his eyes toward the ground ahead.

A hulking man ambled down the street ahead of them. He sauntered with a swagger of a big man that threw his weight around and wanted everyone to know it. He wore a faded gray private's coat and a bushy beard splayed on his chest. Wolf considered crossing to the other side, avoiding him, but decided it would appear even more suspicious.

"Keep calm," he whispered to Roberts.

"I be as calm as I can be," Roberts hissed.

As the man got closer, fear expanded in Wolf's gut like a hot air balloon preparing to take flight. That mean, vacant face was unmistakable.

Roberts passed, keeping his head down, but the man stared at Wolf as he side-stepped around. The big man slowed and stopped, a long dagger at his belt, a cudgel on the other side. A bottle of whiskey was clasped in his other hand.

His voice came like a howitzer belching forth a hot shell. "You boys look family like. I know you?" His words froze them in their tracks.

Roberts was quick to respond. "You sure do know us. We're on the other shift. Jesus, Mary, and Joseph, our sisters know one another."

"They do, sir?" Griff scratched at his beard with a thick finger. His eyes narrowed a bit as he tried to recollect.

Fast-talking and lying were two of Roberts's fortes. These things came easy to him as his everyday survival depended on it growing up on the streets. "Sure do. Met in school, they did."

"My sister's down in Martinsville."

"Well, sure, she is."

Wolf nodded eagerly.

"What's your sister's name?" Griff asked.

"Josephine."

Griff thought for a moment, shaking his head. "No, I don't remember her." He pointed a finger. "But I know you."

"Like I said, same shift. Best carry on. We're in a hurry." Roberts bobbed his head and took a step.

"Wait," Griff commanded, freezing the men in place. "You be Union boys," he said. He took a few steps closer, straining for a better look in the dark.

"Nope," Wolf said.

Nodding, Griff reached for Roberts's uniform touching it. A bold move for a man of lower rank either stupid or confident in his assessment. "New uniforms too. Where'd you get those?"

Wolf hadn't realized his hand had made a fist. His knuckles were flying through the air long before it even registered he'd leapt into action. His fist punished the man's jaw in a wicked surprise hook.

The towering guard's eyes rolled into the back of his head, and he went crashing onto the street like an oak tree falling to the ground. The bottle hit the cobbles with a smash, sending booze and shards everywhere.

Roberts stared at the unmoving guard and then back at Wolf. "Now that's a waste."

Ignoring him, Wolf quickly searched the man, robbing him of his long dagger. He secured it on his belt where it belonged and drew the knife from its sheath. "Should slit his throat and do everyone a favor." The blade was a dull gray in the night.

From the alley shadows came a voice. "What happened here?"

Wolf's hand squeezed the hilt, and he prepared himself to kill whoever spoke. "Beat my sister, he did. He only had what was coming." He sheathed the knife but kept his hand over the hilt.

A silhouette stepped closer, becoming a man. *He must have seen the whole thing.* Wolf's hand hovered closer to the hilt. *How much force was needed to keep this man silent?* His face was covered in grime like he worked with coal or in a factory. He had a thick mustache on his upper lip also stained with soot. "I think I know your sister."

The two escaping men shared a glance. "Say, would you happen to know where she is?"

The man hurried closer and grabbed Griff by an arm. "Help me get him off the street. Then I'll take you there."

They dragged the hulking guard into the darkness of the alley where shadows and criminals reign supreme. Griff's head banged off the ground as they dumped him.

"He knows us," Wolf said to the man.

The man's eyes grew larger, the whites multiplying in size. "He knows you?"

"He's a guard at the prison. Takes a liking to beatin' us," Roberts said.

The man shook his head. He took a step back and wiped his brow. "No, no. We shouldn't be here. I knew this was a bad idea. We'll get caught."

"We're already out." Wolf reached for him. "I ain't going back there."

Dodging Wolf's swipe, the man stumbled into the wall of a warehouse. "She's in the public square." Bracing himself off the wall, he ran from the men. His footsteps chased after him.

"What public square?" Roberts called after him. Both men watched their guide flee and their chances to escape dwindle.

"Goddamnit," Wolf muttered. They looked down at Griff's unconscious body. "Can't be here when he wakes up."

"Maybe he shouldn't," Roberts added. Killing a man when he was knocked out wasn't any different than killing a man when he was awake except easier. "He sure was a mean bastard."

Wolf eyed his tormentor. This brute of a man was responsible for so much misery amongst the prisoners. His removal, however it was accomplished, could be the difference in whether or not a man could make it through the horrors of prison life. "You ever murder a man?"

Roberts shrugged his shoulders. "Sure, we killed men. You were there."

"No, I mean murder."

"Guess I haven't."

"What do you think Berles would do?"

A mischievous grin took shape on Roberts's face. "Not get caught in the first place."

Wolf felt the bone knife handle in his hand, releasing it inch by inch. *I should end this bastard's life. It's the right thing to do.* Drunken voices grew closer, staying Wolf's hand. Men passed by the alley. Sailors or workers, soldiers or clerks, it mattered not, all were enemies.

The escapees knelt next to Griff, remaining still until the men passed. "It ain't right to kill a man while he sleeps, but I'll be damned if I let him go with just a beating."

The two men stripped Griff down, removing all his clothes. They tied him up with his socks and left him to be found with his favorite whipping stick in an especially uncomfortable place. They dumped his garments nearby and moved back to the main street.

"How are we going to find this square?"

"I don't know."

They walked along following the same route they had trudged as prisoners after getting captured. Lanterns illuminated street corners. The neighborhoods became noticeably nicer. Manicured bushes and lawns. Tall ostentatious homes with elaborate sprawling ornate awnings and porches.

A man in a top hat tapped his cane as he escorted a woman in a fine blue dress and bonnet, nodding to them as they passed. Both Wolf and Roberts kept their eyes downcast and nodded in return, trying not to make too much eye contact.

"Figure if we keep walking, perhaps we can walk on out of here," Wolf said.

"Fine by me," Roberts said.

Maintaining their current direction, they navigated into the heart of Richmond.

Chapter Five

Evening, April 29, 1864
Richmond, Virginia

Elizabeth Van Lew took two different routes to reach Richmond's public square. Each path took her around the plaza in a relative figure eight. This gave her the lay of the land and an opportunity to make sure no one was tailing her.

Her route was carefully selected and would force men or women following her into bottlenecks. If in fact they were onto her, this would draw them out, or in some cases, she could lose them by slipping into a tavern or stopping by a friend's house.

If she did catch someone on her tail, like she had those grimy looking Plug Uglies, she would utter the most ridiculous things and, if needed, reverse her route. This always threw anyone following her into a tizzy, fumbling over themselves to scramble out of the way.

But Seamus MacAllister was good at his job. He was a natural man of the street and he tended to blend in anywhere. The only thing that could have drawn him out was a random stop at the bakery. His partner was an adept detective as well, but she hadn't survived this long by taking chances. No, one could only survive with precise caution when operating in a city that would rip you to pieces if they discovered your deceit.

She swallowed down the fact he might have wanted her to know, and that scared her. Not knowing what his purpose was and how much he knew ate at her courage. But she didn't have time to be frightened. The prisoners needed her help, and now they were late. So behind schedule that she had taken a seat on a park bench in the largest square in Richmond.

Women of her social status shouldn't be alone in a public square, even less so at night, but she was a crazy woman. A woman like that could be anywhere at any time because social norms didn't apply to the mad, crazed, and disturbed.

A group of drunken boys loudly made their way through the square. Brothels and bars had found their way into every nook and cranny of the city as it had more than quadrupled in size since the beginning of the war. And this was in addition to the numerous prisons, hospitals, and military camps. Vagabonds and invalids from the hospitals would lurk in the parks and squares at night, sometimes committing petty theft or harassment.

She started to hum to herself and sway in place. One of the young men hefted a small stone and chucked it at the stinking body across the way. The others laughed and took up the rock fusillade.

Their propped-up victim would never retaliate because he was a corpse. Colonel Ulric Dahlgren had suffered at the vengeful Richmonders' hands. The poor boy and his poor family.

His father had requested the return of his body for proper burial for weeks. She'd even gotten Major General Benjamin Butler to ask on Admiral Dahlgren's behalf from the Confederate government. Everyone's hands were tied. And there the corpse sat, well, more stood.

The coffin was propped upright like a book on display. His body was still slightly slumped in the coffin for he only had one leg and his wooden prosthetic was missing. It had most likely been taken as a souvenir by one of his killers. He leaned on the side like a drunkard fallen asleep.

She kept rocking to make herself seem crazier as the young men walked by. A few looked at her and laughed then proceeded onward. She brought herself to rest, watching them from the corners of her eyes.

The weight of the Derringer pocket pistol inside her dress tugged at the fabric on her shoulder. The secret pocket concealed the weapon and was readily accessible.

Mr. Henry should have already arrived with the prisoner. Ross had given the candlelight signal. It should have taken no less than forty minutes to make the trek through the streets. That was thirty minutes ago.

Sighing, she took another view around the square. Two men rounded a corner, disappearing from sight. A man and a lady walked brazenly through the middle of the square apparently to view the vile corpse of the enemy.

The woman hiked her dress a bit too high, revealing an ankle, but pretending she was trying to avoid splattering it with mud. Mr. Dulany and Miss Tennyson. Not Mrs. Dulany. A nice little tidbit of gossip. She bet the old dog would still be sitting in front pew of St. Paul's Episcopal Church on Sunday morning singing at the top of his lungs. It appeared that he had much to repent for.

Perhaps she could use that for leverage against the man in some way. She filed that piece of information back into her brain for later. It was amazing what you could learn by just sitting back, being quiet, and paying attention to everything going on around you. People tended to loosen their tongue and speak freely around her because they thought her mad. Confederate officials dismissed her but paid enough lip service because of her social status. Little did those men know this woman was sabotaging their every effort.

A cool breeze washed over the streets, the few towering oaks in the square ruffling in the night. The days grew warmer, but the nights still remembered winter.

She sighed and removed a timepiece from her dress and clicked a button on the side. The lid sprang open and she glanced at the watch face. Late. Her mind began to race with contingency plans. *Who bailed? Ross? No, he was a staunch Unionist. Mr. Henry? Reliable. He could be bought for the right price.* After all, he'd been bought by her.

Was there trouble with Colonel Wolf? Illness? It was a possibility. He was in bad shape a few weeks back. A fever almost took him. But Ross had communicated he was able, and if she didn't liberate him now, he may languish the rest of the war in a Georgian prison. And that could be years, or it could be months. Regardless, it would be a futile struggle with illness and starvation until one inevitably took him like taxes enacted by a government, certain and permanent.

However, if she hadn't acted, she would have backed out on her promise, and she wasn't a woman to do that. If Henry didn't get the prisoner here, she would back out on two promises: one to Wolf and one to Admiral Dahlgren to reclaim his son's body. She wondered if she could carry the corpse on her own. It would be a difficult task to accomplish.

How much more time should she give them? She closed the pocket watch and slipped it back inside her dress. Five minutes? Ten? She sighed, eyeing a rough-looking man with a long drooping mustache coming her way. He passed in front of her then turned to ogle her.

"You Miss Van Lew?" he asked.

"I am," she said. Her voice conveyed a level of social status and let it be known that one such as himself shouldn't be speaking to her. She gulped, keeping herself composed. This breakout could be turning into a heap of dung.

"Late night to be out without a chaperone."

"That is none of your concern."

"I am only concerned about your well-being."

"I only convene with the true Lord our God. He guides my hand!" She stood abruptly, raising her hands in the air. The man took a step back.

"He speaks to me all the time. Whispers the truth."

The man settled with his hands in his pockets. "Remember it ain't safe out here at night."

She leveled her eyes on him. "God watches my back."

A creepy grin filled his lips. "You have a good night, ma'am."

They are all over this. I must return to the mansion. Send someone else to collect the prisoner. But we are already behind. The boat captain might not wait any longer unless he wants a better payout. Then he'll wait, she thought to herself.

The man strolled away, his hands holding low on his lapels. He whistled a soft tune. She averted her eyes and started for the far street while mumbling incoherent things and throwing in a mix of rhetoric about God, fire, brimstone, angels, and demons. It mattered not as long as it sounded like the insane driveling of a mad woman. *Which of my servants should I send back?*

Bowser was the only one she truly could trust with this mission but risking her when she was already in such a fruitful position would be unwise. But if these prisoners were caught, she might lose Ross and Mr. Henry. *Information from the Confederate White House or helping those brave imprisoned patriots? Which one was more important to our cause?*

She reached the edge of the square and two men in gray rounded the corner, making her heart leap. She kept her head down and mumbled to herself. The two men stopped, staring at her. *Soldiers? Have they come to arrest me?*

"Ma'am?" the taller of the two said.

She glanced at them, making sure to stare through them. "Fire will reign from above and the seas will boil from below. The dead will walk the earth, having been released from hell," she hissed at them.

The two younger men wore rebel gray. Both lieutenants. They had scraggily beards and the flesh around their eyes was gaunt. They looked like men on hard times, men who lived on the streets, only much worse. Parolees? Sick? Injured? The bigger soldier had a limp.

"The Lord cares for all his angels," she said. She wavered her hands toward the sky like the most fervent of his worshippers. Waving her hands, she went to move past them until she felt the ironlike grip of the larger man grasping her arm.

"How dare you touch a lady!"

He leaned near her ear. His stench was sourly ripe like a man who hadn't washed a day in his life. "Van Lew?"

She lifted her chin with haughty indignation. "Yes."

"A friend sent us."

She turned, looking him in the eyes. They'd only met twice, but she remembered now. "You are Wolf."

His eyes darted around scanning the square. "I am." He released her.

"Where is Mr. Henry?"

"He left us."

"Who is us?"

"Captain Roberts and I."

She eyed the smaller man. He had dark hair and a mischievous countenance to him like he'd steal a pie from her kitchen and not even bat an eye as he ate his fill. "I was only expecting you, Colonel. Not two. Your passage is only booked for one."

"I will not leave him."

She studied him for a moment. There was a sense of stubborn nobility about him. Or was it a righteous ignorance? He knew not what his demand forced her to risk when she'd already risked so much to free him. "Then we must move quickly for you both are late. And hold yourselves like military men. You are my escorts for tonight."

She led them around the square. Seeing that it was sufficiently empty, she guided them toward the open-faced coffin propped against a tree. A torch on either side burned, illuminating the dead colonel.

An audible gasp came from Wolf. "Ma'am? What are we doing?" Their feet squelched in the mud as they drew near.

"That's Dahlgren," he whispered.

The ground here was beaten from thousands of feet. It wasn't every day a dead man sat in the square. It was still even grander to have a dead enemy raider on display. An enemy that had come to ravage their city only to be killed by Richmond's brave defenders.

Dahlgren's body leaned to the side in the coffin as if he'd passed out on a wall, but it was because his prosthetic leg was missing along with his single boot, revealing a lone bare foot.

Black flies buzzed around him. His sky-blue Union officer's pants were on, but everything else had been stripped away. After he had been displayed in such a way for only a few days, complaints came from Richmond's fine ladies about how it threatened their sensibilities. In turn, authorities clothed him in a new shirt and a U.S. Army blanket to hide the grotesque wounds that covered his pallid, bloodless torso.

But now Dahlgren had taken on a greenish hue. His head had been laid to the side so only the entrance wound from the bullet was exposed like a coin had entered his skull. The other side was a mess of frayed skin and bone where the bullet had broken free. Maggots toppled over one another as they consumed his flesh. No one wanted to see that.

She glimpsed at them from over her shoulder. "Take him down."

"Surely we can't take him with us," said Wolf.

"He is your guide north. You don't go without him."

The two men exchanged looks before Roberts said, "Don't look like he can guide much of anything in his current state."

"Not sure I'd want him guiding us again anyhow," Wolf said.

She settled her eyes on him. "Let us put his soul to rest. Give his father some peace. He has paid for your passage."

"All right. All right," Wolf said.

The two men moved forward, covering their noses with jacket sleeves. "No offense ma'am, but he smells fierce," Roberts said. They struggled to hoist the rigid man from the coffin.

A voice cut through the night. "Crazy Bet."

She turned to see Seamus MacAllister standing nearby watching her escapees.

"And what are these fellers up to?" the Plug Ugly said, nodding his bald pate at the two men.

Best to be out with the truth. "These men are removing Colonel Dahlgren's body for transportation north."

Wolf and Roberts stopped and set the body down. The body lay malleable, taking the shape of the ground.

"And on what orders are these brave rebel officers acting?"

Both the prisoners stood silent.

"President Jefferson Davis."

Seamus's eyes widened with surprise, and he scratched at his jaw with a dirty fingernail. "Really? These men were ordered to sneak into the square at night and remove this body with the town crazy lady?"

"I have the orders right here. I act as a messenger of good will. You know this, Seamus," she said. She held out a letter written on cream-colored paper.

"You mean as a Union sympathizer." He snatched the paper from her hand. His eyes scanned the document, and she was surprised the cretin could read. If indeed he could, he would recognize the letter was in fact signed by

Jefferson Davis. It was amazing what she could get her hands on with a spy in his house.

Seamus's voice grew pompous. He held the paper out, reading aloud. "The person who bears this letter is on official business of the Confederate States of America. Do not impede their mission under penalty of treason." He waved it into the air. "These are some serious orders."

She reached her hand out, but he kept hold of the paper, grinning at her. "So how did you come across this? Thieve it?"

"It is of none of your concern, aside from the fact that I conduct his official business."

"So you're telling me that tomorrow when Richmond rises with the sun, President Davis is responsible for removing this stinking body from the square? When the papers report the corpse is gone, he won't be surprised one bit that Miss Elizabeth Van Lew and her Confederate officers buried the body or wherever you are going with it?"

"That's true."

Seamus took a step toward them. "So when I go and find the Home Guard and imprison you until morning everything will be just dandy? I will look a fool and you will be set free?"

"Yes, you will most likely be removed from your station."

Seamus laughed. It was a hard harsh sound much like himself. "My station? Lady, you are fucking crazy."

Her mouth stayed flat and she shifted her hands over her stomach, nearing her pistol.

"If I am to believe this crock of shit." He took his time tearing the paper in half and then quarters until it was mere confetti on the ground. "That's what I think of your 'orders.'"

"You've done yourself a great disservice, Seamus. You should go back north from whence you came. Forget you ever saw us here."

He laughed again. "What unit you men with?"

"Stuart's."

"Your unit is Stuart? I said which unit?"

"1st Virginia Cavalry."

"The 1st Virginia Cavalry. Really? Where are you camped at?"

Wolf gulped, his throat moving with guilt despite his best efforts to hide it. "Charlottesville."

"Charlottesville. Interesting. Pretty far from there."

"On official business."

"Just like our town crazy old maid."

Van Lew put her hand under her dress grasping for her pistol. One shot. Put this infuriating man down then they run. He must die though. He knows too much. Her fingers found the short handle barely large enough to fit in part of her palm.

Seamus must have seen something in her eyes because he was faster on the draw. He closed several feet before the pistol escaped her dress. He pressed a knife to her breast with a wicked smile. "Who would have thought Crazy Bet was a spy? Seamus MacAllister is the one who uncovered Richmond's most notorious spy ring." He turned to face the men. "1st Virginia is camped near Fredericksburg. Your accents don't belong to loyal sons of the South, but somewhere further north. Wisconsin or Michigan? In fact, I bet if I marched you two over to Libby Prison, we might find that two of their rats escaped."

Wolf slowly moved toward them.

"Ah. Hold it right there or Bet gets it." The tip of his blade pressed painfully into her chest causing her to gasp. A droplet of blood formed at the blade's point, growing in size before it trickled down her breast leaving a thin red stream in its wake. "Nice and slow, you boys get on the ground."

She eyed them, the scowl on Wolf's face expanding.

"Just have to sit tight here until Jimmy and Ben finish making their patrol. It'll be the best breakup yet. Caught in the act."

No. It won't be. She grasped at his arm, throwing her body weight into it. His eyes grew larger, and he flung her to the side. She felt the pain as she hit the mud-caked cobbles but ignored it.

Wolf was upon him, and the two men slashed and jabbed at each other with knives. Seamus laughed as they circled one another. "You hold that like it's an axe."

Darting forward, Wolf thrust with the pointy end while Seamus parried with slashes of his own. Roberts tried to flank the man, but without a weapon, his part was limited.

She pushed herself seated. Her hands found her pistol and released it. It was surprisingly light, almost like a paperweight in her hand. "Seamus!" she said.

The Plug Ugly turned her way, his brutishly intelligent eyes shifting toward the single round barrel of violence.

The pistol shook. She'd never shot a man. She'd never killed a man. She knew she could, but could she really do it?

"Stop," she said. He stood more upright. He tried to turn her way before Wolf rammed his long knife into his belly. The sound was like a butcher chopping into a piece of meat. Seamus gasped as Wolf closed on him, getting near his face as he forced the blade deeper.

"You cheatin', dirty bastard," Seamus muttered, gritting his teeth.

"Never doubt a desperate man." Wolf removed his blade with a flourish of crimson, and Seamus fell to the ground holding his abdomen. Blood flowed over his hands like a red river breaking free of a dike.

"Finish him," Van Lew said. She slipped her pistol back into her sleeve. "We don't have time before his compatriots return."

Wolf bent close to the Plug Ugly.

"Do it, you bastard," Seamus spit.

Cupping the man by the chin, Wolf ran his blade along his neck, and Seamus gurgled and coughed as he bled out on the cobbles, a pink grin gaping from his throat. She helped the men shove him into the coffin, upright and on display for the world to see their crime, but not until morning.

The two prisoners eyed her. Her breath came sharp and she could feel the slash across her breast. The warm blood ran along her skin and soaked into her black dress. She felt it with her fingers then forced them down upon the cut like she was trying to keep it all in.

"Ma'am," Roberts said.

"I'm fine. Follow this street. It twists all the way to a safe location on the river. There will be a boat there. The man's been paid. You can trust him." Her head felt a bit fuzzy and she tried to blink it away.

"Let us escort you back home."

"I know where it is well enough. When Seamus's gang returns, the city will be crawling with them. You make sure Ulric's body finds its way back to his father. Do you understand?"

"Yes, ma'am."

"I can take care of them here. Now go and take care of yourself." She took in a breath. She'd been stabbed. Mary would help her at home. "Tell Butler I think of his embrace often."

"We will. Thank you," Wolf said.

"You have our best," Roberts added.

"Godspeed."

The men disappeared down the street, the limp body between them swaying.

She didn't think she could die from this wound, but she best get it bandaged or risk passing out next to a dead body. She could explain the entire assault away and how brave Seamus tried to stop the Northern brigands but fell to their evil blades. He'd been a hero. She stopped and ran her eyes over the Plug Ugly.

His eyes were open. Blood saturated his shirt and coat as if he'd been caught in a red rainstorm. His ugly head was covered in scars. The man was cruel, and he probably deserved to die long ago. One knife fight too many. For him it was only a matter of time; the odds were against dying an old man in bed.

She'd have to be more careful. She was known to his associates, and she knew they would come knocking. She gave him a slight tilt of her chin. Their game had ended in blood.

Chapter Six

April 30, 1864
Fort Monroe, Virginia

Their guide hadn't said a word through the night. He had only given the terse command to sit and be quiet. Then he tugged his cap low over his eyes, leaning on the rudder almost as if he were asleep. Wolf and Roberts did as he bade, and with the rising sun, they crept upon the fortress.

Fort Monroe was an irregular bastion fort with seven bastions. It was constructed on a narrow isthmus that stuck directly into the James River. The formation of the land itself led to a natural control of the waterways, something realized early when the United States were British colonies. It was positioned to control maritime access to the James and York rivers as well as the bay leading to the Rappahannock and Potomac Rivers.

The fortress was built into the interior of the isthmus with ten-foot-thick brick and masonry walls and had an eight-foot-deep moat. Numerous red-brick support buildings sat outside the defensive position as well as docks and a harbor. Newer crude hovels made from pieced together wood peppered the landscape, filling in any open space, and giving it a shoddier non-military look.

Originally it had been designed and built after the War of 1812 as part of a series of coastal fortifications to protect the coastal interior of the United States. It was a lesson learned in American blood, sweat, and tears after the British sailed through the Chesapeake and burned the White House and Washington, D.C.

It had been in Federal hands throughout the entirety of the war, having been a starting point for McClellan's Peninsula campaign. Now it headquartered Major General Benjamin Butler's newly formed Army of the James.

The boatman steered the small single-sail skiff toward a dockside harbor under the watch of a cannon mounted in turrets along the walls like metal sentinels.

Colored men fished with makeshift fishing rods off the docks. Others unloaded cargo from a steamship, carrying crates and pushing carts. They all wore coarse linen, wool, or jean cloth shirts, mostly drab in nature of browns and whites that hung loose on their torsos and baggy trousers or breeches. A few wore hats made from plaited straw or wide-brimmed brown hats that Wolf had seen rank-and-file rebel soldiers wear.

"You ever seen so many?" Roberts said.

"I haven't." They'd seen slaves while on their foray near the rebel capital as part of Kilpatrick's raid and even more from afar on the docks in Richmond from the windows of Libby Prison, but here there were so many. "Must be freemen."

Roberts grinned and slapped him on the back. "Just like us."

Wolf cringed as pain spiderwebbed over his back.

"Sorry. Forgot," Roberts said.

The boatman let his vessel reach a dock, and he hurled a rope to a young barefoot colored boy who was waiting. The boy moored the boat, and the boatman tossed him an apple. Catching it with both hands, the boy flashed a grin. He turned and jogged away.

"I can't stay long." The guide gave an irritated glance at the decaying corpse of Colonel Dahlgren. He lay across the width of the ship covered in a blanket. "Hurry along now."

Wolf and Roberts climbed onto the dock and the boatman helped them lift the corpse. The more they moved the long-dead colonel, the worse he stank. Roberts gagged as they untied the watercraft and their guide steered his small craft back down the James, giving a steamship a wide berth.

Voices behind them murmured then grew into a din. Colored workers and children eyed the two gray-coated men with mistrust and fear and even anger.

Roberts spoke from the corner of his mouth. "They all like this?"

The crowd was growing as more came to gawk at them. "We're wearing reb jackets," Wolf said.

"No, no, no," Roberts called at them waving his hands. "We be Union men."

"We escaped!" Wolf said, trying to reason with them.

A few of the freed slaves held sticks and clenched fists. Wolf and Roberts took a step back. He didn't think they'd go after white men, even ones in rebel uniforms, but who knew? If they thought they could get away with a good rebel beating, they may.

"We come in peace," Wolf said. His hand fell on the hilt of his blade. He wouldn't take a beating if he didn't have to, misunderstanding or not.

"We're Lincoln's boys. True Union men. Loyal to the United States thru and thru. Not a secesh bone in our bodies."

The crowd crept forward with an excited energy. A man shouted something intelligible in the back.

"Take your jacket off," Wolf said. Both the men scrambled to remove the rebel coats then tossed them on the docks.

A man yelled as he made his way through the congregation of people. "Move on now, contraband. Get outta the way." The freemen parted ways as a man in blue nudged through. He wore a captain's uniform and a kepi with long bushy sideburns. He folded his arms across his chest.

"Well, what do we have here? A couple reb spies?"

***

An hour later, they stood in Major General Benjamin Butler's study. He was a short squat man, reminding Wolf of a stretched barrel. He gave into going bald with very little grace, and while the top of his head was free of hair, along the crown and down the back it hung to his collar. His mustache drooped like it was depressed to be his, and he held the appearance of a stubborn yet intelligent mule with ambition.

His military reputation was poor despite having some of the first successes of the war. His Federal oversight of the captured Southern port of New

Orleans had earned him the nickname "Beast Butler." He'd forced a series of draconian laws on the citizens which had made him popular with radicals in the North and subsequently politically palatable in the Union. Now he'd found himself at Fort Monroe leading the relatively insignificant Army of the James. He viewed the young men from the side with one of his eyes.

"Heard you boys had a bit of a mix-up on the docks," Butler said with a slimy grin.

"We did, sir," Wolf said.

The major general's study held more than the regular opulence of a general's status indicating wealth from outside the military command structure. Fine gold candlesticks adorned his desk. A stack of oil paintings leaned on the wall in a corner. A large wooden chest rested behind him, secured with a heavy metal lock.

Butler took a seat and stared at them as if he expected a story. "Well. Did Bet say anything about me?"

"She mentioned you, sir."

A grin belonging to the devil himself formed on Butler's lips. "Of course she did." He licked his lips fiendishly. "Anything specific?"

Roberts glanced around uncomfortably. "That she thinks of your embrace often."

"Just grand. Just grand. Been almost six months since I've seen her. Let me tell you, it cost me an entire shipment of confiscated cotton to get her from Richmond and back again. But it was worth every dollar."

"Not sure I understand, sir. You shipped her here?"

"I think you understand perfectly well," Butler said with a broad grin on a button-like mouth. "She is a grand woman."

In Wolf's mind, anyone who helped him escape was the grandest of people. Her fortitude and bravery with a knife pointed at her breast made her exceptional. "She's a brave woman. Forgive us. We didn't spend much time together."

Butler continued to smile. "She is." He sighed, looking them up and down. "I can see how that lot outside thought you were rebels. Starving, ugly, and desperate."

The two former prisoners stood silent.

Raising his eyebrows, Butler continued. "Humorless lot. Suppose that's what Libby does to a man. I trust Ross wasn't too hard on you."

Both men exchanged a glance before Wolf found the words. "He was convincing."

Holding a piece of paper close to his face, Butler read it with one of his eyes. "Van Lew tells me you kept the Dahlgren letter secret."

"I did." *And I paid for it with my flesh and blood*, he added in his mind.

Butler nodded. He had no idea the scars Wolf's body bore for the Union. "Wouldn't put it past the Southern bastards to lie about it. You did good on that. Colonel you say?"

"Colonel Wolf, sir." The words sounded empty on his tongue and he gulped saliva down a dry throat.

The major general rummaged through a stack of papers in a drawer in his desk, flipping through a few. Wolf's lie hung over them like a woolen cloud, and he prayed that Butler couldn't hear the fear in his voice. The general licked his fingers before turning a page over. "Hmm. I don't see you on my list of potential parolees." He studied them again. "But your regiment is a relatively new one, and my list hasn't been updated in some time." He let the paper fall, and the tension shrank into the corners of the room. The major general folded his hands together. "I have secured you passage back to Alexandria where you can fall back into your parent regiment. I suppose you can accompany young Dahlgren the rest of the way."

"It would be an honor," Wolf said. The stench of the man still lingered in his nose and any thoughts of meat were out of the question despite that being the only thing he could fantasize about while imprisoned.

"Thank you, sir," Roberts added. Even he looked a bit green at the thought.

A knock sounded at the door. Butler rose, lumbered over, and answered it.

"Do you think they know?" Roberts whispered.

Wolf shook his head. "I don't think so."

"When do we come clean? You know. Tell them we was faking it."

He had no idea what the penalty was, but impersonating an officer had to be punishable by something severe. This was a mostly volunteer army, so perhaps they would be lenient. Imprisonment. Flogging. Surely nothing capital like they were deserters. Heck, they were trying to escape back to their regiment to fight. "Best to ride this out. Get back to the 13th and blend back in. We tell 'em we escaped and want back into rank."

Butler clapped Wolf's back as he passed. The spot where his hand struck stung, and Wolf grimaced for more than just the pain. He hoped Butler hadn't overheard anything they spoke of.

"Well, we will get you men out of those rags and into your proper uniforms. Then back to Alexandria." Butler stood behind his desk, placing his hands on it as if to prop up his extra belly weight. "It is a pleasure to meet you men. You did a very good thing and I assume that Admiral Dahlgren will want to greet you upon arrival to commend you." He flipped open a gold-trimmed cigar box, exposing finely rolled, rich smelling cigars. "Take one on me, boys. You just remember to vote for me when the war's over."

"Vote, sir?"

"Well, I don't suspect you boys will relocate to Massachusetts, but when the time comes, perhaps a vote for president."

Holding the cigar beneath his nose, Roberts took in its rich scent. "You betcha!"

"Of course, sir," Wolf said.

"Those are my boys. Now, if you'll forgive me, I have some business to attend to."

They left his office. Other men waited outside, each dressed like a civilian ship captain. Long frock coats. Puffy caps. One had a red scarf around his neck.

Wolf and Roberts were shown to an officer's quarters by a cheeky, portly artillery captain and given new uniforms. They were guided to steaming hot bathtubs where the men soaked and puffed on their cigars, enjoying the finer things in life.

A smile found its way onto Wolf's face for the first time in weeks. The wounds on his back were healing. His thumbs didn't ache. And the rich cigar smoke and a glass of whiskey helped the men drift into a deep sleep.

They slept for over twelve hours in beds, and neither man could remember a time they'd slept better. The next day, an officer came and got them, guiding them back to the docks. Everything was golden in their new Union blue uniforms even if they were living a luxurious lie.

Men had even saluted them, and Roberts got a big kick out of saluting back. He even reprimanded a private for slouching at his guard post.

At the docks, they boarded the USS Hunchback, a converted New York ferry. Black smoke puffed from her smokestack, and they sailed their way north toward the capital.

Chapter Seven

May 3, 1864
Potomac River, Virginia

Black clouds billowed from the USS Hunchback's smokestack and clogged the air with a bitter coal stench, and Wolf couldn't care a lick in the whole world. A brisk wind whipped off the waters of the Potomac. In every way it was the opposite of Libby. It ruffled his hair and beard, and even his jacket collar shifted under its fresh, free, and wonderful spell. He closed his eyes, enjoying the clean air.

The steamer had a crew of twenty-two men, including the captain, almost half of which were colored men. The ship was a converted side-wheel ferry that looked more like a swimming turtle than a floating instrument of war. Battered and dented armaments protected the wheels that propelled the ship along the sides.

A single 12-pounder Dahlgren smoothbore howitzer mounted on an iron carriage rested near the rear of the watercraft. More stationary Dahlgren smoothbore guns bristled from places on the steamer that once held passengers, horses, and carriages as a ferry in New York City.

The crew worked well together, and there was no dissension among them. They treated Wolf and Roberts with respect, and they had dined with Acting Master E.K. Valentine, who acted as captain, on their way from Fort Monroe north.

After days on the river, the trees on either side of the Potomac were already burgeoning from petite buds to lush greenery, another retreating of spring before a summer campaign of war. As they sailed closer to Washington, Wolf had found himself in a precarious situation. He needed to find a way back to his unit without attracting too much attention. Otherwise, who knew what awaited him. The thought had preoccupied Roberts incessantly as the ship chugged north. The men stood near the bow, basking in the stench-free air.

"We could go west. Land as far as the eye can see. Perhaps find some gold. I heard of men making it rich there."

Wolf's voice dropped. "You mean desert?"

"I see it as mustering out early."

Wolf shook his head. "If they found out, they'd send the marshal to hang us."

"*If* they found out. That's a lot of land they'd have to search. A man could simply fade away into the wilderness."

"I ain't looking over my shoulder for the rest of my life."

"We could go north to Canada. Hunt beaver or bear pelts. Heard of men doing that."

"I'm no deserter. The army gave me a life. I ain't turning my back on it."

"The army might turn their back on you. The army might hang you from a gallows until you were done dancing your jig."

"They won't." They absolutely could but he believed they wouldn't. Prayed they wouldn't. "When we reach the port, we shed these uniforms and walk our way back. Keep our story straight. No problems."

"What's our story? We walked out of prison?"

"Aye, we did."

"They're going to want to meet the men who lifted Colonel Dahlgren's body north. His father. Butler thought maybe even old Abe himself."

"Not if we're nowhere to be found. Just two lowly enlisted back in our unit."

Roberts stared out, his dark eyes reading the treed shores. "As much as I hate prison, it's been nice having everyone respecting us like."

"A small price to pay for freedom."

"Just to get killed fighting somewhere else. Suppose that was always to be the case." He gripped the rail, looking like he might throw himself over.

"Colonel Wolf!" Valentine cried. "Captain Roberts!" The commander of the ship climbed down a ladder from the wheelhouse and straightened his frock coat as he walked. "Don't suppose you gentlemen would like to share a cigar with me before we land in Alexandria? It's a bit of a tradition."

The two free men exchanged a look. "Enjoy it while it lasts," Wolf said.

"It would be a pleasure, good Captain," Roberts said with a slight bow of his head.

Valentine removed three cigars from an interior pocket and handed them to the men. Striking a match, he lit his then handed the flame off.

All three took in the scenes of a busy harbor and enjoyed the warm breeze. Dockside buildings came into view. Double-sailed schooners and steamships with giant wheels propelled passed them. Small fishing boats darted in and out and between the larger vessels. The Hunchback plodded along, carefully navigating through it all.

Alexandria was the closest Southern-occupied city to Washington, D.C. It was right across the Potomac River from the nation's capital, and when Virginia seceded, they were never given even an inch of freedom. Soon after Virginia's defection from the Union, Federal troops poured across the river, seizing control of the important Potomac port. Rebel flags were torn down, and the citizens had been under the Federal government's yoke ever since.

"Slow her down," Valentine called at his wheelhouse. Wolf didn't see how they could go much slower than their current rate. The ferry wheels churned a fraction slower in its circular rotation. Black smoke diminished from her stack. The Hunchback's speed decreased along with its soft wake in the brown waters.

Valentine puffed happily. "Alexandria used to be a quaint town. Now look at her. It's no more than a swollen belly of the Union Army." Wagons rolled munitions. Brand new cannons were offloaded from ships. Union men in blue uniforms directed colored workers on the docks. Every part of the town bustled with activity, all of it seemingly related to the war effort.

"She's full of Union men."

"Aye, she is. Many are sick and wounded. Lots of missing limbs here. Must be almost thirty hospitals. See there."

Roberts and Wolf turned and scanned the city's waterfront.

"Those three buildings in a row." He pointed out a four-story redbrick structure. "Used to be a bank and two stores. Now it only sells hands and feet." The captain shook his head. "This war is changing us."

Wolf stretched his back and then pulled up on his rusty brace. The war was changing him too. He felt seasoned, like he'd seen enough for ten men. Then again perhaps he had. He knew one thing; he wasn't going back to Libby. He'd die before that. He'd gained an acute understanding of Captain Yates's desire to never return to the rat-infested prison and held the same distinct belief.

"Used to trade and sell slaves here too. One of the main places to do it in the upper South. Kept them right over there before auction."

"Used to," Wolf said.

The captain wavered his head. "May come back someday. If the South wins."

Wolf puffed on his cigar. "They won't." He would see to that. He would see the nation's ship righted her course or at least do whatever the army sent him to do, and win or lose, the army would have something for him to do.

"I heard a lot of men say that. You should have seen them forcing everyone to sign the oath of allegiance. Ha. It was like pulling teeth. Hollering and screeching. Those will be some tough people to bring back into the fold."

"Captain, you sound like you may have Southern leanings yourself?"

The captain placed a hand on his chest. "I am a realist. The Union pays, I sail for them. Either way, countries need ships and men to man 'em. Trade happens regardless of who wins, and I will continue to be employed."

"You'd think with your kind of crew that you would be a Union man through and through."

The captain surveyed the colored men working his boat. "Let me tell you a secret. Those men over there work harder than any white man I've had on my crew. Many of 'em are stronger. Don't grumble, just do what they're told. I'd take them all on if I wasn't afraid of getting hung with 'em if we got captured. I ain't no John Brown."

"No. No. Of course not," Roberts said.

"We appreciate you taking us with you," Wolf added.

"The Hunchback goes where she's told to go. No more, no less." Valentine eyed the slips. "When this all cools down, might head west. Country's growing. Westward."

Roberts nudged him with an elbow. "You see, Wolf? I told you west was the way to go."

"Ain't nowhere else to go but the West," Valentine said. More sailors traversed the deck now, prepping mooring ropes and preparing to dock. "But I'm just a man of the sea. Not sure how I'd fare with all you landlubbers."

Wolf eyed Roberts for a moment. Perhaps his friend was right. Maybe they should just head to the West and leave this god forsaken civil conflict to somebody else. Let other people bleed for this land.

Valentine continued. "Fortunes to be had. Gold and land. What else do you need?"

"There's Indians out there," Roberts suggested.

"Where do you think you boys are headed after this here war?" Valentine looked at them. "If you stay in, you'll go out West. Clear the way for the settlers."

"You think?" Wolf asked.

"If you wasn't fighting each other, you'd be rounding up those redskins and driving them out."

The captain's words rang true. The country was spreading. Land was being gobbled up. Immigrants came by the boatload like Wolf's people had in the recent past. The native peoples would continue to be driven away to make room for the newcomers.

"But I'm just a sailing man. What would I know?" Valentine pointed at the wheelhouse. "Bring her in to the slip, Rodney."

The Hunchback began a slow eking turn into the docks. Over twenty ships lined the slips, some sail, tall masts poking toward the sky like bayonets, others steamships. The Hunchback bobbed its way into the slip, and colored men waited to help them moor. Ropes were flung between the ship and the quay. Once the ship was secured into place, the sailors stretched a gangway to the dock, and goods began to be unloaded.

"We made it," Roberts said. He smiled at Wolf and clasped hands with him. The men got closer and hugged, relief washing over them like a warm rain. Finally, they were back in the safe embrace of the Union capital region, far enough from the tortures of Richmond and the tens of thousands of troops and forts between them and any rebel armies.

Valentine grabbed Wolf's shoulder, sending him a painful reminder of his time with Captain Marshall Payne. "Welcome back, gentleman. Where would you like the good colonel?" He pointed at two Negro sailors holding a crude wooden coffin between them. Much to the appeasement of everyone, Butler had the body placed in a coffin in a cool place as to slow the decomposition and mask some of the stench.

Wolf pointed out. "On the dock over there will be fine. We are expecting someone from the Admiral Dahlgren's staff to pick him up."

"Very well. Until we meet again." Valentine took his leave and joined his sailors, issuing orders at a shout.

The two men collected their meager belongings and disembarked. The docks reeked of fish. They were surrounded on all sides by the active sounds of a wartime harbor. Horns blowing. Seagulls calling overhead. Men yelling to one another as they worked. On the streets, carts clanked along redbrick roads.

"Now we have to ditch these uniforms and find out where the 13th is camped," Wolf said.

"What if they aren't here?"

"Then we find a way there." The quay felt solid under his feet, but Roberts's continuous worry was driving him mad.

"I dunno. Maybe we should run."

Turning on him, Wolf grabbed by the scruff, hissing. "Where are we going to go?"

Roberts raised his eyebrows. "West? I ain't got no family to go back to."

"I ain't going back home to tell my father I'm some sort of coward. I'd rather die." He released his friend, smoothing Roberts's uniform then clapping his shoulder. "We'll go back to our command. We can't let our brothers down. That's our family and it ain't right to desert them. Besides, what would Berles think?"

"I wouldn't want to let the sergeant down. He's taken care of us."

"Me neither. I apologize for getting angry."

"Well, you ruffled my fine uniform." Roberts pulled away. "You should treat a captain with more respect."

"We ain't no officers. We're just us."

They moved down the docks with a bit of pep in their step.

"Excuse me." An officer waved at them from the edge of the wharf. He was young with a clean-shaven face. His uniform was spotless, and he dodged around a pool of water to come closer. He peered down at a piece of paper before he spoke. "Colonel Wolf?" He lifted a hand in a hasty salute, and for the briefest of moments, Wolf forgot he was playing the colonel. "You came in on the Hunchback?"

Wolf saluted back. "Yes, Lieutenant."

"Lieutenant Fox, sir. I am here on behalf of General Custer."

"Dahlgren's body is on the dock waiting for transport." Wolf pointed behind him.

"Someone else will collect that. You are Johannes Wolf, are you not?" His eyes squinted as if he questioned his own words.

Wolf felt the blood drain from his face. His gut churned like he had contracted a severe case of the Virginia Quickstep.

The lieutenant turned toward Roberts. "And you are Ira Roberts?"

"I am." Roberts gulped and seemed to shrink in his jacket.

"You came from Butler at Fort Monroe?"

Wolf side-eyed Roberts. "We did."

Fox lifted his chin. "We've been expecting you. I'd like to welcome you back to the Army of the Potomac."

A breath escaped Wolf's lips, and he relaxed for a moment. "It's good to be back."

"Come this way," Fox said. The lieutenant was a quick walker, and Wolf had to hurry his pace so as to not be left behind. They walked over a redbrick road. Carts bustled past. Fox sidestepped a suspicious puddle again. A squad of infantry marched down the center of the street, muskets on their shoulders.

Halting, Fox lifted a hand and spun on them. His eyes narrowed as he spoke, causing Wolf to tense. "By the authority placed in me by the United States, you men are under arrest."

Wolf and Roberts stopped, frozen in the street. Their eyes searched for a way out. Filthy brown water lapping around the wharf could provide an escape. The infantry squad halted. The sergeant on the edge of the formation lowered his hand. "Ready!" The soldiers raised their muskets to their shoulders.

The lieutenant lifted his chin in righteous authority. "You men come peacefully, and that will be taken into consideration during your trial."

Wolf's hand slipped to the knife on his belt. Neither man had any other weapon. They were mere passengers until they had a chance to be refitted by a quartermaster.

Spit flew from Fox's mouth. "Do not try me, Corporal. I will not ask again."

"Aim!" the sergeant shouted. Gun barrels were sighted upon them, waiting to breathe forth fire like slender dragons. The soldiers squinted on the other side. At this short distance, they would make quick work of them.

"I ain't trying to die today," Roberts whispered.

"Surrender or get shot. Take your pick," Fox called to them almost as if he dared them to run.

"Maybe they'll just flog us?" Roberts squeaked.

"Corporal, surrender," Fox called at him.

Citizens and passersby began to gather, chattering to one another and pointing at the confrontation near the docks: Union men preparing to shoot Union men.

Wolf sighed, letting his hands lift into the air. "We surrender."

"Sergeant, restrain these men," Fox said with a sneer.

The infantrymen jogged forward, using the butts of their muskets to usher the prisoners along. Wolf's blade was taken from him again.

"I'll be getting that back."

The private smiled at him. "Dead man don't need no things."

"I ain't going to die."

"Private," Fox ordered, "give that over." His face darkening, the private handed the blade to his commanding officer. There was always a pecking order among soldiers, thieves, and clergy.

The squad marched the prisoners around a street corner to a three-story redbrick building. Its sides were whitewashed, and a single-story brick warehouse was attached. A strip of white had been painted above the doors. The outline of letterings read Price, Birch & Co., Dealers in Slaves. A Union man lounged in the doorway, leaning against the frame. The doors were open to the interior.

Fox nodded to the man. The man smiled with blackened teeth. "Got some fancy boys today."

"Do not be fooled by their coats. They are enlisted, Corporal Mack. I place them in your custody."

"Follow me then."

Wolf stopped in the doorway. A sharp buttstock into his lower back propelled him through. The interior of the building was dark and had a couple of desks inside. A rusted cross-barred iron gate was open, and Mack stepped through into the adjacent warehouse.

"The one on the end will do for these two."

The warehouse held a long row of cells; each had a thick wooden door with a latch and lock. The floor was planked and stained with mud. There were chains and hooped rings on the walls along with manacles. They were rusted and empty, dangling reminders of the trade in human flesh.

Mack noticed them staring at the chains and spoke. "When we first arrived in Alexandria, there was still one of them darkies chained up there. Half-dead like they'd forgot him. That's how quick those rebs ran out of here."

Wolf and Roberts were shoved into the holding cell. The door closed behind them. The room was almost entirely dark with an overwhelming damp musty smell. The only fresh air or light came through the small cutout holes in the door hardly large enough for a man to fit his fingers through. There were no benches or beds, just a plank floor and a leaky bucket.

"Corporal, I will return when it is decided how to proceed with them."

"Oh, you know. They ain't goin' nowhere." Mack grabbed the door and shook it. "Strong oak." He looked through a hole at them. "What you boys in for?"

"Impersonating an officer," Roberts said.

"Ha, where'd you get that idea? You know they don't like nobody like yourself in their club."

"We only done it to survive."

"They don't care why we did it," Wolf said.

"You be a smart one. But not smart enough to not hang," Mack said.

Wolf slumped down the edge of the wall.

Mack shook the door again, and it wasn't clear if he was testing the security or tormenting his prisoners. "You boys holler if you need anything. I like to keep my tenants happy."

"Maybe some food?" Roberts asked through the holes.

"You really are dense, aren't ya?" Mack said. He chuckled and left the room, snickering to himself as if the answer was so clear and easy.

"Back in a cell," Roberts muttered.

"Just traded one for the other."

"You leave me out of this, Wolf. It's the last time I listen to you."

"Ah, probably is."

Roberts took a seat across from him, and both men put their heads down in silence. They'd escaped only to become prisoners of their own army.

Chapter Eight

May 6, 1864
Near Todd's Tavern, Virginia

Brigadier General George Armstrong Custer adjusted the collar on his blue sailor shirt beneath a black velvet hussar-style jacket. His red necktie chafed his skin. It was a unique style to himself, a style that had been adopted by his men. Red neckties were worn throughout the ranks, displaying a bond of respect he'd built with his men.

Officers from the Army of the Potomac's Cavalry Corps filled the old farmhouse where Major General Philip Sheridan had chosen to meet and strategize with them. As in any costly war, especially one that was so uncivil, new faces lined the rows of men both sitting and standing.

There were newcomers from the Western Theater, but most were men that had risen through the ranks earning their commands with tact and guts or in some cases bad luck. Not many were left in command that had fought at Gettysburg.

The rotation of faces was quicker than a dance around a Maypole; every time they met, there were new officers. Those that had disappeared had been displaced, dismissed, transferred, killed, or wounded.

Shake-ups had occurred all over the Cavalry Corps after Grant's arrival a few months prior. Judson Kilpatrick had been sent west after the debacle of his raid on Richmond. Custer wasn't sorry to see the blowhard and brash commander go. Ulric Dahlgren was dead. He hadn't known him well, but the man was Kilpatrick's lackey, so his loss wasn't terrible. Then there were those that would be missed. The most highly thought of and distinguished cavalry officer in the Union, John Buford, had died of a fever the previous December.

It was a rotating carousel of command. Alfred Pleasonton, once Custer's benefactor, had been shown the door in place of a bandy-legged short Irishman with a neatly trimmed mustache who went by the name Philip Henry Sheridan, known to the men as "Little Phil." It wasn't this man's appointment that bothered Custer. No. Colonel Alger of the 5th Michigan spoke highly of the appointee. But the men that had been appointed at the divisional level over Custer left much to be desired.

There had been a succession crisis in the eyes of the men when the 3rd Cavalry Division was given to Brigadier General James Wilson. He was an engineer until only a few days ago, and starred after Custer, Davies, and Merritt, making him ineligible to command senior officers by virtue of time in grade.

Custer had known Wilson from West Point, and Wilson was not a man he could fathom serving under. In fact, he loathed the man. He'd made that very clear to Sheridan, and the corps commander responded by moving Custer under the 1st Division whose command now fell to another unexperienced cavalryman, Alfred Torbert. However, taking into consideration the alternative, a slightly more likable fellow.

The divisional shuffle had cost Custer one of his favorite subordinates and artillery commander, Alexander C.M. Pennington, and the esteemed 1st Vermont, both of which he had fought tooth and nail to keep under his command. However, Sheridan hadn't budged, and when Custer pushed harder his superior offered him a fine string of curse words that would put a sailor to shame.

Torbert sat near Sheridan, a degree of haughtiness settling on his face. He resembled a younger version of General Ambrose Burnside with his bushy sideburns connecting with his mustache. For all his pompousness, the man could hardly ride a horse and carried himself like he was a gift from the Creator himself. *We will see how far he can ride.* The table they sat around was only so big, and most of the junior regimental officers stood. Custer's men lined the wall behind him.

In his own Michigan Brigade, the faces had almost all changed. Colonel Town of the 1st Michigan had departed back for his home state. The combination of consumption and campaigning had taken their toll on the cadaverous colonel. Custer didn't think he would live long.

The 1st fell to Lieutenant Colonel Peter Stagg, a capable soldier who had stepped in for Town on many occasions. He kept his thick jaw free of all facial hair and had piercing blue eyes that could read the terrain in a moment. He held steady reins on the veteran regiment.

Then there was Colonel William D. Mann of the 7th. Custer never had any love for the wild-bearded man. A man with a beard and a crazy-eyed gaze should have been well suited for war, but in fact, he was much better suited for solving logistical needs. His patented invention to assist the way soldiers carried packs and equipment with adjustable straps had actually been a worthy improvement.

It was enough that Custer looked past his dislike and supported the colonel and his product. The Ordnance Department felt otherwise. Of course it was all financially oriented, so much so that he was surprised when they had begun issuing more of the repeating Spencer carbines.

Mann hadn't gotten his way and resigned his commission, which wasn't a huge negative in Custer's mind. His replacement, Major Henry W. Granger, stood to Custer's left. He had a broad face, a commanding voice, and a thick bushy beard that reminded him of a grizzly bear.

A youthful face stood on the other side of Granger. Major James B. Kidd of the 6th Michigan had become Colonel Kidd after Colonel Gray had to seek rest for a bad back.

Bad backs and horsemanship did not go hand in hand. But God bless the man if he didn't try his hardest on countless occasions to return to his regiment. His Lieutenant Colonel Thompson had been wounded in Hunterstown, leaving Major Kidd as the next replacement. He'd proven himself sound and energetic. Time and luck would tell how far he'd go.

Then there was the portly Colonel James F. Moore of the 13th Michigan.

He'd managed to find a seat at the table despite only leading a regiment. He stared longingly at the major general as he spoke. Custer trusted him about as far as he could throw him, which wasn't a great distance, yet somehow the commander with the least innate abilities and minutest martial prowess had survived and maintained his position within the Michigan Brigade.

The man standing on Custer's right was the only other man who had been with him since the beginning, Colonel Russell A. Alger of the 5th Michigan. A handsome man with dark hair, he held no love for Torbert but respected Sheridan, and that was enough for Custer to trust the man as well.

"I'll tell you one thing about Meade. He is an old grandma in general's clothing who doesn't have a goddamn sense in a bone of his body. He lacks innovation. He lacks guts," Sheridan spat. "And if I had half of a man as a superior, this war could be done."

Torbert's face took on a less than comfortable tone. He had been appointed by Meade. He was also at the root of the conflict. His men had relinquished Todd's Tavern under Meade's orders that had superseded Sheridan's orders. Now rebels had entrenched themselves at the critical crossroads, and Meade had directed the cavalry to take it back. Men would die on the morrow because of the confusion.

Custer peered at the short brown major general with long arms and bandy legs. His neck was hardly enough to hang the fellow. His rival, Wilson, didn't look much better. He had been bested during the opening engagements of the Battle of the Wilderness. On the opposite end, Custer's Brigade had been met with success once they escaped the drudgery of baggage train duty. He'd had but only a moment to scribble a letter to Libbie about it.

Oh my love, I wonder what you are doing now? Do you think of me as I think of you? He couldn't remember a time before her delicate embrace. He tried to shove the thoughts of his lovely wife into his heart and focus on the task at hand.

Tomorrow would be bloody. Men would die crawling over the rotting fly-covered corpses of horse and man alike. The army had most likely lost the initiative to wedge itself between Lee and Richmond, which meant infantry would again be thrown into the meat grinder that could have been avoided.

But tomorrow Sheridan's command would retake Todd's Tavern, clearing the way for Grant's army.

"They don't call him Old Snapping Turtle for nothing, sir," Wilson said.

Sheridan sighed, shaking his head. His face was heated with agitation. He'd been going on and on for over an hour about his distaste for Meade. "If he hadn't recalled my orders, we could have gotten the jump on them."

"They are on the defensive, sir. We will break them on this rugged ground and take Richmond," Wilson said with an assuring smile. Charming and likable words wouldn't make up for a weak performance in the field, at least that was Custer's take on it. Then again, these men were the ones promoted.

"Granny Lee will see that we can't. Or we will turn around and march back home. We need off our leash. We have over 100,000 men in this army. We have over 10,000 cavalrymen. Let's use them."

"Grant won't back down. He's promised this much, but I cannot speak for Meade," Wilson added. He'd been a former aide to Grant and was apparently making sure everyone was aware of his close relationship with the Union Army's top dog.

Sheridan slammed his fist into the table. "I don't give a damn what Meade thinks. I am trying to whip the devil out of some rebs and win this damn war. We don't have time for cautious maneuvers."

A captain stepped inside the room. He stood with his black slouch hat underneath his arm.

Sheridan licked his lips. "We need to draw them out. Destroy them. Stuart doesn't have the men or the horses to sustain any kind of engagement with us."

The officers raised their voices in agreement with the fervor of their commander. "Ayes" and "Yeas" came from them. Not one wanted to appear timid in front of their new commander.

Sheridan licked his lips. "One of you needs to give me something. Something I can take to Grant to convince him this is possible. Think on it tonight men; tomorrow come to me with your plans. We have a long road ahead."

Custer ran fingers over his mustache, massaging it down. A suitable plan was a good way to gain favor and make his rival Wilson look worse by stealing the show. He must write Libbie before he laid his head down to rest. Surely she would have some profound input for a plan, if she was here with him.

The officers took their leave, one by one filing out.

"Autie, would you care to grab a drink?" Alger said.

"Not tonight. I must get a letter to Libbie. It's been too long."

"It's been only a few days since we left." A small grin took over his lips beneath his closely trimmed ebony-colored beard.

"I wouldn't expect you to understand a man in love."

Alger's grin became mischievous. "You're a changed man."

Custer matched his grin. "You, my good man, will never change."

"You sure I can't pull you away?"

"I would only be a distraught and miserable drinking partner. My mind is elsewhere." An idea struck him and he blinked. *That's it!*

"I've seen that look before," Alger said.

"I think I have an idea."

"Should I be nervous or excited to get back into the thick of it?"

A slight smirk formed on Custer's face. "I'd say a little of both. I'll let you know later."

Alger understood his meaning: leave him in private with Sheridan. "You stop by if you want some sleeping medicine." He nodded to Sheridan as he left.

The major general eyed him. "General, do you have something to say?" With a tiny irritated shake, he said, "I swear to God if you are going to complain about Torbert's command, I will shove my boot so far up your ass." His eyes read Custer, and satisfied that he wasn't going to protest, his tone softened. "You did well out there today."

"Thank you, sir. But no need for any boot shoving."

Sheridan held up a finger. "You aren't getting Pennington back either."

"A damn shame but not what I wanted to talk about."

Leaning back in his chair, Sheridan said. "You have a plan for me already?"

"You know me, sir. I love a good scrap. You point me in the right direction, and I will bring those rebels to heel."

"I want to dismantle the rebel cavalry piece by piece," Sheridan said. "Give me something to convince Grant to let his dogs of war off the leash."

"I've been going up against Stuart for a long time. His subordinates are well-versed and high-quality horsemen." Custer's smile deepened. He'd bested Rosser, a friend and roommate from West Point, all afternoon. The big dark Texan was an admirable rival and an excellent commander. They would have still been close if they fought on the same side.

But alas, that wasn't how this war worked. Sloppy, dirty, and personal. Except nobody knew it would be like that when the war began. He wondered if the country still would have tread the same path with the knowledge they held now. "They are cool-headed, and they don't want a true fight if they know the odds are against them."

"Tell me something I don't know, General."

"You see, I have an idea. One that will bring Stuart out. Force him to fight. Act rashly and without thought."

Sheridan's eyes narrowed above high cheekbones. "And how would you accomplish this?"

"I simply thought about what would drive me mad." He paused for effect. "And there is one thing that would drive me and all other men madder than a rabid dog. Miserable and mad enough to risk everything."

Sheridan spoke quickly. He wanted the answer to his problem now. "And what might this be?"

"May I take a seat?"

"Of course. Get on with it," he said, ushering him to sit.

"I have two prisoners we didn't have time to deal with before we departed Stevensburg. They're actually still in Alexandria."

"We have plenty of prisoners."

"No, Union men."

"Deserters?"

Custer shook his head to the negative. "Not one bit."

"What got them there?"

"Impersonating officers." Sheridan did not appear impressed, but Custer continued onward anyway, hoping he hadn't jumped too far out of line.

74

"They went on that Kilpatrick raid and got themselves captured wearing officers' coats. Escaped Libby. Made it to Fort Monroe. Butler had them shipped to Alexandria."

"That cross-eyed prick had no idea?"

"He thought they were telling the truth."

Sheridan leaned forward patting his coat for a cigar. He reached back, searching a different pocket. Finding one, he plopped back into his chair. "I don't see what this has to do with getting us off Meade's leash? Destroying Stuart's command? Winning the war?"

"Well, you see, I have an idea."

Chapter Nine

Early morning, May 7, 1864
Near Shady Grove Church, Virginia

Major General Wade Hampton III rubbed the brim of his black slouch hat. Dust cloaked the edge, and he ran a thumb over and over it in an attempt to correct its imperfection. There was increasing heat this May morning, and the heat brought dryness and dust which made a soldier appear flustered, weary, and unsoldierly. Lately he had been all three, but his officers and servants were cognizant enough to not test him.

He had been the richest man in the South before the war. Despite his father and grandfather having been war heroes, the need had never arisen for him to take up arms until the North had decided to force all the South into a rebellion.

He'd outfitted his own legion—composed of infantry, cavalry, and artillery—and had risen through the ranks to major general. His rise was marked by his calculated and aggressive maneuvers that earned his soldiers' respect. And now while he should be leading an entire division in the battle taking place up north, he'd been regulated to an effective squadron of about two hundred men. Barely two hundred men.

A woman's laughter caught his ear, raising his blood pressure even higher. In an adjacent room sat two of Stuart's aides digging through mountains of paperwork. The larger of the two, whom he recognized as Henry McClellan had a tall frame and a thick chest, looked up, shaking his head. The smaller bookish man with spectacles continued surveying the documents with great interest.

Hampton had been waiting for over an hour for his commanding officer to meet with him, and while they were in the middle of a war, he'd made a romantic rendezvous with his wife.

Giggles, amorous laughter, and charming sighs had leaked from the room with seemingly no end in sight. Each youthful sound of pleasure dug him deeper into his pit of anger. Yet he waited in a dining room along with the ghost of his brother, whom he ignored, and another officer.

The man across from him sat erect. He was slender, older than Hampton, and white covered most of his head. He was handsome with an imperious and intelligent air to him. Surely another aristocrat turned officer of the South. His gray uniform was pristine as if it had seen neither weather nor war.

Hampton stood abruptly, causing the man across from his to shift uncomfortably. He started to pace, his large riding boots thumping the floor. It drew the attention of the older and spectacled aide. He glanced from his papers. Hampton glared in his direction and the man eagerly went back to reading. Pacing was the only action he could do to contain his unsettled frustrations.

Many men called him the Brute, most just Wade or Hampton. Rumors ran through his tiny command that he'd fought a bear and won. Like most rumors, much of it was false with slivers of truth and fact.

In actuality, he'd shot the bear first then ran it through with his hunting knife. Oh, how the grizzly had bellowed, scaring him, but he'd done it. Not with his bare hands like the gossipers held, but he let the men have their fun and create their heroes.

It kept their minds off the task of living and dying at his command. It held them in check. Lack of respect for a leader could quickly disintegrate into mob rule, and he made sure that they felt his respect in return. *I will not lead them where I do not wish to go.* And he wished to go and fight Grant's monstrosity of an army, an army that had moved below the Rapidan River searching for a fight.

They'd been surprised when the Federals had stuck around after the bloodletting at the Wilderness, an area that was so thick with foliage one couldn't tell friend from foe, and he was sure the Southerners feared that land more than the invaders.

The door creaked open from a bedroom. Hampton's eyes zeroed in on it with expectation. The other men glanced toward it as well.

A woman's form filled the doorway. Her hair was dark, almost black, parted down the middle, and pulled back into a bun. Her lips and mouth were average and her nose more round than sharp. Her white, black, and gray dress was long and patterned with crisscrossed lines and her collar lined with lace. She wore tiny gold hooped earrings, and her brown eyes regarded Hampton with friendliness. She smiled when she saw the colonel quickly approaching them.

"Edmund. It is such a pleasure to see you again."

The colonel stood, bowing his head. "And I you, Flora."

Her smile didn't fade as she turned to Hampton. "General, it is good to see you again. I trust your hip has healed?"

Hampton pushed down his own angry feelings at having to wait and placed a gruff smile on his lips. A woman's smile could always soften a man's inner turmoil. "It has, ma'am. Thank you." The truth of it was, it nagged him every time he mounted and dismounted his horse not to mention sitting for any length of time. In the end, he supposed it was a small price to pay to stay in this world.

He noticed her clothing was lighter than normal instead of mourning black. She had been publicly grieving the loss of her daughter to a fever for over two years. "You look well-rested, ma'am. I trust all is well with the family."

She gave him a slight grin. "It is nice to be back on my feet. Little Virginia and Jeb Junior are well."

"Happy to hear it."

She stepped closer. Her smile held confidence, but uncertainty crept upon it. "You will watch out for him. My Jeb?"

Hampton bent down from above. She stuck out her hands, and he gripped them carefully as a porcelain teacup. "Of course, my lady. He has my love and that of the men. We would never let harm befall him."

She blinked rapidly and her smile broadened. She gulped before she spoke. "I will hold you to your word." She cast a brief look at Fontaine and released Hampton's hands. "I am holding you from your business with my husband."

Hampton lowered his head in respect.

"Come Flora, we must make haste for Beaver Dam. Maria and the girls cannot wait to see you. Lucia and Rosalie have a gift for you and Virginia."

"Then let us not tarry."

"Flora," came a voice. The bearded major general, J. E. B. Stuart, the Knight of the Golden Spurs, also known as the Beauty, and all around dashing legend of the Confederate Cavalry Corps stood in only a shirt buttoned halfway up. He wore no weapon. No ostrich-plumed hat. He looked like a plain country gentleman just having awoke from slumber, not a man leading a corps in the middle of a war.

He held out his arms for her and she swooned to his side and they embraced. He cradled her cheeks as they kissed deeply. After a moment, Hampton averted his eyes to give the two privacy. A few long seconds later, the two separated after repeated pecks to each other's lips and little terms of endearment like "Honey" and "Buttercup."

Stuart pointed at Fontaine. "Do not delay. It is not safe here."

The colonel nodded and led Flora outside the home. Holding his hat, Hampton approached. The love-stricken general watched his wife and her cousin leave with longing eyes, ignoring his subordinate. Stuart sighed like a schoolboy smitten for the first time.

"It's been a tough few years for the both of us."

The ghost of his brother Frank still sat in the dining room watching the living with indifferent sunken eyes. Hampton didn't want to console the general on his personal losses. He was here for business, but he understood the sense of loss from the war. It lingered around them all like a pale fog always engulfing them.

They'd both lost friends and family in this war. Hampton's two sons under his command had been spared both illness and injury. For that he was blessed. He had an intimate understanding of what loss could do to a man. Stuart's loss wasn't on the battlefield, but it plagued his family no less, especially his grieving wife.

Hampton glanced at the ghost of his brother and sighed. "It has, Jeb." He paused. "But that's not why I am here."

Stuart's eyes regarded him for a moment as if Hampton's true form pulled him from the Avalon of better times. "I know why you are here, General." He turned and went for the dining room table.

"Then you understand why I chafe to be without a division while we fight against Grant's invading leviathan."

"I appreciate your concern."

Do you? "I need the Laurel Brigade at my disposal now."

"I know you do. They would already be under your command, but I needed them to stymie Meade or Grant, take your pick, so we could secure defensive positions."

Hampton's voice grew in volume a hair. "I do not want to give up Gordon either. With only one brigade, I will be smaller than a junior division commander."

Stuart blew hot air through his mustache. "Do not bring that up, General."

"It is a most egregious slight." Hampton's voice dipped back to a hushed bark. "Does Marse Robert lack so much confidence in my abilities?"

The major general pounded the table. "He does not."

"Then why does he slight me so?"

They locked eyes. Hampton knew what he was to say, but he wanted him to say it out loud. Recognize the unfairness of the situation. Admit that Lee treated him different than his own kin. Acknowledge there was nepotism. "I've written both yourself and Lee many times now. Have I fallen out of favor?"

"You have not. Marse Robert is irritated with so much whining, but he has not lost faith."

Hampton stood taller. He towered over his commander as well. He wasn't one to be told he was a complainer. He was a doer, taking what he had and getting the job done, but what could be accomplished with two hundred men? He could do something, but his full weight could only be felt with the proper command.

"Then I ask. Why do I sit command-less?"

"Good God, man. What do you want me to say? Rooney deserves a division. He is a sound commander. That division needs one of their kind to lead them."

Virginia rules the roost while the rest bear the brunt. "At the expense of senior commanders? Men that are proven at a divisional level?"

"He was a prisoner for God's sake. Give the man some space."

"You did not answer my question."

Stuart shook his head, having been broken down to the truth. "It's Lee's son. What more of an answer do you want? Of course, he's going to be given responsibility. If he has an ounce of genius that his father has, we are better for it."

Hampton closed his mouth. Actions and results were not enough to garner favor. Rooney had good commanding qualities, but the South prided herself on respect of a man's quality, and he knew he was Rooney's superior. He also knew pushing Stuart wouldn't accomplish much. If only they would have shipped him west like had been requested by Johnston and then Longstreet. He wouldn't have been stripped down as his regiments were sent away for refitting in the winter, leaving him almost without a command to turn away Judson Kilpatrick. It was like he was being held back because he was too valuable but lacked the right pedigree to be rewarded.

Stuart stared up at him. "I've instructed Rosser to return here. He will fall under you, but you must give Gordon to Rooney."

"You know I protest this exchange. I don't even have all of Young's men. Half don't have horses." The railroads were as much of a determent as they were assistance. A patchwork of weak infrastructure that the Federals seemed to take great joy in destroying made transportation of troops a logistical nightmare for the rebels.

There was little fight in Stuart's voice. "I understand your dilemma and note your protest."

"I have less than two brigades. My effectiveness will be hampered."

"You will do what you always do, which is lead and win."

"Of course, sir."

"Can we conduct our business now?"

Hampton dipped his chin in concession.

"I believe that stubborn drunk Grant means to continue his debacle of a campaign. He's trying to flank us to Richmond. If he can control Spotsylvania Court House, he will have easy access to the capital." Stuart nodded, studying a map on the table. "But he isn't infallible. His corps comes in pieces from the Wilderness. One at a time. There is our opportunity. We just need to slow them down."

He tapped the map. "Federal Cavalry has been seen here. Todd's Tavern. A disgusting little hovel. If we can bottle them up here, that will give Lee a chance to shift his army from the Wilderness."

Hampton scrutinized the map. "Lee has a much farther way to go."

"He does. That's why I need you."

"As soon as I make contact with Rosser, I will move out to see what can be done."

"Very good, General." Stuart sighed. "I know this can be trying, but Grant is Lincoln's last hope. If we can defeat him here, we can win."

"I share your optimism, sir."

"Very good."

Hampton took his leave. The door opened before he reached it. A man stepped inside. His almost black beard was short along the sides but in a longer rectangle around his chin. His receding hair had been brushed to the side of his head and was kept in place by sweat and natural grease, flaring outward from his ears. His eyes had a slight downward slant, making him appear worried. His cheeks were thinner than Hampton remembered, a combination of his recovery from Gettysburg and his subsequent imprisonment, but his nose was still too round, giving him a slightly more proletarian appearance. His mouth pursed when he recognized Hampton.

"General Hampton."

"General Lee."

Both men regarded each other coolly for a moment.

"Come on in, Rooney. I need to speak with you," Stuart said.

Hampton gave him a thin smile. "Congratulations on the promotion, General."

"Thank you. If you forgive me, I must see Jeb."

Hampton nodded and walked outside. He wanted to curse the man. He wasn't used to being the one men looked down on, but these damn Virginians stuck to one another as if they had all the answers.

A young lieutenant with a black mustache peered at him as he came outside. He stood at the ready as Hampton approached, but his smile faded when he recognized the anger on his father's face. The young man was his son, Thomas Preston Hampton, but he'd always called him Preston.

He was his second son from his first marriage and had been at South Carolina College when the war began. He was an impetuous young man with a knack of finding a fight, which drove his father mad and simultaneously made him extremely proud. Hampton kept him close when he could and worried about him endlessly when he was out of sight. His other son, Wade Hampton IV, served on the staff of Joseph Johnston and the Army of Tennessee.

Preston handed him the reins to his favorite horse, a burly bay named Butler.

"Is everything all right, father?"

Hampton regarded him for a moment, his anger subsiding with a glance at his son. "Everything is fine."

"Your meeting with Stuart? Did you get your brigade?"

Both men mounted their horses.

"We have enough. Enough to wage a war. Come."

Father and son spurred their horses for Young's camp.

Chapter Ten

Morning, May 7, 1864
Alexandria, Virginia

For four long boring days, Wolf had expected to be taken in front of a military tribunal in Washington, D.C. Surely they had courts in the capital for such things during wartime, but they hadn't crossed the Potomac to the heart of the Union. Instead, they passed prestigious church steeples built in the colonial period as they headed the opposite direction.

They had an escort of six troopers, including the smooth-faced prick, Lieutenant Fox, and the prison guard, Corporal Mack. Both the prisoners sat in the back of a cart like boxes of dried hardtack destined for the army.

Chains jangled as Roberts positioned himself upright to get a look at the city around them. Their hands had been manacled and chained to one another like they were common criminals or slaves. They'd left their feet unchained, but to escape six men on horseback would be a most difficult endeavor.

They passed by Christ Church in Alexandria, the horses' hooves clopping over the bricked streets lined with stately mansions and beautiful townhomes. Christ Church was the same one Robert E. Lee and George Washington used to attend when they resided near or in the Virginia port town.

It was a two-story church with a tall bell tower that rose in three parts, each smaller than the last: rectangle, octagon, and at the top, an even more compact capped octagon with a red dome. Wolf had never seen a church like it, but he supposed it looked the part enough.

The unit continued through the Alexandria streets, passing stately mansions. They all had a similar Georgian style to them, everything in symmetry and balance. The doors usually sat in the center. The windows were of considerable size and equally spaced apart as if on a grid and were enclosed by plain exteriors.

The horses clopped off the brick streets until they reached a muddy road lacking any structure. They took this west until the land became familiar and turned into the recognizable campgrounds of the Army of the Potomac near Stevensburg, Virginia.

However, as they entered the camp it was clear that something was very different. It was devoid of almost all people. Sick men with gaunt depleted looks stepped out from huts. A man with an amputated arm, his sleeve rolled to the elbow, waved with his other. There were more wounded soldiers on crutches, some missing feet or entire legs. They all watched with sullen faces.

Trash littered the ground. A gust of wind tossed paper into the air, rolling it like a tumbleweed. An empty tin cup lay on its side forgotten. White tents, empty of soldiers, flapped in a soft breeze.

There were seemingly more women than normal. They tended the wounded and cooked food. Sutlers still had their row of tents and goods stacked, awaiting the armies return so they could gouge the soldiers on simple things they couldn't live without.

A few companies of logistical personnel who maintained the supply depot remained, but even most of them were gone. The military camp was missing its mounted branch. The Cavalry Corps had departed with the rest.

Wolf and Roberts were shoved into a house's cellar which had been cleared out of everything but bugs, dirt, and a bucket. It had a low ceiling, and the men were forced to sit for comfort. With no candle for light, they may as well have been in a coffin.

Every now and then, heavy boots would traverse the floor above, sending dust into a clouded frenzy around them and make Roberts sneeze.

Wolf tossed a pebble in the dirt as he sang loudly in the dark stuffy air. "I'm a Yankee Doodle Dandy. A Yankee Doodle, do or die."

"Will you shut up?" Roberts called at him.

Wolf made sure to face the direction of Roberts's voice. "A real live nephew of my Uncle Sam's."

Standing, Roberts grunted as he smacked his head. "Now I told you once to be quiet."

A guard pounded on the cellar door. "Shut up!"

Getting to his feet, Wolf edged closer to Roberts, hovering his face near his friend's. Roberts shifted away, his feet shuffling. "Your breath stinks."

He grinned at him making sure to enunciate every word. "Born on the Fourth of July."

"I have half a mind to throttle you," Roberts snarled.

"I'd like to see you try."

"If you hadn't made us put on those damn jackets, we'd never be in this mess."

In his own fashion, Wolf's comrade was correct. His back wouldn't have been burnt. His face broken. His thumbs popped in that *device*. The thought of that press made his stomach churn and a cool sweat break out on his neck. They'd never have been beaten and abused. They wouldn't be back in Union territory. They'd be stuck on Belle Isle with all the other enlisted men, freezing in the cold, dying from exposure and starvation alike as if it were a competition to see which one killed them first.

He wasn't sure which was worse: a slow wasting death or being strung up like a traitor from the end of the rope. Both had their perks. One was quick and dishonorable. The other was an inglorious drawn-out affair. And both led to a shallow grave.

Wolf backed away from his friend. "You're right. I gave us a shot. Didn't work out. But at least we'll hang over starving."

"You always were a real downer," Roberts said, sitting back on the floor.

Wolf rested his head on the wall, glancing at his friend he could hardly make out in the darkness. "Sorry, I got you into this." He kicked at the cellar door.

Their guard's voice belted through the cracks. "I'll come in there and whip ya!"

Malice filled Wolf's eyes as he stared at the door. Light blazed through the cracks, casting slivers of visibility on the floor of their prison. If the man didn't use a weapon, he could probably best him. He banged his head on the stone wall. "I'll tell you one thing. If we ever escape, I ain't never going back in a cell. Never."

Roberts's head bobbed as he agreed. "I'm sorry too, brother. When we escaped, I thought we would be free. Not just locked up on the other side."

"Well, I ain't rotting in this jail," Wolf said and then spit.

"What're you planning to do?"

"Whatever it takes to get us out of here."

***

The two men plotted for hours. They contrived all sorts of plans. Faking an illness to force the guards to open the door and beating their guards and escaping. Digging out with a piece of metal from around their piss bucket. There was much angst between the two when Roberts decided to use the piss bucket for the other bodily function.

Breaking apart the bucket for metal digging tools was deemed a poor idea. One, it would take too long, and two, they would be destroying their waste pail, forcing them to relieve themselves on the floor where they sat. They threw around a series of other ideas, all of which in the end left them sitting on the ground fantasizing about the food they'd eat and the girls they'd meet until the afternoon came knocking with the jangle of their cellar door's chains. The two lifted their eyes.

The door rattled from the other side, causing both men to gaze up in far-flung hope. To their dismay, it was Corporal Mack's muffled voice. "Wake up, my generals!"

He had taken a clear interest in the men, personally escorting them back to the encampment. Wolf suspected the additional duty alleviated some of the boredom of his Alexandria post or perhaps relieved him of even worse guard duties.

Wolf couldn't think of a guard duty that was worse, but like in any soldier's life, there were always tasks that were worse than your current one.

Everything was relative. He'd much rather stand picket duty than dig a latrine. He'd much rather dig a latrine than fill a latrine. He'd rather fill a latrine than bury the bodies. But he supposed some men may feel different. Not that any of it mattered. Soon they'd stretch his neck from a rope.

Roberts and Wolf slowly got to their feet.

Mack peered through the cellar doors at them. "Good. You ain't dead." He smiled with his blackened teeth.

The door creaked as he opened it, and the light of a thousand suns poured inside. Wolf and Roberts shaded their eyes with their arms.

"They decided already?" Roberts asked Wolf softly.

"I suppose so," he responded.

Mack yelled inside. "Well, come on out. I ain't got all day."

They walked out into an unknown fate. "Go on. We got a nice man here to see you."

The two men shuffled over stone steps into the daylight.

A man in a pristine cavalry captain's uniform stood waiting, his black slouch hat underneath his arm. He regarded them for a moment, his eyes scrutinizing their haphazard appearance with a touch of disdain. He glanced down at a piece of paper he held. "Corporal Wolf? Private Roberts?"

The two men nodded. "Aye," Wolf said, still squinting from the bright daylight.

"Aye," Roberts echoed.

"Corporal Mack, I will take them from here. Here is the appropriate paperwork."

Mack examined the paper as if it were a Bible written in Latin. His eyelid twitched as he read incredibly slowly. After entirely too long, the captain sighed. "Do you need anything else from me?"

Mack scratched his head, looking up at the captain. "Everything looks in order. That be Sheridan's signature?" he said, turning the paper toward the captain.

The handsome captain spoke with finely enunciated words, marking high education and social status or both. "It is."

The guard grinned, revealing all his blackened teeth at once. "Good luck, my generals. Remember a tight hangman's knot is better than a loose one."

The captain nodded to the jailer and waved at Wolf and Roberts to follow. Ten cavalrymen sat atop horses surrounding a wagon. Two more dismounted troopers waited for them along with smooth-faced Lieutenant Fox.

"Shackle them," the captain said.

Rusted metal manacles were placed on their wrists, instantly chafing their skin, and they were led to the wagon. They half-laid half-leaned in the back.

"Men, forward," the captain commanded, and the unit with the prisoners left at a trot.

"Where you taking us?" Wolf asked the officer.

"I believe you should be ending that sentence with sir, or is that too far below you now?"

"I believe a man should know where a group of armed men are taking him, *sir*."

The captain studied him for a moment. He was weighing the prisoner's worth for engagement, and the scales tipped in Wolf's favor. "You men are going south to the Army of the Potomac."

"For judgment? Sir," Roberts added.

"I do not know, but what I do know is that we have orders to make all due haste." He turned to the men around him. "Let's take it up a notch. Double-time."

The wagon jostled as the team of horses picked up their gait to a canter, and they headed south, the two prisoners falling over one another as the wagon flogged them over the rough roads.

Chapter Eleven

Dusk, May 7, 1864
Todd's Tavern, Virginia

The sun started to set as they rode south. They crossed rivers, passed tiny hamlets and towns, and trees growing large bright green leaves. But all of spring's growth was soon shattered by the smoke.

Blackened smoke shrouded the road like a thick sea fog. The men in the escort coughed. Others covered their mouths with scarves and sleeves, keeping hats low over their eyes to prevent the stinging bitter wind from biting them. The air here took on a swollen, oppressive feel and smelled burnt and used up. Soon after they navigated through baggage trains and ambulances.

Wagons overflowed with what could barely be described as men. They were blackened and soiled as if they'd come from the earth itself. All of them had downcast eyes or white vacant stares. They moaned like the dead and cried like the living.

Ambulance drivers whipped their horses like escorts to hell, but the road lay jammed with wagon and men. They stalled, surrounded by the densest foliage Wolf had seen. The black forest acted like an army of succubi, accepting men inside and quickly making them disappear.

The narrow clogged lane slowed them, but it wasn't long before they removed themselves from the conflagration of wood, man, and beast. They reached a humble tavern at the crux of a crossroads. The sickly revolting scent of rotting flesh hung in the air, clawing at their noses.

Mounds of dead horses lay where they'd fallen, the stench oozing from the dead animals. Cries of the wounded filled the air like a cloud of buzzing flies.

It was clear multiple battles had been fought here. Men carried other men, taking them to surgeons and makeshift field hospitals. Two colored laborers led a team of horses to haul away the carcass of another slain horse. Their team was skittish from the stink of death hanging in the air, and they whipped the poor beasts to keep them focused. Campfires dotted the surrounding area, and Union men rested around them.

The Cavalry Corps flag and its Divisional flags flew on poles outside the building. A white and red guidon with opposing stars on either half hung limply alongside a blue dovetailed guidon with white crossed sabers and a large red C in the center of the sabers. Next were the Divisional flags of the 1st Division, crossed crimson sabers on a field of snow white and the 3rd Division, Union-blue crossed sabers on a white background.

"This is a corps commander's headquarters," Wolf said.

Roberts's chains jangled as he nervously scratched his head. "We be screwed. I knew it. They brought us out here to make an example out of us. So the whole army could watch. Don't get too far above your station, laddies." He shook his head. "There's an us and a them. And they will keep us down to make sure they are obeyed without question." He tried to bless himself by making the sign of the cross but was hindered by his shackles. "Oh, Lord."

The tavern sat, worrying Wolf like some sturdily built gallows. His companion's words rang true. What reasons could they have other than something public and capital?

"Help them down," the captain said. Dark rings had formed under his eyes, but he still held himself straight and proper.

Troopers hauled them down from the wagon, and the captain led them to the door. He knocked and entered, ushering them inside followed by Lieutenant Fox.

"Wait here," the captain said pointing. Fox took a seat in a creaky chair, listening to the men talk inside.

Cigar and wood smoke clouded the air of the house. Men's voices rose in fierce discussion. And the two prisoners stood in the foyer, still in chains.

Officers came and went, and the pair received more than their fair share of ugly glares and curious glances. A short rotund man brushed past them and swung open the door like he was trying to rip it from its hinges. Before he disappeared, he stopped, turning on them. He cocked his head to the side as stared. His eyes blackened with utter revulsion.

"Colonel Moore?" Wolf said.

"Corporal," he said. "I do not want to even hear your explanation. It's preposterous what's been done." His chubby cheeks bounced as he shook his head in anger. "If it were up to me, you'd both be flogged until you were dead." Without another word, the colonel departed.

More heated discussion could be heard coming from the other room.

"You think they're deciding how to do us in?" Roberts asked.

"I'm sure they wouldn't put this much thought into it. Rope and a tree will get the job done."

"Ahh, Wolf, I can't stand this bad luck."

He peered hard at his friend. "You won't need to worry much longer."

Roberts wavered and he looked like he could cry. "You ain't making it any better!"

The captain returned to the foyer. "Come."

They were shoved into a room filled with aides and two men of high rank. One Wolf recognized instantly as Brigadier General George Armstrong Custer, the man that had led them to victory on countless occasions. The man that had given them pride. A man they'd bled and died for. A man they'd been defeated with. A man they'd retreated with. A man whose life they'd saved. Would he return the favor? His blue eyes held no clue. His flaxen mustache fluttered as he recognized them.

The other general they didn't know. He was short with a trimmed black mustache and had two stars on his shoulders. His eyes were deep brown and just above his high cheekbones. His demeanor was one that wanted to be impressed, but you probably were never going to live up to the task. "These them, the impersonators?"

The captain spoke, "Yes, General Sheridan, sir. These are the men you instructed us to bring."

"You remember these fools?" Sheridan said to Custer.

Custer cocked his head to the side. "Can you forget the face of a man that saved your life?"

"Can't say I've ever needed it," Sheridan retorted with a chuckle. "Can you men explain to me why you're here?"

Both Wolf and Roberts started talking at once. Everything came out as gibberish. There was mention of Yates and Dahlgren, letters, widows, rapers, Libby Prison, and escaping.

The generals sat, silently watching the men make every extenuation available to prove their innocence. When one excuse didn't illicit a response, they would jump to something else.

Sheridan raised his hand, and they stopped talking. "I've heard enough. So you're telling me that you gave Dahlgren's secret orders to assassinate Jefferson Davis to a Southern woman that you saved from being raped who mailed it back to a dead comrade's father in Michigan. Then under the instruction of your captain, you pretended to be officers to ensure better treatment. You were then tortured in an attempt to find the letter which you did not yield. After which you elicited the assistance of Union spy Elizabeth Van Lew to coordinate your escape. Then you masqueraded as officers, tricking Butler before anyone in the War Department could figure out you weren't actually officers to send you back to Alexandria. Is that all?"

"You forgot the part where we stole Dahlgren's body and replaced it with a Richmond thug," Roberts said.

Sheridan nodded, irritated. "Of course, I forgot that part." His voice exploded in a fast-paced harangue. "Do you honestly in the name of goddamn Jesus Christ Our Savior of Nazareth expect me to believe one fucking line of this fairy tale? Who do you think you are, the Brothers Grimm? Your lives are on the line, and you feed me this dung heap of a story? Do you understand the repercussions?" He didn't wait for a response, carrying on immediately. "Let me tell you. The War Department wants to let you rot for a few months then hang your asses from the gallows with a bag over your head." He paused, glancing at Custer. "And your commanding officer doesn't think very highly of your rebellious exploits either. He has cited multiple actions that are punishable in the military code of conduct. Insubordination. Failure to follow orders. Drunken on Duty."

Wolf knew he could count on Moore for just about any damning piece of evidence he held to be given freely and without reserve. Despite the truth to all his statements, there was still more. He'd also robbed a woman. Burned people's homes. Shot a prisoner in the back. But he wouldn't give the general more ammunition to stretch his neck with. He was tired of it all. Tired of being jerked around and imprisoned by anybody and everybody with a gun and a jail. "You know, if it ain't the rebs going to do it, it might as well be you guys." Sheridan's eyes became larger circles, and Wolf continued anyway. "You should get it over with. We were fighting and surviving out there. Any man with half a pair would have done the same. And if he didn't, then he doesn't deserve to live." He paused. "Sir."

Sheridan twisted in his chair, eyeing Custer. He jabbed a finger threateningly at the prisoners. "I can't believe you led me to believe these men were a solution to my predicament. Remove them from my sight."

"Perhaps they were not the right fit for this mission," Custer bowed his head in deference to his commander. He had stuck his neck out for his men and had lost favor.

"Wait!" Roberts dropped to his knees and held up a hand in need of mercy. "Hear me out, sir. We're just tired of being imprisoned. What Wolf's been saying is real, the whole story. I can prove it."

"I will entertain this for *ten seconds*, but then we have a war to win."

Roberts quickly stood, tugging at Wolf's coat. "Take off your coat."

Wolf shook his head. "I ain't."

"Take if off or we'll hang." His eyes pled with Wolf to obey him.

"If you think for a second I am going to hang or rot in prison for the rest of the war, you have another thing coming."

Sheridan's eyes gaped and then he sneered. "What would you do?"

"Fight. Escape. Die if need be, but I ain't going back."

"Rot you will!" Sheridan shook his head. "And you too!"

The captain grabbed Wolf by his arm and he shook it off.

"Take off the coat," Roberts hissed. "I don't want to die."

"Unlock me and I'll do it."

Everyone turned to Sheridan awaiting his response.

The major general sighed. "I cannot believe I am entertaining such a thing. Do it, Captain."

"Captain?" Wolf held up his shackles. "You don't think you could help me out, do ya?"

The weary captain gave him a dry stare and pulled a key from his jacket. "I can't say I've ever heard a story like yours, Lieutenant." The key clicked in the lock and the shackles fell to the floor. The captain collected the fetters.

Rubbing his wrists for a moment, Wolf shouldered off his coat followed by his shirt. He stood shirtless before the generals.

"I see a skinny man," Sheridan said. "Take them away."

"Turn around," Roberts ordered him desperately.

It was Wolf's turn to shake his head. He spun, facing the other way.

"Look here, General. Right here." Roberts tapped Wolf's back over the branded skin. Audible gasps came from the general's lips. "There is no truer man to the Union cause. We ain't lying. You go on and send a telegraph back to Washington. Dahlgren's body is there."

A harsh sigh came from Sheridan before he said, "You men must be true to endure such punishment. Sickens me." He shared a glance with Custer then looked back at them. "You may clothe yourself again."

Wolf buttoned his shirt, facing them. "We ain't yellow, sir."

Sheridan held out a defending hand, allowing no more debate on the matter. "I believe you men. Unlock the other one." The captain moved to comply, releasing Roberts from his chains.

"These might be the ones we need," Sheridan said with a nod.

A short grin formed on Custer's lips. "They might be."

The major general went back to his table and took a seat. "I should probably disavow you from this military, send you to a prison to rot, or let someone else deal with you. But I think your commanding general may be correct in his original assessment." Sheridan took out a piece of paper and began writing over it with sweeping penmanship. He didn't look up as he wrote. "Corporal Wolf, I am going to promote you."

Wolf blinked. His ears must have deceived him. Such a reversal of fate did not exist for a man with his shitty luck. "Excuse me, sir?"

"You didn't mishear. I am promoting you to lieutenant and giving you a command." He looked from his writings. "You cannot fail me. Right back into the cell with you if you do."

"I already told you I ain't going back."

"Very good, Lieutenant. That means I won't need to see you in circumstances like we're in again."

"What would you have me do?"

Scratches and scribbles sounded out as the general wrote. "You are going to make Jeb Stuart come out to fight."

Wolf laughed, looking at Roberts for assurance he'd heard the man right. "Surely, he can do that on his own."

"He will not. It is up to you to draw him out and distract him so I can defeat him."

Wolf was flabbergasted. He went from rotting in a cell to going on a suicide mission. "How do you propose we do that?"

Sheridan grinned with a glance at Custer. He took the pen and stuck it back into its inkwell, pushing it away from him as if he detested the idea of writing. "They're your men. You tell them."

"Well, boys, how do you drive any man mad?"

"Dunno, sir," Wolf said.

With a short cough into his hand, Custer smiled. "You're going to kidnap his wife."

Chapter Twelve

Dusk, May 7, 1864
Todd's Tavern, Virginia

"You're mad! How on earth could we kidnap her?"

"It can be done," Sheridan said. "Boy, this is the army. We can move mountains even if it's only pebble by pebble and takes a lifetime."

Sheridan stood and Wolf felt taller than he had moments ago. "BMI is telling us she traveled north of Richmond with her husband but has been sent to stay behind their lines as Lee engages Grant, but not far from the front. We know the home she resides in."

Custer took a step forward; he was almost the opposite of Sheridan. Tall, golden-haired, and athletic. "You sneak south, snatch her, and leave this note." He handed it to Wolf. The name *J.E.B.* was scrawled over the envelope. "She isn't to be harmed. After all, we aren't monsters."

"Stuart and Lee don't know it yet, but this isn't a campaign for Richmond. This is a campaign to destroy their army man by man. And in order to do that, we must force them off-balance and to fight on our terms. Toe-to-toe where our numbers can come into full effect," Sheridan said. He dipped his chin, confident in the plan as it was explained. "I am willing to let you handpick your men, but you must take the man who knows the home."

"Bring him in," Sheridan called into the other room. A man stepped inside. He was tall and lithe with curly brown hair and a charming smile. "Mr. Wolf and Mr. Roberts. It's mighty fine to see you again," said Hogan.

BMI Agent Martin Hogan had been their guide along with a few others for Kilpatrick's doomed raid. His presence was appreciated by the officers and men due to his knowledge of the South and his clandestine abilities.

The last time Wolf had seen him, he had been wrestling a rebel in the ambush near Garnett's Mill. The same ambush that had resulted in Wolf's capture and Dahlgren's death.

Wolf couldn't help but smile. "Hogan, you yellow-bellied son of a bitch."

"I believe I could say the same for you."

The men shook hands with one another. "You made it," Wolf said in amazement and a bit of envy.

"And I am sorry to hear about your imprisonment; however, that is bloody well better than how our poor colonel ended up."

"Some might say that." Only Wolf and Roberts knew the true details of Dahlgren's final moments.

"No one hates Libby more than me," Hogan said. "So what do you say to another run down south?"

"Let me talk to my companion alone for a moment."

Sheridan nodded. "You get one minute to make up your mind but remember the alternative."

Wolf bent near Roberts. "What do you think?"

"I think we are going to get killed out there. Think about it, first we have to get down there. Find her. Then whisk her away. You think that the Beau Sabreur is going to sit by while we galavant through the countryside with his wife? Are you insane?"

"They're going to either send us to prison or hang us or both. If we succeed, we're free."

"You can send my ass back to prison."

"We could be free. Clean slate. We ride in, ride out. Nobody knows any different. Really easy when you think about it like a stroll in the park."

Roberts sighed then shook his head. Understanding that there was no other way crossed his boyish features. "I ain't going to let you get killed by your lonesome, but. . ."

"But what?"

"But how come you get the promotion and I'm still some lowly private? It's disrespectful."

"We're about to change that," Wolf said with a nod. "All right, General, we'll do it."

"Very well, men," said Sheridan with a smile. "I am not issuing you any formal orders. This mission is strictly unofficial. This is a dangerous task with no room for error."

"We have some demands," Wolf said loudly.

"Demands? Did my assholes for ears hear that right?"

"Yes sir, your assholes for ears did."

"You goddamn son of a bitch. Bunch of upstart bastards you are. Hurry now, what are they?"

"My comrade here wants a promotion too. What do you say, a corporal?"

Roberts leaned over and whispered. "I always thought of myself as a sergeant kind of man."

Wolf turned toward Sheridan again. "He wants to be a sergeant."

"Done," Sheridan said. "Enough?"

"And I want Spencers for F Company of the 13th."

Sheridan snorted a laugh shaking his head at Custer. "This guy's got some brass balls coming in here and asking me to outfit his old company. You have your hands full, General."

"Yes, I do. But I wouldn't mind getting the 13th up to standard. They are listed as a saber regiment, but another regiment armed with Spencers couldn't hurt," Custer said. "The 5th and 6th Michigan have performed exceptionally well with them."

"Why don't we make it the entire 13th?" Wolf said with a glance at Custer.

Sheridan shook his head. "Don't push your luck, son. I will make sure your company is outfitted, and we'll put your regiment on order next time they are back in camp. Will that do, Lieutenant?"

Wolf nodded with a smirk. "That will do just fine."

Sheridan quickly scribbled out the order for weapons and a commission letter and handed it over to Wolf. "Then you must depart immediately. Mr. Hogan will go with you back to the Michigan Brigade. I will see you on the other side."

The newly promoted men saluted the generals and they saluted back.

Wolf turned toward the captain. "Your man has a knife that belongs to me."

The captain hesitated, stiffening under the other officers' scrutiny.

"Do you have his knife, Captain?" Custer said.

The captain raised his chin. "Lieutenant Fox does, a man under my command, sir."

"Lieutenant Fox!" Sheridan called through the door.

The smooth-cheeked officer hurried into the room like a beckoned dog.

"Give the man his property back."

"Property?" Fox said his voice cracking.

Sheridan could hardly stay seated. "Give this shaggy-faced man's goddamn dagger back now."

Fox hurried, removing the blade and sheath from his belt and handing it over. Wolf held the blade for a moment, enjoying the lethal weight of it in his hands, and then secured it on his belt.

Sheridan showed them the door. "Hurry. These armies are on a collision course again, and you don't want to be stuck in the middle."

"I'll ride with these boys back to camp," Custer said.

"Me as well," said Hogan.

Custer and the three men left the house. Their noses were pummeled by the stench of rotting flesh outside. The general flagged down his aide who went in search of mounts.

When some were procured, they accompanied the general on horseback through the camp. They met with the division's quartermaster where they acquired one hundred Spencer carbines for F Company. The bald man wanted nothing to do with them and their request. He even resisted the general, but when he produced Sheridan's orders, the man begrudgingly complied with a good deal of cursing under his breath. A wagon with the weapons and ammunition in them was transferred to the men.

They continued back to the Michigan Brigade's bivouac. Troopers in blue sat around campfires with picketed horses nearby. Custer raised a hand as they passed, returning the friendly waves of his men.

Wolf couldn't help but notice the predominance of red neckties that many of the men wore like their general. It seemed that his bond had only tightened with them since the ill-fated Kilpatrick-Dahlgren raid.

"I took a big risk on you two," he said as they passed more fires and men speaking words only meant for themselves.

"Big risks for big rewards, sir," Wolf said.

"No wiser words have been said, Lieutenant. I knew you would understand. A daring raid, a noble mission, great rewards. I wish I was riding with you, but alas, the war continues while you go south. But we will be close behind. Grant's given the go-ahead over Meade to embark on our quest. Your raid will precipitate the campaign of over 10,000 troopers that are to deal the death blow to Stuart's command."

"Is that everyone?" Roberts asked.

"May as well be. The Cavalry Corps rides with Little Phil to victory!" Custer said with some vigor. He breathed in. "You smell that, boys?"

The odor in the air was a combination of horse dung, sweat, and the dead, a level of relative stink just above gagging.

The general continued, his eyes suddenly saddened. "We are close to the end. Then where will we go? Where do men like us go when the bugles cease, the flags furl, and the soldiers put away their swords?" He gestured as they walked. "There's no glory in banking or farming. Only numbers, red and black, and crops, good or bad. No. No glory there. Our nation will have little need for men like us. We will fade with the setting sun until we are forgotten."

"West, sir. West we will go," Roberts chimed in.

"I suppose we will," Custer said, regarding him. "There may be yet some glory in the West, but we must grasp all we can here and now before they are through. And they will be through. Your mission will chop an arm off Lee." Custer threw out a hand like a knife. "Piece by piece we will hack from him until he has nothing left but the old broken horse beneath him. No cities. No plantations. No armies. Nothing."

"Yes, sir," the men echoed.

They rode in silence the rest of the way to the 13th Michigan campgrounds, contemplating their general's words. They stopped at a spacious command tent with the regimental colors stuck in the ground out front.

Custer stayed atop his horse. "Colonel Moore," he called. They waited more than their fair share of moments. "Blubbering bastard. Colonel Moore, come out here."

The portly colonel emerged from his tent, his face red with exertion. He muttered under his breath until he saw it was the general calling his name.

He bowed his head. "General, sir. How can I help you?" His eyes crossed over, settling on Wolf and Roberts. They narrowed a bit. "Are they to be flogged? I never liked them. Terribly disobedient and horribly undisciplined wretches. I can't be held responsible for their vagrant behavior. And who is that?" Moore said, gesturing at Hogan.

"Bureau of Military Information Agent Hogan, sir, at your service." He removed his hat and gave the colonel a slight bow.

"What the bloody hell are you doing with these miscreants?"

Custer raised a hand, cutting off Moore and giving him an unamused grin. "This is your new Lieutenant Wolf and Sergeant Roberts. They are to be given every accommodation and pick of your men."

"I beg your pardon, General, but under whose authority?"

"Major General Sheridan himself. Now you would do well to keep such insubordinate questions to yourself or perhaps you should be the one being flogged. I see you aren't wearing your arms. Do you have an explanation?"

Moore's face brightened like a ripe tomato. To be dressed down in front of two men he despised made it even worse. "We are in camp, sir. There are 100,000 men in this army."

"We are in a running battle with a wily and smart opponent in their home territory. You would do well to not deviate from my advice of being armed at all times."

Moore lowered his head. "Of course, sir, my apologies."

"Where is F Company?"

But Wolf already knew. He saw their black and red guidon down the row of tents, its gold wolf head snarling in the breeze.

"General, we can take it from here."

"Yes, you can. My orders are for you to pick your men and leave as soon as you can." Custer raised his voice. "You are not to be interfered with." He turned his horse and walked it away. "Good luck! We are counting on you."

Moore's beady eyes watched him go, making sure he was far out of earshot. His voice dripped with deadly venom. "I don't know who you think you are. An upstart that's for sure. Don't count on getting any further up the military ladder. Save that for the men of good breeding. Not the dumb Dutch and immigrants."

Not baring any teeth, Wolf smiled his way. "It's been good seeing you, Colonel. I will report back when our mission is complete." Wolf and his companions turned their horses away toward the company guidon.

"And what mission is that?" Moore called at them.

"None of your concern."

Chapter Thirteen

Dusk, May 7, 1864
Near Todd's Tavern, Virginia

Wolf and Roberts walked their horses through the unknown troopers of the 13th Michigan with Hogan trailing close behind them. Men eyed them with curiosity. There were so many fresh faces, most young and all dirty. A few they'd seen before, but no one called out, "Hail, friend!" or "Good to see you, brother!" They only watched, wondering who these haggard latecomers to the regiment were.

Wolf ignored them, making for the wolf-head guidon. Pieced together from material in his home by his sister, the wolf's head belonged to his father. It was a larger version of the one in his pocket that came from his ancestors long ago. Like the company's flag, it too was ripped and stained with blood: some of it theirs, some of it their enemy's, all of it earned on the field of battle.

The man that stood closest to the standard puffed a pipe as he watched them approach. His curled mustache held strong, and bluish-gray clouds snuck from his mouth. He had a powerful frame and build, but he wasn't heavy. Gray hair trailed his sideburns to the top of his head. His sergeant's coat was unbuttoned, revealing a white shirt underneath. A saber and pistol rested on his hip.

Wolf stopped his horse in front of him.

A slow smile spread on Sergeant Wilhelm Berles's lips, causing his cheeks to crease. "I never thought I'd see the day." He shook his head in disbelief, and puffed harder on his pipe. "I was sure you were dead."

"Came close," Wolf said down to him. "Many times."

Wilhelm's smile grew. "Why don't you come down here so I can see you?" He peered around at the other rider. "And Mr. Roberts. By God, it's good to see you." He nodded. "Mr. Hogan."

"Sergeant," Hogan replied.

They dismounted their horses, and Wilhelm embraced Wolf like a father would his son after a long journey. He squeezed him tight for a moment before releasing him. Wilhelm's bottom lip twitched, and his eyes glazed over for a moment like they may have deceived him. It was as if he saw Franz standing there instead of Wolf. He gulped back the memory. "You look absolutely terrible."

"We've been in prison."

"Captured?"

"Seems of late everyone is looking for an excuse to lock us up."

Wilhelm gave Roberts a quick hug and shook hands with Hogan.

"I'm afraid I must depart, but I will return soon," Hogan said. He mounted his horse and walked from the camp.

"What happened?" Wilhelm asked watching the BMI agent depart.

"Long story, but you're not the only one who escaped are you?" Wolf said. "I need a squad of men."

Wilhelm looked briefly at him. "For what purpose?"

A laugh escaped Wolf's lips. "Well, you are looking at F Company's newest lieutenant."

"And sergeant," Roberts chimed in.

Wilhelm puffed on his pipe, grinning. "Must be quite the tale." He flipped the pipe over and tapped the end of it on the ground.

"Wolf!" came a shout. A hulking man came running across the bivouac. He hardly had time to brace himself before he was hoisted in the air by Dan Poltorak. The large Polish man was joined by his brother Bart. They hooted in their native tongue, smiles visible beneath round noses and cheeks.

"You got small," Dan said. He wrapped a hand around Wolf's arm and shook his flesh like it was a disappointingly thin kielbasa.

"Prison does that to a man." His whole body moved as Bart clapped his back multiple times. They found Roberts and proceeded to lift him in the air like he was a child.

"Little man!" Dan said squeezing the air from Roberts. He set him down only to have the process repeated by Bart.

"You guys are going to crush me!" Roberts breathed.

Van Horn emerged from a tent, a fraction of a grin on his dour face. Then the old abolitionist Zachariah Shugart joined them. He grabbed Wolf's arm and smiled. "I prayed day and night for you boys, and God has rewarded us with your safe return." Tears welled in the corners of his eyes and he gulped. "The whole unit was devastated by what we thought was your loss. God is truly great!"

More men from F Company showed up to see their lost comrades. Hands were shaken, backs clapped, and much merriment took the men. Captain Peltier emerged from his tent. His frock coat was unbuttoned. His black beard had a few stray grays making their appearance. His English was laced with a slight French accent. "This is a great surprise. I'd had you men labeled as casualties in the regimental rosters. It'll be a pleasure putting you back on."

Wolf handed him the commission letter from Sheridan.

Peltier's dark eyes read quickly then he glanced back at him. "Many surprises indeed. I welcome a new second lieutenant to the company. Our numbers have continued to dwindle. Illness and Kilpatrick's raid have beaten us down over the winter. Glad to have you back."

Wolf looked over his shoulder. "Not sure everyone feels that way. The colonel."

"I understand," Peltier said, nodding slightly. "I will do my best to run interference with him, but he is our commanding officer. We follow his orders."

"I'm afraid we won't be here long."

"I see this letter says to give you handpicked men and for you to depart immediately."

"Yes, sir. We must make haste."

"I can't say I like losing ten of my men on the eve of an engagement, but General Sheridan commands the Corps."

"Maybe I can sweeten the deal."

Peltier's bushy eyebrows lifted. "How so?"

"You see that wagon right there?" Wolf pointed over at a mule driven cart. "I do."

"I got two crates of Spencer carbines and enough ammunition to last for a campaign on it."

Peltier cocked his head. "No?"

"Yes, Captain. Go take a look."

The captain walked to the wagon, a cluster of the men following him. He tugged a crate off the back. "Get me a bar." A trooper brought him a metal bar to pry it open. The wood snapped under his hand, and he threw the lid to the side. A smile settled on his lips. He dug his hands into the crate and removed a Spencer carbine, holding it in the air for all to see like he'd discovered a golden nugget.

"Now look at what we have here boys!"

Cheers went up from the men as Peltier started to hand them out. The weapons were pristine and clean, the wood finish smooth, and the barrel oiled with a slight sheen. "Now we have the upper hand."

Troopers raced to form a line to receive their new guns. Excitement and joy shone on their faces. For so long they'd been treated like a second-class company by Colonel Moore. He'd shoved all the men he didn't want together and then given them second-class weapons despite their sacrifice and heroics on the battlefield.

"So you made it out, Wolfie?" came a voice from behind.

Wolf turned to face a shorter man with a dark complexion. His black hair was ruffled, his looks handsome, and his eyes flinty like charred wood. His uniform jacket had tears around the edges. A short smile stuck on his lips.

"Adams."

The man eyed him for a moment. "You return and you bring us gifts? Now this is an interesting surprise." He stopped. "And a promotion? An officer at that." Envy flashed in his eyes. It had been rumored that Private Adams had once been Lieutenant Adams of the 1st Michigan before the burning of Elmira, New York, in which numerous people were injured and slain in the altercation gone wrong. Since they were veteran troopers, the War Department had turned a blind eye in order to usher them back into the fight just when the Union was having a reenlistment crisis due to enlistment terms ending at the same time.

The worst of the bunch had been split up and distributed among the other Michigan regiments to mitigate any revivals of the debauchery. The two men that had ended up in Wolf's unit were cutthroats and brigands who didn't bat an eye at putting someone down in any situation.

"It was earned with blood."

"Some men I guess are just suited for it."

"Where's Nelson?"

Adams flashed another smile that didn't touch his eyes. "He's around. Won't be too happy to see you above ground and kicking."

"Feeling's mutual, but I'm taking you men into my unit."

Adams snorted a laugh. "What? Why?"

Wolf stepped closer and the other man lifted his chin. "'Cause I need you. I need your expertise."

"Expertise? That's what we're calling it? Men that do what you need them to do. Men that don't flinch at getting their hands dirty."

"Call it what you want, but you're coming with me. No troubles."

"Never from me. I am a good little soldier I am."

"We'll see."

The cutthroat shrugged his shoulders. "Grandpa Berles and Old Man Shugart won't like it, but it beats riding around here. You won't get no trouble from me. Nelson?" He shrugged his shoulders again. "I can't be held responsible for what he does."

"Good. We meet in an hour."

"Off to get me a new rifle. You're too kind, Wolfie. Must be my birthday," Adams said, sauntering his way into line.

Is bringing these men a mistake? No, he needed men who walked hand in hand with survival. He needed men who could carve their way out and not blink. He needed them, but could he control them?

Chapter Fourteen

Dusk, May 7, 1864
Near Todd's Tavern, Virginia

Wolf's ten men stood before him in a line. Each man held his new Spencer carbine as if he were afraid someone would steal it from him. Even though the days were growing longer in preparation for summer, they were losing light in the afternoon sky.

Captain Peltier accompanied him as they inspected the men for the mission. Anything easily distinguishable as Federal had been done away with. Wilhelm still had his kepi and coat, but the other men looked civilian enough. Black, brown, tan, and gray jackets, sack, and frock coats. Top hats, pork pie hats, broad slouch hats adorned their heads.

Wolf had elected to wear a slouch hat. Black and wide-brimmed, the same as Custer wore. His jacket was short and black to make it easier to draw his pistol. If the coat was too long, it would need to be unbuttoned or risk riding up on the horseman, restricting his movement.

His men appeared uncomfortable and too militant to pass as true civilians. It may do from far away, but close-up, they looked rough.

Wilhelm anchored one end of the line with his chest puffed out and his back straighter than a bayonet. Next to him Van Horn wore a beehive style hat, making him look even more like a farmer. He was a bit taller than Wilhelm and looked like a rain cloud followed him everywhere. The happiest part about him was the way he held his new firearm.

109

Next to him were the two Polish brothers, broad and thick like a pair of oxen. On their other side was Private Jacob Hale, a new recruit from Kalamazoo, with reddish hair and a pointy nose along with Private Gregory Pratt, who had black curly hair and a hooked nose. Both were young and lacked experience, which made Wolf hesitate to bring them on.

"You're sure, sir, that Hale and Pratt can handle it? We'll be going hard and fast."

"I think they will. They are eager and good horsemen. They will not lag."

"Hey there, laddies," Hogan said as he trotted up atop a bay-colored mare. He had three other men with him. Two wore blue coats covered in dirt and had reddish-hued skin and pitch-black hair. Beaded bandolier bags hung around their chests. The last rider, apparently having been lifted straight from the frontier, had a long beard and a dark buckskin jacket.

"Can't leave without us," Hogan said.

"We never would have entertained such a thought."

Hogan grinned. "I was able to secure a few additional recruits I thought may help our mission." Each man carried long rifles in their hands. "K Company, 1st Michigan Sharpshooters."

The three men nodded toward Wolf, and Hogan pointed in turn at each one.

"This is George Greensky," Hogan said, gesturing to the taller of the two. "And James Ashka—" The Irishman scratched behind his ear words trailing away.

James finished his own name. "Ashkanak."

Hogan sat straight and gave Wolf a wink. "They're Indians."

"I can see this. Welcome to the platoon, gentleman. I am Lieutenant Wolf." This brought a smile to the three men's faces.

"Why are they smiling?" Wolf asked Hogan.

"I don't know."

George grinned. "We have a good friend, Payson, who is known as Wolf."

James leaned closer. "You don't look like him."

"Suppose not," Wolf said and they all laughed.

Wolf had no problem with adding these men from the northern Michigan tribes to his command. Most of the men in his unit had found their way there from being an outcast in one way or another. Men that had chips on their shoulders and something to prove. He'd started that way. Now he had to prove himself or risk finding himself back in a cell. That wasn't an option for him, so it was win or die.

"Step in line with the others." The two native sharpshooters walked their horses over to the other men.

"And this backwoods specimen is Irwin Skinner. One of the only white men allowed in K Company," Hogan said with a flourish of his hand.

The frontiersman pressed a wad of tobacco into the corner of his mouth. "Pleasure to meetcha. Half-injun, I am. My ma was Odawa, my pa a bear." He let out a sharp laugh. "Nah, he was some kind of English." He leaned closer. "You need something taken down from far away I'm your man. I prefer to work alone, but those two be good men. Quiet. And quiet's good for our kind of work. Not as good a shot as me, but better than everyone else. Been huntin' our whole lives." He spit a black glob on the ground. "Marching with the army got me itching to get out into the woods again."

"Good to have you."

Skinner nodded and walked his horse back to the row of troopers.

"Let me assure you, Wolf. There ain't too many men with a better shot than any of those three on either side of this war," Hogan said. "And the government wouldn't let them fight until recently. Sitting on a gold mine, they were."

Wolf sucked in air through his nose. These were his men. Their lives depended on the decisions he made. And his mission was to march around behind enemy lines and survive long enough to kidnap their enemy commander's wife. Damn. This will be a waste of men if we don't succeed.

"Captain. This is them."

Peltier saluted the men, and they all returned it. "We will see you when this is done." He snapped his hand down. "Wolf, I hate to see these men go, but you have done us a great service with the new carbines. You have my thanks. I want you to take the company guidon."

Wolf shook his head. "I can't. The company must keep it."

Peltier shook his head in disagreement. "I will not hear it. We will get a regulation flag for the rest of the campaign. You must fly this one. You are a part of the company."

"But the men surely will be disappointed to not carry their standard."

"They will," Peltier smirked, "but will take solace in their new guns."

"Sergeant Berles, will you carry the guidon?"

"Sir, yes, sir." He marched to the flagpole and lifted it from the ground, carrying it over to the men.

A grin formed on Roberts's face and he gave a fierce shout. "We are Wolf's platoon!"

"Wolf's platoon!"

"Wolf's platoon!"

The only man not chanting was Nelson, a fire burning in his eyes.

***

The mounted men walked their horses out of camp. To the untrained eye they were a squad getting ready to go on patrol. In an active campaign area, they were one of many.

The main army hoped to beat Lee to Spotsylvania, but Wolf somehow thought they wouldn't. Nobody ever really got the jump on Old Marse Robert. Not in his experience anyway.

The armies were on a collision course in the same area Wolf had robbed the old woman of her husband's pocket watch a few months before. Soldiers would clamber through their small town again, taking refuge in their houses and plundering their food stores. It would be a wonder if there was a scrap of food left in the entire region with Grant's 100,000-man army.

But Wolf's men were ahead of the main army, most of which was still north in the wilderness. Hogan guided them in a different direction, away from the battling cavalries. They swept directly to the east from Todd's Tavern and away from both Grant's army and Lee's as they leapfrogged south in an attempt to outmaneuver one another.

They traveled down an unnamed road.

Wolf led the unit from the front with Hogan by his side. "You know where this leads?" In the dark, it was possible to be traveling in the opposite direction of the way they needed to be going. It stuck out in his mind like a thorn because it had happened on Kilpatrick's raid. The combination of unfamiliar terrain with the night was always a test for the men.

Hogan grinned, bobbing his head. "I know where this doesn't lead. Spotsylvania. We have to get around the rebel cavalry. 'Cause I tell you one thing: we aren't going through them, and we'll never make fast enough time if we try to navigate the forests around them. We have to go around. Lucky for us, we are fifteen men and they number in the thousands. That and they are getting ready to bed down after a long day of fighting," the Irishman gave him a wink, "and we are relatively well-fed and rested. At least me and my mates are. You?"

"Been a prisoner twice now in the past few weeks. Let's just say I've been fed better."

"Captured twice. Not many men can tell that tale."

"No, they can't." *And it won't happen again.* "Where is she? We go around the rebels, but to where?"

"Where's the Beau's belle?" Hogan said with an almost singsong voice.

"Stuart keeps her far from the battlefront but within a day's ride for comfort. Our boy is a lover."

"And a fighter."

"Very true. But he is a lady's man. And the women of the South love him dearly, especially his wife. She's staying with some family near Beaver Dam Station. A Colonel Edmund Fontaine and family. A second cousin of Flora."

"How do you know that?"

Hogan swayed with his horse as they walked. "Not all Southerners are friends of the South. Let's just say some people can see the writing on the wall."

"The Fontaines are spies?"

Hogan neither confirmed nor denied the information. "Flag, sir?"

Wolf peered back at Wilhelm and the guidon carried in one of his hands. "Sergeant, furl the colors. And while we're at it, let's strap those sabers to your saddles. Try and look the part."

With a quick nod, Wilhelm dismantled the pole and removed the guidon from it, shoving it in a bag on his saddle. Wolf hated to see it go, but he understood they were venturing far from Union lines in an active war zone. Secrecy was going to be paramount. The rest of the men went about strapping their sabers to their saddles so they looked less like a cavalry patrol or at least a Federal one. They tucked the sabers and sheaths under their left legs, running the straps through rings on their saddles.

"Like this," Roberts said to Pratt. "You have to angle it right, or it'll rub. By the knee."

Roberts was embracing his new role as sergeant nicely, showing the younger members of his understrength platoon the tricks of the business.

"Putting away the flag already, Wolf?" came a voice from the line of horsemen.

Wolf slowed his horse, letting it fall back through the few ranks. He recognized the voice. It was strong and deep like a rocky well. "I trust not having the guidon flown is not a problem for you, Private Nelson?"

The mountain of a soldier didn't bother to acknowledge him while he spoke. "I don't prefer riding under any flag. Just like Dahlgren."

"You do thrive without company or army."

"I thrive everywhere and anywhere as long as there's a fight."

"That's why I selected you to come with me. I need men that can fight."

"I remember a scared little boy." His voice rose higher pitched. "I can't shoot a man in the back, boohoo."

"I'm not that man anymore."

"Still a boy?"

Wolf turned to stare at the big trooper. His beard was thick and his shoulders broad. His hands were ham hocks, but they were scarred ones. "You remember this, Nelson. I ain't getting captured. I ain't going back to prison."

"Boy's gotta death wish. Well, let me send you along then. We got unfinished business."

"Try it and I'll kill you."

"You ain't the first man to say that."

"But I'll be the last if you push me. I picked you for this mission because we need men willing to get their hands dirty. I know you and Adams have that in you."

Nelson grinned like a bear before a stream filled with salmon. "We do."

"You ain't off your leash, but your leash got longer." Wolf let his words sink in. "You and me ain't the same, but we want the same thing."

"What's that?" Nelson said, his grin spreading to his hairy cheeks.

"We want the army, and we want freedom to do as we please."

Nelson chewed his words in silence before he spoke. "Maybe I'll hold off killing you for a while longer." He turned to Adams. "You hear that? Wolf here is going to make us indispensable to Uncle Sam."

"I heard him. All that talk about not being the same, Wolfie. I told you all along we are just alike. Even more now than ever."

Wolf didn't bite on the man's remarks. They had made their break.

He tread the narrow path of a soldier. It was a gray path where any wrong step could turn into a quicksand of savagery and despair. He'd been close to sinking into those depths, but had come back into the fold.

The line between them had been drawn, and he would keep it that way. A line that Wilhelm had taught them despite their resistance. No women and no children. And now they marched to kidnap a woman. Her well-being would be his responsibility and he would protect her from harm until his last breath. But her husband would fall for that was the way of war.

Chapter Fifteen

Early Morning, May 8, 1864
Near Todd's Tavern, Virginia

In the darkness, Hogan brought his horse to a halt. Wolf held a fist and his men followed suit. They were wise enough to keep their mouths shut. Only the creak of a saddle was heard and the occasional stomp of an impatient hoof. Hogan gently urged his mount forward further into the recesses of night, until he became only a gray shadow ahead.

Wolf found his hand falling back on the handle of his pistol. The darkness kindled that spark of caution in a man. Being the victim of an ambush brought it out even more because what could be in store for them was seared into his brain. The spark of caution turned into a flame of permanent wariness because bullets and death hid in the dark. The only comfort was knowing you had a chance if you were quick on the draw. Being surrounded by some mean soldiers didn't hurt either.

Hogan returned, his form growing larger, and the tension in the air gradually decreased. A mosquito buzzed near Wolf's ear and he brushed it away. He eyed the agent and spoke softly. "Reminds me of the last time we were on a dark path in the woods."

"Don't put a hex on us like that. We're back on Brock Road behind the rebs. But they be close."

"Quiet now. Rebs are close," Wolf whispered back to Roberts and he passed the word down the command.

They started forward again, but the pounding of hooves brought them all to a halt.

"To the woods!" Wolf half-shouted.

The unit drove their horses into the dense brush, kicking up dead leaves and dirt. They waited as the riders drew closer with each pounding hoof.

A company of cavalry thundered past toward Spotsylvania. Moving like enraged ghosts, they passed, unknowing that the enemy hid in the trees within harm's reach.

"We got them ahead of us now," Wolf said to Hogan.

The guide scratched behind his ear, eying the way they'd come. "We could go back. Ride closer to Fredericksburg and follow the rail south that way, but it will add at least twenty miles. Or we follow them and hope they think we're with them. But that isn't up to this laddie, no siree."

In the night, both ways were the same, densely forested roads in enemy territory. The longer they spent away from the main army, the more chances they had to run into rebel forces. He glanced at Wilhelm, and his sergeant gave him a nod.

"We follow them. Darkness will cover our pursuit."

Wolf led the way to the road, kicking his horse's flanks to move her along. The men drove their mounts from the forest and followed at a trot. The slower pace should put enough space between them unless the enemy horsemen returned by the same route. His gamble paid off, and their pursuit of the rebel cavalry went unanswered. Miles disappeared and gave way to the town of Spotsylvania.

The structures and homes appeared abandoned as if the people who lived there had packed their belongings and moved to a less volatile place. It seemed to be the crossroads of the war, a distinction no town wished to have.

Wolf lifted his hand in the air, and the riders reined in their mounts to a walk as to not engender any additional scrutiny. They crossed between lifeless home after home, shadowed and dormant like a cemetery of houses. The men kept their heads low and scanned their surroundings for the enemy. But they found neither horse nor rebel as they traversed through the town.

They passed the home of the matron Wolf had robbed during Kilpatrick's raid months before. He eyed the yellow clapboard-sided home, wondering what had become of the elder woman who had resided there with her slaves.

In hindsight, he didn't regret robbing the woman of her husband's pocket watch. That watch essentially ensured his freedom from Libby Prison. He wondered if Gratz's father held it as the last treasure of his son, unknowing that a comrade had stolen it, stuffed it in an envelope along with the secret orders to kill Jefferson Davis, and had a widow who they'd saved from being raped smuggle it north. Perhaps someday Wolf could explain it to him in person. Then again, Wolf doubted he would make it that far.

They came to a crossroads, and nothing stirred around them. Wolf's men steered their horses onto a southern road.

"Hi there!" came a shout.

All of their eyes darted toward the voice. Shadows moved in the darkness, turning into marching men. Canteens jangled, boots thumped the ground, and the quiet coughs and words of tired men doing the infantry trudge filled the air. Hundreds of marching men in butternut and gray.

"Dear God," Wolf muttered.

"That my friend, is a rebel infantry regiment," Hogan said.

Wolf's heart rate accelerated. An officer atop a horse waved at them. "Keep moving down the road," Wolf said harshly.

His men continued forward, nervously eyeing the approaching infantry, but keeping their horses at a walk.

The officer on horseback raised his voice, cupping a hand around his mouth. He was a portly fellow with a black beard, and Wolf almost felt bad for his horse. "You boys with Fitz Lee?" He lowered his hand, and when no one responded, he spurred his horse into a trot to meet them.

Wolf drew his pistol and aimed at the silhouette. *Bang!* The Colt Army .44 revolver kicked in his hand like an angry mule. The officer reared his horse on two legs. The animal screamed in terror, and the rider toppled from his saddle.

Angry shouts sounded from the marching soldiers. They eyed the homes for enemies and the riders in front of them. A musket popped, fire exploding from an unseen barrel followed by the bark of a sergeant.

"Ride!" Wolf called to his men. And they were off into a gallop. Houses blurred past them. Wind engulfed them. Horse manes fluttered in the night.

A distant ripple of gunfire crackled like a dry pine log on fire. Wolf squinted behind them. Orange blooms opened up in the darkness, but the bullets weren't close enough to buzz or zip past the men. It was more a vengeful response from being surprised.

They pushed their animals for almost a mile. Wolf made frequent checks behind him as they rode to ensure his unit stayed together and that the enemy did not pursue. They couldn't sustain the pace, not and save their animals, but they could keep it up long enough to stretch out from the town and the infantry within.

"Whoa!" Wolf said. He slowed his horse and his men followed his lead. "No use in burning them out before we need to."

"Whose idea was it to shoot at them?" Hogan said with a hasty breath.

"First thing that came to mind," Wolf said.

"Remind me to get out of the way next time."

"Remind me to take the long way around next time."

Roberts spoke up behind them. "What about that company we saw earlier? They could be on this road."

"We'll deal with them if we have to. Looks like the rebs are getting into position at Spotsylvania. Which means we just threaded a needle in our nightly pass thru."

"Aye, that was an entire regiment of the bastards, all right," Hogan said.

"You see the look on that reb's face when Wolf shot at him?" Roberts said.

"Practically shit himself," Pratt said.

"Before he fell off his horse," Hale added. The two young men laughed at the rebel officer's misfortune. The young men didn't realize how close they'd come to getting captured or worse.

Wolf's eyes swept the night for more threats. Another ten minutes and they would have run smack into that regiment. Right now, they were probably trying to decide if it was a case of mistaken identity or actual Federal cavalry this far south.

"They won't pursue," Wilhelm said. "Too much going on ahead of them. We're irrelevant."

"Let's hope so, Sergeant," Wolf said, patting his mount's flank.

They pressed on into the night.

***

As the dawning light rays eclipsed the horizon, he brought his men to a halt. He'd estimated they'd traveled over fifteen miles and put enough distance between themselves and the two armies.

"We're going to take three hours. So catch some sleep. Tomorrow will be even longer." He climbed from the saddle, adjusting his reins. "No fire."

There were a few grumbles, but everyone knew that fires were like a signal to anyone that people were near, and they didn't want to advertise their whereabouts in enemy territory.

"Loosen the girths but keep them saddled." Wolf patted his mount's back. "Sorry, girl." As soon as they had stopped, the flies and mosquitos found them and descended upon them with an irritating vengeance. The horses' tails flicked and their skin twitched, trying to keep the winged menaces away.

He took a sack of feed from his saddle and gave her some, letting her eat out of his hand. No matter the demand of traveling far on horseback, there was always as much strain if not more on the mount. And a mountless cavalryman was just infantry. A crippled mountless cavalryman was just a slow-moving prisoner.

She munched loudly, nibbling at his hand. He wiped his hands together, and the horse nudged him for more. "Be calm, Sarah." He made sure to wrap her reins loose enough so she could reach the leafy green brush. She nudged at him again and he stuck his hand back into the sack and fed her a bit more grain.

The sounds of men curling up on the ground and tending their mounts was hushed save for the intermittent creak and scrape around them. Men could never truly be quiet. After his horse finished eating, he patted her nose with a soft sigh.

He thought about his previous horse, Billy. He'd bolted in the woods where they'd been ambushed and captured. Most soldiers went through multiple mounts during a war. Roberts had been through two. Hell, General

Custer had been through five already. The Michigan Brigade was notorious within the War Department for being great "horse killers."

But Billy had been Wolf's first mount, and like him, the horse had been rejected as being suitable for service. They'd proved everyone wrong as they'd raced across the fields at Hunterstown to save Custer then charging twice near Gettysburg.

Billy had given him legs. He had let a man who never thought he would run again sprint across fields and leap over streams. He could never forget him and their bond. He sighed. But in war, everything was subject to change at a moment's notice.

A friend could be with you one moment and gone the next. Life was this way too, but war expedited the process. It was like living at a full gallop, everything and everyone blurring by. He wondered how many of these men would even be here in a few days. There was no way they were going to escape this endeavor without a fight.

When this mission was over, they'd be back in ranks with the rest of the company. And after passing through the destruction surrounding the Wilderness and Todd's Tavern, there was plenty of fighting to be done in this war.

He loosened the strap and rubbed his hand underneath the saddle. "You'll be fine, old girl. A few more days of this and we'll be back in the slow-moving Army of the Potomac." Sarah didn't say a word, only stood with her head bowed.

"Johannes," came Wilhelm's voice from behind. He said his name with perfect inflection like his father would at home. It brought back a flood of familial memories that he wished to embrace and fall back into, but for now, he brushed them aside like a fly. These men were his family now. They must hold his every attention.

"Yes, Wilhelm."

The sergeant studied him for a moment with cool blue eyes like he'd seen a boy who'd transformed into a man before him. "My apologies, Lieutenant."

"Please, you've known me for a long time."

Wilhelm shook his head no. "You should call me sergeant."

"You know I'm not like that. Hell, I only just received a promotion and I'm not sure I even deserve that. I got it for surviving."

"Sometimes surviving is how you get promoted. Grit and a bit of luck."

The two regarded one another. Between them hung the lifeless body of Wilhelm's son, Franz, a young man who shouldn't have ever been to war. A young man cut down that neither of them could save, but that was saying that you could save someone from this war.

After a moment, Wilhelm spoke, "May I speak frankly, sir?"

Wolf was about to rehash the whole conversation over again but held his tongue. "You may." But he already knew what was coming.

"You shouldn't have brought them."

Them. He referred to Adams and Nelson. The two men Wilhelm promised to get court-martialed from the service, something that fell on deaf ears despite the soldier's claims.

"We need them," Wolf said.

"No, we do not."

"I need men that aren't afraid to get their hands dirty. I need fighters. I need survivors."

"Do you, sir?"

"I do for this. We are going deep behind enemy lines. We are kidnapping Stuart's wife for Chrissake. Is that not dirty? We tread a fine line between war and criminal."

"It's a bit unorthodox, yes, but those men aren't fit to be out of chains."

"Then we are their chains. I need men that dig themselves out of a tight spot."

Wilhelm's eyes flashed the disagreement of a father to a son as if Wolf needed a lesson with a sharp tongue or a switch, but he restrained himself, keeping his face calm, his mustache straight. "These men can do that. They are easy killers, but not soldiers. Being a true soldier takes pride in what you've done."

"These are the kind of men I need." He got closer. "I trust you, Wilhelm. You've gotten us this far. I intend to bring us all back. But this war must end, and we need these men to do it."

A slight nod of Wilhelm's chin was his only consent.

"I need you to watch them." Wolf dropped his voice. "If need be, we'll put them behind us, say the rebs shot 'em. But if they're going to kill, I'd rather have them with us than against us."

"You seem to understand the situation well then."

"Sergeant." The word felt wrong on his tongue.

"Yes, sir?"

"I can't do this without your support and guidance. But we will carry out this mission. We will."

Wilhelm nodded fully. "Yes, we will, sir. You're the right man for this job."

"As are you."

"Until the war is done."

"Until the war is done."

Chapter Sixteen

Late Morning, May 8, 1864
South of Spotsylvania Court House, Virginia

The sun crept in the sky, nearing its apex, although it was hard to tell with the overhead greenery blocking out its warming rays.

Wolf's men were quickly saddled and ready to depart at his command. The fifteen horsemen left little in their wake. No embers of a dying fire, only rustled and overturned brown and black leaves where they had rested their heads in the fading coolness of morning.

They rode south surrounded by thick foliage. If they'd wanted complete secrecy, they would have attempted to trailblaze through the secondary growth forest, an impregnable undergrowth of shrubs, tangled vines, and fast-growing trees sprouting skyward. But that way would be slow going, and they'd risk injuring their horses, so they stuck to the roads for speed, leaving them exposed to the glaring sun and potential enemies.

"It's a hot one," Wilhelm said.

Wolf eyed the sky. Clouds dissipated and the humidity grew more oppressive by the minute. "Aye, it will be blazing in an hour."

"We'll have to keep the horses well-watered if we're going to push them hard."

"I agree. About six miles and we'll make our way to Anderson's Ford. Isn't that right, Hogan?"

The BMI agent nodded his agreement. "There we can cross with little notice."

"I don't want us going across no bridge."

"Well put, Lieutenant. There's always eyes and ears around bridges," Hogan added. "In a river, not as much."

"Then we go around Beaver Dam Station to the good colonel's home."

When they reached the North Anna River, sweat caked the horses and riders alike. The sun had beaten them mercilessly, causing Wolf to go for his canteen with its lukewarm water three times.

They dismounted, watering their horses in the shallows. George and James quietly took a rest beneath the shade of the nearby trees away from the group. They crouched in the undergrowth, their dirty blue jackets acting almost as camouflage, and they carefully studied the woods along the opposite shore.

Wolf removed his hat and wiped the beads of sweat from his brow. "We made good time," he said to Hogan.

"We did." Hogan took his canteen and held it under the water. Bubbles floated to the surface.

"Should be there by tonight." Wolf scanned the opposing embankment of mud, grass, and trees. A few rocks were stuck in its side like earthy fruitcake.

"It's the next part that will be tough." Hogan took a swig of his water. He gestured with his head. "Once it's done, we're going to be riding even harder."

"These men can handle it." Wolf took a swig from his canteen. The water was tepid at best, but anything was gratifying in the heat. "But it's going to be a sprint."

"You be good at running, Yellabelly," Hogan said with a grin.

Wolf cracked a smile in return. "I'm probably the worst runner here."

Hogan emitted a stifled laugh. "Not too fast on two legs, are you? Never asked you how that happened. Gettysburg?"

"Father's shop, before the war."

"So no Southern man can claim to have maimed the great Lieutenant Wolf?"

"I been harmed plenty by the bastards. One in particular more than most." Payne's face came into focus and he found himself gritting his teeth as he relived the pain he had experienced at his enemy's hands.

Hogan blinked back his words as if he relived some hardship as well. "I'm sure plenty of the bastards want my head for something or another."

Wolf nodded. "I've earned my own hate too I'm sure."

"Where there's war, there's men seeking retribution. That's why when your golden-locked general brought up your special circumstances, I immediately endorsed such a mission."

"All of my special circumstances dealt with survival."

"And protecting our cause."

He never thought he'd done more than any other man. It was natural to deceive the enemy if it could be done. He never could have known the impact his defiance would have on the war effort.

Hogan hooked his canteen back onto his saddle, speaking over his shoulder. "That's the kind of men we need for this type of war."

"Plenty of men in this war," he said, patting his mount's flanks.

"No, that's not what I meant," Hogan said, turning. "I meant in this type of war. The irregular type. Ones without big armies and cannons. Ones that are more secret if you will."

"You mean like something the Bureau of Military Information would be interested in?"

Hogan's smile became fierce. "Exactly." His voice changed to a Southern drawl. "Actions behind enemy lines."

Wolf straightened his reins and tugged his knee brace upward. The damn thing always seemed to slip down his pant leg. Sarah dug her face into the river water, hardly stopping between laps to swallow. "I'm interested in a long career in the army. One could say I finally found something I'm good at."

"You mean you finally found something you could do."

"I suppose that's why I'm good at it."

A sharp whistle came from down the riverbanks, drawing their immediate gaze. The head of every man in the party went upright. Hands went to pistols and carbines. Most stood motionless, their eyes surveilling from left to right. They knew danger came with movement.

Wolf gazed down the line of men and horses. George and James had all but disappeared into the undergrowth, long rifles to their shoulders. Skinner was all together missing.

They could hear the roll of wagon wheels over dirt, the clink of horses' harnesses, and the intermediate flick of a whip upon horse flesh. A man called out, "Get up," every now and again, his voice muffled by the layers of trees.

A team of horses pulling a wagon behind them emerged through the timber. The wagon brimmed with stacked boxes. The driver wore a faded gray rebel coat and a brown wide-brimmed hat that was folded in the front. Behind him, clopped another team. They didn't stop at the sight of the raiders but pressed on, the teamsters driving into the river.

The horses splashed into the water, high-stepping in the shallows. As they ventured further into the river, the horses' legs chopped the flowing currents. Water pressed dangerously upon the wagon.

The driver flicked his whip, and it hissed in the air. "Come on now!" The horses continued to strain against their harnesses, but the wagon was too heavy, bogging down into the muddy river bottom. He whisked his whip, biting at the backs of his team. Standing half-way up, he tried to get a better view while keeping his balance. Noticing the riders, he shaded his eyes before he shouted, "Could you give us a hand?"

Wolf exchanged a glance with Hogan and Roberts. "What're they hollerin' about?" Roberts asked.

"They're stuck and want our help," Wolf said.

Nelson frowned. "We should tip 'em."

"Prolly taking something to the rebs," Hogan said.

Water rushed around the wagon, and the horses screamed, the terror of being hitched and stuck in the water spooking them. The teamster whipped them again. "Get on now."

"What do you want to do, Lieutenant?" Hogan asked.

It was comforting for a soldier to know his very own sharpshooters had sights on the enemy. With the tiniest of gestures, he could have the drivers shot and they could burn whatever was in the wagons or let the river take it. Then again, terrorizing behind Lee's lines while appealing would only lead to a hunting before they wanted one.

If they failed at their primary task, then not much would matter. They'd be no better than some ineffectual ill-fated raid. They'd probably be dogged like Dahlgren through Virginia until someone like Pollard devised an ambush for them in an unnamed forest near a small village. No, all was for naught without completing their primary mission.

"Help them across. Hogan, you do the talking. Your fancy Southern bit."

"Be a pleasure, sir," Hogan drawled.

His men mounted, pushing out into the ford that should have been shallower than it was. The swirling waters rose slowly around their horses' legs, noisily gushing.

Near the middle of the river crossing, the driver stood, watching the back of his wagon dip lower than the rest as it sank into the mud.

"Praise Jesus for you boys. Toss me a rope here."

Wilhelm tossed his picket rope to him and Wolf did the same. They wrapped the ends over their pommels and let their horses do the work.

"Come on, girls!" the teamster shouted.

"Git, Sarah," Wolf said, urging his horse.

They tugged and pulled the wagon, leading them across. Roberts led Dan and Van Horn to the other wagon, and they followed behind.

The driver eyed his comrade slowly making his way across the ford over his shoulder. He grinned at Wolf and then gave a curious glance at Wilhelm.

Hogan smiled, his voice changing accents to a much slower Southern dialect. "You sure are lucky, good sir, to come across us."

"You gave us a start there. For a minute, I thought you were Lincoln's ilk." He nodded at Wilhelm. "That one in the blue and all, but we know our boys take what we can. Fight with what we got." His eyes lingered on the Spencer carbines on their backs and saddles. "That's some fine weaponry you got there."

Wolf gave a short smile as his hand went to his pistol on his hip, tapping the handle.

Hogan quickly drew attention back onto himself. "We are a resourceful group. Lifted those right off some very dead Union cavalry."

The driver nodded glancing back at his man in the other wagon. "Suppose there be plenty of them nowadays."

"Always happy to add to that number."

Wolf and Wilhelm sat silent, keeping their eyes away from the man or risk engaging.

The driver laughed. "Ain't that the truth." He eyed the Union men sitting quietly atop their horses. "Say, you boys sure are quiet."

"Long ride. Long war," Hogan said.

"We're headed that way now with extra ammunition from Richmond we been sending by rail up here."

"Is that so?" Hogan said. His eyes darted for Wolf. Every tidbit of information helped. Raiding and destroying ammunition meant for the front could have an immediate impact on the war, but alas, this was not their mission.

"Yes, sir. This ford here be the fastest way. We were told to make all due haste, so we're leaving as quick as we can get loaded." He gestured back toward the river road. "More be coming down that road. Slowed down by a bunch of Yank prisoners. They ship ammunition north and prisoners south. Haha."

Wolf's eyes steeled as he heard the word prisoner, and he knew immediately what he had to do. He would not allow the prisoners to befall the fate of so many men before them.

"I see. Well, be careful. I hear there's a lot of Federal cavalry in the area."

The teamster gulped. "That so? Damn. You boys wouldn't want to give us an escort now, would ya?" He nervously scratched under his hat, his eyes searching for Union soldiers in the trees.

Hogan eyed Wolf again, an action the driver noticed. "Say, why you looking at him? He your commander?"

"Nonsense. I am in charge here."

The teamster wrinkled his nose. "He some sort of dumb?"

Hogan grinned and one of the men stifled a chuckle. "Dumb yes, but excellent fighter."

"Say, what unit you boys with?"

"Wickham's," Hogan retorted.

The driver turned on Hogan, friendly surprise lighting on his face. "Wickham! You be Virginia boys? I'll be damned. I got a brother up with Wickham. You might know him. Henry Gates. You know him?"

"Can't say I do."

"Well, that's a shame. He's a fine lad. Younger brother you see."

"But I'm afraid we must be on our way," Hogan said.

"Thanks for the help, boys. If you see Henry, give him my best."

"It will be my pleasure," Hogan said with a slight bow.

Wolf tipped the brim of his hat at the man. The driver nodded back, and with a creak of the wheel and a flick of their whips, the drivers drove their team onto the forest road, disappearing under the stomp of hooves.

"Close call there," Hogan said. He eyed the opposite embankment. "We'll have to hurry past here before more arrive and avoid the train station at Beaver Dam. If we're careful, we can pass around unnoticed."

"We're going to Beaver Dam Station," Wolf said clearly.

Hogan cocked his head. "Now listen, this wasn't a part of the general's orders."

Wolf twisted in his saddle and scanned his men. "We ain't leaving those boys to get shipped to Richmond like a bunch of goddamn cattle. We're breaking them free."

"The mission, Wolf. If we raise the alarm too early, we could lose her."

"No. We free the men. Then we find her."

"Christ, give me guidance," Hogan said with a peek at the sky.

Wolf would be damned if he was going to stand by while those men could be freed. He knifed a hand toward the train depot. "Forward, men!"

Riders splashed into the ford, and Hogan closed in on him. "You're making a mistake."

"No, I'm not." He drove his horse into the water, wading to the other side. With the crossing of the river, his decision was set in stone.

Chapter Seventeen

Late Afternoon, May 8, 1864
West of Todd's Tavern, Virginia

The alarmed bleating of cattle almost overtook the pops of gunfire through the woods. A bullet buzzed past Hampton's ear, and he slightly jerked his head to the side. The day was fading fast and dusk crept upon the forests surrounding him. Every additional minute diminished his ability to see.

"Would you look at that?" Preston said. He glanced at his father for confirmation that the sight was indeed worthy of comment and it was.

Hamstrung cattle stampeded their owners in blue, causing a rapturous rout as the Union soldiers fled down the road back toward Todd's Tavern. Victorious cattle swung their tails back and forth as they chased their captors. It made Hampton want to grin, seeing the scared looks upon the Union soldiers' faces as they avoided getting run down. His attack had faltered as well, but for different reasons.

His men had captured a Union baggage train and camp. Wagon after white-canvased wagon lay uncovered as his men ransacked them. Men in butternut and gray surrounded the wagons, tearing into boxes of hardtack and dried meats while ducking Union bullets sent by their retreating enemy on foot.

Standard military consensus was that pitting dismounted cavalry against infantry was a poor idea. Undermanned cavalry were never able to withstand a concentrated infantry volley, at least in theory. But then again, Hampton had learned how to fight in the saddle and not in the classroom.

If he could wait for the conditions to fall into his favor, he would pit his men against infantry any day. But how could he stop his men from looting? How could he keep a hungry soldier from eating? They were not regularly supplied. He watched a man collapse as a bullet thudded into his chest, crackers tumbling from his hands as he hit the earth. The men next to him crouched onto their haunches below the wagon, shoving food into their mouths.

A weak staccato volley popped from the trees, sounding like a symphony orchestra failing to crescendo at the right time. Acidic smoke clouded the air amidst the eruptions of fire from musket tips. Despite the terror brought on by stampeding cattle, these men would not give their ground without a fight. He maneuvered his mount to the side, waiting impatiently for his hungry men to feed themselves.

The Union forces they'd sent scurrying were Miles's Brigade under Hancock's 2nd Corps protecting the rear of the Union Army. Miles was an advance element attempting to stretch their reach away from Todd's Tavern; Hampton and the recently arrived General Mahone sought to keep Hancock tied up while the rest of the Cavalry Corps and Anderson dashed to Spotsylvania to beat Meade and the Army of the Potomac to the crossroads. Breastworks and entrenchments layered Laurel Hill, commanding the area from the defensive position. More rebel infantry were on their way to reinforce and create a nice surprise for the Union 5th and 6th Corps.

The more time Lee had to rush his men to Spotsylvania the better, and making the Federals think the threat of attack could come from the north and west could achieve such a task.

"Young, form your men in a skirmish line. We need some space between these wagons and our men."

Pierce Young, a long-mustached brigadier general of one of Hampton's brigades, took the flat end of his sword and began wielding it liberally on the backs and rears of his looting men. The dismounted men snarled in response but hustled to obey. The other officers took up the shout, and soon, a loose skirmish line traded fire with Federal infantry that gave ground.

However, Young's attack lacked staying power. The Union soldiers were stiffening despite being forced to battle on duel fronts.

"Let's get those batteries going," he said to Preston. It was a necessary order and one that would remove his son from the brunt of the upcoming assault and keep him out of harm's way. If Preston had any inkling of his true intention, he may balk at the order, but it was an order of importance. "Then I need you to ride to Mahone and tell him we are preparing to drive them back." *There that should keep him occupied until we are through.*

"Yes, sir," Preston said, his eyes flashing a familiar fierceness. He disappeared toward the artillery in the rear. Within minutes, his artillery opened up on the retreating blue-coated men. Over a half mile through the thick forest near the Northern flank, the distant crackle of an infantry on infantry struggle could be heard. It was much more prominent than his skirmish line, and he knew Mahone was doing the hot work.

The boom of his cannon roared like a crashing ocean wave upon the shore. Trees and leaves shook in response, and the ground trembled before his guns. This seemed to hasten the Union men, and they gave ground in fits and starts. A cluster of enemy soldiers screamed as a shell burst over them.

"Sir, look!" Pierce shouted.

Hampton squinted; his eyes seemed to become worse and worse every month. He saw men moving in the distance. "What is it, Pierce? I can't see that far."

"Regiments are moving down the road from the entrenchments. Green flag with a harp." Pierce's horse shifted nervously beneath him and he tightened the reins to bring the animal under control. He shifted as he tried to find a better view. He studied the advancing men as if he were judging a cotton crop in his very own fields. "They're rallying the other regiments. I do believe Hancock intends to drive us off."

"The bloody Irish." Stubborn. Ghastly. And willing to die by the handful for a worthless piece of dirt. A brigade of them were leaving the safety of the entrenchments near Todd's Tavern. "Hancock isn't any better than the Irish. Stubborn fool," Hampton said. He dismounted from Butler and handed over the reins to an aide.

133

He joined his dismounted men in the trees. They crunched down noisily on hardtack. It was unadvisable to hurry when eating the tooth-dulling biscuit, but hungry men wouldn't be denied their fill. They waited in a skirmish line, loosely positioned in the trees near the supply wagons.

Blue regiments adjusted their course to flank Mahone's men from the north, and two additional regiments maintained their march west to keep Hampton's men at bay.

Smoke and darkness threatened to end the fight soon, but he would push an advantage if one could be found. His men were good for it. His gunpowder-covered, stinking, hungry men were good for it. He'd ask and they'd give their all. Hit the enemy and run. Make the enemy think you are in the thousands when you numbered barely a hundred.

He drew his Manhattan ivory-handled engraved pistol, unbuttoning the flap on his other holster holding the same style weapon.

"How many Yankees you kill with it?" Pierce asked.

"I'd say seven."

"Had to have been more than that?"

"Seven that weren't running."

Pierce smiled. "Of course. They do run often."

"Not often enough."

Seven notches were cut into the handle of his revolver. By the setting of the sun he would be adding even more.

Whirling clouds of gun smoke obscured his vision, and his men waited impatiently for the enemy. He rested a hand on a nearby tree, using it to take some of the weight off his feet. His eyes never stopped scanning for the enemy. Each gray billow and white swirl were an elaborate hoax taking the shape of his opponents.

He didn't need to check if his pistols were ready to fire. He knew they were loaded, but he glanced down at them anyway. Percussion caps were atop their cones. Paper cartridges were loaded and ready to fire. His other pistol was a plain Navy Manhattan revolver with a more rugged wooden handle. His favorite pistol held five shots and his secondary six. He scrutinized the smoke for the faintest of movements.

Cannons thumped, sending shells and shot far over the trees before crashing through limbs and slamming into the earth. They left trails of death in their wake.

Depending on the type of projectile, some shells were set with fuses prior to firing. At the right distance, they would explode and rain death among the enemy. Albeit, the enemy's ordnance was usually of higher quality and had much more accurate fuses while his men were stuck with wooden fuses with paper lining the inside. It made Southern artillery work a much more precise and delicate process where experience and attention to detail were absolutely necessary.

The cannon fire slackened and then became silent. He looked behind at where he had placed the battery. *They can't make friend from foe, so they've stopped. They are close.* He couldn't help but let out a brusque sigh as he steeled himself for the coming combat. *The bloodletting will be soon.*

A dozen men pushed emptied wagons across the road and tipped them on their sides, providing additional cover for the men there.

"Do not give ground," he called around him. Most were too tired and hungry to even glance his way.

The soldiers next to him continued to eat their crackers. The closest soldier, finishing one, slipped another into his mouth, breaking off a chunk with his molars, irreverent to the battle taking shape in front of him. A sergeant in a patched gray jacket laughed at something long and hard as if he'd lost his mind.

Misty shadows became a blue mass then turned into silhouettes before taking shape as nameless faces. Tightly packed men weaved through the dense timber trying to hold their line in proper formation. Union men were urged on by their officers to stay brave as death was but a hundred yards away. Color bearers whipped a green flag and a blue Pennsylvania flag near their center.

Hampton was taken aback when a song belted from their lips. It wasn't a high-pitched battle cry like the rebel yell, but an actual song, yet it remained unnerving. He couldn't make out the words and soon realized they were singing in their native tongue of Irish Gaelic. The melody was brave and sweet, holding touches of sadness, and although he couldn't understand them, he could feel the meaning of their words. It encompassed the sad memory of home and those that were gone with the beat of a battle march.

He could feel the men around him become nervous as they continued forward, singing in the unknown language. Heads turned, eyeing each other, and his men took courage from his brothers in arms around him.

He held his pistol in the air. "Time to put a stop to the brave bastards."

The Irish regiment was still over a hundred yards away, calmly singing as they came onward. One of his captains looked at him. Nothing about him designated him as an officer aside from the orders he barked at the men in front of him. He thought the men were from Cobb's Legion. Georgians. Tough sons of bitches.

They made eye contact, and the captain gave him a short grin. He was missing his front two teeth. Then the air screamed above them for only a second before it concussed spraying waves of thunder and metal rain.

Hampton crashed into the forest floor as if he'd been thrown from his horse. He rolled onto his back, his officer's jacket now decorated with leaves and crumbly dirt.

His wounded men writhed on the ground like worms after a rain. The captain laid facedown, blood trickling from the top of his skull. A jagged piece of metal had replaced his hat, protruding defiantly outward.

The man lying next to him coughed hysterically, sucking in air but never getting enough. Another soldier crawled away from the others, leaving a bloody trail like an injured snail.

Yet he was still in one piece. Grasping his pistol and a handful of dirt, he ignored the ringing dinner bell in his ears as he shouted, "Let 'em have it!"

His men opened up on the Irish regiment. The forest had split the blue mass into clumps of men. The clusters of Union soldiers withered before the hot lead balls but held rank. Their dead were left in bloody wakes behind them. They continued forward and came on like a harpooned whale, barreling ahead despite mortal injury. He took aim now.

He could make out individual faces. Fierce eyes. Scared eyes. Mostly the eyes of young dirty men kept together by fervent orders and staunch veterans, who knew to fold and run in the face of the enemy brought death, and more importantly, shame.

A Union officer on horseback paced behind his men. He swung a straight infantry sword in circles, urging his men forward. "Faugh a Ballaugh!"

Hampton sighted his pistol on the officer. A very long shot with his pistol, over sixty yards, but if it drifted low as it sailed for its target, it had a chance of striking the line of men hurrying to form.

"Faugh a Ballaugh!" the officer shouted again. Curly hair stuck from the sides of his Union kepi. A thick mustache entrenched his upper lip. He continued to bark orders at the men in front of him.

Hampton's men fired at will. It sounded like a giant oak splintering in two, inch by inch. His pistol leapt in his hand. *Bang!* Smoke wisps drifted from the end of his barrel.

Union soldiers collapsed as Minié balls entered their bodies. Their hands rose to their chests, trying to keep their own blood inside. More went down screaming, but all the cries of the men were drowned out by the guns banging as Hampton's men did their deadly work.

He squinted an eye. Everything was a blurry haze at best. His eyes just weren't what they used to be, and he let his finger depress the trigger again. *Bang!*

As the blue-coated men continued to march toward Hampton's, he thought for a moment they were simply going to charge him. Yet no bayonets were fixed on their muskets, and at this distance, they should have already begun their charge, but their line halted. They stood no more than fifty yards from his men instead. It was impossible to muster any kind of legitimate volley in the thick green foliage.

Hampton took aim, letting his thumb drive the hammer of his revolver backward. Smoke had almost enveloped all of them as if they'd stepped into a cloud and fought in the heavens. The enemy looked more like ghosts than men. It made it easier to kill when they were mere shadows and helped a man deal with the harm he inflicted.

Might have time for one more shot, but he held his finger. Instead he shouted, "Take cover!"

His dismounted men hid behind trees. Others hit the forest floor, covering their heads with their arms. He crouched down onto his knees, using a tree to protect himself.

The Union officer's voice rose like a rocket sailing thru the sky. "Fire!"

Flames burst from the opaque guns, smokelike wraiths shaving steel over flint stone. A fraction of a second later, the bullets came for Hampton's men. It became indiscernible if the deafening sound of tree branches snapping was from the onslaught of bullets or the forest absorbing the lead.

Trees shook as bark was stripped away by the buzzing balls. Men screamed as the gunfire struck home. Holes punched through their bodies as easily as spoons dipping into bread pudding.

The man next to Hampton's head kicked back like the victim of an errant hoof. The impact toppled him backward, and he slid over the dead leaves.

A cluster of cavities riddled his body. Hampton frowned. It looked like he'd been hit with a shotgun blast. The Irishmen were shooting muskets? Filled with buck and ball shot? He'd heard of their use at Gettysburg in the Wheatfield but hadn't seen it in action. No man would opt to use a smoothbore musket when the rifled ones provided not only topped them in range but accuracy, yet here these men, who had ample access to better weaponry, chose the smoothbores.

Bitter powder smoke singed the nostrils, trying to burn the hair away from the inside of his nose. Hampton aimed quickly from behind his tree. "Let 'em have another one!"

He pulled the trigger, his revolver rotating through the remaining shots like a clock at work. His men followed his lead, firing into the Union line. The opposing men let out another volley, but this one lacked the power and command of the first. It was a single hive of bees instead of twelve buzzing past, over, and into his men.

He holstered his pistol and drew the other. Six shots. His enemy was fragile, cracks forming in their ranks. They were a locomotive that had lost their steam. Now was the time to send them running back to Hancock. He full-cocked his pistol. "Give them the blade!" He scanned the men around him to make sure they still had enough fight for it. Wild eyes stared back. Men in the heat of killing. Men that were capable of deadly and courageous feats. *Brave boys.* He bellowed at the top of his lungs. "Charge!"

Bounding forward, he jogged at a blue clump of men. He didn't bother to make sure he was followed. His men would. Whether it was honor or order that drove them to charge an enemy, it drove them nonetheless. His hip nagged at him, but his blood boiled in his veins. The smell of bitter gun smoke and coppery blood filled his nostrils, inciting a deep howl from his bowels. He was a wolf culling the herd of brave sheep.

The Union soldiers in front of him attempted to reload faster. They ripped paper cartridges with their teeth, spilling powder onto blackened fingers and dry cracked lips. Wordless prayers crept from their mouths.

He stopped and aimed, letting his pistol bark. An enemy soldier clutched his breast, sinking to his knees as if he suddenly wanted to repent for all his sins. A second later, Hampton drew his long straight sword. Double-edged, heavy, and deadly. He'd need it soon, he only had four shots left in his pistol.

He was close now, no more than twenty feet from the enemy. He closed the distance with another call of the wild. His men were there around him, surrounding him like a medieval king as they protected their liege.

A Yankee captain screamed at his men to get their guns up, his sword wavering over the closing rebels, but his men were preparing for the incoming melee. A few of the enemy soldiers quickly fired shots, the balls mostly going high with a whip and a snap through the leaves.

Hampton felt the hot breath of a bullet's wind on his neck, and he shrugged it off like a death maiden's kiss. With loud calls to steel themselves in mortal contest, the rebels crashed into the Union men.

Swinging his sword into a gun barrel, Hampton sent the smoothbore from the man's hands. It clanged as it hit the undergrowth. Weaponless, the man tried to cover his face. The Union soldier next to him howled, baring his teeth and winding his weapon backward to bludgeon Hampton.

Hampton's pistol popped. The assailant's hands leapt for his throat. He followed his shot by running his sword through the other man's belly. The sound was a damp slap as the point punctured him. The young man's face shook as he screamed for mercy. Hampton shoved him backward, forcing him off the blade.

From the other side, a new Yankee took a swing at Hampton's head, using his gun like a stick. He didn't bother to duck. He towered over the man but deflected it easily with his sword. Shoving his pistol into the man's breast, he pulled the trigger. Fire mushroomed from the barrel. The Union soldier's eyes bulged as the bullet seared through his flesh, ripping out his back.

With a snarl, Hampton turned toward the incoming gallop of a horse's hooves.

"Mallacht Dé ort!" shouted the Union officer atop his steed. He thundered at Hampton, rearing his horse as he neared him. Hampton hardly had time to meet his blade with his own. If he had been but a hair closer, the man would have bashed his skull in. The officer swung again, and Hampton deflected his blow to the side with a clang. He tossed his pistol to the ground. As the man continued past him, he lunged and grabbed his belt.

Roaring like a grizzly bear, Hampton yanked the officer from his horse and into the air. He landed atop him and pummeled him with his cannonball-sized fists. The two men struggled, but Hampton was ever the larger man. He beat the officer's face until he went limp, his face mangled and shattered.

Teeth were missing, an eye swollen shut, blood filled his mouth like a freshly dug water well, and his remaining eye rolled into the back of his head. Hampton closed on the other officer's face, yelling at him with every ounce of rage held within his large body.

He blinked, realizing a war still raged around him and that he was responsible for not only his survival, but also for his men's.

He shoved the beaten officer onto the ground and crawled over the forest floor, searching for his sword. Leaves crumpled in his hands.

A charging Yankee staggered as a shotgun blast ripped into his side. The sergeant grinned as the man spun onto the ground. He held his shotgun at the ready. "I'll cover ya, General. Get your sword," he said, and pulled a cracker from his pocket, stuffing it in his mouth with a grin. "And yer pistol."

Hampton retrieved both, and his men trailed the Yanks as they fled back toward their entrenchments closer to Todd's Tavern.

Night charged upon the land like a horseman clad in all black. It darkened the terrain and shadowed the forest around them. The smoky fog of war surrounded them like a misty morning, the battle lingering around them.

They pursued the fleeing soldiers knowing that more enemies lay ahead, but not where. They all slowed their pursuit, peering hard for movement, anything to understand where the most danger came from. His men stopped their yelling and became quiet hunters, stalking prey instead of chasing it. They could feel the ominous presence, the oppression of men waiting in ambush.

He walked in a thin line with his men. Carbines and rifles, pistols and swords, were held ready to fire or stab at any moment. Every now and again a soldier would stop, either finishing off the stragglers or capturing them. It mattered not. The Yankees would fill their ranks with more poor bastards. The more his men destroyed and routed the Yankee armies, the more seemed to pop up in line, ready to die for their Republic.

Dusky shadows covered the length of the forest, stretching and reaching for his men. Everything was a haze. He put a hand down as he hopped over a log. Every few moments, a single shot would go off as a retreating man turned and fired harmlessly at his pursuers.

The air tightened. His breathing became condensed. His heart went faster. Every man felt the pressure.

"Get ready, boys. They're close," he said to the men around him. Raising his pistol almost level with his shoulder, they stalked further into the war mist. Hampton scanned the timber and spotted a small drop in elevation ahead. It wasn't a ravine, but more of a cut in the land. Roughly thirty feet to the other side, the ground sloped upward. Trees clung to the slanted angle of ground.

His men traversed downward. A man on his left tripped and fell onto his rear, sliding into the cut. The forest held its breath. No animals called or insects buzzed.

"Fire!" screamed a voice through the smoke.

The volley was controlled and ready. The man who'd covered him only minutes before took a bullet to the chest and collapsed under the violence. With ragged breaths, the man tried to stay alive. More of his men disappeared, finding their place on the ground and being thrust against trees like they'd been blown over in a windstorm.

Hampton blinked at the casualties around him. Only pure divine interest in his survival had saved him. One of his men held a friend. Another went down as he dragged a man rearward.

He shot his pistol up the hill. "Fall back!" he shouted. "Fall back!" He clambered up the cut in the ground, making for the safety of his original lines.

They fled before the entrenched Federals. The darkness and smoke covered their retreat. His men reached the point where they'd overtaken Miles's brigade earlier. They took cover, waiting for Hancock to send more infantry after them, but as the mantle of night embraced them, the threat dwindled. He set out pickets in case Hancock wanted to get a bit frisky, but his opposing general was acting timid and unsure. Probably because when he'd expected cavalry, he'd run into infantry as well.

His men cared for the wounded, and despite some additional casualties, they were still happy to be well-fed, especially off Yankee supplies. Delicious barrels of pork and beef were discovered in the captured wagons and the men ate like kings.

Later in the evening, Hampton was rejoined by Preston and the diminutive General William Mahone as their men traded foodstuffs around campfires in the dark. Mahone's beard was long and his cheeks thin like an old forgotten prisoner, and his eyes were restless and observant.

"Sure gave those boys a whipping," Mahone said. He gnawed the edge of a cracker. The fire gleamed off his face with an orange glow.

"We did," Hampton said. He sighed, staring into the flames. "Kept them in place."

"Old Hancock doesn't know what he's got."

Hampton stifled a laugh by smoothing his beard.

"Damn it feels good to be out in the field taking it to the Yanks." His son gave him a tired but true smile, and the men around him nodded their heads with approval.

"The 2nd Corps is one of their better ones too," Mahone added. More grunts of agreement. Nothing like the beginning of the war with so much optimism and hope. These men were seasoned and worn-out, just plain tired of fighting and killing, yet they marched on anyway because not a cowardly bone resided in their bodies.

Hampton nodded. "Hancock is a commendable soldier and leader. Now he sits entrenched."

"I thought they might just leave a few regiments. But Hancock's entire corps is there. Should be reinforcing the other corps," Mahone said. He tilted his head as he tried to chew his hardtack.

"He'll keep them that way."

"Suppose I should get my men to the courthouse while they sit themselves out," Mahone said. The wily small-statured general quickly rose to his feet, brushing crumbs off his jacket.

Gun and cannon fire rumbled the ground they had rested on for the last hour. A much larger fight was taking place southeast of their position. "General, I will see you near Shady Grove Church." Mahone gave a quick nervous salute. "A true pleasure working with you and your boys today."

Hampton gave a brief nod and returned his salute. "Good to send some Yanks running, but then again, there's always tomorrow."

Mahone's mouth creased around the edges. "Tomorrow we shall begin anew." He regarded the cannon groaning in the distance like giants tossing stones at one another. "Or tonight." He bowed and placed a black slouch hat that appeared too big atop his head.

As good as getting back into the fight felt, Hampton worried. He finally had a couple of good brigades at his back, and he couldn't help but worry. He eyed his son for a moment. Preston bent over and tossed a log onto their fire. *He is a good lad. Smart and resourceful. He may outshine is predecessors one day.* But that did little to alleviate his worry.

Rosser's men had been fighting almost nonstop, and despite their prowess and that of their commander, they'd suffered casualties. Many casualties in man and horse flesh. It didn't seem to matter if they thrashed the bastards or not, the Yankees came onward, and that kind of will worried a man.

It concerned a commander that cared for his men, especially when his son was within his ranks. For he couldn't lose them all, but it felt like he was. He knew he couldn't lose them all for that would mean the loss of his son. He mustn't allow it to go that far, but he couldn't evade the feeling that they would all pay for their rebellion in blood.

Chapter Eighteen

Late Afternoon, May 8, 1864
Beaver Dam Station, Virginia

Wolf's men followed a road toward Beaver Dam train station. It was a rough and root-laden five miles from the ford. The countryside was forested and rural with a railroad running along the route.

The railroad was a vital vein through the Confederacy and was operated by the Virginia Central Railroad. Originally, it was built to serve the farmers of the region to expedite the movement of goods. Now it served by connecting the Confederacy's eastern armies with the food supplies from the farmers in the Shenandoah Valley. A critical function to continue the war effort.

The Virginia Central Railroad traveled directly to Richmond, cutting through Hanover Station where goods and personnel could move to a new track of the Richmond & Fredericksburg Railroad and travel north.

With the relative positioning of the armies, it made sense that the rebels weren't shipping goods through Hanover north. Most likely the goods would have ended up in Union hands, something the supply-strapped South could ill afford.

"We're close now, Lieutenant," Hogan said.

"Dismount and into the forest," Wolf commanded.

The thick brush made quick work of them and brought his unit to a slow walk. His men struggled through the undergrowth plagued by vines, roots, and grasses trying to snare them.

When the harsh outline of the rail structure came into view, Wolf pointed at Hale and Pratt. "Horses."

The two young men appeared irritated to be stuck with passive dismounted duties but took the reins from the other men.

Slowly, the unit stalked closer to the train station.

Wilhelm joined Wolf, walking by his side. "Eventually you're going to have to let the new men in on it."

"When they prove they can handle it," Wolf muttered, his hands firmly wrapped around his new Spencer carbine. The shiny polished stock held seven metal cartridges. The gun barrel was clean without a touch of rust. It was a true thing of beauty.

"How can they prove it without a chance?"

"They can prove it by holding the reins and staying quiet. I don't have time to mentor them on a mission like this."

"I seem to remember another young man who often wanted to prove himself in the face of the enemy."

Wolf tried to mask his sigh by breathing out his nose. "A young man who dug enough latrines and sat on enough picket duties until he saw the elephant."

"They're good lads. When the time comes let them do their job."

"They'll get their shot." He kept his eyes ahead, watching the depot. If there were prisoners there, they would be freed.

The men neared the forest's edge, spreading out in a skirmish line. Beaver Dam Station was a new structure composed of freshly cut tan wood. A white sign that was charred around the edges hung on the front and read Beaver Dam in black letters.

No one had bothered to paint the building that had clearly been rebuilt. A few buildings that acted as storage surrounded the train depot, but the station was the most prominent.

A loud hoot sounded from the tracks. A single-stack locomotive rested on the rails. An upside-down cone formed the chimney stack, and hot steam leaked from the top. Two large wheels, linked with coupling rods which the engine rotated to propel the train forward, was probably fueled by wood fed into the furnace.

Men rushed to and fro, unloading supplies from cars into wagons. A team started off in the direction of the ford they'd recently crossed. But it wasn't them that drew Wolf's attention, it was the bedraggled defeated men seated on the ground under the watchful gaze of guards holding muskets with long fixed bayonets that shone in the sunlight.

As he lay in the brush, he counted the number of guards.

"How many do you see, Lieutenant?" Wilhelm said.

"A company or so if you count the lot of 'em."

"Psst," Roberts hissed, drawing Wolf's attention. The small man pointed toward the rear of the station. An artillery piece rested, limbered to a team of horses near the rear. An officer wearing a red kepi stood nearby smoking a pipe.

"Goddamn artillery," Wolf spat.

Wilhelm spoke from the side. "Looks like a 12-pounder Napoleon smoothbore. But they're limbered. There's probably a few more onboard that train. If we operate quickly, we can be in and out before they can unlimber and fire."

"A company of men with a battery. All we need is a company of cavalry to show up to complete the defense."

"There's a way to win every fight," Wilhelm said.

Wolf racked his brain. Right now, he had few things in his favor. The most important was surprise. They could move fast. He also had over three hundred allies sitting there eager to escape. Weaponless, yes, but able to fight. He didn't have the time to wait until night to strike.

The conductor climbed inside the locomotive. More steam puffed through the stack. The guards began to bark at the seated prisoners. There wasn't much time before they were carted to Richmond's Belle Isle and beyond. May as well have been a death sentence.

"Sergeant, we need to move fast. Do you think we can blow the train? Can't take those boys south without an engine."

Wilhelm sighed, eyeing it. "We need something to blow it up with."

"Plenty of ammunition in those wagons?"

"How about that cannon?" Wilhelm said with a slight grin beneath his curled mustache.

Wolf shared his destructive enthusiasm. "How about it?"

***

Wolf gave the two young men a task he thought was fit for their current lowly station. It was a risky order but vital to the plan's success. Hale and Pratt would be riding into the depot after his sharpshooters started the attack. And as much as Wolf had protested Wilhelm, he insisted on going with them. The three men were to scream and yell while shooting their pistols and carbines in the air like a band of wild Indians until the rebels decided to give chase.

The key was impressing upon the rebels that they were under attack. If all went to plan, they would unlimber and load that cannon for Wolf and his men, who could turn it on the locomotive. After that, chaos would reign supreme leading to freeing the captured soldiers.

Hogan crawled on all fours to where Wolf laid. Both men spied on the rebels going about their business of loading wagons. The guards were having a particularly difficult time getting all the Union men on their feet. Angry gestures with bayonet fixed guns was only getting them so much compliance. "You know I disagree with this."

"I do."

"This isn't why we're here. Our mission is of the utmost importance. These men, to put it frankly, are not. You know I wouldn't just leave them behind if our cause wasn't greater."

"I will not sit by while these men are submitted to the brutality of a rebel prison."

"If we fail, you could be extending the imprisonment of thousands more. Our mission will expedite the end."

Wolf ignored him. The sharpshooters were still positioning themselves in the forest surrounding the station. Soon he could see how good of a shot they actually were.

"Prepare yourself for battle, Mr. Hogan," Wolf said. The BMI agent may be right, but he would be damned if he didn't free these men.

Hogan grabbed his shoulder. "Wolf. Listen to me. You don't have the authority to do this."

Wolf glared at the man then down at his hand. "Last I checked Sheridan put me in charge." He shrugged himself from the other's grasp. "We free them. You can file a formal complaint with Sheridan when we return. But these men will be released today."

Hogan's mouth shut with a shake of his head. Another wagon traveled down the road away from the depot. The sun beat down on them through the leaves. The musty smell of dead leaves and damp forest rot filled their noses.

He adjusted his Spencer. Seven .56-56 copper rimfire rounds lay in the magazine stock of the weapon ready for rapid fire. All of his men had them. They could seem like a company of Union infantry in the woods, not fifteen cavalrymen. He settled in eagerly awaiting the first sharpshooter to make his mark.

It wasn't long before the first gunshot cracked the air like a monstrous sheet being torn in half. The rebels around the locomotive didn't respond. Wolf supposed they assumed it was the engine or a man shooting at a deer in the woods. It mattered not.

The guard went rigid, straight like a musket, and then collapsed onto the ground. A puff of dust clouded the air where he once stood. The prisoners all gaped in awe at the dying guard. The rebel cried out as he died in a pool of his own blood.

Wolf's raiders hastily made their way back to their waiting horses. Two more gunshots fired in the distance, and more guards fell. The conductor of the train peeked out his window, and a shot took him in the shoulder. He squawked inside his driver's compartment. This set the depot alight with armed men.

Wolf pointed a finger at Wilhelm with the young soldiers. They galloped toward the station, firing shots with their pistols as their horses pounded the ground beneath them.

Mounting his horse, Wolf waited. Wilhelm's men made a big ruckus as they shot their pistols dry. Rebels haphazardly fired back. The prisoners ebbed and flowed in their mass. Rescuers had arrived. The remaining guards were jabbing dangerously at them to keep them back with bayonets. Gray-coated infantry were forming in front of the train.

Wolf's men walked their horses carefully through the woods, circling to the other side almost perpendicular to the locomotive. He kept stock of his trio of riders wheeling their mounts. A volley blared out from the rebels, and Wilhelm turned his riders around. A victory shout carried forth from the rebels. Yet the sharpshooters continued to bring down individual men.

The artillerymen went about unlimbering the 12-pounder next to the infantry. The sharpshooters continued to bang away from the forest and the rebels moved their line back adjacent to the locomotive for cover.

"Clever," Wolf said.

"Veteran men," Hogan said nearby.

"Get them out of there," Wolf said under his breath. The gun's crew started to prep the cannon. He didn't know where they'd shoot. Perhaps in the woods would be enough to scare away most raiders despite the inaccuracies, but soon it became clear they were aiming for Wilhelm and his men.

Wilhelm guided them to the edge of the forest. All three had their carbines out firing away at the rebel infantry. Working the lever to chamber a new cartridge, Wilhelm was much faster than the young men. Cock, lever, fire. Infinitely easier than a muzzle-loading musket, and much more efficient than the Sharps or Burnside carbines, a Spencer enabled a good soldier to fire over twenty shots off in a minute. Smoke surrounded the riders from the carbines. That was the gun's only determent in Wolf's eyes: too much smoke. One couldn't hit what they couldn't see, at least on purpose.

The three riders presented a prime target for the artillery piece. They were over three hundred yards away and in the open, unlike the sharpshooters landing hits among the rebels in spite of the distance. A canister shot could shred them.

The cannon finished prepping, and the red-hatted sergeant pointed vigorously at the horsemen. A solid shot rang out and the earth trembled.

Wolf thanked God that it was a solid shot instead of canister or a fused shell. The shot burst through a tree near his men, sending shards of wood-like brown rain into the sky.

Wilhelm turned his horse in a circle and retreated. A platoon of infantry followed at a run. The artillery sergeant was taking no chances, and he pointed at his corporal who brought up a new shot. This was the time. Rebels started to tend the wounded guards. The sharpshooters went quiet.

"To the cannon!" Wolf shouted.

His riders burst forth from the trees with their pistols in hands. He dug his heels into his mount, ensuring she understood now was the time for speed. He let out a whoop as they charged the cannon from the rear. The sergeant's red kepi turned their way. A new round of cheers went out from the prisoners.

"About face!" the sergeant screamed. "Turn that goddamn cannon rearward!"

Straining red-faced artillerymen heaved, trying to rotate the artillery piece to face the new threat. Blood burst from the sergeant's chest as one of the sharpshooters found his mark. He sank onto the wheel, collapsing onto the ground. Wolf's men closed fast.

He fired his pistol once, twice, three times. Each shot lifted the barrel into the air with the power of the shot. He leveled the revolver and set his aim again. The fourth shot struck the gunner in the chest, misting scarlet into the air. He fell onto his back, his hands seizing in pain. The rest of the artillery crew stopped everything and gawked. Their corporal screamed at them, but they couldn't peel their eyes from their comrades. Bullets screamed at them for a few more seconds before they ran in a frenzy, seeking cover down the tracks.

"Get that gun around!" Wolf shouted. His men hopped from horses. Bart, Dan, and Nelson had the piece spun in a matter of seconds, the brute strength of the men equal to twice maybe even three times that of regular men. All the while Wolf kept his eye on the rebel infantry.

The remaining rebel infantry were adjusting their line. The other platoon marched back from the forest having lost Wilhelm and his riders to the road. They hadn't realized they'd been duped into pursuit. Chaos is the master, he thought. Time to buy us some breathing room.

Wolf kicked his horse in the flanks urging her toward the prisoners. A startled guard took aim and smoke erupted from the muzzle of his musket. *Buzzzzz!* The bullet passed by Wolf dangerously close.

He hugged his mount and aimed his pistol as he got within twenty yards. *Bang!* The bullet hit the man in the leg, and he collapsed, his hands leaping for the wound. The prisoners had seen enough. They lunged for the remaining guards. The guards fought back with blade and musket but with little success. The prisoners swarmed over them, grabbing fallen muskets to arm themselves.

Wolf spun his mount around. "Fire that cannon!" he yelled at his men.

The rebel platoon near the forest had seen the revolt and moved quickly to put it down, double-timing their way back to the depot.

"Fire the cannon!"

The conductor jumped from the driver's compartment and ran from the train. Standing to the side of the cannon, Wilhelm ripped a lanyard.

Boom!

The cannon blasted smoke and fire from its iron lips; the solid shot hit the engine in the side. A fiery inferno erupted into the air. Men jumped to the ground, and Wolf ducked.

Metal and wood shot outward with deadly purpose. The energy was powerful, and every single man stopped what they were doing to stare.

Wolf's horse reared into the air, and Wolf held on as best he could to her neck. "Easy, Sarah!"

The wreckage burned, and it lost its spell over the men.

"Thank you!" shouted a Union prisoner. They bolted for the forests. Rebels fired at the fleeing men. Sharpshooter fire kept the rebels pushing backward. Hundreds of men in blue ran for their lives, scrambling through trees and over logs to escape.

Wolf watched them run. *Godspeed, good men.* "Roberts, collect them up! We ride."

Quickly remounting, Wolf's raiders soon galloped again in the opposite direction of the fleeing Union prisoners. Confusion ruled the depot, and the rebels didn't know which men to follow. Eventually the easier target remained, and the rebels chased after the prisoners into the surrounding forest.

Wolf's raiders galloped down a road and halted. Pistols and Spencers were reloaded as they waited for the rest of their men to rejoin them. Wilhelm's men trotted up first. Hale and Pratt's eyes were agape, but Wilhelm appeared as calm as an old dog about to nap on a sunny porch.

"How'd they do?" Wolf asked.

"Adequate," the sergeant said.

Wolf spoke to the two young men. "Very good. I expect an excellent next time, boys."

Hale and Pratt nodded vigorously. "Yes, sir."

They didn't have to wait long before they were joined by the sharpshooters. "Excellent shooting, men," Wolf said.

"It's gonna take dem boys three days to round all them prisoners up," Skinner said.

"Let's hope some of them reach the Army of the Potomac."

"Ah, I'm sure a few will."

"Then we've done enough."

Wolf turned to Hogan. "You may lead us to the Fontaine house."

Chapter Nineteen

Early Morning, May 9, 1864
Near Beaver Dam Depot, Virginia

A morning fog rolled over the land, smothering the trees and hovering over the ground like an unsettled snow. The mist surrounding the white plantation mansion only added to the mystery of who resided within.

Wolf's men dismounted and stuck the two new members of their unit, Hale and Pratt, with watching the mounts. If the two young men were disappointed, they were hiding it now. The danger involved in riding with Wolf was beginning to show itself to them, and perhaps staying with the horses was a noble enough cause.

Wolf had decided thundering in on horseback would spook the people within and potentially lead to a chase. He pointed at George and motioned him out into the forest then sent James in the other direction. To Skinner, he made a half circle, meaning for him to round to the other side of the manor house. They would ensure no one fled on foot.

Then he settled beneath a tall oak and watched the building in the quiet of the morning, waiting for the men to get into position. His civilian-dressed troopers spied out from behind trees.

The plantation mansion was a Georgian style home with redbrick chimneys on either end with symmetrically spaced windows and a door centered in the middle.

Wilhelm hovered near Wolf. "Everyone yet sleeps. Now is a good time to strike. Groggy men make poor fighters."

"I would agree, but look," Wolf said. He gestured with his head at a colored man standing outside his humble cabin near the edge of the property.

The slave wore a white shirt and loose brown trousers. He carried a hoe in one hand and strolled toward a nearby field. He hummed to himself, his melody accompanied by the soft swick, swick, swick of him digging the tool into the earth.

"We must move fast. Before the house is abuzz with activity." Speed and surprise were always desired if they could be attained in any military endeavor. "Sergeant Berles, you take your men around back. Sergeant Roberts, your men stay with me."

They would cross almost fifty yards in the open before they reached the house. Wolf would have to hobble. His men would beat him there, but he would be with them when they charged inside. With a short nod, Wilhelm's men ran through the cool early summer dew.

Staying low, his men followed across the open ground. The man in the field kept his head down, digging away, oblivious to the raiders racing for the home of his masters. Wolf fell behind his men, but he stayed with them as best he could.

When he reached the side of the home, Nelson and Adams lined along the side of the door while Roberts and Shugart assembled on the left. Each man held a pistol in his gloved hands. Their chests heaved despite the short run.

Wolf joined them along the wall. Nelson peered through the window. The stone-faced man gave him a curt shake of his head. No one awake. Very good. Nothing fancy. Bust the door. Charge inside. Round them up. Take the woman. Be on their way.

Wolf counted down on his fingers for the giant trooper. Best to use a man who likes the destruction to do his part. *Three, two, one...* He clenched his hand into a fist.

With a snarl, Nelson spun on the mansion door and laid a heavy boot into the doorjamb. The frame crumbled beneath his weight, and he took a step back as the other men raced inside.

Roberts ducked through the door followed by Adams then Wolf. Each man went a different direction, pointing his pistol. A few seconds later they could hear the back door cracking under Dan's shoulder.

The heavy footsteps of Wilhelm's men pounded out as they rushed inside. Shouts of alarm came from the upstairs. Wolf hooked into the kitchen with his pistol aimed in front of him. A slave emerged from her quarters attached to the kitchen.

Her head was wrapped in a turban-style cloth and her dress, made of a rough-spun cotton blend, was a checkered orangish brown. Her eyes lit up when she saw Wolf's with his pistol pointed at her.

"Shhhh!" he held a finger to his mouth. She sucked in short breaths but was too terrified to take in enough air. "We aren't going to hurt ya." His men quickly covered all parts of the lower level. He grabbed the woman by her arm, forcing her into the parlor.

"Wait here," Wolf hissed.

An older gentleman's voice echoed down the stairwell. "Who goes there?"

Wolf's men hid behind corners, waiting to ambush him. The voice turned into a man, and he ambled down the stairs from the second floor, holding a shotgun in his hands. He squinted around the room for an intruder.

"Freida? What's going on?" the older man called out.

Wolf eyed the slave girl. She trembled behind Nelson, too scared to cry out. Wolf held a hand to his lips. His eyes leapt back to Nelson. The big trooper gave him a cutthroat signal running a hand across his neck. Wolf shook his head no and holstered his pistol. Nelson's eyes flashed otherwise.

"Colonel, sir?" Wolf said, stepping out. His boots echoed off the polished wood floor. *Go too fast he might shoot you.* He tried to put on a calm friendly demeanor, masking his anxiety over potentially taking buck and ball to the chest.

The elder white-haired Colonel Fontaine narrowed his eyes, traversing the last few steps with his shotgun held loosely to his shoulder. "Do I know you, boy? Why are you in my home?" He looked past Wolf and into the kitchen, his words taking on a more authoritative voice. "Frieda? Did you let this man in?"

With a loud thump, Nelson pistol-whipped him from behind. The colonel gasped and collapsed on the wood floors; his body rolled still. Roberts snatched his shotgun. Wolf motioned to his men, and four of them hustled up the stairs.

Women's screams echoed through the hallways and down the stairwell. Wolf grabbed the colonel by the collar and dragged him into the parlor.

"Set a fire," he ordered the slave girl. He propped the old man in a chair and searched a nearby desk. He found a decanter of whiskey and poured himself some while he waited. The women's screams pierced his ears, and he cocked his head, letting the alcohol scream down his throat. "Fine whiskey, Colonel," Wolf said in tribute to the passed-out man slumped in his own chair.

Four women and two children were manhandled into the parlor from the upstairs. Three of them ran to the unconscious colonel, tending him, waving their hands to cool him, and tapping his cheeks trying to resurrect him. "What have you done?" cried his wife.

"He'll be fine, just a headache."

The last woman stood defiantly, eyeing Wolf and all his men. Her dark brown hair hung around her shoulders. Her mouth held average lips, and her nose was more round than sharp. Her eyes contained honest anger. A light green wrapper was draped around her, hanging down to her bare feet. Her form was slender, bordering on shapelessness.

"Who are you? Why are you here?" she demanded, rocking an infant in her arms.

Wolf met her eyes. "We're here to take you into our custody."

"Your custody?"

Adams and Nelson laughed. Her eyes speared them, but the troopers couldn't care less.

Wolf handed the decanter to Roberts, who grinned from ear to ear and took a swig. He raised his eyebrows and nodded in satisfaction. "The good stuff." Appreciating the fine alcohol, he emptied the bottle into his canteen.

Wolf's bad leg thumped the floor as he got closer to her. "Yes, ma'am, that is one way to put it."

Her hands gripped her babe tighter with every step he took. "Do you know who I am?"

Thump. Thump. "I do. You're the wife of Jeb Stuart. Flora, I believe, if my man Hogan is correct."

"I am correct," Hogan said with a smile.

Flora snorted and shook her head. "So you're a Union dog. The North's depravity goes even further than I could imagine. Do you *know* who my father is? I assure you, you wouldn't be here if you did."

Wolf cocked his head. "Can't say I do."

"General Philip St. George Cooke."

"Sounds familiar, but I don't know him."

Hogan leaned in, whispering. "He be the one in the cavalry manuals. Union general."

"Her father is a goddamn Union general?" Wolf asked with an angry glare for the agent.

"That he is. Out of the field now." Hogan chuckled a bit, inspecting his nails. "I believe he sits on a board for court-martials among other administrative functions."

"He sits on a board for court-martials? Dear God." He had no doubt who would be sitting on the board if he failed or if something ill befell his daughter while in his custody. Any way it played out, he expected to hang.

"Nothing like a bit of incentive to succeed."

"Aren't we up a spout." Those generals had tricked him into doing their dirty work, hadn't they? It hadn't seemed he had much of a choice in the matter. Now he was up a creek in a leaky overburdened canoe with a dozen men caught in a crossfire between Confederate and Union sharpshooters. Hell, throw in a few Parrott guns to use them for target practice.

"I believe Sheridan has the paperwork already signed to release you of any incrimination if you succeed."

"But if we fail, I'll surely hang." He got closer to Hogan, pointing at Flora. "If something happens to her, we hang. There are no orders. It will look as if we're rogue bandits."

"For you, yes. The rules are slightly more relaxed for someone in *my* position."

"So we're just a bunch of Jonah's getting damned to hell."

"Desperate men, desperate times."

"Excuse me," Flora interrupted. "What do you intend to do with us?"

Hogan leaned back in near Wolf. "You really have no choice but to succeed. Perhaps more caution was due with the prisoners now that this has all been brought to light."

Wolf shook his head in anger. "I suppose not, huh, but I'd rather hang than see those men imprisoned."

Hogan grinned. "A brave raid indeed."

Wolf thought about punching the Irishman straight in his lying mouth. The man hadn't lied but deceived him of all-important information that may as well have been spitting in his face. *What else might the man know that he held in reserve?*

"Gentleman," Flora said louder.

They both turned. "What?"

"What are you going to do with us?"

Wolf sighed, his angry eyes leaving Hogan and focusing on her. His words boomed into the silence. "We're going to kidnap you, ma'am."

Her jaw dropped as if he'd smacked her across the face. She was too shocked to say anything before she uttered, "You are wretched men not even worthy of my scorn."

Wolf ignored her biting words. He'd expected anger, but hardly such a viper's tongue. "Roberts let her change into something a bit more suitable for riding."

This brought on another round of sobs from the children and women, but they did not resist. She handed her babe to one of Fontaine's daughters and kissed her boy atop his head. She forcibly removed his hands clutching her dress. "It's okay, little Jeb," she whispered. She brought herself in front of Wolf. "Take me if you must, but do not harm these people. I command it."

Wolf raised a hand. "I don't suppose you have much of a say in this." He locked eyes with her. Her brown eyes held fire and brimstone. His blue eyes drowned out the flames like a tidal wave of water.

Flora's voice came out with enough conviction Wolf almost believed her. "I will fight you every step of the way. I will call out every chance I get."

"We'll gag you."

She sighed heavily. "Give me your word on as a man, however cheap that may be. You will spare these people. They've done nothing wrong."

"They will not be harmed," Wolf said. He turned to Adams. "When they return, we burn this house."

Adams pursed his lips considering the orders. "With them inside?"

"No, get them outside," Wolf said with a scowl.

Flora's voice demanded to be heard. "Jeb will hunt you down like the dogs you are and have you killed."

"He's welcome to try ma'am, but we're hard men to kill. Roberts," Wolf said, ushering his friend toward the stairs.

She held her ground, and her chin shook in defiance. "Even better. He loves a challenge."

"Get her out of here," he growled.

Roberts and Flora disappeared out of the room to the second floor. Wolf stuck a hand in his black coat and removed a letter. He handed it to Fontaine, who was waking up with hazy eyes. "Colonel, when we leave here, you go on to the nearest telegraph office and send this message to Stuart? Do you understand?"

"Bah, you renegades. How dare you come into my home like this," Fontaine said, his voice shaking. "You are no better than thieves and criminals."

Wolf grabbed the elder colonel by his pristine uniform coat. "I said, do you understand? Do not push me. I hold your family."

Fontaine's mouth opened and closed, and his nostrils spurt hot air. "I understand." He blinked and gained an ounce more of courage. "You'll hang for this."

"I assure you you're not the only person who wants me in a noose." Perhaps his men would be spared by the Union high command for only following their commander's orders. Most likely they would hang alongside him on the gallows as war criminals. One thing was certain. If they failed, they would die by noose or bullet.

"Best get your family out of this house," Wolf said. "You have only until my horse gets here." More wailing came from the women and children, but Fontaine read the razor glint in his eyes and hurried them outside.

Wolf followed his men to the outdoors. He waved over his head at the distant trees and the two rookie troopers led their horses onto the lane leading to the mansion.

Steel scraped flint, emitting sparks on a rag-wrapped stick. The flicker grew into a flame and the torch glowed yellow in the dewy morning air. Adams awaited his command to burn the house.

Flora emerged from the front door Roberts in tow. Her riding dress was white, gray, and black checkered with flowery white lace around the collar. Her hair was split down the middle and arranged into a bun on the rear of her head as was the style for the time. She sported white gloves and black knee-high riding boots.

"I trust you are ready to ride," Wolf said.

"I am what I must be," she retorted.

"Torch the place." Adams gave a wide smile, marching forward. He broke windows and stuck the torch inside. Fire scrambled up the curtains. Flames quickly engulfed the house.

"You'd think he'd done that before," Roberts said.

"Pretty sure he has."

The blaze roared around the house. The family wailed as their lives disappeared into a thick black smoke. The plantations slaves had all emerged from their shanty homes. They too watched the structure burn. It was hard to read them as they showed neither joy nor despair, just a regular indifference to it all.

His sharpshooters rounded the house with a horse for Flora. In the distance, the rest of the plantation's horses galloped down the road.

Wolf hobbled over to Flora and offered her his hand. "My lady."

Her face twisted in disgust, but she took his hand. He seized it in an iron grip.

"Hey!" she shouted.

He quickly wrapped a rope around her wrists.

"How dare you touch me like that!"

"For your own good."

"I cannot mount like this," she said.

He gripped her by the hips and lifted her atop her horse. "There." Turning back to his men, he said. "Mount up!"

It was time to run.

Chapter Twenty

Mid-morning, May 9, 1864
East of Laurel Hill, Shady Grove Church, Virginia

J. E. B. Stuart's general staff stood inside the tiny single room of Shady Grove Methodist Church near the town of Spotsylvania. It had been founded almost twenty years earlier and most likely had never seen so many men, never as many men in uniform, perhaps never a man as distraught as the one before them.

The man before Wade Hampton was in shambles. Stress surrounded his eyes and mouth like heavy bags of grain. His lips quivered beneath a bushy well-formed beard. His shirt was untucked underneath his dirty gray uniform, and his plumed hat lay tossed in a short-backed pew. He began to pace, his arms folded over his proud chest.

"Sir, I beg of you. The battle is here. We protect Lee's flanks. We bleed Grant day after day here, but we must not let them flank us. Even now Hancock searches for a way around."

A finger pointed at him, shaking fiercely. "Do you not understand what I told you? She's *gone.*"

Hampton eyed the pulpit and the plain wooden cross behind it. The telegram had come from a reputable source, but its contents were no less disturbing than if it had been an evil jest. Stuart's wife Flora had been taken by a band of renegades. His words came slow and assured. "I understand what you've told me. It is dire news."

162

Stuart wiped his cheek, glaring. "Union cavalry is departing their lines en masse." He shook his head. "This sequence of events is no coincidence. They smell rotten, my dear friend." His lip quivered in anger.

"Marse Robert wants you to intercept Sheridan?"

"I want to kill Sheridan if he is behind such treachery!"

"What did he say?"

"I am to pursue as I see fit. Defend Richmond if need be. But how can he ask that when my wife, bless her fragile soul, is missing!"

"But the battle is here, sir. This is where we fight it. We bleed them enough through this wilderness, they will yield to our cause."

Stuart shook his head, not listening to Hampton's protest. "No, I must get her back. What kind of man am I if I cannot even protect my own family?" His eyes pleaded for understanding. "You have a family. Can you imagine? What if Mary were taken? Would you not make every effort to secure her?"

The man begged to be assured he was making the right move.

"I would on my honor."

"Then you understand my reputation is at stake here."

Hampton pointed out a window that ran along most of the church wall. "But we are fighting for something larger than our personal honor."

Stuart's mouth stood agape. "There is nothing greater than a man's personal honor. Without it, we are mere beasts, apes, soulless creatures."

"And with that comes causes higher than oneself. Liberty. Justice. Freedom. Surely those things mean more than a single man's honor?"

Stuart's face twisted, his mouth forming a snarl. "How dare you? It is my wife for Christ's sake."

Hampton stood his ground, keeping his cool. "We bleed the Army of the Potomac and check Meade's every move."

"Grant."

"Whoever leads that godforsaken inept horde. This war will end. The North doesn't want or need this war. They are tired of this war. They want a way out. Lincoln knows it. Lee knows it. Grant knows it. Even that curmudgeon Meade knows it. If we deny him Richmond and make him pay for every inch of Southern soil, we will win the war."

Stuart shook his head. "War is honor. I will not have mine befouled before my eyes. But I wouldn't expect a businessman such as yourself to understand the marital ways." His words stung his subordinate.

Generals Pierce and Fitz Lee regarded Hampton. They'd been quiet as the two juggernauts battled over strategy, and now the contest had grown even more personal.

Grinding his teeth, Hampton stood a bit taller. It was something he liked to do when a man threatened his honor. He was like a bear standing on his back legs and loomed over his opponents or friends.

He was more than capable, an outstanding commander in his own right having come into his own during the war. Stuart was right about one thing; Hampton was a businessman. But the warrior's blood ran in his veins. He was the third of his name. The third to take up arms in the defense of his nation from overzealous and tyrannical governments both foreign and now domestic.

His friend's words stung him nonetheless. He had given so much for this war and to have it shoved in his face made him angry. "Go to hell, Jeb. I bled. I lost. Just like you." He pointed a finger. "And I get no respect from high command. I could lead the corps just as good as you."

Pierce gulped and Fitz's brows narrowed, but Hampton didn't care what the man thought. His words were true.

"Yet you don't."

"I don't, but I am still a servant of this nation first. I go where I am needed. Not where I want."

Air expelled from Jeb's nose. Then he closed his eyes for a moment and nodded, followed by a heavy sigh. "Wade, I'm sorry. I spoke falsely. You see. It's Flora." His eyes squinted. "You understand? I haven't run afoul of you?"

Hampton gave him a terse nod. "No, sir. You have not. This war is taking a toll on all of us. Has made us act in ways that aren't natural for our bond."

"Then you appreciate why I must go?"

"I do. Very much. I might not agree with it, but I understand it."

"Very well. I bid you farewell, good General. Fitz." Fitz Lee took a few steps closer to Stuart. His long black beard pointed near the center of his chest.

"Sir?"

"I want you hounding Sheridan everywhere he goes. Depart immediately."

Hampton cut in. "Jeb. Let me help."

Stuart nodded to Fitz. "Go. Yes, Wade?"

The men locked eyes. Stuart's held so much pain that Hampton knew he must attempt to alleviate his friend's suffering.

"I have a captain. You may know him. Marshall Payne. He has a talent for this kind of work. Let me send him. He'll track them down." He admired the young man despite their sparring of late. Stuart had a gravitas that most men would only dream about, like a Julius Caesar in modern form. If he could assist him, he would. Both their honors were at stake. If he would not help a friend in need, who was he?

Stuart shook his head in disbelief. "I stand corrected in your shadow. You are a giant in more ways than one, Wade Hampton. More honor resides in your little finger than in the rest of us." Stuart lifted his chin, becoming composed and dignified like a warrior poet of ages past. Then he smiled. "Are you sure that you aren't a Virginian in exile?"

Hampton grinned and placed a hand over his heart. "I am not only a servant to this nation and to my brothers but always a South Carolinian thru and thru. First to secede."

"And a true friend." Stuart bowed deeply. He walked forward and stretched his arms around Hampton.

The gesture was both uncommon and abnormal for the men. Gradually, Hampton embraced his commanding officer with a pat on the back. "We'll get her back."

"I know we will." Stuart released him. "I'm taking Gordon's Brigade, and Fitz Lee's Division will depart soon. More than enough to handle that cheeky Little Phil and his band of rigid horsemen."

They shared a laugh at their opponent.

"I will gather Payne's men and send them on their way."

"Very good, General."

The men saluted one another, and Stuart said, "I will see you soon." And he stormed from the church.

Hampton glanced back at the cross. "Watch over her. For all our sakes."

***

It took him less than thirty minutes to find Captain Payne and his company of Red Shirts. Every Iron Scout he had with him in his command trailed him, along with one of his aides. Men rested in the bivouac eating whatever they'd stolen from the Yankees the day prior, but maybe even more important was the out-of-saddle rest they were getting now. Many slept on the ground, their caps and hats blocking out the morning light.

The captain gave him a subtle wave as he approached. "Gave them Yanks a fine go of it yesterday, didn't we, sir?"

"We did."

Payne sat around a modest campfire with a cluster of his men. Most had their jackets hanging; a few held them over the fire as they roasted fleas and lice from their clothes. A few slept beneath a nearby tree.

His men were all first-rate specimens, well-bred soldiers. All looked strong despite the lack of supplies. All looked athletic, no deformity, and those that had been wounded bore their scars with pride.

"I must speak to you now, Captain."

Payne leisurely rose and walked over, swiping long brown curls behind his ears. His saber wavered as he strolled to his commander. A smile took his lips, not touching his fierce eyes. "How can I help you, General? Gentleman." He nodded at the Iron Scouts.

"Good day, Captain," Dan Tanner said. He was the handsomest scout of all of Hampton's men. With his fine clothes, trimmed beard, and petite features, he blended in with men far above his station. His brother, George, tipped his broad farmer's hat, and Hampton suspected that while they said they were brothers, either their father or mother were not the same.

George had a plain forgettable face and a wide nose. The rest of his face was engulfed in a brown beard that hung off his chin.

The last of Hampton's Iron Scouts spit on the ground.

"I don't believe I know you?" Payne said.

166

"Name's William Scott," he said and spit again. He was a feral-looking mountain man and seemingly despised the well-fed and fancy-clothed Red Shirts.

"Charming fellow you have in your employ, sir," Payne said with a grin.

Hampton didn't have time for all these things, these niceties. He needed to make sure they won this war, but instead, he found himself politicizing between the men, stroking egos and putting out fires.

"I need you to take a platoon of your men and my Iron Scouts and track down a woman."

Payne's eyes lit up with intrigue. Hampton could almost read his mind. *Oh, the noble general has himself some lustful urges he needs satisfying.*

"I do say the plot thickens, General."

Hampton ignored his curious gaze. "It does. You are to head south."

"South? The enemy is the other way."

"Yes, to Beaver Dam Station."

"If you desire a quality horizontal refreshment or two, General, I know of some nice clean, fancy girls that can cure your every ailment." His eyes settled on Scott's. "Not something the rank and file can get their grimy paws on."

Scott tongued his front lip and spit on the ground again.

"I do not need any horizontal refreshments, Captain. This woman is the wife of a general."

Raising a hand in defense, Payne smiled. "No need to say any more, but surely this mission is better left to your scouts."

"Enough, Captain."

Payne tightened up before the general's anger. Hampton pressed his horse closer to his man. He let him off the leash on occasion when the war called for it, but not in the presence of others. "You would do well to know that the woman you seek is Flora Stuart, the general's wife." He eyed the men in the camp around him. "Only take men you can trust to keep their mouths shut."

Payne nodded his head in understanding. "I would say this is a bold endeavor we undertake on your behalf."

Hampton leaned down and hissed. "She is missing."

"I do declare. This is most disturbing news. Bloody red Indians?"

167

"No. We think they're bandits. Possibly Yankees, perhaps escapees. I do not know, but whoever and whatever those men are, they are to be dealt with using extreme violence. This does not go unpunished. Do you understand?"

"I do." Payne's smile almost unnerved Hampton.

"You are off your leash. Conduct your mission as you see fit, but you get that woman back and in one piece. Do you understand that?"

"I do."

"Then make haste."

Payne grinned. "We shall not tarry." He faced his men. "Red Shirts! Gather on me."

Chapter Twenty-One

Afternoon, May 9, 1864
Near Hanover Junction, Virginia

Wolf's raiders avoided Beaver Dam and the chaos of the rebels there clearing the tracks and attempting to corral escaped prisoners. Instead, his small band rode hard for Hanover Junction to the east. There they would cross the North Anna River and make a wide berth near Spotsylvania then for Sheridan's last known location. After that, he'd hand over Flora to Sheridan and see what Stuart did.

Assumedly, this would draw Stuart into a hasty attack to liberate her or send in his own men to whisk her away in the night. As long as it kept Wolf out of a jail cell, he could live with that. He tried to keep his mind focused as they rode. The most important thing was reaching Union lines again.

They made quick work of five miles, and Wolf brought them to a walk with a loud, "Take 'er down now, boys."

The soft clops of hooves over the dirt road echoed in the air. Cottony gray clouds crowded the sky above them. It was hard to tell if it meant rain or not, but it did mean some well-appreciated reprieve from the sun.

He glanced over at Flora, who hadn't balked at the difficult pace he'd set almost immediately. She appeared unfazed by the ride, displaying herself as an excellent horsewoman. She kept her face forward and her chin high as if their very smell offended her.

"Are you okay, ma'am?"

She stared ahead, not daring to even peep at him. "Do you even care?"

"I do." He supposed he did in his own right. Her safety was paramount to him not getting hung by her prominent father or her vengeful husband.

She snorted in response.

"I do not wish any harm to befall you."

"Fancy way of showing that, snatching me from my family's home."

"It's all a means to an end, ma'am. Just business."

"Your business is one with the devil then."

He didn't know how to respond to that. He didn't feel particularly devilish. He also didn't feel like hanging or going back to prison either. But her concerns were a woman's worries, and he wouldn't expect her to understand the warlike reasons of men.

They rode in silence for a while, but Wolf couldn't hold his tongue. "Why would you betray your true nation and your father's love?"

"Don't all women betray their father's love by taking the love of another?"

He had difficulty comprehending her words. To him, they sounded like some high-minded philosophical retort, probably disrespectful. "What I mean is, why did you marry Stuart, wrong side and all?"

Her brown eyes regarded him from the side like she was whipping a stubborn mule. "Why does anyone marry? For love, of course. Clearly not a venture for all men." The last words were a barb aimed at Wolf.

He narrowed his eyes at his clothes. His black jacket was not fine by any means, but it wasn't of poor construction. Truthfully, he probably could have used a bath and brush, but then again, he was a soldier in the middle of a war. "I am not married."

"Don't ask me how I can tell, but one could start with the smell."

Grinding his teeth, he tried to piece together a retort, but her tongue was like a whip cracking the air.

"Or your hair is tangled and in need of a cut." Before he could respond, she continued. "And your mouth isn't fit for a saloon let alone to be wagged in front of a proper lady. Not even good enough for one of your *camp* women." She regarded him for a moment before continuing. "Probably don't have a dime to your rotten name."

Hogan and Roberts chuckled nearby. Wolf gave them a nasty glare, and they closed their mouths.

"I got more than a few dimes." He'd saved almost thirty dollars since he started, money that had been taken when he'd been captured. Now that he thought about it, he really didn't have anything to his name. "Someday I'll find a nice girl. One that don't care much about money."

"Exactly my point. Girls. Girls. You, Lieutenant, will only ever be with girls because you are about as civilized as a man raised by wolves."

This brought a few smiles from his men, and Wolf grinned as well. "Well, as a matter of fact, ma'am. I was raised by Wolfes."

"Did you not go to grammar school?" she said sounding out the next phrase. "Wolves."

"My name is Wolf, ma'am."

She closed her mouth; he'd caught her in a verbal trap of his own. "A fitting name for a savage man."

He dug into his pack and pulled out a piece of hardtack. Breaking it in half, he handed her a part of it.

She took it in her hands, and a general air of disgust surrounded her.

He shoved the tack into his back molars and gnawed on the sheet-metal-like cracker. The trick with hardtack was to dunk it in coffee or soften it in some stew before you attempted eating it. Since Wolf had neither, he sucked the edge before trying to crush the "bread."

"My tooth!" she complained.

"You have to soften it, ma'am."

She held the hardtack, staring at it with vengeful eyes. "How do you eat the stuff?"

"You get hungry enough, it'll be enough. And the army will make your belly growl mighty fierce."

"Glad I'm not in the army."

"At the next stop you can dunk it in some coffee."

She attempted to embrace an angry air, but responded with a short, "Thanks." Then after a moment she spoke again, only softer. "When we met there wasn't this divide."

"Met?"

"When Jeb and I met, the nation was still whole." She raised her hands and flung them outward. "There wasn't this mess."

"My life would have been much different without this war," he said.

"Mine as well," she muttered.

She thought he meant about how much better, but what she didn't know was that this war, despite all the pain and suffering, presented him with purpose. He would be no better than a beggar on the street without the war.

In fact, he could have been already dead and not a soul, save his family, would care. It made him think of his father, Bernard, back home in Grand Rapids, hunched over in his furniture shop carving wood. He wondered if his father still thought of his only son in the wilderness of Virginia fighting a war that neither of them were native too.

It was a war to cure a wound that had been festering in the background of a young nation since its inception. The unanswered questions of equality and power had brought men armed to the field of battle ready to shed blood on this claimed soil. In this war, some men gained, and all men suffered.

"Do you still speak with him?" he asked.

"Who?" she snapped.

"Your father."

She adjusted her reins under her uncomfortableness. "No. He hasn't even seen our youngest yet."

"That must be difficult. I haven't seen my family in over a year."

She softly shook her head at him. "My father fights against my husband in a war that will never end. The two men whom I love the most in this world are trying to kill each other. Difficult is an understatement. Every day I wonder which note I will receive from the front, my father or my husband slain in the service of their nation."

"Meant no disrespect."

Her demeanor hardened again, any rapport or common ground he'd built up slipping away like quicksand. "Ha, coming from my kidnapper. Disrespect. I will tell you something right now. I look forward to the day my husband catches and hangs you." She twisted in her saddle haranguing the men. "Hangs all of you. My heart will leap with joy as I gaze fondly upon your corpses with all the respect a dog is owed."

Nelson snorted like a bull, but the rest of the riders ignored her. Wolf didn't antagonize her any further. "You call out to anyone, I'll gag you," he added as a reminder. Last thing he wanted was her shouting out to the nearest rebels the first chance she got.

She humphed in response but held her tongue.

Hogan pushed his horse near Wolf's other side. "You really have a way with the ladies, Yellabelly."

"Bah. I only try to ease her captivity," he said loudly.

She didn't bite but kept her eyes forward.

His voice lowered. "We will not keep her after the deed is done."

"I suspect we won't." Hogan dropped his voice. "Can't say I'd want to keep her." He finished with a mischievous grin for Wolf.

"Stuart can have her!"

***

Hanover Junction was a critical intersection of two railroads, the Virginia Central Railroad and the Fredericksburg-Richmond Railroad. It acted as a junction between the east and west running line and the north and south line.

None of the prewar railroads were built with war as a concern. The South didn't have the supply or manufacturing capability to do more than just maintain what was already in place. What was in place was a mishmash of railroads built by different business ventures with only their own profits in mind. Infrastructure that over the course of the war crumbled without replacement parts and inadequate repairs.

The tracks were different sizes. In some towns, different railroads had built their own lines to avoid having to use a rival railroad's tracks. This had caused all sorts of issues in the infrastructure-deficient South, and Hanover Junction with their crossing lines was critical to the Southern war effort and by proxy, a crucial target for Northern disruption.

The east-west running tracks brought in food and supplies from the

Shenandoah. The north-south line gave Southern troops the mobility to travel north to fight.

A station sat near the crisscrossing tracks. The depot was painted red like a barn. Wood planking lined the sides, and with the current campaign going on, rebels crawled all over the depot.

Wolf's men took position in a nearby forest, scouting the junction for navigation. He dismounted with his men for a more concealed view of the station.

"More graybacks on them tracks than Robert's hat," Adams said. He gave Roberts a wicked grin.

"I burned 'em off," Roberts said. He took his hat off, inspecting it for the crawling critters. "I can't help that they keep breedin'."

Adams nudged Nelson. "If only his mother hadn't bred him."

"But cunts like to breed," Nelson said, chuckling to himself.

Wolf was glad Flora was back with Shugart and the horses so she wouldn't be subject to such uncouth conversation.

"Ain't right to talk about a man's dead mother if you ask me," Roberts said, shaking his head.

Hogan took stock, counting softly. "Must be two, three companies of the graybacks."

His count was no exaggeration. Groups of infantry milled around waiting to change trains for the journey north. Some sat, others dozed, a cluster drank coffee, and a few sat around a campfire cooking bacon.

Wolf knew if he had to, he could get the jump on these men. What happened after that was the problem. He had no means to sustain a prolonged engagement with the rebels, and as they mobilized, more and more pressure would be put upon his small unit.

He could have the sharpshooters focus on taking out their officers and noncommissioned officers, hoping to create chaos among them, but again, they had no means to sustain any action. Surely he would lose men, and he wasn't here to lose men. He was here to acquire a lady and wreak havoc on Stuart's psyche.

"You think we can make it past?" Roberts said.

"No. Wilhelm." Wolf waved the broad sergeant his way. He bounded down their line, dropping to the ground near Wolf with a grunt. "Lieutenant?"

"What's your assessment? That's our route north."

Wilhelm's blue eyes regarded him for a moment. "We can't go north without a fight."

"Aye, and we can't go west without running into Beaver Dam Station."

"I warrant they will be ready for us this time. I think you have your answer."

Wolf continued to eye the rebels lounging in the distance. The thought of dashing through and around the junction with sabers and pistols drawn like a band of desperados faded away as quickly as it had come.

"If we can't escape north, we will be trapped south with the rivers." Wilhelm knew this. They all knew this. "If we go in the other direction of our army, we could be signing our own death warrants."

Wilhelm's cool eyes studied Hanover Junction with methodical logic as if he balanced their odds on a scale. Going north meant they would face a suicidal battle cutting their way through the junction. Then they would still have to circumvent Lee and reach Sheridan. All together not a great prospect for success. On the other side of the scale, he could recall the doomed Dahlgren raid, fleeing across enemy territory with their hounds nipping at their heels. *"Das Beste kommt selten hernach."*

Wolf understood him right away although it had been some time since he'd heard his native tongue. *Bad is the best choice.* The idiom summed up the entirety of their situation.

"Hogan, can we get south?"

"Taylorsville is about two miles south of here. From there we can cross the Little River then the South Anna." Hogan got closer to Wolf. "We will be far from home if we go that way."

"We don't have much of a choice. If Stuart hasn't already found out, he will soon. And when he does, he'll come looking."

Hogan rubbed a tired eye. "Yes, but we are supposed to go back toward Sheridan."

"Can you think of a way through? We'll be cut to pieces if we try to go through there. The only path we have is further south."

Hogan eyed the train station, gulping. "We can try and follow the Pamunkey River, ford there, and then swing north toward Fredericksburg."

Flashbacks to Dahlgren's fleeing men flickered in Wolf's eyes. "Like we did before?"

"It's a way back where we can cross without confrontation."

"Then that's what we do."

His men mounted their horses. Flora judged them with indifferent eyes. "Finding things tougher than you imagined, Lieutenant?"

Wolf struggled a moment to secure his disabled leg's foot in the stirrup. It always caused him grief, but the added angst of Flora made it worse. It was like she was not only judging him for being a horrible person but a cripple too, something that he never really understood until after the accident.

"Things are just fine, ma'am."

"Really? Is that why we are going south instead of north to your invading horde? Seems to be the opposite direction I'd want to go if I were in your godforsaken shoes. Or perhaps you have a death wish? If that is the case, you would do well to turn yourself in now to those brave soldiers at the depot and put this expedition to rest."

He glanced at Flora Stuart with her treacherous tongue lashing out this way and that like a menacing overseer with a bad toothache. No wonder Stuart was so beloved by the South's womenfolk. Anything to put distance between him and Flora.

"Everything is going according to plan. If I were you, I'd prepare for a hard ride."

Chapter Twenty-Two

Late Afternoon, May 9, 1864
Near Beaver Dam Station, Virginia

Payne's men were some of his finest. He'd left the rest of the Red Shirts in the capable hands of Lieutenant Samuel Hendricks, a friend from childhood and trusted comrade from a rich family outside of Charleston. The Red Shirts would be fine while Payne handled this task for Hampton and Stuart.

Every man in his platoon knew enough to keep their mouths shut after the task was complete. Stuart's image and his pride would be damaged, perhaps even indefinitely, if the incident was leaked to the Southern or Northern Press. The press on either side were a bunch of journalistic vultures hovering above a distraught man. It needed to be handled with a brisk but delicate hand, one that swung a saber into the bare necks of the enemy.

He galloped in the lead of his platoon, their mounts a thundering cloud of Southern vengeance. Their horses were fine Southern stock bred for speed and endurance, the best and most expensive that they could purchase. Each and every one paid a dividend in the field.

His platoon was a full one, not like the decimated companies, regiments, and divisions that languished in the regular Army of Northern Virginia. Even while the commands of other captains dwindled from illness and combat, the ranks of his company had always been kept at a hundred men. His men were always replaced with the best the South had to offer.

The Red Shirts were men of class that had been raised in the bosom of privilege. Most came to them wishing to join, some were recruited in ones and twos, the reputation of the company enough to draw them in.

They had taken men of lower standing within their ranks, men of moderate societal stature and wealth, but nothing of the lower classes that filled the Army of Northern Virginia's coffers. His men were nothing like the men that populated the Iron Scouts, a much more salt-of-the-earth type.

The Iron Scouts were usually poor men with the unusual ability to go and be anywhere relatively unnoticed. There was a certain discrepancy between his men and the Iron Scouts. But all men had their use, even to him, so he accepted the Iron Scouts for their unique capabilities.

No matter how long they'd fought in Virginia, one could not replace a man who had lived there his entire life. He was familiar with every nook and cranny of the land. Every hideout, farm, village, sympathizer, waterhole, tavern, and trail.

William Scott was one such man. His blackish beard was streaked with gray. Of average height and build, he had a wild glimmer in his eyes, not a calculating violence like Payne himself. No, Scott wasn't capable of what Payne could do. In fact, he'd never really met a man "like" himself. Scott was more like a mountain lion, extreme violence bred into him, but out of necessity. He wasn't a man who enjoyed the violence, just a man who could use it.

He carried a long-rifled musket on his back. Payne had never seen one longer, and it would be wildly inefficient for horseback. It was so long that the Red Shirts had started calling him Tiny Will Scott. That nickname would have caused a least a dozen fights by now if Payne hadn't threatened to cut everyone's balls off. His men quietly continued the mockery, sending Scott for the knife on his belt every so often. As long as they focused on the enemy, he wouldn't have to punish anyone.

Altogether, he had twenty-four superior horsemen along with three of Hampton's Iron Scouts. They would overtake the renegades and he would administer a slow justice. *How dare the Northerners operate with such sinister impunity!* The thought made him smolder inside. The enemy would scream under the knife no matter how hard their constitution.

"We cut through here, and we will be on the house before a mile," Scott called at them as they rode.

Payne gestured down the deer path with a sharp hand, slowing their gait. He trusted Scott, but if they lost a horse, they lost a man because they could not wait for him to acquire another.

They trotted through fresh green leaves that grew thicker and fiercer by the day. Spring growth would soon transform into a fertile summer. An early wet spring had seen to that.

Back home they would be planting. His family's 220 slaves would be working the fields, and that was only on their main plantation. They had almost another hundred slaves they rented to other smaller farm operations. George Archer and Jeremiah Richie would have been on horseback directing the field hands.

Richie had taken a Minié ball at Second Manassas, and Archer had died of a fever before Gettysburg. But there were always new men, younger or disabled ones from the war, to take their post.

Men trying to improve their status. Men who would try to save enough to buy their own land and own slaves and live the blessed life of a plantation owner. Easier said than done, but men toiled the earth, scratching together wealth while clinging to dreams of a better life only to find they'd been digging their own graves the whole time. He would have to write his mother and ask who ran the fields in their absence.

The rich smell of burnt wood filled his nose as they grew close. He couldn't see anything at first, but his intuition told him that it came from something much larger than a campfire, more of a conflagration. It reminded him more of the Battle of the Wilderness where acre after acre of dry woodland had gone up in flames, turning it into a holocaust with wounded men screaming in the orange and yellow flames.

As he neared the edge of the forest, hazy black tendrils dissipated into the sky above the treetops. They emerged from the path and into an unplanted field of brown dirt and grass. No slaves worked the open land, and the spots where the earth had been tilled revealed dark soil. The wreckage of the plantation home on the other end of the field appeared complete as if it had grasped at its last throes of existence.

"Come on!" Payne shouted. They galloped over the field, turning the topsoil in the process. The charred, blackened skeleton of a once beautiful mansion greeted them. Formerly redbrick chimneys still stood in the framework of the giant smoldering carcass of wood and stone.

Payne glided from his saddle to the ground followed by Scott and Dan Tanner. They walked the premises, searching for clues as they went. His Red Shirts spread out over the grounds searching for anything that would lead them to their prey.

The fire consumed everything it could and died away. Only the aftermath remained. Payne squatted down and dug out a handheld mirror that surely belonged once to the lady of the house.

The glass had bubbled from the heat and lifted around the edges. It reminded him of how human skin bubbled under just hot enough flames. Not enough to sear the skin clean off, but enough to blister. He chucked the mirror back into the rubble.

A lanky rider came up. George Turner had a long face with a trimmed brown beard and wore sergeant stripes on his sleeves. "No bodies in the surrounding area."

"Slaves?"

"They're gone too."

Payne gave him a quick nod. Local men would round up the slaves. They were of little threat to Payne and his men but perhaps held important information. More importantly, the telegram possessed a level of truth. The people of this home had fled or were taken. He turned his eyes to Scott.

Crouched on his haunches, the scout studied the ground. "Looks like two groups. One atop horse." He spit tobacco on the ground. "I'd say 'bout ten, maybe fifteen of 'em. Mounted. They went east, but there be footprints that go west. Little ones too."

"Couldn't have gotten far with children. They will know what this is and who's responsible."

His men mounted, following the tracks to the west. A little over a mile away they came across another more modest country mansion. With two-stories, clapboard sides, and short steps leading to the door, it was more of a farmhouse to Payne.

He quickly dismounted, marching with some urgency. He planted a fist into the door, pounding in three loud thumps. His men remained mounted. He glared back at Scott. "You sure this is the right spot?"

Scott lifted his chin with a challenging eye. "This be where the tracks went. I'm sure of that."

Payne pounded away again, vibrating the door. "Open on up." He stood back looking at the second-story windows. White curtains blocked any sight inside. "I am Captain Marshall Payne, Hampton's Red Shirts. We need to talk." He scanned from window to window. "Well, Mr. Scott, it appears that no one is home." A curtain trembled as it fell into place. "Or everyone is too scared to make themselves known."

"We mean no harm. We are loyal Southern gentleman here." Payne stood waiting. He would hate to have to kick in the door to get answers, but there were worse things that could befall these people. Yankee brigands for one.

The door cracked open and a wary eye stared out. "We already took the letter to Beaver Dam Station to telegraph. We don't want any more trouble."

Payne close-lipped smiled at them. "My good sir, we are here to rectify that situation. We are here to make things right."

The door shut, and he could hear arguing on the other side. "We are here on behalf of Major General James Ewell Brown Stuart. I believe you know the whereabouts of his wife?"

The door opened, and an elder gentleman with a stained double-breasted colonel's frock coat stood inside. His face had been wiped clean of soot and smoke, but the rest of him was filthy. His whitening hair stuck out to the sides reminding Payne of a duck's tail feathers.

He stepped outside and tugged his coat down. "I am Colonel Edmund Fontaine, and that was my home they burned."

Payne glanced back toward the out-of-view smoking mansion. "I truly am sorry for your loss. I would love to catch those men that did this and put this inconvenience to bed."

"Inconvenience? By God, I am in ruin."

Putting his hand over his heart, Payne said, "Dastardly and depraved, and I want to bring these men to justice."

"They were heathens the lot of them. Brutish monsters. Ambushed me they did. In my own home," he said, his eyes growing larger with each unthinkable thought.

A short smile lifted on Payne's left side. If they'd wanted him dead, he'd be dead. "Mischievous devils, huh? Can I come in and chat?"

Fontaine became agitated, shaking a bit. "If it please you, Captain, just yourself. The children and womenfolk have had quite a scare."

Payne removed his gray slouch hat and brushed his long curly brown hair back behind his ears. Taking off his fine gloves, he slipped them through his belt with all due care.

"Not a problem at all." He turned back to Scott. "Take the Tanner boys and head back to the good colonel's home. Follow the tracks as far as you dare. We won't be long behind you."

"Yes, sir." Scott and the Tanner brothers spurred their mounts in the direction of the plantation home.

Payne stepped inside, his boots echoing. The colonel stunk like he'd been tending a fire for two weeks. And Payne was sure that was not something he did without the help of a slave.

"What can you tell me, Colonel?"

Fontaine's eyes shifted under the question, drawing Payne's attention. "To be fair Captain, I was knocked unconscious right from the very beginning." His eyes lowered in shame. "I didn't see the men who did this. There was one that spoke, but I can't recall him."

"Did anyone see them?"

"Oh yes, my wife and the children."

Payne gestured almost as if he were offering his hand to the colonel at a ball. "Do lead the way, my good colonel."

They stepped into a parlor where there was an elderly woman and multiple younger women, all covered in soot, along with two young children. One wrapped her protective arms around the boy, and the matron held the girl, who could have been no more than a year old.

All were in various states of distress. Watery eyes peered at him as he entered. More tears flowed on the young ones' cheeks.

"Maria," Fontaine nodded to his wife and then his girls. "Rosalie and Lucia, this is Captain Marshall Payne, one of Hampton's most loyal lieutenants and sent by Stuart."

"You have nothing to fear from me," Payne said with a charming smile. But they had everything to fear. Their weakness disgusted him, and that made it hard to disguise on his face. He forced it down. He would protect them despite their feminine frailty. They had things he wanted, so he would attempt to be kind. After all, these were his people and well-bred.

He took a seat across from them, resting his hands on his elbows and leaning in. "Please be brief. Every moment we give them, they slip further from our grasp. What can you tell me about who did this?"

Maria coughed dangerously into her hand. "Sorry, the smoke." She composed herself and rocked the little girl on her hip. "They were horrible monsters."

His grin didn't fade. "Aren't they all?"

The Fontaine matriarch waved him off. "No, more heathen than the usual Yankee."

"What made this roving band of brigands different?" Every piece of information could be used. His eyes focused on her with his unusual intensity.

"There were redskins."

"You mean Indians?"

"Yeah, that's what I meant. Two or three of them."

"Indians did this?"

Her eyes scolded him. "You talk too much. Now quiet down and I'll tell you."

Payne grinned at her. *If she was my property, she would not have a tongue like that in more ways than one.*

Her eyes narrowed a bit at him as if she could read his mind. "Some of them were hulking brutes, a few were Dutch—I could tell by their *ugly* accents, and a few were redskins. All of them were horrible, disgusting men."

"Did they wear uniforms? How did you know they were soldiers?"

She shook her head. "No uniforms. They were dressed like regular people."

Payne filed the information back into his mind. He rolled over the "civilians" that would coordinate a kidnapping on one of the most important generals of the Confederate army.

Union sympathizers? It couldn't be. They would never be so brazen. They'd be burnt out in a week's time and hung from the gallows with some swift Southern justice. Brutes and immigrants didn't surprise him. Red men? That wasn't unheard of in Virginia, but most of them had been coerced westward years ago.

"How did you know they were soldiers?"

"They acted it well enough. Called each other sir, and the like. Fancy guns. Talked about Sheridan. Isn't he that chunky Northern general from out west?"

"Little Phil Sheridan is the commanding officer of the Army of the Potomac's Cavalry Corps." Perhaps they were the escaped prisoners from Beaver Dam Station.

"Did they mention anything about being prisoners?" It seemed far-fetched in his mind. These men had been well-armed, mounted, out of uniform. Aside from the uniform, all those things went against them being escaped criminals on the run.

"No, captain. I heard none of the like."

"Was there anything unusual about them. Anything that sticks out in your mind?"

"Aside from the savages and the Dutch riding together? No." She thought for a moment. "Well, their leader had a bad leg."

Payne blinked several times before he spoke. *Bad leg?* "What do you mean *bad leg?*"

"He wore some sort of metal brace around his knee."

Payne leaned in even closer. His eyes took on a hard cutthroat glint. "Did you catch his name?" *It can't be him. He's in Libby Prison. Where I'd left that mangled pup.*

"Can't say I caught it."

He eyed the other women. "Did any of you catch his name? The man with the brace? What did he call himself?" He stood, scrutinizing everyone in the room. A house slave avoided eye contact with him, a clear form of deception. "You? What do you know?"

Fontaine chimed in. "Answer him, Frieda."

"I dunno nothing, massa."

Payne walked over and grabbed the slave by her arm, letting his grip do the talking. "What do you know?" He squeezed her arm harder and harder, his fingers pressing painfully into her flesh and muscle. His hand would leave bruises, but who would rise in her defense? Bruised slaves could work as well as others.

"Please, I don't know nothing." She turned her face away from him.

"I know his name," squeaked the four-year-old boy.

"Hush now, Junior," Rosalie said.

With a slight shove, Payne released the slave girl. He stepped over to the younger woman with her hands atop the boy's shoulders.

"And you must be little James E.B. Stuart. Is that right?" he said, squatting down next to the young boy.

The boy stuck out his chest and lifted his cherubic chin, imitating soldierly toughness. "Named after my pa, Jeb."

"Yes, you are." The boy was too young to remember he once held a different namesake: Philip St. George Cooke Stuart, named after his grandfather and "Father of the Cavalry." But that was before the war.

A series of humiliations had driven Cooke behind a desk, some of those coming from his estranged Confederate son-in-law. *Must make for fun family holidays.* The war had plunged a wedge into their family like it had so many others and showed that no one was immune from the divide.

The boy squeaked. "My pa's gonna save my mom."

"No, that's what I'm here to do, son."

The boy stuck out his lip in defiance. "He's gonna do it. He's my pa and he loves my ma. He can do anything in the world the best. He's the best soldier, and I'm gonna be the best soldier just like him."

"I'm sure you will." Payne's tone hardened. "So what did you hear, young cavalryman?"

The boy puffed out his chest. "I heard one of the big men call him Woof, sir."

"Woof?" Payne narrowed his eyes in confusion. "You mean like a doggy?"

"No, Woof." The little boy shook his head, angry at not being understood. "Wooolf," he sounded out.

Payne heard him clearly now. "Wolf you say?"

"Yes, sir."

Payne stood upright. "Wolf." He eyed the slave with hostility. She avoided his eyes again, confirming the young boy's story. That was the thing with slaves; they were always hiding something, sneaking something, slacking on labors, or being deceitful. He assumed it was in their nature, and it was necessary to keep them in constant check.

If she were his property, she would be promptly beaten for not sharing all she knew. She deserved a reminder for next time, a going-away gift. However, each man must handle their property as they see fit.

He respected that common courtesy and didn't raise his fist in anger. Instead, he turned on the colonel.

By the looks of Fontaine, his slaves probably had free reign of his house and lands. This "soldier" lacked the strength to properly control his people and that included his wife. Payne didn't think it was age that had caused this laissez-faire attitude but a fundamental weakness of constitution. He was deficient in all traits required to be an effective plantation owner.

"Colonel Fontaine, I suggest you discipline your slave accordingly."

Fontaine paled to an almost sheet-like white. "I will address it." He averted his eyes away from Payne's.

Payne searched the man for some sort of strength, a will-to-do preserve but found nothing. He let his eyes crawl over the other man's body and dig deep into his soul, seeing every cowardly fiber in his being. A quick grin snapped upon his lips like the crack of a bullwhip. "I am sure she will be taught her due respect." His unfeeling eyes fell on her, and they removed flesh from her back with their gaze.

"You take care of Stuart's kin. He's coming like wildfire back down this way, and I've never seen a man itching for more of a fight than him. You would do well to remember he wants to fight Yanks, but he'll kill a man who lets harm come to his kin. You understand, Colonel?"

If Fontaine could pale himself into a ghost, he'd already done it. His mouth quivered around the edges. "I would never let anything happen to his kin. We are one and the same."

"Yet here we stand." Payne shrugged his shoulders. "Sometimes it is better to fall in defeat than live with its shame."

Fontaine dropped his eyes to the floor.

"Do not speak to him in such a manner, Captain!" Maria said.

Payne snapped his fingers and pointed at her. "Enough, woman."

Her mouth drooped closed. Fontaine's eyes remained downcast.

Payne stepped closer to him, smelling his disgusting weakness. "Do not fail him or you will be seeing me again." He let his eyes speak volumes, telling what he was capable of, and all they spoke of was vicious calculated violence. "Very good." He stared down his nose at the boy. "We will bring your mother back, little Jeb. You have my word," Payne bowed to the child and marched from the room with a swagger. That kid had more guts in him than the grown man protecting him. Stepping outside, he donned his slouch hat and gloves. His eyes skimmed over his men still in the saddle, waiting impatiently.

"Looks like we have a Wolf hunt, boys." His men did not know about his interrogations at Libby, but they smiled all the same. They had Federals to hunt down and bring to heel and send to hell. Something these men were bred for.

Chapter Twenty-Three

Night, May 9, 1864
South of Taylorsville, Virginia

Wolf awoke to the soft crackle of the campfire. The night pressed in around him like a quicksand of darkness, sucking away the light.

His heart leapt in his chest with the sudden departure from the world of dreams. His blood pumped, a giant horse galloping in his veins. It was as if his body knew something he did not. An unseen threat was near.

His fingers closed around the handle of his Army Colt .44 caliber pistol as he scanned the campsite searching for the cause.

Lazy flames lapped the air like an ocean's waves but with less force. Orange embers glowed. Aside from the fire, the forest stood still, holding its breath. His thumb crept overtop the hammer of his pistol. The gun's click cracked the air much too loud. Without exhaling, he waited a moment before he moved it into full cock.

The forms of his fellow soldiers didn't move; they were lost in an exhausted slumber. His eyes shifted from man to man, searching for the culprit until they found a person in the trees.

They locked eyes, and Wolf almost snapped his gun in their direction, but recognition slowly took over. *George.* The sharpshooter put a slow finger to his own lips.

There was something else, something in the distance, a faint sound chipping at his ears. It grew into a low rumble, a rolling nighttime storm.

Then little by little it became more apparent. The drum of horse hooves.

His eyes snapped to the woman sleeping nearby. He'd respected her privacy as much as he could, giving her her own blanket and space, but kept her rope wrapped around his wrist.

He rolled quickly to the side and reached for Flora, covering her mouth with a free hand. Her eyes shot open in terror. Mumbles of distress leaked out from beneath his palm.

He held his pistol to his lips and shushed her. "I'm not going to hurt you." He hoisted her upright by her tied wrists, and they made for the trees. The other men were awake now, rushing to mount their horses.

"Into the woods!" Wolf half-shouted. His men were quick to obey, leading their horses away from the campsite. He hobbled over to Roberts, who held Flora's horse.

"I can't mount a horse like this," she said. Taking her by the hips, Wolf boosted her atop the animal.

"Hey!" she complained. "I will tell all of my degrading mistreatment."

"Quiet," he growled. Then he tossed her rope to Roberts then said, "Take my horse. Continue west about a half mile and wait. George and I will catch up on foot."

"All right." With a hand on Flora's reins, he ushered their horses away to the soft clip clop of hooves.

They disappeared into the forest, and Wolf joined George's overwatch of the camp.

"They've been on and off since Taylorsville."

Wolf eyed the darkness unable to make out a thing. "On and off?"

"They've been tracking us. I've done my best to cover what I can, but these men are good. They are no novices."

It was no surprise that Stuart would send men after them. After all that was the point: to take his mind off of Sheridan. To make him lash out unnecessarily. To force an excellent commander to make a hasty mistake. Why wouldn't he send his best trackers? But they had come so quick. He'd expected at least a day's head start on them. *Perhaps we've underestimated Stuart's resolve?*

They waited in the darkness, watching the dying flames of their campfire. Wolf's belly churned with nervous agitation and a little tired nausea.

He looked back the way his unit had gone. They would have to wait and then circle back behind their hunters. Perhaps they could cut west. It felt like the noose was tightening around his command, and they'd only just begun.

George continued to stare out. A finger went up to his ear, and he softly tapped it. Wolf realized it too. No more pounding hooves. No more riders. They'd stopped somewhere, and that meant men now stalked the camp on foot.

Wolf's breathing became shallow as he waited, knowing full well the rebels crept through the surrounding forest. George took his rifle and propped it up on a tree branch. The move was slow and deliberate in order to deceive any enemy eyes. Wolf gripped his pistol harder.

The fire continued to cast flickering shadows on the trees and brush around them, an inviting scene to any nighttime followers. A fire was an easy identifier in the rich ebony night, a signal beacon to friend and foe alike.

Wolf's strained, trying to make out the enemy closing in before him. He almost didn't see the man as he slithered into the camp. He crept quietly along a series of trees, almost circling. He was followed by another and another. They were rebels; they had to be. Dressed in civilian gear, they were easily confused with Wolf's men. Two held pistols and the leader, a long rifle. They circled around one more time, their eyes feeling the darkness before they walked into the light.

"They be close," the one with the long rifle said.

"We just missed them," a handsome man in fine attire said.

"Aye, look at these tracks," the homely one said. The three men studied the ground. Using the firelight, they walked with their heads down.

The most savage looking of the three stopped where Wolf had slept. He dug his foot into the ground. Eyeing the forest suspiciously, he took a knee. He placed his face near the ground. Brushing aside dead pine needles and leaves, he carefully crawled to where Flora had slept. He turned his head toward his comrades. "This be them. See. Those feet be lighter than the rest. That be a woman."

"And here," the homely one said. "Multiple heavy tracks. Those be the brutes Captain spoke about."

"It won't be long now. We'll catch the traitors," said the handsome man, flashing white teeth.

A loud twig cracking under the pressure of a boot drew all of the men's attention. Guns were trained in its direction. The men held their aim, and Wolf held his breath.

Men in gray emerged from the shadows. Blood-red shirts stuck out beneath their fine Confederate cavalry jackets. Black, brown, and gray slouch hats along with a few gray kepis with yellow bands adorned their heads. Wary glances rested upon proud faces, and their eyes scanned constantly around them. They held their weapons with the confidence of men who knew how to use them. The tension released from the three men, and the groups greeted one another.

A slow gulp trickled down Wolf's throat. He recognized them immediately. He'd faced them once before and they were a deadly foe: battle-tested veterans, filled with an elite confidence and élan that oozed from their every pore. They had been forged in battle and it seemed that their ability to conduct war was genetically ingrained in them, passed from generation to generation.

Those men were Hampton's best and led by the vilest man that roamed the earth. Could have been gray-clad kin to the devil himself. The man that had tortured him. The man that had branded him like a common criminal. A man that Wolf knew he would have to kill before the war was over. A kill that would satisfy the very essence of his soul. He could think of nothing more gratifying that he had left in this life than to kill this son of a bitch.

The ranks parted, revealing a shadowed man. He strolled into the campsite clearing, and the swaggering gray shadow transformed into Captain Marshall Payne. Even with his eyes masked by his slouch hat, Wolf was sure it was him.

Payne's brown curls brushed the tops of his shoulders. A lengthy umber goatee grew from his chin. Blue eyes hid under that hat, eyes that had been filled with cold-rimmed ecstasy as he pried secrets from Wolf's flesh.

All his secrets save one, a letter from Abraham Lincoln to assassinate Jefferson Davis, head of the rebel government. That secret Wolf kept inside, and with it, his only shred of dignity was denying the enemy the fruitful public relations victory to expose the plot.

Payne regarded his trackers as if they were servants and not equal free men. "I thought you said we'd caught up to him."

The feral-looking guide spit on the ground. "I'm telling you they're smart. Covered their tracks back there very well. Them Injuns must be helpin' 'em. Won't matter, I can add a few more scalps to my wall when we catch 'em. They be clever, but I always find me prey."

Payne grinned like the devil in the flame light. "Scott, if you weren't of such poor English stock, I'd let you join my Red Shirts."

The Red Shirts chuckled and laughed. Murmurs of Tiny Scott echoed from the men. Scott glared at them angrily.

"My name be Scottish, and I wouldn't join a bunch of fancy cavaliers that do more pony tricks than fightin'." This caused a few angry comments from the Red Shirts.

Payne spread his hands wide. "Ah yes, you are of *Scottish* stock. Figures." He shook his head. "Our pony tricks are a part of our allure." He appeared pleased with himself and spoke matter-of-factly. "Which direction did our prey flee?"

"Well, it was hasty. But they want us to think they went further south, but I think they went west through the forest. Got a woman or a child with 'em. Either way somebody lighter."

"Very good. Just as we expected. Through the forest." He rested a hand on the hilt of his sword. "Hmm. Those sound like the movements of a desperate wounded animal." Payne sniffed the air loudly. "I can smell their fear." Then he let out a fierce laugh. "And fear us they should. Right, boys?"

His men laughed.

"Gordon, take Baker and bring up the horses. We shall take whatever ground we can from them tonight." Two men peeled off the back of the platoon and disappeared into the forest.

Wolf didn't realize his hand shook until his own ears heard the pistol rattling. Unfocused, he aimed his revolver through the trees, its bead sight level on the harsh outline of Payne.

One slight squeeze of the trigger, and the man would be dead. He'd never know who killed him. Never have any idea of the man who'd claimed his revenge from behind a log at night. A man who would relish his death as he watched his blood soak the earth. He could reclaim a piece of his soul by sending the other's to hell, extinguishing his life's flame.

A soft hand rested upon Wolf's arm, bringing him back from his fantasies of revenge. He turned toward George and he whispered, "Enemy."

The pad of his fingertip applied pressure to the slender trigger.

"Not now," George said quietly. "Too many."

Wolf blinked back his anger. Sweet revenge was so close he could almost taste its tantalizing and succulent flavor. Who could have thought the death of another could give a man such gratification? But something held his hand back.

He lowered the pistol. "Not now."

It wasn't some sense of honor. It wasn't good enough to assassinate the man in the dark. No. No. That could never be good enough for Payne. Wolf wanted to watch the life leave his eyes, a blade through his belly. He wanted to savor his enemy's demise. Drink in his pain. He wanted revenge, up-close and personal, and he would seize it.

Chapter Twenty-Four

Night, May 9, 1864
South of Taylorsville, Virginia

Wolf and the sharpshooter slowly backtracked away from the fire like skulking thieves. They found the others almost a half-mile away waiting in the dark like wanted men.

They walked their horses, single file away from the camp until the sun began to creep on the horizon, and two roads stretched lazily before them.

"Hogan," Wolf softly called down the dozing line of horsemen. They'd been at war long enough to know to capture whatever rest was available to them. Despite Flora's discomfort—even her head bobbed up and down—she slept in the saddle.

The Irishman brought his horse near Wolf's.

"They're between us and our way east."

"They are."

"Which way do we go now?"

"This here route runs north to south." Hogan sighed, eyeing the dusky dirt road. "North will take us to Stuart and Sheridan. Depends on who's getting the jump on who, but if I were a betting man, which I am, I'd bet on Stuart. So north is still no good until they engage in battle. Then we can try to circle around to Sheridan's lines." He eyed the other way. "That leaves south, mile by mile closer to the enemy capital."

"Do you know of a place where no one can find us? A place where we can hide until the armies meet?"

Hogan swatted a mosquito on his neck as he thought. "There's an inn outside of Richmond. Sometimes we use it to meet with informants and the like. No one should come looking for us there."

"That's where we go then."

"Closer to Richmond puts us at risk."

Wolf shook his head. "We need to get away from the Red Shirts and off this road. It won't be long. We only need enough time for Sheridan and Stuart to fight."

"Red Shirts?" Hogan asked.

The horsemen perked up at the sound of the enemy's name. "Aye, those are the men who follow us. Hampton's Red Shirts."

Roberts rubbed his eyes. "Wolf, those be the men from Gettysburg?"

"They are. Not all of them, but enough."

"You're not saying he's with 'em are ya?" Roberts asked. "The bad one?"

Wolf stared at his friend, comrade, and brother. He hadn't told Roberts much. The physical pain of torture was excruciating enough for Wolf, but Roberts knew that the captain had done the deed with wicked efficiency.

"He's here."

"Dear God, he's here. This changes the game."

"Yes, it does. I'm going to kill him."

Roberts nodded fiercely. A worried look took hold of him, but his words rang true. "I'll help you. Least I can do."

"Never doubted you."

Hogan held up a hand. "Now, gentlemen. Wait a minute. We are here to keep Mrs. Stuart company until the battle's done." He lifted his eyebrows high. "Until Stuart's demise, we aren't to be riding off getting ourselves killed for some feud."

Wolf considered the BMI agent. This man had no idea the trauma that had come at Payne's miserable hands.

"I'm not sure you understand. We're going to kill that man. You cannot stop me."

The BMI agent's head went back as he searched the heavens for any sliver of succor. "That wasn't the deal. We are close, Wolf. So close to doing this thing right."

"I didn't say I'd break my word, but when we're finished, I'm going after Payne."

"What about your orders?" Hogan asked.

"Bugger your orders. I'm going to kill that man."

Wilhelm came near, talking lowly to Wolf. "I want revenge on these men for what they've done, but we must stay focused. We're in enemy territory. One misstep could bring about our ruin."

Wolf met his eyes. "Sergeant, I already told you. When we're done, I kill him."

"Yes, Lieutenant," Wilhelm said, his mustache quivering with dissatisfaction.

"Sounds like quite the fellow to draw such a sour reaction from all you fine men. I'd like to see him myself," Adams added. "Maybe I'll kill him."

"You will not, Private," Wolf said.

Adams grinned at him. "Sounds like a challenge. Who can kill a man first? A game if you will. Care to place a wager?"

"Bah, he's prolly a fucking coward," Nelson said. "Hurt your feelings, did he?"

"He's mine," Wolf said.

Nelson nudged Adams. "The boy lieutenant looks so serious."

"He does, don't he? Must be quite the bastard," Adams said, an impressed look on his face.

"Which is why he's mine. When the time comes, you let me take him."

Flora's voice chimed in, higher pitched than the rest. "What makes you men think you have a chance? If my husband sent them, they will find you and will kill you." She looked well-satisfied with herself.

All the men turned to stare at her.

"That's if he doesn't want to do it himself. He is an excellent horseman and well-versed in both saber and pistol. Better than you lot."

Wolf's men exchanged glances. A slow grin crawled over Nelson's face. "With all due respect, ma'am, I'd rip your husband's head off and shit down his throat. He'll pity the day he meets us."

Flora's mouth dropped open. "How dare you speak to me that way!"

"Private," Wolf said.

"You gonna tell me to be a more righteous man? You gonna tell me how to do my fucking job? Huh, Wolf?"

"I'm gonna tell you to shut the fuck up. Nobody talks to Flora but me. Uncle Shugart can pray for your soul later."

The thick trooper ground his teeth, the muscles around his jaw flexing. "We'll finish our words later, Wolfie."

"Private," Wilhelm said.

Nelson eyed the veteran German soldier.

"You'll maintain order as long as I am alive."

"Don't tempt me, Dutchman," Nelson said with an evil grin.

"I'm the only Dutch here," Van Horn added.

Nelson turned toward him. "And I don't like either of ya."

Wolf's eyes didn't leave the hulking trooper. "Do we need to hash out who is in command here?"

Nelson's eyes gleamed, and he flexed his hands into fists. His lip curled beneath his beard. "I ain't got a quarrel."

"That's good," Wolf said, reluctant to take his eyes off the dangerous man. He turned back to Hogan. "Take us to your inn."

"Yes, Lieutenant," Hogan said. He maneuvered his horse to the front of the understrength platoon.

"Take us at a trot," Wolf called after him. He stayed behind Nelson in the short column where he could react quicker if need be. He'd hate to have to put down one of their own, but that was the risk in bringing a man with fire in his veins.

He heeled his mount's sides, and she increased her gait to a trot. The raiders rode into the morning light.

***

It was almost midday when they reached Hogan's inn. It was a ramshackle structure with a slight lean to the left. Clearly, it had been abandoned at some point. Boards had been nailed over the windows. The front porch was missing planks. A hole gaped through the second-story roof, revealing gray weather-beaten wood. The place was so run-down Wolf thought it might not even stay upright in a harsh wind.

"This is the place?" Wolf asked.

"Locals call it Yellow Tavern," Hogan replied.

"Ain't much of it yellow," Roberts said. Any semblance of color on the tavern had been bleached by the sun, wind, and rain as it had been left unattended by men.

"Used to be."

"I was expecting something a bit more accommodating," Wolf said.

"What better place to be than one nobody wants to go? Even now it's our island in a sea of enemies. Stables are out back."

The raiders stabled their horses, ensuring feed bags were secured. There was no way they wouldn't need the animals well-rested after such a continuous ride or risk making them lame. Hogan led them along a dirt path overgrown with tall swaying grass and entered the tavern through a back door.

The door creaked on rusted hinges as it struggled to open. Inside were overturned tables, a few broken chairs, and a dust-caked bar. Cobwebs ran rampant over every corner and ceiling space available. The fireplace was dark, and the brick surrounding it chipped away. Stairs near the front entrance led to the second floor.

Hogan walked over behind the counter and pulled out an oil lantern. Removing a box of matches from his jacket, he lit the lantern, illuminating the ramshackle place.

The men uprighted tables and chairs, clearing areas.

"That collapsed room will make a good place to see any approaching riders," Skinner said.

Wolf nodded the go-ahead and Skinner carefully navigated the stairs upward, trying to hold back his weight for fear of breaking through the steps.

"A fitting place for men of your character," Flora said, eyeing the surroundings. She looked much too exhausted to be causing so much trouble for Wolf.

"Flora, remember our pact. You talk too much, you get the gag."

Her mouth closed, and he smirked.

Dan offered her a chair at a table with a smile. She didn't say anything but sat down with her arms draped over her belly, her wrists still tied.

"I'm not going to run. You can remove these," Flora said.

Wolf judged her words, weighing her to see if she told the truth. He gestured at Dan with his chin. The big Polish trooper leaned low and unknotted her ropes, unraveling them.

She nodded her thanks to Dan, and he smiled sheepishly. "Thank you," she said loudly.

"There's dried goods underneath here," Hogan said from across the room. "Tack and the like."

The men checked their weapons and ammunition. They set up their bedrolls. Dan, Roberts, Adams, Pratt, and Nelson sat at a table playing cards. Adams shuffled like a master, flipping the cards along his fingers. Some men were about to lose whatever valuables they had.

Hogan joined Wolf at his table. "I am going to meet up with one of my informants." He draped his brown coat over a chair and put a gray officer's frock coat on. "Nobody get frisky when I return," he said to the men around the room.

For the most part, they ignored him. The sharpshooter in the nest above would notify them of anything before he got close enough for them to riddle him with lead.

"Where are you going?"

Hogan smirked, running a hand through his curly hair. "Don't you worry about where and who, Lieutenant. I will return before nightfall." Hogan turned, and James rose to join him.

"No, James. I do this on my own."

James gave a terse nod and sat back down, leaning his head on the wall.

Hogan exited and a gallop of hooves followed.

Wolf studied his men. *Am I doing my men a disservice by not having a better idea of where I am? Am I doing enough to protect my men?* Reconnaissance was critical in the field. Every engagement showed the truth of that principle of war. "Shugart."

The elder abolitionist slowly stood as old men do and made his way to Wolf. "Young sir?" His words were said with no ill will, but none of them were really young anymore. Young in age perhaps, but war aged a man beyond his years.

Wolf gave him a faint smile. "I want you to scout the area. Get poor Pratt out of that game. I want to know who and what is around us. Most importantly, I want to know ways to retreat. We don't know when we'll have to run again."

The tuft of hair atop Shugart's head fluttered as the older man bobbed his head. He gave Wolf a warm smile. "It will be good for the boy to be separated from the vile influences of gambling." He shuddered under the thought. "I, of course, will counsel him on the virtues of a sin-free life."

"And you are the one to save him."

"My work is never done. This will be a sober unit by the time the war is over. I can tell you that."

Wolf couldn't help but laugh. Despite the fact he laughed at Shugart, the old man grinned; he looked like a skeleton with his thin cheeks and ghostly cobweb-like beard.

Shugart's jaw settled into a stubborn defiance. "I will never stop trying to save your souls."

"We appreciate every prayer, Uncle." Wolf clapped his hands together in mock prayer.

This made the old man grin. "And all my prayers are freely given." He clasped Wolf's upper arm fondly. "We will be back before dark with your report."

"Thank you, Uncle."

Shugart disrupted the men playing cards. Pratt's brow was already creased. Only a single green dollar still sat in front of him. There was no way any of the other men at the table would ever let the young man win a hand. In fact, if he thought he was winning, he was losing. They were all just setting him up for a bigger fall.

"Come, Private Pratt, we have more scouting to do."

Pratt rolled his eyes to the other men. "We only just started."

Adams grinned at him. "Yeah, Uncle. Let him play a little longer."

"He gets better every hand," Nelson said. The brutish man eyed his hand over the top of his nose, his thick fingers engulfing the cards.

"Leave this poor lad from the corruption of your sinful vices. He still has a chance for redemption."

"Better just leave that dollar, Pratt," Adams said. Pratt snatched his last dollar and shoved it in his pocket. "I ain't even got a chance to win my money back."

"Yeah," Adams said. "One more hand?"

Shugart glimpsed back at Wolf, and he shook his head no. "No, we must do this before dark."

"I will go with them," James said. His eyes were dark and serious. "It is not safe. The enemy is close."

"You may join them."

The troopers gathered their carbines and were joined by the native sharpshooter.

"Are you a churchgoing fellow, Private?" Shugart asked Pratt.

"Of course, raised Catholic."

Shugart regarded the Indian with a bit of suspicion. "And you, James? Are you a Christian?"

"I've been baptized."

"Very good, James." Shugart turned to Pratt again. "And you've accepted Christ, Mr. Pratt?

Pratt nodded. "Well, as much as any other man. My parents put the water on me when I was a babe." His voice trailed as the door closed behind them, and James gave Wolf a wide-eyed glare.

The man had elected to go; his fate was his own. And old Shugart would have him singing hymns by the time they returned.

Wolf settled in his chair across from Flora. He leaned his chair back into the wall. He put his boots on the table to stay semi-reclined. Flora studied him with tired eyes.

"Get some rest, ma'am," he said.

"I will do as I please."

Wolf gave her a short grin. He tipped his hat over his eyes and snoozed away the afternoon.

***

He awoke from his snooze to the *schwing, schwing* of metal over stone. Placing a finger on his hat, he pushed it upwards. Skinner sat on the floor in the corner sharpening a knife. Nearby, Wilhelm inspected and cleaned his Spencer carbine with a rag.

The poker game had ended, and Adams licked his lips as he counted his money. Not surprising. The man had a knack for swindling others.

Flora's head was dipped before him. A strand of hair was loose from her bun and dangling in front of her face. Dan and Bart tended a fire in the fireplace. Van Horn and Hale dozed on the floor like fallen soldiers on the battlefield.

Skinner looked up at Wilhelm. "Fight's coming. Can't hurt to be ready."

Wilhelm grunted. "You and I share the same sentiment."

"Sentiments? I ain't sentiment one bit."

Eyeing his weapon with pleasure of a craftsmen his favorite tool, Wilhelm smiled. "We are of the same mind, friend."

Skinner grinned, scratching beneath his hat with his knife. "Yes, we are, my German friend."

"Hogan's coming back," George called down from the upstairs observation nest.

Galloping hooves soon followed his words, and Wolf stood. He straightened his bad leg. It always seemed stiff, which complemented his hardened and scarred back. He put a hand on his lower back and forced it outward.

Hogan entered, closing the door behind him. He gave a small grin. "Appreciate the lack of bullets when I rode up."

"You can thank George."

"You have my thanks," he called up the stairs.

"Almost shot you myself with that gray coat on but decided you didn't ride well enough to be a Southerner," George retorted.

"Saved by my lack of equestrian prowess." Hogan gave the men a bow.

"What's the news?" Wolf asked.

"Quite marvelous, in fact. Stuart has taken the bait. Over half his force is frantically searching for our dear lady over there. He's near Taylorsville now, racing around like a mad man. Sheridan is taking his sweet time, marching straight for Richmond. Custer's taken credit for burning Beaver Dam Station, and both are preparing for a fight."

"This was all a way to get him to fight?" Flora said.

The men turned and looked at her.

"That is none of your concern," Wolf said.

She lifted her chin. "Then may he never find me."

"It's too late," Hogan said. "He's already bitten the hook. Soon Sheridan will take him."

She laughed high and haughty. "So he thinks."

"As is done, ma'am. There will be a battle here soon enough."

"And my husband will win."

"Your faith is well-placed, but this will not fall in his favor," Wolf said.

"Then you don't know him."

"We know him very well." Wolf let his eyes do the talking. She had to realize the truth of his words. Everything they'd done so far was because they were familiar with how the dashing Stuart operated. He was a man that would never let his wife's kidnappers go unpunished. A man who frantically and aggressively searched for her made mistakes. He should be setting up defenses not galloping around from town to town.

She blinked and averted her eyes away from him.

"Did you see Shugart or James?"

Hogan's eyes read his for an answer. "Can't say I'd see James unless he wanted me too." Hogan gave a short grin that disappeared. "Where'd they go?"

"I sent them to scout the area."

"It's good you sent James with them."

"I know, but they should be back." Wolf went to the window and peered between the boards. "We can only wait."

Chapter Twenty-Five

Evening, May 10, 1864
Near Yellow Tavern, Virginia

Tracking was a slow and precise business and Scott had lost the trail for most the day. The dense woodlands had foiled him for hours before he located the trail again, and it led them here to a rural country road. Payne sat atop his horse, watching the scout with disgusted impatience as he tried to find their scent like an overused bloodhound.

Scott walked lightly over the road, holding the reins to his horse as he studied the ground. The man would walk one way then drop to his knees eyeing the earth, sometimes even sniffing it like an actual beast of the forest. Then he'd stand and either follow the tracks farther or turn back around and tread his steps back to the group before starting the whole process anew.

"What can you see, Scott?"

"It's hard to tell. You see, this is a common road. Many riders have gone through here. It's hard for me to say which way our prey went."

"Let's spread our net." Payne waved forward Lieutenant Fickles and Sergeant Turner. "Take your men north then split covering east and west. I'll take the rest south. Let's run down these wild pigs."

The men parted ways in a cloud of dust. He kept Scott, the best tracker of the group, to guide his men. They traveled south down a forested road toward Richmond. He didn't understand why Northern raiders would travel deeper into Southern territory, but Scott seemed sure enough about the possibility.

They stopped at a few homes and talked to the people there, asking if they'd seen any groups of men. They came up empty-handed.

"Well, Scott?" Payne demanded.

The scout eyed the road ahead. "Don't know, sir. Thought we'd have run into 'em by now."

"Yet we haven't."

Scott eyed Payne for a moment, a mountain lion sizing up an alpha wolf. He knew the scout wouldn't strike first. He would adhere to the military hierarchy. But if he did, Payne would bring the wild man down with calculated saber strikes. If the man wanted to shoot it out, it would happen close. In that case, he would beat the Scott on the draw, solidifying his own victory. He was prepared for the conflict but was sure Scott would not act.

"Let's return to our rally point. Perhaps Mr. Scott can take up the trail again."

Scott's lips quivered in anger, and Payne ignored him. His men turned their horses around. "Let's walk 'em back. Give our mounts a rest."

Their horses' hooves tapped out a muffled drumbeat along the packed dirt road, and his men were quiet. Even though his men wouldn't complain, being in the saddle for such a long hard pursuit was surely wearing on them. He'd hate to lose such fine horseflesh for no cause. Despite their excellent breeding, the animals and his men weren't tireless.

In the distance, riders appeared like lonely ghosts. Payne regarded them for a moment. His men must have found something. He raised his hand in a wave.

The other riders drew their horses to a stop.

He gave Scott a side-eye. "Must be Fickles or Turner's men." He waved again over his head.

"There's only three of them," Scott said.

The two groups watched one another from afar. Payne let his hand fall to the pommel of his saddle. He peered over his shoulder for a moment. The road was clear. The forest on either side of them buzzed with insects. Both parties judged the threat of the other. *Must be Turner. Can't be them. Can it?* His nose twitched and he squinted, letting his hand embrace the familiarity of his pistol handle.

The horsemen twisted in their saddles, spinning their mounts in the opposing direction. Tails swished and dust clouded as they galloped away.

A quick grin flashed on Payne's lips. He pointed with his reins. "Those be our wild piglets." He raked his horse's flanks with his spurs. "Let's get 'em!"

The rolling thunder of hooves drummed in pursuit. Shouts and whoops came from the men around him. It had been too long since his hounds had been blooded. The wind whipped his long hair and tugged at his open officer's coat. Gracefully, he drew his pistol from its holster in one fluid motion.

The riders ahead turned down an intersecting road and disappeared from view behind trees and shrubs. Unable to see the prey drove his men on even harder. Payne gave his horse an extra kick.

Never let the foe from your sight. His men crouched low on their mounts as they turned the corner. They would run down the cowards.

Every stride closed the distance like wolves hunting newly born fawns. It was only a matter of time before they were caught.

A pistol flashed a fiery report back at them, the shot flying harmlessly overhead. The rider lacked natural equestrian skill. The shot was so poorly aimed that Payne's men didn't even duck.

Fighting on horseback took practice. Hell, riding a horse took practice let alone engaging the enemy accurately while in motion. His men, who had grown up in the saddle, had mastered the skill. Their horse tactics could rival any of the tribes of the Great Plains.

As they drew even closer to the fleeing horsemen, Payne took aim. It took skill to hit anything atop a horse, at a gallop even more so, but it could be done if the horse was excellently trained and the rider confident. In his case, he had both at his disposal.

Patiently, he waited for the wavering of his pistol to fall in line with the rider's back, all while prepping his trigger ever so slightly. It was really a matter of hurrying up and then waiting for the precise moment to release the tension. *Bang!* The bitter smoke from his shot instantly dissipated behind him.

The rider ahead arched his back with a scream, instinctually pulling his reins hard. His mount reared on two legs and sent the rider tumbling from his horse. He emitted a loud huff as he hit the ground.

The front rider didn't glance back, only demanding more from his poor beast. His partner slowed his horse, spurring it back toward the fallen man. *Ah, yes, a bleeding heart for his fellow man.* Finally, a little contest.

The rider galloped in his direction, charging Payne's men; his pistol blared at the rebels. A soft whizz tickled at Payne's ear as a bullet passed by. He beat Payne's men to the fallen and struggled to dismount his horse as he reached his comrade.

"Hold your fire!" Payne shouted. His riders threatened to run the men over with their mounts, but they slowed and encircled the men, pointing their guns at them.

"What about the one ahead?" Private Matthew Gordon said, his pistol in hand. Gordon came from a family who owned three mills near Charleston. Handsome lad with a dimpled chin.

Payne studied the escaping rider as he got farther away, kicking up dust as he went. "Later, Gordon. We have all we need," he said, mouth twisting into a smile. "I will accept your gracious surrender, gentlemen." He emphasized his words by cocking his pistol.

The two men froze. The old man with a beard like white hanging moss strained with the effort of holding the injured man beneath his armpits. He struggled to simply keep the younger man in his arms, and they both sank to the road in defeat.

"We are loyal Confederates," the old man said.

Payne's men laughed. "Is that so?" He eyed their mounts. Cavalry saddles. Fine long guns strapped to the sides. The younger man gritted his teeth, trying to hold his back with his hand. His chest shook, and he whimpered in pain. The elder stared at them defiantly.

"You will pay for what you've done. We will go to your commanding officer."

"Do not threaten me with false bravado, old man. You are the ones in my possession. And by the looks of you, you are just the men I was searching for."

A distant crack of a gun sounded off like a firework faraway. It drew one's eyes upward as did any gunshot. His eyes had less than a second to locate the perpetrator before warm wetness splashed across his face: a summer rain. His cheek twitched and he raised a hand to wipe it away. The liquid smeared between his fingers like crushed berries. Blood. Thicker bits of tissue congregated in rugged globs. But not his own.

Next to him, Private Gordon teetered in his saddle as a drunk man would before he collapsed on the road. His men took cover, and Payne quickly hopped from his horse. He scanned the road over his mount's back.

A rider stood faintly in the distance barely visible to the naked eye. *Much too far for a shot. From the saddle? Much too far.*

He turned and peered down at Gordon. He lay in the road, coughing blood on his chest that was masked by his crimson-colored shirt. His hands flapped uselessly as he tried to stay moving. His mind hadn't caught up to the reality of his impending doom. He had no chance at survival. Death would come quick.

The distant rider turned his horse and fled. *He shot that from atop a horse at that distance? A lucky man indeed.* He would take pleasure in cutting the man down. Maybe he'd take his fingers before he died. Or would he take his eyes instead? Hard to tell which one meant more to a man like that.

Most men wouldn't survive that long in a battle, but when he did catch that rider, he would make sure to take him alive. That way he could be assured he would die screaming. Then he would see what the man valued more. Eyes or fingers. He bet on eyes, but who knew? Sometimes men surprised him.

"Get him." Payne pointed at Gordon. A few of his men hustled to his body, hauling him by his arms toward the brush. Blood bubbled from Gordon's mouth, his eyes wide with fear. The man left a dark stain on the ground like a horse had pissed.

"That was a mistake." His eyes regarded the two men sitting in the center of the road.

"Sir, you should take cover," shouted Corporal Thomas Cook. He was a blond freckle-faced young man from Spartanburg. His family owned modest lands and only twenty or so slaves. Payne almost hadn't allowed him entry into the Red Shirts, but as the war wore on, his entrance was all but assured. He was a crafty fighter, an expert with a hunting shotgun.

"He's gone, Corporal."

"Could be more?" Cook tried to peer down the country road.

Payne made a grand gesture of bending down near the two men. He scanned over their heads. No man, no matter the shot, would try it over the heads of his two comrades. "Can't be too safe now." He gave a charming smile. "Now who are you two?"

"We aren't anyone of note," the elder man said.

"My man is bleeding out on the side of the road bound for a date with our heavenly father. Do not tell me you're nobody. Nobody's don't shoot my men."

"We're true Southerners. Loyal we are," the elder man said. "Thought you were Yanks. They're all over these roads."

Payne gave an understanding nod. It was an expected response. Lie, lie, lie, make counterarguments. "You're right; they are." He lifted his eyebrows. He supposed he would entertain them for a moment in time. "So you originated in these parts?"

"Yes, we're from Hanover," the young man cried.

"Really? What's the name of the church right on the outskirts of town? Can't miss it. Nice white steeple."

The young man blinked. "Methodist."

Payne pretended to believe them, watching the boy's eyes light up, only to shake his head in disappointment. "Close, but wrong. You sure you're from these parts?" He tried to give them an unalarming smile. "Boy, I can ease your suffering. I know a good doctor around here. About three miles up this road, lives next to a tobacco plantation."

The young man's eyes lit up. The elder man shook his head vehemently. "Don't say anything, Pratt. These men aren't going to treat us fairly."

Payne's cold eyes watched them without feeling. "Of course, we will. We are all Southern gentleman here. We're honorable. Men of high standards and moral code."

Pratt held up a hand soaked in blood. "I yield. We're Union soldiers. Please take me to the doctor."

"Really?" Payne said sarcastically. His men chuckled from the trees.

The older man sighed and eyed the ground. "We're lost from our command."

"No, you're not."

The young man frantically shook his head. "We're on a mission."

A grin formed on Payne's face. With enough suffering, a man would talk and talk. Tell you anything you wanted to know. He was almost disappointed with how easily they'd broken. "Are you? Do tell me more, boy. Doctor ain't far."

Pratt blinked at his companion. "I need help. I been shot," he beseeched. "Uncle, the pain is fierce."

Shugart grabbed him by the shirt. "They ain't going to help us, boy. So keep your mouth shut and die a loyal man."

Payne drew himself upright in front of them, holstering his pistol. "Let me tell you. You boys seen better days." He showed them his weaponless hands. "See? No harm." He tried to smile again like he would at a friend. "Where is she, boy? You tell me, and I'll take you right over to the doctor."

Shugart lunged for him, swinging his fist as hard as he could. Payne had seen it coming a mile away. His backhand cracked a bony cheek and sent the old man onto the ground. "Now, you be careful, old-timer."

"Oh, God," Pratt said. He had collapsed on the ground, emitting a high-pitched moan. "It's so bad." His chest heaved. The old man crawled to him, placing a hand on the scarlet flow escaping Pratt's body. "It's okay, boy. Keep breathing."

"I do declare this is unfortunate. Let me assist you, boy," Payne said. His hand eased a knife from its sheath.

"Yes, thank you." The boy moaned, struggling to stay still. Payne slipped his dagger into the boy's neck. His eyes bulged, and blood spilled from the wound like an unblocked spigot.

Shugart held his convulsing body. "You killed him!"

"I helped him on his way."

"There's no doctor," Shugart said, tears forming in his eyes.

"No doctor."

Payne wiped the blade on the dead man's coat and sheathed it. Blood could corrode a blade if one wasn't careful. The boy would have never lasted long enough for a full interview, but the old man would. He held the same information. "Let's get to know each other, old one."

Shugart studied him with fearful eyes. "I have nothing to say to you."

"But you will."

***

The light from the fire danced across the hanging man's thinning head of hair. His flop of hair reminded Payne of some sort of malting bird, unruly and wild. He wiped his blade on the old man's brown jacket, darkening the shade.

He didn't hang in the traditional sense, by a rope or tether around his neck. He wanted the man to be able to speak, so hanging was counterproductive. No, he needed him to stay in place while in massive amounts of pain but still be lucid. So he simply nailed the man's hands to the tree above his head.

Soft chatting from his men drifted from around the campfire. Turner was telling the story about when he killed a bear with only a knife. The part he always left out was that he'd shot the beast three times before he "slew" it with his blade. He danced and jabbed and dodged imaginary swipes from the animal to the other men's delight.

The men had distanced themselves from Payne while he worked. Most men didn't have the stomach for this kind of thing. But Payne was sure of one thing. He'd always had a stomach for it. Ever since he was young, he had felt different. He had this extra spark that other men didn't have. The spark of a killer.

Having been raised as a hunter and horseman, it had been easy to disguise his glee at the kill. When he entered the war, it was harder to mask his pleasure with the opportunity for it all around. It was like giving an alcoholic uninhibited access to a bar that was restocked daily.

Some men liked fighting and thrived at it, viewing it as a contest. Other men had that extra piece, the one that helped them turn off their brain and slog through the dirty gory work until it was done. But few took as much pleasure in it as much as he did.

He enjoyed it enough to where he could excel in other areas like interrogation. The suffering of others gave him a sort of ecstasy far greater than any sexual encounter. Not like with a woman. No, not like that, but similar. It was more like ultimate control over another: control where he could flick his wrist, the blade would bite, and the man would die. Control over every bit of relief they had from the pain. Control to escalate a man's pain to the point where he would say anything to escape its fiendish grip.

They were always defiant at first, much like this old man. The next phase was the crying and bemoaning. The mind was a far worse enemy than the blade during this phase. A man would piss himself before Payne had done much of anything to make him cry. Then the poor man would start the begging and pleading.

It was a pitiful sight, but it was in this phase that he'd procure most of his answers. The key was to not stop when they begged. No, no. When the man begged, they were close. The man's ego searched for a way to save his own skin and his pride with empty words of promise and faith.

He would inflict even more pain on them then. He would steal the ego's voice and reveal the truth hidden below. It didn't happen often, but for this mission, he had been given permission to go as far as he wanted. It was kind of Hampton to let him indulge.

His captive, Shugart, had screamed and called for God's help when the nails bit through his flesh. Payne imagined Christ must have done the same. But when he was finished hammering, the man became quiet, calming himself as he drifted into a trance-like state.

Even after pissing himself, Shugart had continued to pray. Fiercely he prayed for deliverance from evil. He never begged, but he did plead with God quite convincingly. Enough to have Payne eyeing the sky and waiting for a response.

But for the most part, Shugart had just gone to a different place in his mind like he had left his own body behind while ignoring Payne's excellent craftsmanship.

Payne had used his knife like an Oxford-trained surgeon, not like one of those hacks in the field hospitals, but a true surgeon practicing real medical precision, not sawing and hacking limbs just to toss them into a pile. In the end, Shugart cried out like Christ on the cross then went limp, his weight pulling down painfully on the nails.

Payne regarded the man. *Was that his last breath?* Shugart's head dropped to his chest. His tuft of hair was almost motionless, the wind causing it to slightly flutter. His skeletal body appeared to have already been hanging for days. Soon the flies would come seeking rebirth in his flesh.

"Impressive." He'd never thought a man of his age could have withstood such treatment.

Barely audible words tumbled from the dead man's mouth, perking Payne's interest. He studied him for a moment like a doctor would a moving cadaver. He'd assumed he was dead.

He stepped closer. Fresh blood surrounded the nail heads like angry red water wells, but enough had flowed to dry into the trunk's bark. He grabbed Shugart by the loose tuft of hair, lifting his level with his own face. "You still have some life left in you?"

"Water," Shugart mumbled.

Payne nodded in genuine concern. "Of course." He snatched up his canteen and unscrewed the cap. His work could be very tiresome, so he kept it nearby. He tipped it back, letting the water flow into the dying man's mouth. Water dribbled down his chin. "Not too much now," Payne said as if he were addressing a child.

"You're evil," Shugart said, his voice hardly audible.

Payne cocked his head. "After I gave you a merciful drink of water?"

"You'll never succeed here. Your cause is unjust."

"Rescuing a man's kidnapped wife?" Payne shook his head. "You abolitionists have such conflicting priorities."

Shugart's chest shuddered. "I go with God. I go with no reservation for the things I've done."

Payne sighed. "More of this." He shook his head. "God isn't coming for you. You aren't going to heaven. You're going to burn in hell."

"My God will take his faithful servant."

Payne patted his arm. Then flicked the blood from his fingertips. "Okay, you win." He stretched the man's neck by tugging his tuft of hair.

Clouded eyes gazed at him. His throat jiggled before he managed a few more words. "I forgive you."

Payne nodded his acceptance of a clean slate and ran his knife across Shugart's throat. Blood trickled down his neck, leaving a crimson trail upon his naked chest. The elder simply let out a loud gurgle and lowered his head in death.

Payne bent over at the waist, getting close to Shugart's face. "Did he take you?"

Shugart's body hung limp, soundless and soulless, a husk of skin and bone.

Payne strolled back to the campfire with a sharp whistle of Dixie. Dixie was a peppy upbeat tune. It truly cheered him on the inside.

Turner glanced at him, finishing his story. His eyes darted down at Payne's bloodstained hands. "Did he talk?"

Snatching a rag, he wiped his hands off. "He talked enough."

Turner grinned, looking over his shoulder at the corpse. "Yank paid the price?"

"He paid dearly." Payne unrolled the cuffed sleeves of his red shirt.

"And? Where are they?" Turner inquired.

"I don't know. He wouldn't say. But they're close."

Turner pushed his slouch hat back on his head. "You mean it didn't work? All that crying and hollering."

Payne's eyes flashed fire at him. "It worked just fine, Sergeant. Sometimes they pass before we can acquire everything we need. It is an art but a delicate one."

"Course it is, sir. You're mighty good at it too," Turner said, with a gulp.

"I am." He took a seat, staring at the dancing flames of the fire.

"What are we going to do?" Corporal McMillan asked.

Snapping a twig between his fingers, he tossed it in the fire. "We wait."

"Wait, sir?" McMillan asked.

The fire sizzled and cracked like an old steam engine locomotive on its last run. If he knew his prey, he'd have them soon enough. "For them to come to us."

Chapter Twenty-Six

Evening, May 10, 1864
Yellow Tavern, Virginia

The tavern door burst inward, and a distraught James barreled inside. Hands leapt for guns and swords. Wolf had his revolver cocked and aimed at the man before he raised his hands in the air.

"Don't shoot!"

Pistol hammers were laid to silent rest when they recognized it was one of theirs. But James's face quietly screamed of alarm.

"What is it?" Wolf asked, letting his chair rock forward. He stood and the chair behind him banged on the wood floor as it rested on four legs again.

"They got them," James blurted out.

"Who's they?" Hogan said. He adjusted his hat on his head, making his forehead seem longer.

"The rebels hunting us. At least ten of them." James took a breath. "That's not all."

"What's that?" Wolf demanded.

"There's going to be a battle. The area is crawling with Stuart's men. He's beat Sheridan here."

"How close?"

"I dunno. Maybe four or five miles."

Wolf's mouth formed a tight line, and he shared a glance with Wilhelm, then with Hogan. The BMI agent shrugged. "It's what we want." He walked around the table, raising a hand in the air. "We could make a break for Sheridan's forces."

"I would love to do that, but I cannot leave those men in Payne's hands." He peered down at his hand. There was a bit of a shake in it as if it remembered the torture. The vile thumb press tightening and squeezing until his thumb broke. He gulped down the horrible memory. "We will not leave them."

"Listen, Wolf, they're probably dead. If that guy is only half as bad as you made him out to be, then they're gone, or worse, Payne and his men are on their way here."

"No. If there's a chance they're alive, we'll extract them," Wolf said, with a shake of his head.

Wilhelm nodded in agreement. "Wouldn't be right to leave them."

"Can you take us back to where they were captured?" Wolf asked James.

"In the dark it will be harder, but I can."

"I need everyone mounted in a few minutes." He pointed at Dan and Roberts. "You two are going to stay here."

"I'll stay with her," Nelson said with an evil grin.

"I wouldn't mind her company either," Adams chimed in. "We really are great guards."

"No, I need you with me." Wolf motioned Dan and Roberts closer. "If we aren't back by sunup, let her go and head north."

"Let her go?" Roberts said, scratching his head then staring at his brown-laced fingernails. "Ain't holding her the whole point?"

"Yes?" Dan said, raising his bushy eyebrows over a thick brow.

"No." He eyed them. "You let her go. She didn't deserve this. She was only a means to an end. We go north, find Sheridan, and tell him we tried."

Roberts gave him an irritated smile. "Lotta good that will do me. He'll throw me back in jail."

"He won't. He's got his fight."

"Easy for you to say since you aren't planning on coming back."

Wolf laughed. "You have to be ready in case I don't. Payne is a dangerous man, and if I can, I'm going to kill him."

"Never could back down from a fight, could ya?"

"Never do."

***

James led them over the dark country roads. They passed dark naked fields and even darker forests. They even quietly passed by homes with lightless windows.

The night enveloped them into her nothingness. Beasts and creatures roamed the timberland around them, but one would scarcely know anything existed beyond the nearby trees as it was all covered by the abyss of night.

The horses became skittish as they approached the spot where Pratt had been shot. The animals tossed their heads and stamped their hooves in irritation as their riders drove them closer. Wolf patted Sarah's neck. "It's okay, girl." Her ear twitched and she let out a soft neigh.

It only took another moment before they located Pratt's pale body lying on the side of the road. The contrast between the night and the lifeless white corpse was stark.

Wolf dismounted, handing his reins to Wilhelm. He walked to the body and knelt near him. Pratt was facedown, shirtless, and bootless. His pants were still on, but his belt had been removed, leaving them bunched and loose. Wolf touched his shoulder, finding the dead trooper's flesh cool. The entry wound was clear and almost in the direct center of his back. Merely an inch away from hitting the spine, it was an incapacitating wound for sure.

He awkwardly rolled the man over. Bugs scurried away with chattering clicks of legs and flapping of wings. The young trooper's eyes were open and a thick line had been carved over his throat like a piece of roast beef. *Must not have given the right answer.*

Gently, he let the body roll to the side. "Let's get him on back," he said with a sigh. Bart helped him lift the body onto the back of his horse. Both the men remounted after Pratt had been tied down sufficiently.

Sarah shifted uneasily beneath him. The extra weight bothered her, but the smell of death did so even more. Wolf brought her reins to the side, trying to bring her under control. "Any idea which way they were heading?"

"We ran into them coming from the other direction," James said. He hopped from his saddle and studied the road with a clear level of intensity. "I think they went back that way, but it's difficult to make out for sure."

"Take us that way."

The men searched into the night. They turned the wrong way once and had to backtrack. An hour passed. Then another. He could feel the demoralized air surrounding them, all brought on by the knowledge that one of their own was being held by a madman. But it was the fatigue of hunting in the dark that really ate away at their courage.

"Stay the course," Wilhelm said.

"It may be futile." Wolf kept his eyes probing the upcoming road, looking for something, for anything to shine light on their predicament. He couldn't see Wilhelm's eyes well, but he knew they sought the same thing. They both knew that no search for a missing man was meritless.

"We could split up." Glancing over his shoulder, Wolf eyed the way they'd come. "Perhaps trace a larger route?"

"I don't think it's wise at this point. With so many enemies in the area, we stand a better chance together."

"But does Shugart?" Wolf asked.

"The old buzzard can take care of himself. Hell, God probably has a special angel that watches over his shoulder."

Hooves rolled, causing the men to turn. George emerged from the murky trees. Wolf hadn't even noticed him leave the group. "There's a fire ahead. Through those trees. I saw men sleeping."

"How many men?"

"Twenty or so."

"Rebs?"

"Hard to tell in the dark, but some had sabers."

Wolf's eyes glinted with revenge. "Very well. Let's pay them a visit." There was no guarantee that the men ahead were even the enemy they were searching for. They could be Union forces.

The unit followed George along a road and astride a path hardly big enough to fit a horse. The trail wound deeper and deeper into the timber.

Only the soft thud of hooves accompanied the men.

After the point that Wolf had thought about turning them around, the sharpshooter held up a hand. "Here we dismount. Less than a mile that way," he said, pointing into the trees.

"Get on foot and spread 'em out," Wolf said softly but with command. His men tied their horses to low-hanging branches, leaving Hale to make sure the mounts didn't become spooked in the night.

As quietly as possible, the rest of the men stalked through the forest, attempting not to be heard. Pinpricks of light grew larger through and around tree trunks. When they got close enough to stay hidden, his men took positions, observing the two midnight campfires.

The fires burned low with muted yellow flames. Blankets layered the ground, and the forms of their enemies resided in their warm embrace. Only a single sentry stood next to a tree in the distance. *Much too easy. They should have at least two sentries, preferably four, watching the night.* Either extreme arrogance or carelessness could lead them to a quick grave, unless it was a trap to lure them closer.

The woods suddenly became a much darker and more dangerous place in Wolf's mind. *Are we the ones being watched?*

He crept to where George overlooked the camp. "I only see one," Wolf whispered. He tugged on his brace.

The Ojibwe sharpshooter's face stayed flat, a slight frown settling on his lips. "The guard hasn't moved since we've arrived. All white men move when standing guard." He eyed the forest over his shoulder. Then back at the camp. "Yet he still stands," George said, gesturing with his head.

"Sleeping?"

"I do not know."

"Could it be Shugart?"

"It is possible he is tied to that tree." But even George's words sounded unsure.

"Then cover me," Wolf commanded. The men around him nodded their silent understanding, aiming their carbines in the night and ready to rain lead into the enemy at a moment's notice.

Quietly stalking through the forest, he drew his pistol and left the hammer half-cocked for easier use. He zigged and zagged for the edge of camp, hobbling as he weaved around the trees. Men dozed around the campfires.

A few snored. One smacked his lips and rolled over, freezing Wolf in his tracks. Shallowly breathing, he waited for the man to stop moving, not even daring to blink.

He continued his stalk around the fringe of the camp, creeping closer to the man near the tree. As the distance faded between them, the surer he was that it was Shugart. But something was wrong.

The form stood at an angle. They must have him tied up. *In and out,* he told himself. *They'll never know you're there.* Maybe he should have his men shoot up the camp now. They were clearly outnumbered by the rebels, but the darkness and surprise would easily swing things in their favor.

He stopped and skimmed the woods where his men hid. One shout and they could do their dastardly deed. He licked his lips. *No, you came for Shugart.* He edged closer, and the form standing near the tree transformed into his comrade. He knew it right away when he could make out the flop of stringy hair on the top of his skull.

But each step Wolf took was like a hammer blow to his soul. Every foot nearer exposed the treacherous violence brazenly displayed upon the man's person.

Dark red crusts caked Shugart's body like a funeral shroud. His arms were entirely maroon where the skin had been shaved off him like strips of bacon. White bone was exposed in some areas, forcing bile to rise in Wolf's throat.

Round-headed nails had been driven with force into his palms. The flesh had torn as more and more of his weight was held by his hands. Wolf's breath struggled as he neared the old soldier. The smell was antagonistic, warning Wolf that evil had been done. Nothing moved about the man who had clearly suffered before he died.

Wolf was afraid to see what had been done to the man's face. He was well-versed in what Payne was capable of, and there were no boundaries to his depravity. But Wolf lifted Shugart's head gently as if he were caring for the old man on his deathbed. He owed him that much.

Shugart's head was dead weight, a mere hanging sack of wheat. His lips were swollen and purple, giving them the appearance of fat earthworms. Blank eyes lay open, yet no spark of life was left inside them. A slender line creased his throat where it had been cut like Pratt's.

"I am sorry, old friend," he whispered. "We shall get you home."

With bitter sadness, Wolf holstered his pistol and pulled Shugart's hands free one at a time from the nails pinning them. He lifted the old man, placing him upon his shoulder. His body was much lighter than he looked, merely a bag of bones in flesh. Softly, he turned around to make for his men.

A shadowed form stepped in front of him. Fire danced across his face like the devil had come to make witness. A grin scrawled on his lips as if he were about to charm a lady. "It's good to see you again, Mr. Wolf."

Captain Marshall Payne's cold calculating eyes studied him with not even an ounce of feeling.

Now that this man stood before him, no weapon drawn, Wolf froze. Payne hadn't called to wake his men or sound the alarm. No. He only quietly confronted the intruder to his camp as if they were long lost friends.

Payne's voice held a level of disdain as if he were disappointed. "I see you've been demoted, Colonel?"

"Never was a colonel."

"You never were a colonel?" Payne shook his head, his long curled hair bouncing atop his shoulders. "Now that is regrettable. I thought we had come to a mutually agreeable consensus on the truth."

Wolf's eyes couldn't leave the man. "I will kill you for what you've done to me."

A smirk flirted with Payne's lips. "You were a fun case. How's your back?"

"It'll heal."

"Mmm." Payne's eyes glowed in the dim firelight. "Must still be raw. And the thumbs? I seem to remember a lot of *begging* to keep those thumbs intact."

"Fuck you."

"You have such a mouth on you."

"Step aside and I'll let you live another day."

Payne placed a hand on his chest. "You'll let me live? I do believe you are in my camp, Lieutenant? Or is that a lie too?"

"That's not the only thing I lied about."

Payne's eyebrows narrowed, and the realization about the assassination letter filled him with sudden malice. Something he'd been so sure of was false. "No matter now. The newspapers took care of that."

"No, it matters. You'll die for what you done to me and my men."

"I think not. I am a hard man to kill," Payne said with a soft chuckle.

"Don't matter."

Payne's step forward caused Wolf to tense. He prepared to throw Shugart to the ground and go for his holstered pistol, a move that surely would be slow unless he could toss Shugart's body far enough to disrupt Payne's attention from his draw.

Payne seemed to sense what he was thinking and stopped, cocking his head to the side. "I am eager to find out just how good you are with a blade? Or would you prefer a duel with pistols? You are an intriguingly stubborn fellow."

"It doesn't matter."

"I must say I prefer a good saber duel any day of the week. Much more personal, don't you think?"

Wolf didn't answer. He could care less about a duel. He would kill this wretched man with blades, bullets, or balled fists, the method mattered not. Only that his evil was extinguished.

"Let me pass."

"Now you know I can't let you leave here."

"You will if you want Flora back." It was his only bargaining chip now, and he threw it on the table to see if his opponent bit on it.

"A shrewd negotiator." Payne glanced over his shoulder. "A quick whistle and this camp comes to life. Unlike your friend there." He laughed softly. "Such a holy crusade he was on. Abolishing all the sins of mankind. Such a noble crusader."

Wolf ignored his slanderous words. "You kill me, and you'll never find her."

"Who said anything about killing? You know me. I like to have a conversation."

Sweat trickled down Wolf's back, stinging its way toward his trousers. "If I don't make it back, my men will kill her."

"You truly have the heart of a monster, Lieutenant Wolf, threatening a poor innocent soul like that."

"What if I said you could have both? Free Flora and get your duel?"

Genuine shock enveloped Payne's face. "You would make me a most happy man."

"All you have to do is let me go now."

"You are a fickle one, aren't you? But you have a reputation as a liar. This puts me in quite the predicament. However should I choose?"

"I haven't come alone. Your camp is surrounded."

Payne eyed the darkness with renewed interest. "Then you should have surprised and killed every last one of us. That is if you were a smart man. Instead you came sneaking in like a dirty redskin."

A knife appeared at Payne's throat. The orange flames glinted on the blade. George's face peered over Payne's shoulder.

"Quiet one aren't we?" Payne said lifting his chin even higher to avoid being cut. He lifted his hands in the air. "Perhaps you should finish me now? Unarmed. A knife at my throat. I assure you, the odds will never be better."

Wolf shook his head at his man. "No, George."

George removed the blade and took a step back. Payne rubbed his neck for a moment. "Such a tender caress."

"Tomorrow at 10 a.m. We meet at Davidson Farm. You'll get Flora back and your duel."

Payne showed him white-as-snow teeth. He bowed low to Wolf, sweeping his hat off on the way downward. "Then you and your friend may retire."

Wolf stepped softly past his most vile enemy. His skin prickled and pimpled as he crossed in front of him. Payne's hand snaked out, and he latched onto Wolf's upper arm like a rattlesnake on a warm summer night. He snarled, hissing at him. "Unhand me."

Payne's face closed on Wolf's until he was only a few inches away. Wolf didn't recoil but lifted his chin at the man. "You hear me loud and clear, Wolf. I will hunt down and kill every last one of you." He took a breath, his voice growing in hostility. "You will all die screaming." His eyes became less fierce and his grip loosened. "Keep your word, and I will show them mercy by hanging them as the common criminals they are instead."

"At 10 a.m., you'll get your chance."

Payne released him, a smile back on his devilish lips. "Then I bid you adieu." Wolf took quiet steps away from his mortal enemy.

George grabbed Shugart and together they hurried away from the camp.

The man wouldn't shoot him in the back. No, it wasn't his style. He wanted to be up-close and personal for his rival's death. And the feeling was mutual.

Payne's words drilled into him one by one. "Sleep well, Wolf, for it will be your last."

Chapter Twenty-Seven

Near Midnight, May 10, 1864
Yellow Tavern, Virginia

A fire burned in the tavern's crumbling fireplace. Stone and mortar had chipped and broken away in disrepair, crumbling in pieces on the floor. Bright orange flames leapt from charring logs.

Wolf sat in his chair, his arms folded across his chest. He was done listening to a word Hogan had to say. It seemed that every man had an opinion on the coming battle, and none of it matched his own.

Hogan leaned on the table. "We didn't come all this way to release her on the eve of battle."

Wolf continued to stare at the fire. "You said it yourself. The battle lines are drawn. Sheridan has his set piece match. We done our part."

"He's right, Hogan," said Roberts with a nod for Wolf. "We done enough."

"I say we just kill her and make for Union lines," Adams said, leaning against a support beam. He stuck out his bottom lip and shrugged his shoulders. "Simple enough."

Flora's mouth dropped, appalled by his idea.

"We ain't killing her," Wolf said. He glared at the swarthy man and went back to the crackle of his fire. These men couldn't be trusted to not kill, burn, steal, or rape anything.

"No evidence is the best kind," Adams said. He glanced at Hogan. "If the

Irishman is right, and we are near surrounded by the secesh bastards then I for one don't want to be found with the *Beau Sabreur's* wife."

"You shouldn't. He'll have you shot," Flora added.

Adams pointed a finger in her direction. "You sure we can't gag her?"

"No gag."

"Sergeant Berles," Wolf said across the room.

The German sergeant stood. "Yes."

"On the morrow, you are to take this unit back to Union lines."

Wilhelm's mustache twitched under his nose. He moved to the table. "Why wouldn't their commanding officer lead such a movement?"

Wolf looked up at him. Wilhelm's eyes clung to the truth, yet he forced the words from Wolf's mouth. "Because your commanding officer will not be with you."

"And where will he be?"

Wolf's eyes darted at Flora before he spoke. "I will be delivering that lady back to her husband."

Wilhelm looked away. "This is not something you can do on your own."

"Wrong. This is exactly something I *must* do on my own. Payne will keep his word."

Wilhelm's jaw tightened in anger. "You know that man is vile. He will cheat you the first chance he gets."

"No, he won't. One of us isn't walking away after tomorrow. It's all a game to him. He wants a duel. He'll get one."

"You should not do this alone." Wilhelm shook his head in dissatisfaction. "At the very least take me with you so I can watch your back." His eyes were filled with pain of loss. Loss that was going to be multiplied as he would surely lose his adopted son on this mission. To have lost one child was more than enough. "I cannot follow those orders."

"You will, Sergeant. I won't lead these men to the slaughter because it gives me a better chance at making it out. No. Let me return this woman and kill Payne then I'll find you."

"Yes, sir," Wilhelm said. His words held the weight of doubt.

"You don't have to yes sir me, Wilhelm. Not now."

"Yes, I do. Especially when you give bad orders."

"Bad they may be, but those are my orders."

Wilhelm dipped his head with a slight shake. "You will do well to survive this."

The fire rippled in the fireplace. Payne was a master horseman, deadly with the saber and pistol alike. Wolf was good with a saber but not the best. His training was practical. Survivable. He didn't have years beneath his belt. The first he'd ever held a sword was in training with Wilhelm as his instructor.

"I've watched you train and fight. Remember to use your horse. Your horse can put distance between you and a man. It can also kill a man if used properly."

Wolf listened intently. His horse gave him a distinct mobility that wasn't afforded him on the ground with his own two legs. He thought Sarah would do her part as long as he stayed mounted. If he was unseated, then he would struggle to keep up with his athletic enemy.

Wilhelm continued. "He'll be quick, but he sounds like a man who enjoys the fight. He will feint and jab to test your defenses. Do not fall for these. Always be moving. It makes it harder on your opponent. Sit still and you'll die."

"I will keep what you've said in mind."

"Good. Then I suggest you get some rest."

"You as well. That goes for the rest of you. Get some rest. Roberts, you're on the first watch."

Wilhelm retired to his blanket on the floor. The man settled and laid still. The other men murmured their goodnights, finding places near the fire. Flora moved over to her corner away from the men.

He wasn't ready to sleep just yet. Can one be ready when such a battle commences with the morning sun? How can he sleep knowing it could be his last night? Shouldn't he soak in every second and enjoy every minute since they could be his last? He fed all his swirling thoughts into the flames, letting his mind come to some sort of equilibrium. One must be at peace with their own death to batter down their fear before a mortal contest.

Roberts added a log on the fire and joined him. He pulled out an unlabeled bottle, setting the caramel-colored liquor on the table. He gave Wolf a sheepish grin. "Heard you talking to Wilhelm. Thought maybe you and me could share a bottle." His dark eyes read Wolf fondly but with remorse. This would be the last time to share a drink as brothers until they met again. If they met again. Wolf didn't fool himself to the reality of the coming battle.

"Ain't no Madam Scarlet Grey's, but then again, we can pretend," Roberts said. He tugged the cork from the bottle's lips and pointed it at Wolf. "Here's to you my friend. Escapee of Libby. Savior of Custer. Survivor of Dahlgren's Raid." He took a long pull then wiped his mouth with the back of his sleeve. "Not bad." He handed the bottle off to Wolf.

Wolf tipped the bottle back and let the warm liquid run down his throat but not too much. He'd learned enough from this war to know he didn't want to fight hungover.

"That all? You gone soft on me, Lieutenant? Rank making you lame?"

Wolf slid the bottle back across the table. "No. Just want my mind to be clear for tomorrow."

"No drinks ever hurt us too much, on account of the practice 'n all."

"No, but I can't be slow or foggy. I'm going to fight Payne tomorrow."

"I heard ya. I'll go with you," Roberts averted his eyes with a nod.

"No."

"You can't go this alone. Let your trusty pal ride with you. I ain't scared of dying. I mean I'd rather live. But no man should have to fight alone."

The fire popped, tossing embers into the air. Roberts's death would be on his hands. It would be selfish to keep the man by his side solely because he didn't want to die alone. Why waste so many lives when one will do?

"This journey I must take on my own." He stood. Roberts's eyes followed him, but he was silent. "Tomorrow is a big day. I must try to rest."

"I got this feeling everything is going to be all right." Roberts corked his bottle and kicked his feet up on a chair across from Flora.

Wolf gave him a sad grin. "Me too." He stripped off his black jacket and draped it on his chair. While unbuttoning his shirt, he contemplated the battle he would surely undertake. His thoughts were a bit warmer from the whiskey, but he knew that he would have to be lucky to win. And he hadn't felt super lucky of late. He laid his shirt over his jacket.

The cool air touching his burnt back still stung the fresh skin more than he thought it should, but the shirt rubbing on it all day didn't feel right either. He rolled a blanket on the ground and sat on his bedroll to remove his boots.

"Lieutenant?" came a feminine voice.

Flora approached him. He regarded her coolly. "Yes, ma'am?"

"What happened to your back?"

"Before this I was at Libby Prison." As he looked at her, the tale of untold horror in his blue eyes discomfited her.

"That happened at the prison?" She stood expectantly, blinking in his silence. "At Libby Prison?"

"Yes, it did."

"You were in a fire?"

He sucked in air through his nose, letting it exhale to calm him. "No, ma'am." He tugged off his other boot, setting it alongside its accomplice. He wiggled his toes, feeling the ecstasy of freedom.

She gulped and blinked rapidly as she began to understand his meaning. "You were burned?"

"They wanted information."

Her mouth opened and closed, uncertain of what to say next. "I'm not sure I can believe that. It's so barbaric."

"It's war, ma'am." His eyes met hers. "War's barbaric."

"Who did this? I will have him arrested. My husband will see to it." She lifted her chin in her staunch moral stance.

"He's a captain in Hampton's cavalry."

Her voice dipped in shock. "He's one of my husband's men?"

"I suppose so."

She gulped again. "I will see that he is notified. I'm sure he doesn't know about what has transpired."

"Thank you, ma'am. Tomorrow you'll see him again."

"You have my thanks."

"I don't deserve thanks. We held you against your will."

She gave him a short smile. "You are not forgiven for that."

"Didn't expect you to be the forgiving type." His eyes weighed her reaction.

"I am a righteous woman. I judge a man by his character. Your character is rough, in need of a woman's touch and a preacher's guidance, but I think you can be molded into a gentler man."

His brow creased. "I doubt that. I think it might be too late for me in that regard. I'm married to the army now."

"My husband does both." Her eyes averted with a stab of shame. "There's always rumors and admirers and the letters. I guess that's what comes with being the famous cavalier." She smiled softly, her commanding exterior melting before him exposing a hidden rawness. "Sometimes I feel like a sideshow. Even when our firstborn died, he was reluctant to return home. I needed him the most then." Her eyes watered as she recalled the lonely sadness. "But this war took everything from him, and in turn, it did the same to me."

Wolf was uncomfortable with her openness. After all, this woman had despised him for days and now chose to open up about her relationship with an enemy general. "I. I don't know about that, ma'am."

She wiped the corner of her eye. "Sometimes it's easier with my enemy than with my own people."

"We aren't enemies, ma'am. We're all Americans. This will end one day."

"I surely hope so. None of us have truly gained anything from this disagreement. Reconciliation would be beneficial for all."

"Your father will take his kin back."

"You do not know the extent of it."

"I know that if he is a man with an ounce of sense, he will accept you when this is over."

"We can hope," she said, brushing the corner of her eye. "You know I'm not from the South."

"I do."

"Well, don't you know everything." She gave him an extra glare. "My father was actually from Virginia but stayed with the Union. Jeb says he will continually regret it for the rest of his life."

"A man must live with the decisions he makes."

"One must. I've committed solely to Jeb and Virginia. I have promised to raise our children—" She stopped herself. Wolf could tell the death of her first child still tormented her. "Our children whom you've ripped me from. I promised to raise them in the South no matter the outcome of this conflict."

Wolf didn't know what his future held. If he did survive his duel with Payne, it would most likely lead to more war, more danger, and more death. "I suppose I'll try to reenlist when the war is done. If I can't do that, I'll go home to my family in Michigan."

"I attended boarding school in Detroit." She smiled a bit. "And lived in about every Army fort there was on the frontier."

"I suppose it's the only real place I've ever known. My family went there when they came to this country."

"German?"

"Yes, ma'am."

"Cherish them. They are the only free thing you get in this life." Her words stung him more than she could know. His death in the morning was almost assured. It pained him knowing that it would happen without saying goodbye to his mother and father and sisters. But he had made his farewell with his adoptive military family, and somehow that seemed enough. Enough to let those men live while he dealt with this.

"I do cherish them, ma'am." She could take his words whichever way she saw fit.

"That's both of us. Sacrifice is necessary in these times."

She didn't know how true her words were to him. "Yes, it is. You'll be back to your children tomorrow. I promise it."

She nodded briskly. "You have my thanks for that despite this situation."

"I must rest, ma'am. Tomorrow will be long."

"Me as well." She stood looking down at him for an extra moment.

He settled on his blanket keeping his back from touching it. "Goodnight, Mrs. Stuart."

"Goodnight, Lieutenant Wolf."

Chapter Twenty-Eight

Midnight, May 10, 1864
Near Yellow Tavern, Virginia

Payne's men camped along the edge of a forested ridge. He'd thought it wise to make a new camp despite the darkness. His men didn't complain. Settling into a new location within striking distance of the Davidson Farm gave him peace of mind. He knew full well that Wolf was a devious foe. The boy was a lying scoundrel that would find his end in a long-drawn-out scream.

Rebel cavalry had been arriving in exhausted companies and squadrons over the past hour as Payne and his men watched. The men staggering in were a haggard lot. Even their beasts lowered their heads, ready to lie down and sleep like the dead. Not a man among them looked prepared for a fight, let alone a battle.

A burly bald major with arms that looked like he could strangle a bull joined him at his fire. "How'd you boys get ahead of us? I thought we were the van?"

"We were on a reconnaissance mission for Stuart."

The major grunted and massaged his mustache in irritation. "I thought we were running reconnaissance for Stuart."

Irritated, Payne put on a fake smile. "You know the general always puts out all his feelers. Will he be here soon?"

"He's a few miles back with General Lomax."

"Excellent. I am sure he'll want to speak with me."

The major lifted thin eyebrows. "You got something for us?"

"Nothing that would concern you."

"You think you're special or something, Captain?" The major's brow creased. "If there's something I need to know, you better well spit it out."

Payne sighed. "You'd best put out some pickets. There's an army headed this way."

The major shook his head. "Say, what outfit you from?"

"Hampton's."

"Figures. I oughta flog you right here and now. Unorthodox bastards."

Payne got to his feet and a stunted smile curved on his lips. "Are you sure that's a good idea?"

The major browsed the red-shirted men snoozing around the fire. Recognition washed over him like an ocean wave. "Wait, you're a part of the Red Shirts?"

"The one and only. Captain Marshall Payne at your service," he said, with a slight bow.

"I spoke too soon." The major rubbed the top of his head in a nervous gesture for a man so powerfully built. "It's been a long night. My boys are tired and hungry. Haven't eaten a whole meal in a couple of days." His hard eyes pled for forgiveness.

"You did speak too soon."

Narrowing his eyes, the major's cheeks reddened. He'd been slighted and tried to backtrack to save face, and his rival had basically spit on him. "You would do well to check your tone, Red Shirt or not."

"I will do as I please."

"This insult will not go unpunished."

"Payne!" came a shout.

Major General Stuart, with his plumed slouch hat, followed closely by the tall Brigadier General Lomax came riding into view trailed by a host of aides and adjuncts. Stuart was off his horse in a heartbeat. "My God, it is good to see you." He raced straight for Payne, and Payne gave him a slight bow.

Stuart's worried eyes scanned the campsite. His voice lowered. "Do you have her?"

Payne blinked. The answer was painfully obvious, but he entertained the man all the same. "I do not."

The major could hardly contain himself at such an opportunity to rectify Payne's insubordination. "General, sir. He has insulted me. This captain is a disgrace to the uniform."

Stuart raised a gloved hand into the major's face. "If you know what is good for you, you will hold your tongue."

"But, sir. This captain—"

Stuart spun on the major. "You, sir, will stand down now!" His eyes darted at his subordinate. "General Lomax."

Brigadier General Lunsford Lomax was one of Fitzhugh Lee's brigade commanders. He had beard-covered cheeks that held extra weight. His eyes were deeply set in his face over a hooked nose. His coat was unbuttoned, and his eyes flashed to quick retributive anger over his corps commander's words.

"Major Tunstall, you will cease your disruption now!"

The major's eyes ran from Stuart to Payne in fury then back to his commander. "Sir," he hissed.

The man should let this go, Payne thought.

Lomax pointed out to the forest. "Major, get your men formed into pickets in those trees running north to south along Telegraph Road."

"We are exhausted," Tunstall retorted. His voice and confidence grew softer, each rebuke damaging both his pride and his confidence.

"We are all exhausted. Do it or risk court-martial."

Tunstall lifted his chin and gulped. "Yes, sir." He eyed Payne with seething anger. "Captain. We will meet again."

"I am held in suspense while I await such a pleasure."

Tunstall marched away under the angry eyes of the generals.

Stuart shook his head. He removed his hat and wiped an errant strand of hair from his forehead. "What news have you, Payne?"

"I have made contact with said Federal brigands."

"You have?" Stuart's eyes lit up again, widening with eager concern.

"I have, sir. Killed a few. They do in fact have your wife."

"Has any harm befallen her?"

"I do not know, but I do not believe they have brought her harm."

Stuart removed his gloves, tucking them into his belt. "Of all the times in my life I have resisted the temptations of alcohol, I would love a drink right now."

"I can have that arranged, sir," Payne offered. "Turner!"

His sergeant peered from the campfire.

"Bring the general a bottle." Turner rummaged through a pack on the ground.

Lomax averted his eyes at the forwardness of Payne, and Stuart waved off the offer. "No, no. I need a clear head. It's already so hard to focus with the thought of Flora in those heathens' hands. Unspeakable treachery."

"It is, sir. Most unfortunate." It was unfortunate for her. Very fortunate for Payne. He now had the opportunity to slay that lying bastard once and for all. Wolf couldn't have more than twenty men with him. Two were gone now. Fool. He would capture them all and cut them apart piece by piece. He may even let Stuart take a few shots at the men. It would garner good favor with the clearly distraught husband and sate his vengeful appetite.

"Well, what did they say?" Stuart asked.

"We are meeting in the morning."

Stuart didn't give him a chance to continue. "I will accompany you."

Payne gave him a wary grin. "I am not sure that is wise. It could be an ambush, and we cannot let anything happen to you."

"No, I am going," Stuart said with a dismissive shake of his head.

Lomax used the opportunity to step in. "If you would excuse me, Jeb, we have to make a plan for tomorrow. Sheridan is coming this way."

"Goddamn these men," Stuart said.

"I would agree, sir. You have a war to run. Let me handle these brigands and see your lovely wife returned to you."

Stuart sighed. "I've asked so much of these men over the past week. My boys are exhausted. It took everything we had to get out in front of Sheridan and between him and Richmond." He rubbed the side of his neck.

"Bring me a courier. We will need Richmond's help."

Lomax turned and waved one of Stuart's aides forward. A fierce looking young man, both muscular and tall, approached.

"Henry, ride to Richmond and ask General Bragg for any men he can spare. I want them to ensnare the Federals in a pincer if we can. Clear?"

"Yes, sir."

"You may, go," Stuart said, waving the man off. Then he gestured at Lomax. The general bent close to Stuart.

"Lomax, as your men arrive, I want them to defend along Telegraph Road. As Sheridan comes down Brook Turnpike, we can defend, and when Wickham arrives, we can hit his flanks or rear. He won't expect it." He forcefully locked eyes with Lomax to ensure he completely understood. "Pickets in the woods in front. Stretch them out as far as we can afford. We'll give them a fight." He made a straight line with his arm in the air. "Wickham will form at a ninety-degree angle on your right along that ridge. When Griffin's battery gets here, he will center our position. We have to give everyone time to catch up and hopefully sneak a moment's rest."

The man truly was magnificent to watch. His mastery of the battlefield and positioning his men even under stress was something of legend. Payne was impressed, something he wasn't often.

"Yes, sir," Lomax said with a nod. "I will get my men into place as they arrive."

"Very good." Stuart turned back to Payne. His eyes blinked back uncertainty. "I'm coming in the morning."

"Of course, sir, but do you think it wise?"

Stuart ground his teeth. "Where is the meeting?"

"Davidson Farm, a mile or so east of here."

Stuart called up to the heavens, seeking an answer to his dilemma. "I am torn between my honor and my duty, life and brotherhood. It is a torturous time."

Payne slithered forward. "Hampton lets me handle these types of *irregular* events. I can assure you of my success in retaining her." The last thing Payne wanted was Stuart interfering in his duel. He would never stand for it. Stuart would as soon capture Wolf or murder him as to let Payne satisfy himself on this man. No, it would never work to have Stuart there.

"We will see how feisty those Yanks are in the morning. You will find me before you depart?"

"Of course, sir."

Stuart put a hand over his heart. "You have my thanks. This causes me great anguish."

"You and me both. A pleasure to serve such a noble cause."

Stuart gave him a nod and a smile. "Captain, I will promote you when this is done. You are far too valuable to keep as a captain. Major or Colonel?"

Payne pressed a hand to his chest. "You are too kind. I would worry about my activities. I am a specialized soldier needing neither rank nor praise to satisfy my needs."

"We may need even more men like you before this war is over. Let's give you at least a squadron, a regiment, if we can find the men."

Payne bowed his head. "I am humbled by your faith."

"And I by your dedication to healing a man's wounded heart." Stuart slightly bowed his head and left him.

Payne walked back to his campfire, settling in. He leaned against a tree. The soft clops of horses' hooves competed with the crackle of fire as more and more horsemen arrived.

He would feign ignorance and forget his meeting with Stuart. It was the only way to get the duel and rescue the wife. If a promotion came with his success, the victory would be that much sweeter.

The fire rippled and waved in the night, and he watched the flames glow without blinking. In the fiery depths, he witnessed a great struggle and a great victory.

Chapter Twenty-Nine

Morning, May 11, 1864
Near Yellow Tavern, Virginia

"Alexander, where is Hampton's captain?"

His aide appeared squeamish at the question. The man always had a faint look to him, but this was more than normal as if he'd eaten a rancid piece of meat and now his stomach roiled.

Alexander Boteler had always had a weak constitution and held himself more like a whipped dog than would seem soldierly, but he was one of the most intelligent men Stuart had met. He was the kind of man that needed to be kept off the frontline because his value far superseded his martial prowess despite his desire to serve.

His aide edged his spectacles onto the bridge of his nose before he spoke. "I sent Lieutenant Wendell to find him this morning, and he said they were gone."

"They were gone?"

"Yes, sir, the Red Shirts."

Stuart ground his teeth, flaring his nostrils. "I told the man to wait. I told him to wait. Is Henry nearby?"

"You sent him to Richmond early this morning to hurry the Home Guard troops along."

Stuart nodded as it came back to him. His actions felt like they were on a predetermined course. He made moves and issued orders, but it was as if he weren't actually there. Almost as if he observed everything from a detached omnipotent state.

Major General Fitzhugh Lee was saddled nearby. He was a stout man with a long pointed beard. His eyes bugged out a bit, and now they were encircled with the darkest shade of puffiness saved for an incredibly tired man, a man who'd barely slept in days.

Fitzhugh, or Fitz as the men called him, was Robert E. Lee's nephew and through that superior distinction, he had the pedigree for military success. His command of the battlefield showed an astute mind for war, and sometimes Stuart was surprised that Marse Robert hadn't reversed their roles. He didn't know if it was something that Lee had seen in Stuart himself as a young man that had catapulted him into his unrivaled position or if a sequence of daring victories and excellent press coverage had propelled him forward to his position of trust.

"Jeb, the rest of my command under Wickham is coming down this road now," Fitz Lee said.

"In a moment," Stuart said, turning away from Fitz's questioning stare.

"Did Payne say anything? Where?" His mind was still a tired blur, running on a horrible repeat of worry for his wife. He could hardly remember what was said despite how hard he tried.

"Something about a nearby farm. North and east of Yellow Tavern. Davidson Farm."

"That old run-down building south of here?"

"I suppose, sir."

"Goddamn that man." He turned toward Fitz again. The general was clearly waiting for orders, but Stuart continued his preoccupation with Payne. "You know Hampton will be held responsible for this man's actions. I will see to that."

"Sir? Where should my men deploy?"

Stuart glared at him again. *This extremely capable general keeps demanding my input. He should know better. But that damn Payne.* "The insubordination of his actions. Damn him," he muttered.

"Sir?" Fitz said. His bugging eyes narrowed in worry. "Sheridan is close."

"Dammit man, don't you see what I'm going through? My wife has been snatched by vile Yankee brigands, and that upstart Sheridan is breathing down my neck."

Fitz averted his eyes, readjusting himself in his saddle. He moved his slouch hat beneath his other arm. A storm was coming in more ways than one. Slate-gray clouds collected overhead, and the Union soldiers were driving farther south.

"Fitz, per Stuart's previous orders, Wickham's boys must go on my command's right. We have the Baltimore Light Artillery in a good position here," said Lomax. Although born in Rhode Island, he was a descendent of one of Virginia's founding families. He had been classmates with Fitz at the United States Military Academy at West Point, and the men worked extremely well together.

They'd beaten Sheridan to Richmond because of his leisurely pace. Stuart's swiftness had served dual purposes though. One of which was to search for his wife, and now when he was so close, the man who knew her whereabouts had disappeared with the rising sun.

"We have a favorable position," Stuart added. "But we aren't ready to give battle yet. We must wait for Gordon's return. Three brigades versus three divisions. Perhaps they'll write a song about us. Will our man Sam Sweeney do it?" He scanned the men around him but didn't see his musically talented banjo-playing orderly.

Waiting for Gordon was the only realistic way to defend. Otherwise they would have to give ground until they reached the earthen walls around Richmond or reinforcements showed.

Gordon's men had served valiantly at the Battle for the Wilderness. The smoke-shrouded forests combined with the yellow fires and the buzz of bullets were enough to break a man even after he had drunk a gallon of water and escaped the place. It had been a burning hell.

Their movements had been frantic as they trailed Sheridan. In Stuart's rush south, he'd left a part of his command. Gordon had done his part by severely delaying Sheridan's thirteen-mile corps. They had faded away as quickly as they'd attacked. His men engaged and had done their part to the point of exhaustion, but he would ask more from them.

His towering aide, Henry McClellan came riding up, sitting tall upon his horse. He was a fierce young man with piercing eyes. His mount danced beneath him, its chest heaving from the ride. "Sir, I have a message from Richmond."

"Yes?"

"General Bragg reports he has adequate men at his disposal for defense. He can send at least Hunton's Brigade to assist, but they will take some time to arrive."

"How long?"

"By midday."

Stuart sighed. "Send him my thanks and hurry them along." He tugged his beard. He was outnumbered three to one, poor odds even for his resilient men. An additional brigade would tip the odds ever so slightly back toward him if they held their position and struck hard when the time came. He may be able to significantly damage the enemy cavalry, but he couldn't help but question if he'd made the right decision. *Have I made a mistake rushing here with only a third of my men?*

The questioning thought confused him. He wasn't an unsure man. He had always been decisive. He'd made a career from making lightning decisions in the heat of battle and bold maneuvers. That was how legends were made. And now he was in shambles with moments of clarity. His mind was foggy and unclear. Worry stabbed his gut repeatedly like a long bayonet. It was a feeling he hadn't experienced much even during this war, and now it controlled and steered him like someone else held his reins.

He was plagued by worry for his wife. But another stressor overshadowed even that. It was an overwhelming sense of dread. His last days were coming. He could feel it deep inside his soul. This war would take him into death's cold hollow bosom.

When a man felt his demise looming, it always was a harbinger of ill. Deep in the marrow of his bones he felt the impending doom. It was almost a premonition fit for an ancient seer.

He'd spoken to Hampton about it passively as gentlemen would, only an offhand remark to mask the worry. All men must die, and if you must go early, then there is no better way than in the service of your beloved Virginia.

"If Wickham goes along the ridge, we will form a Y along Telegraph road." Fitz said. "I understand that. Then Sheridan will be forced to address us in pieces where we can hammer his flanks. Perhaps capture his whole command."

Stuart eyed them. He had duties to his nation. He could never reunite with the Union. His nation would live, or it would die on his shoulders. He ran a hand over his hair, joining the men. "Yes, yes, Fitz. Well done. That is what I had in mind."

Fitz regarded him with tired chocolate brown eyes. "Thank you, Jeb." He looked like he would say something else before settling on. "I am sorry about Flora. Hampton's men are some of the best. If she can be found—"Fitz said. He gulped.

"She *will* be found, Fitz."

Fitz lowered his eyes for a moment for fear of hurting his commander and friend. All his trusted commanders knew now. They were all so close. Lomax stood a bit straighter, getting rigid under the weight of an uncomfortable situation.

"Of course she will, sir. The Yanks will pay for their dishonorable actions," Lomax said.

Have I focused too much on my wife and not the coming battle? His men were some of the finest soldiers in the war, but they needed their leader. His doubt in his own command made him squeamish.

Stuart shook his head, trying to orient himself. "It's a good position. Fitz, make sure Wickham hurries. If you can get word to Gordon, make sure he comes even faster. I will not retreat to Richmond." Retreat was not in his wartime vocabulary. He hated anything that looked weak in front of the enemy. Sure, placing his men behind earthen walls and harassing Sheridan's men was a path to success, but it looked weak, and he couldn't stand the thought of weakness. He wasn't going to leave his wife in the clutches of evil men while he hid behind a wall.

"I want pickets and skirmishers in those woods about four hundred yards from Lomax's men. The battery will hold the center. It will have clear shots on them if they push back our skirmishers. We'll force Sheridan to commit here, and as the reinforcements arrive, he will be pinned between our two forces. Then the fun can begin."

Fitz gave him a short smile. "This is good, Jeb."

Stuart flashed a smile he didn't feel inside. "This will do while we find my wife."

***

He rode with Lomax along the length of Lomax's Brigade lining the Telegraph Road south. Carbine fire popped off inside the woods ahead of his position. The battery at the center waited patiently to fire upon the Federals after their own men were clear. Between the picketed forest and his wooded position along the road was a field of three-inch corn and a land in full bloom. A land about to be devastated by war.

A bullet screamed past, cracking a tree behind them. All the men ducked down. "I see Sheridan's boys have started to roll in," Stuart said. The gnaw of his missing wife ate at his soul as he let himself be seen by his men. The bullet pulled him slightly closer to reality, focusing his dull senses.

Lomax's skirmishers were in a mad dash for friendly lines. Men in butternut and gray didn't even bother to shoot back as they sprinted. Dismounted blue-coated men barely visible moved through the forest and settled on hesitantly lining the edge of the trees. Death awaited them over the open field before they reached his men along the road.

"Fire that cannon!" Lomax called over.

A shot rumbled forth from the battery. The shell sailed into the tops of tree canopies then exploded with a loud pop. Leaves, blooming buds, and metal fragments rained down on the Union men beneath the trees. A few fell screaming to the ground, shrapnel having pierced their flesh.

Two more cannons boomed from Griffin's Baltimore Light Artillery, showering the men in the trees. Pulling his field glasses from their case, he eyed southwest of their position.

More Federal cavalry were arriving and shifting into formation. Sheridan was beginning to reveal himself in whole. *Damn, I need Gordon here. Two brigades won't be enough.* He checked one of the flags.

The Union Army had settled on conforming their standards and flags, making it easier to communicate on the field of battle. It also made it easier for their enemy to know who they were dealing with.

First Division, Second Brigade. Must be Devin. Formidable cavalryman. Not quite on par with his men but stout. He would admit the enemy had gotten better over the course of the war, but that only meant his men must perform to an even higher standard.

In the same direction as Devin's men lay the abandoned Yellow Tavern and much farther to the east Davidson Farm, the last known location of Payne and, God willing, Flora. He still hadn't heard anything, each painful minute ticking onward battering his heart and soul.

Skirmishers were reaching their respective commands. A few were bloodied. They spit white foam from dry mouths and guzzled water from canteens, their chests heaving. Black soot covered their faces, and most looked ready to keel over to embrace the ground in exhaustion.

"Be a ton of the bluebellies over there," said one. He smeared sweaty gunpowder residue over his forehead with the back of his hand. "Whole ton. Came at us like wild Comanches," he breathed. He turned back, seeing his commanding officers. "Sir!" he said, removing a brown farmer's hat.

Stuart eyed him angrily, pointing with his field glasses. "You rally here, soldier. You make them pay for every inch of ground."

The man straightened shouldering his rifle. "We will, sir!"

"I'd rather be whipped than give this ground! You hear me?"

"Yes, sir!" came a chorus of shouts.

"They're forming on our flank," came a shout from farther down Lomax's line of dismounted cavalry.

Stuart turned his field glasses in that direction, but he didn't need them to see the threat. Hundreds of sabers glittered in the sun like sparkling diamonds. The dazzling mounted force trotted their horses within a few hundred yards of their left flank.

Spurring his horse, he rode in their direction. "Wheel that line!" he shouted, gesturing madly. The 6th Virginia boys began to realize they were in danger. Heads turned away from the enemy in front to view the enemy forming on their flank.

"Wheel that line!" he called again.

A lieutenant gawked in confusion in his direction. Stuart jabbed his hand wildly at the advancing enemy. As if the rival horseman saw him trying to rally his troops, a high-pitched bugle sounded the charge. It was an upbeat and choppy sound, one to inspire bravery in the face of danger.

The lieutenant turned when hundreds of hooves announced the coming storm of sabers and bullets. His men scrambled to reposition in a cut along the road. They were painfully slow in their adjustment. Stuart drew his pistol, slowing his horse. He pulled the reins, and his mount made a circle. He twisted in his saddle to keep his eyes on the charging enemy.

He pointed at the dismounted cavalrymen from the 5th Virginia, who anchored the center of Lomax's line. If the 6th was routed, they could be as well, but if they formed properly, they could withdraw in some semblance of order. Chaos destroyed an army. Order maintained it. "Wheel ninety degrees. Defend your flank!" He needed time to adjust Lomax's line.

Colonel Pate of the 5th took up his orders and called to his men, "One more round, boys, then we'll get to the ridge." He gave a quick glance at Stuart. His eyes said one thing: you are asking me to die here. You are asking me to get my men slaughtered. Pate turned back toward the enemy. His sword was drawn, and he understood that their stand would blunt the Yankee charge with flesh and blood.

The 6th Virginia scrambled past Pate's men, who held their fire for fear of hitting their own. Everything worked in the enemy horsemen's favor, giving them time to charge without suffering losses.

The Yankees whipped their horses, gaining on the fleeing men. A few swung shining sabers into those too slow as they passed by, and their steeds ate the ground like locomotives at full speed.

Pate's men were quick to obey, assembling and forming nearly as quick as the galloping horsemen. They were experienced soldiers. But they didn't have time to breathe before the enemy was too close or make sure the hammer was cocked or finish a reload and aim at the enemy.

Within seconds, the blue wave poured into the cut like a flood. Mounted men urged their horses among Pate's, swinging madly with sabers into the rebels.

The back of Pate's skull exploded as a pistol bullet blew it out. He crumpled over himself backward. Then the slaughter began. Hooves trampled his men. The dull thud of sabers atop heads repeated itself over and over. A horse screamed as a man stabbed it with his sword, sending its rider to the ground.

Stuart grimaced. *I sacrificed them for the Cause.* He lined his LeMat pistol on his enemies, nine shots total, not including the underneath smoothbore, short-barreled, 16 gauge single-shot shotgun. A flip of a lever on the hammer and the gun would fire the lower barrel, sending pellets screaming at anyone in close range. He fired a single shot and then another.

Smoke clouded his vision, but a rider flinched, and he was satisfied with the result. The battle was quick, and he turned his horse around as to not get separated from his own men. *How could I have not seen this coming? No matter, we must adapt.*

A yell went out from the opposing tree line, drawing Stuart's attention away from the road. A squadron of dismounted cavalrymen charged forth toward Lomax's line. A golden-haired man urged them onward but within distance of Wickham's men. "Brave fellow," Stuart muttered. "Trying to roll us up."

The cries of Pate's men chased him along. Some fled. Others still fought. Stuart galloped along the rear of Lomax's line. "Hold the line! Hold the line!" His aide was by his side.

"Get that battery to push them back in the center." Boteler disappeared in a cloud of dust as he made the half-mile to the guns. He would apply pressure to the center of Custer's dismounted men. When they fell back, it would leave the men flanking Stuart exposed. The flankers would be forced to retreat or risk a thrashing. *Perhaps I can bring the 1st Virginia up and rout them?* He hated the idea of using his reserves so early in the day, but if things continued to go poorly, he would do as he must. They would have to concede Telegraph Road and reposition on the ridge.

The 6th Virginia was attempting to reform behind the blood and guts of the 5th. The 15th was concerned about protecting their flank while defending themselves from the assault in front. *That bold bastard Custer.* But if Lomax's boys were repositioned, eventually Wickham would be able to pressure Custer's dismounted men to withdraw.

He found Lomax near the 15th Virginia. "Make for the ridge," he shouted. Bullets thudded in the trees around them, buzzing as they passed. The dismounted 15th returned fire with more Federals sneaking across the field.

"Sir, we must get you to a safer location," Garnett, another aide, shouted.

"Make for the ridge. Set your defense there in line with Wickham's new line."

Buzzzzz! A bullet whip-snapped past his ear. *That one was close.* He sucked in air greedily. The snap always meant it was close. *Was that the one meant for me? Will they get closer and closer?*

"Sir, this isn't safe," Lomax agreed. "You should ride ahead."

"Not to worry. You'll be fine, Lomax. Carry out my orders. Don't let them reach Richmond."

Lomax blinked his deep-set eyes. "Of course, sir. We won't."

"Look, sir!" Garnett said. He pointed out at the field. The Baltimore Light Battery was laying excellent fire, and the Yanks in the center were retreating for cover. Stuart surveyed the length of Telegraph Road. Those Yanks knew it too. They were disengaging with the 5th and riding away.

All of his men that were left carried themselves back down Telegraph Road toward the ridge. The Yankees maneuvered in the opposite direction, a host of prisoners under guard as they fell back.

"Reform them on the ridge. Protect the battery. They are a favorite of mine." He glanced that way looking for them. "It's a good position. Trust your judgment, it is sound."

Lomax squinted in confusion. "Yes, sir? I don't understand, sir."

Boteler returned appearing unstable atop his mount. "The battery is trained on them, sir."

"Very well then, good sir." Stuart cocked his head to the side. He could hear the faint ringing of church bells. "Infantry from Richmond are on their way. Good luck!"

Stuart yanked his reins toward the Davidson Farm. He would not, no he could not let his honor be besmirched by classless Yankee bandits. It was downright deplorable. *These men grow bold while I am forced to battle them and my fears for my love.*

"Sir? We retreat to the ridge."

"Boteler and Garnett, with me," he yelled at his aides. The two men exchanged looks with one another.

He galloped his horse along the rear of a humble ridge running perpendicular to Telegraph Road with his aides trailing behind him.

Chapter Thirty

Morning, May 11, 1864
Near Yellow Tavern, Virginia

Overhead morning clouds threatened to storm. A breeze followed along, daring to grow into a wind. Leaves rustled around them fresh and green, shaking under the unseen currents.

"Smells like rain," he said to Flora. They were alone in the gray morning light.

"It does."

Every time the sound of carbine fire rippled to the northwest she would eye that direction nervously. It was accented by the low rumble from artillery. There were only a few bass drums of death, pounding out their morbid march. It was nothing like the earth-shattering barrage on the third day of Gettysburg. Her worried eyes searched for shells and balls heading for them. But nothing came their way.

Hoof thunder in the distance as mounted men repositioned themselves worried Wolf more. A random patrol from Union or Confederate forces could pose an obstacle. So much so, every time they heard riders, he would lead them off the path and wait for the rhythmic beating of hooves to pass. The riders, friend or foe, would never even notice them in the forest. Then they would carry on.

"Is the battle close?" Flora asked.

"Close enough." They continued to ride in silence, the battle serenading them from afar. Wolf's eyes continually scanned for anyone and anything in the distance.

"Are we in danger?" she added. The woman was clearly worried and rightfully so. An errant cannon shot sailing overhead could explode, impaling them with jagged shrapnel. A sharpshooter could think them officers or the enemy and take careful aim, sending bullets through their skulls. And depending on which side they ran into, they could mistake them for the enemy. A woman would most likely stay a soldier's hand, but Wolf might be done for, friend or foe.

"No, ma'am. Not much. The battle is about a mile away."

"Can a cannon shoot over a mile?"

Wolf cocked his head to the side. "There are guns that can shoot over a mile. Pennington could shoot a shell through a window from that distance, or so they claimed. Can't say I seen it."

"But there are guns that could shoot that far?"

Wolf shrugged. "Yes, ma'am."

"So we could be in danger."

"Suppose we are." He briefly regarded her with a fraction of amusement. "It would have to be a mighty lucky shot, ma'am."

She visibly relaxed. Their horses' hooves clip-clopped the ground on the path they traveled. Hogan was sure if they rode east until they found a creek then followed that north, they would reach the Davidson Farm. After following the creek for some time, they exited the timber and entered an overgrown field.

Stunted grass grew in the field, swaying back and forth in the wind. With no trees to deflect the wind, it ran unchecked over the land. The tree line cut north at a ninety-degree angle where the farmer's land must have ended. The timber grew like a natural fence. Then on the far side of the field, stood the Davidson Farmhouse.

His eyes found the single horseman standing motionless in the distance. His coat was gray along with his slouch hat. The red of his shirt was brazen and vibrant, sticking out like a lone rose in a field of dying wheat.

"Is that him?" Flora asked.

"I believe it is. Do not be afraid, but there will be violence here today."

"Would you break your promise of my freedom?"

Visions of the hot poker hovering near his flesh almost made him puke. He daydreamed of ramming his sword into Payne's gut. "When this is over, I will return you to your people."

She lifted her chin, satisfied with his answer. "You are a reprehensible man. No gentleman. But no man has brought me harm in your care. And I wish you perseverance over this man despite his association with my husband's army."

The rider began to trot toward them. Wolf tracked him, unbuckling the flap over his pistol.

"Thank you, my lady. Glad we aren't leaving on poor terms."

She gave him a terse nod with her chin, yet her eyes watched the tarnished man who'd come to rescue her. Freedom lingered on the edges, bringing her to an outward peace.

The rider came closer. His brown locks flowed as the wind whipped them about. His fine gray officer's jacket was unbuttoned to reveal his blood-red shirt underneath, a signature of his elite company. His sleeves were cuffed in yellow, and a scrolled yellow braid traveled to his elbow, designating him as an officer.

The braid followed a French design. It was thinner than those officers holding higher rank and thicker than those officers holding lower rank. When he drew even closer, Wolf could see the three yellow bars on his collar designating him as a captain. A maroon sash was wrapped around his waist.

Every inch of him oozed aristocratic confidence. He smiled under a finely groomed goatee when he stopped his horse. "My lady," Payne said, with charm thick enough to suffocate a man. When he addressed Wolf, his voice turned mocking. "Lieutenant Wolf."

"I've brought her as arranged. She will be escorted to safety after our personal affair is decided."

"No, no, Wolf. Our affair is not personal, it's only business."

"What was your business, Captain?" Flora asked, her voice filled with conviction.

Payne grinned at her, avoiding her question. "My business here today is to escort you back to your husband. After I slay this woefully lacking criminal."

She pressed him further. "Are you not responsible for greater crimes?"

Payne's eyes flashed and only cruelty remained. "Our little pup has been telling tales. I assure you that was interrogation. We needed answers so we expedited the process."

"I've seen his back, Captain. Is that your handiwork?"

"My lady, you've seen his naked flesh? I know your husband has many *admirers*, but who would have thought his wife would be one in kind with Jezebel?"

Flora's cheeks reddened like she'd been outside too long in winter. "Nothing indecent happened."

"I'm sure the papers will take your side of the story."

"Jeb will believe me."

Payne cocked his head a bit to the side. "If only you believed him."

"Do not speak to me of my husband. I will be telling him of your actions here."

"It would be a shame if you were hurt during this duel," Payne said, smiling at her.

Her eyes went wide. "How dare you! You...you are no savior, but a monster in fine clothes."

"I am but a tool for the Southern Cause." He gave a slight bow. "But if harm befouls you, it is this renegade's transgressions that have caused it through no fault of my own. Alas, it is the truth."

"Enough, Payne. Do not threaten her in my presence. Her safety has been assured."

Turning his way, Payne squinted. "Has it?"

"It was agreed on that you get Flora and I get my duel."

"So eager for the next world, Lieutenant? Usually men cling to their pitiful existence a bit longer, breathing the fresh country air. Heart beating. Blood pumping."

"You must promise her safety if I fall."

"I can make no promises."

Wolf studied this treacherous man. He was as charming as he was depraved. He peeked at Flora from the corner of his eyes. She had paled with the talk of her potential harm from the man who'd come to rescue her.

She settled her hands on the pommel of her saddle. "Lieutenant, I wish you luck against this man."

"You have my thanks. No harm will befall you while I still stand."

"And yet you will fall, Wolf. I have been trained in the art of saber fighting since I was old enough to hold a sword. Some may call me a champion of sorts," Payne said. With a quick hand, he drew his barely curved cavalry sword from its sheath; it screamed as it was released from its prison.

It was a custom blade much finer than the Union cavalry standard M1860 sabers. It shone despite the clouds overhead, its metal slightly oiled and both edges sharp. "My father had this made for me in Spain. I believe the town is known as Toledo." He held the sword outward, marveling in its beauty. "As light as it is beautiful. Been blooded plenty of times too." He shouldered the weapon with a smile. "Whenever you are ready, Mr. Wolf."

Wolf's heart picked up a beat in his chest. It was always like this before any kind of fight. There was anger there too. It burned in him like Payne searing his flesh, bubbling around the edges and eating his insides until it would burst from him hot, bright, and violent.

It was a pain that needed to be unleashed upon someone, and this man, no, this animal in man's flesh, deserved all of Wolf's rage.

Wolf tore his saber from its sheath. The sword sang its song with a loud *shashing*. He rotated it in a circle back and forth to warm up his wrist and shoulder.

"On foot is customary," Payne said, gesturing wide with his saber. He tilted his head, glancing at Wolf's leg. "Hmm. But doesn't look like you could perform on foot. No matter, horseback will do."

Wolf ignored the man's insults. "Flora. When the duel starts, ride away from here and don't look back."

She nodded her head brusquely.

He gripped his saber's hilt. The leather was smooth yet worn beneath the skin of his palm; the weight of the sword was both balanced and light. It would be his tool for dispatching this vile man. He pointed the sword at his enemy. "Payne, it's time."

He didn't wait for a response but kicked his mount's flanks. "Ja!" Wolf called. He absorbed the horse's sudden change in stride. Payne's eyes alighted in a fierce delight as he spurred his mount.

The distance between the two men was short, and it was only a moment before their swords met with a clang. The blades crashed into one another like a blacksmith's hammer pounding an anvil. The men shifted and when their blades met again, it sent shivers through Wolf's wrist.

Payne steered his mount past Wolf, and Wolf rolled his wrist in reverse as he passed. He was not above stabbing this man in the back, and his lunge missed. The blade swooshed through the air with no jacket or flesh meeting its edge.

Wolf tugged Sarah's reins to face his opponent, and as Payne was already there, the luxurious blade darted across his body. *The bastard is already here*, his mind barely managed to eke out, before he had to dodge another attack.

Ducking low near Sarah's mane, Wolf felt Payne's sword twisting back over his head, swiping dangerously down at an angle. The air from the blade's razor edge cooled over Wolf's head and neck. He raised his sword again only to defend himself. Now only capable of bitter defense, he desperately deflected another series of attacks.

Every attack was precise. Spurring Sarah, he rode away for a moment. *He's excellent.* He needed to catch his breath and settle his mind. Only luck was keeping him here on the battlefield.

Payne turned his horse gracefully and grinned at Wolf. Taking a deep breath, Wolf shouted, "Get out of here, Flora!"

She urged her horse toward the farm, and he didn't bother to watch her. He held his sword over his mount's head and kicked her hard.

"I'll grab her when we're done here," Payne called.

Muscles rippled in the horses' flesh as both riders picked up speed. Payne skillfully pointed his saber at Wolf. It was the best way to pierce an opponent while keeping the sword pointed in a direction to avoid ones' comrades while charging the enemy.

In a rank-and-file cavalry charge, there was no space for wielding the sword about safely. At least in the initial charge after you struck home with the enemy, swinging was unavoidable. But while riding at full gallop, it was the easiest way to break an enemy. It required no timing. Only pointing. A skilled rider could slash or crush a man's skull as he rode by, but it was more of a guessing game, and he had to ensure he didn't strike his mount by mistake.

He stayed hunched over his horse, Payne matching him stride for stride. When the men neared one another, Payne turned his sword outward, shifting himself in his saddle. Wolf went painfully past, his point reaching nothing but air. He slowed Sarah down and circled his horse back around.

A wetness ran along his side down and into his pants. At first, he thought it must be sweat. Then the pain started to ebb with the flow. It wasn't bad; his blood boiled too hot for pain, but it burned all around the same area. He felt his ribs through his jacket.

His fingers explored a slice in his coat, through his shirt, and found the long and thin split skin that lay underneath. His own blood was warm on his fingertips like a half-eaten bowl of soup. Nothing could be done now. Only win this fight.

"My sword calls for more of your blood, Lieutenant!" Payne smirked, inspecting his blade.

Rage filled Wolf's eyes. "Ja!" They quickly turned into a gallop. Wolf's blade aimed for the center of his chest. Payne's eyes were wide as they met. He was sure to land a blow this time. Payne steered his horse and ducked, and Wolf's saber went over his shoulder. In a fraction of a second, Payne flicked his wrist to the rear, slicing at Wolf's leg. The sword clanged back at Payne.

Saved by the brace. Who would have thought that damn thing that's hindered my existence for years save me? I must change the game, or I will lose. Wolf yanked his reins closing on Payne before he had a chance to settle for another charge. Wolf slowed, and both the men jabbed and sliced at one another. Wolf hammered a blow upon Payne's saber, sending the rear of his saber back into his nose.

Payne spun his horse away. Shaking his head in a daze, he screamed, "You will pay!" The two men met again. This time Payne struck quicker and with more anger. His blade slipped and slid off Wolf's like a serpent's tongue. It took every ounce of Wolf's being to keep the man's sword from biting his flesh. But the more they battled, the more tired each man grew.

"I grow tired of this contest," Payne said. He hacked his sword near Wolf's head with enough force to cleave it in two. It caught the side of Wolf's wide-brimmed hat, deflecting the blow.

The two men were so intent on destroying each other they didn't notice more men galloping their way.

"I command you to stop!" shouted the lead rider. He had a thick bushy brown beard on his cheeks and an ostrich plume in his slouch hat. His sash was buff colored, and he wore three stars surrounded by a wreath on his collar. The center star was larger than the other two. A Confederate major general. Wolf blinked, and Payne's swipe caught the bottom of his ear, sending his lobe flying through the air.

The general drew his saber, deflecting the men apart. Wolf and Payne circled their horses.

"Stuart. Do not interfere! This is my duel!" Payne shouted.

"Where is she?" Stuart yelled at Payne.

"She is safe," Wolf shouted. He touched the bottom of his missing earlobe. "Goddamn," he said to himself.

Stuart's face twisted in anger, pointing with his saber. "Are you the bandit responsible for this? Captain, stay your blade. He's mine."

Wolf tried to catch his breath. A fresh man to fight, the Knight of the Golden Spurs at that. His time here was numbered, but he could become a legend if he somehow survived.

Payne shook his head. "Do me this honor. This scum will die here today."

Wolf stood no chance against two of the finest horsemen in the war. But he steeled himself while the other two men argued over who would have the honor of killing him.

"You will step aside, Captain. He has done me grave injustice and shall pay," Stuart said, pointing his blade in Payne's direction. "That is an order."

"I will not. We have history, General, and he must die at my hand."

"You will step aside, Captain Payne."

"You dare disobey your general?" shouted an aide.

"The general has no right to be here. This is my kill."

A gunshot rang out from the woods behind Wolf. The men turned their horses in surprise, looking for the culprit.

Payne's eyes raged. "Treachery!"

Wolf lifted his saber in the air, holding his reins high for Payne to see. Sarah danced beneath him. Foam lined her mouth, and she let out an irritated neigh. He didn't care what the man thought, but if this turned into a gun battle, things looked even worse. Four guns to one.

Stuart placed a hand on his abdomen. He grimaced as he held his hand in front of his face. Crimson saturated his white gloves. He let out a low groan as he slipped from his saddle. The ground broke his fall with a damp thud. His aides holstered their pistols and rushed to assist him.

Wolf turned. Faint horsemen emerged from the forest, pistols drawn.

"Hurry! Get him on his horse!" shouted a bookish aide.

Payne charged Wolf but reined his steed into the air as Wilhelm and the rest of Wolf's unit came into view.

"You deceiver! You brought your men. Coward!" Payne shouted.

"Forward, platoon!" Wilhelm shouted. Wolf's unit charged from the wood line into the field. Pistols blazed in their hands as Stuart and his aides hastily galloped away trailed by Payne.

Wilhelm wheeled the unit back toward Wolf. The men congregated around him with smiles. They were all there. All his men. Even the ones he was tepid about: Adams, Nelson, and young Hale.

"I thought I gave you an order, Sergeant," Wolf said, watching the backs of the fleeing rebels, including the man he still must kill.

"An order you knew I wouldn't follow," Wilhelm said.

Wolf stifled a short laugh. "No, I suppose you wouldn't." He turned, eyeing the men around him. "Which one of you made that shot?"

A slight man with a mischievous grin raised his hand. "I did," Roberts said.

"Do you know the man who you just shot?"

Roberts shrugged his shoulders. "Nope. Saw some fancy lad sitting there with an ostrich feather on his cap. Thought maybe I'd thieve it from him after the battle was over."

"That was Jeb Stuart."

The men shared a brief glance with one another. Wilhelm squinted at the riders. "We should go get him. His capture could change the war."

"No, he should see his wife."

"Wait, Wolfie," Adams said, eyeing the fleeing rebels. "You mean the Jeb 'the Beau Sabreur' Stuart?"

"None other. Him and Payne were arguing over which one was going to kill me."

"I'd like to take a swing at him," Nelson grunted. "Been too long since I slew a man worth a damn."

"There's more," George said, pointing. Every man's eyes saw them. Riders drew up into formation near the farmhouse. Not a large force but clearly larger than them. Gray coats and red shirts labeled them as the enemy.

"You're not going to have to wait long."

"Maybe one of these baby men will give me a chance."

Wilhelm shook his head. "Roberts shot the best cavalryman that there ever was." He glanced at Wolf. "Did you see the other general?"

Wolf knew the man he spoke of. The brute Wade Hampton. As a subordinate of Stuart, he may be close. "No, just his aides."

"And now Payne's entire command."

Wolf lifted his chin. "We are not finished."

"Didn't look like you were doing too well," Wilhelm said.

"I was surviving."

"Barely."

Hogan pushed his horse near Wolf. "You're sure that was Stuart?"

"There was no doubt."

Hogan squeezed his arm. "Do you know what we've done? His death means supremacy for our mounted forces."

"Does it? He was but one man. Surely there are other capable men."

"The blow to morale will be insurmountable. I must tell Sheridan immediately."

Wolf gave a slight nod, but he was distracted by the force of men straightening their line ahead of him, preparing to run them off the field. "I believe we have more pressing events on hand."

The Red Shirts formed a tight-knit line in the field across from them. Disciplined and confident veteran horsemen. Payne rode in front of his men directing them into position.

"Form up!" Wolf shouted. His men maneuvered their animals into a long single line. He had enough men to give them a fight. He hadn't asked them here, but he wasn't leaving without Payne's head on the tip of his sword either.

"Uh, Lieutenant. I don't mind ridin' and all, but I'm a better shooter from the stationary position than from atop a horse," Skinner said.

Wolf regarded him. "You may take a dismounted position."

George joined Skinner, both kneeling in the trees. They sighted through their scopes and twisted their eye pieces to adjust for the estimated range where the two forces would meet in their deadly contest.

"James?" George called to his friend.

James lifted his chin at his enemy across the way. "I ride with these men."

"You are a sharpshooter not a horseman," George said, his face twisted in consternation.

"I am a warrior. It matters not." He pulled a pistol and a long knife from his belt.

Wolf steered his mount in front of his men. He pointed at Wilhelm with his saber.

"Unfurl our colors, Sergeant."

A broad grin spread across Wilhelm's face, and he reached into a bag hanging off his saddle, removing the wolf-head guidon. It had a dark red upper half like each stripe on the American flag, and the jet-black bottom was emblazoned with the golden wolf head in the center.

"Sergeant," Skinner called out. He tossed him a long straight branch.

Wilhelm fastened the guidon to the pole. Raindrops began to fall from the sky in a tired drizzle. Then he raised it into the air. The wind whipped at it, making it snap in its freedom.

Wolf growled with a glance at the darkening sky. "Let 'em know who we are."

Chapter Thirty-One

May 11, 1864
Near Yellow Tavern, Virginia

Wolf walked his horse in front of his men. Sarah's hooves dug into the soil with each step. The rain pattered them gently. Fate had given him another stab at Payne that made him feel relaxed about what was to come. If he wasn't meant to kill this man, then why present him so soon after their previous engagement?

"I needn't tell you why we fight. Each man has his own reasons. Uncle Shugart fought so other men could be free. Some fight because their family fights." He nodded at Wilhelm. His sergeant's face hardened into a vengeful glower. "Other men fight just to fight; it's in their blood. There's no harm in that. A nation needs fighters." He turned his horse back down the line. "Some fight for a better life. Some fight to go home. But I'll tell you why I fight."

All of their eyes were upon him, ignoring the enemy. "I fight for you. I fight by my brothers' side. I tried to send you men away to spare you this battle, but you returned." He glanced at Wilhelm again. The German sergeant stared forward. "You came back for me. Which means we fight for each other regardless of what this day brings or what our differences are." He eyed the stone crag of a man, Nelson. "We fight shoulder to shoulder united against a common foe. We fight as one, one sword cutting the life from the enemy."

His men cheered, raising pistols and sabers into the air. Wolf pointed across the field with his saber.

"Those men will show you no mercy, so you will give none. Let me be true to you. This is a live-or-die trial. They think they can overpower us with numbers." His voice rose in volume and into a snarl. "Well, I say let them try!"

His men gave a resounding cheer. They didn't resemble a traditional Union force, more like a band of partisans in their civilian attire, but their flag marked them as men with a common tie and bond, a shared interest and brotherhood. They would ride and fight under the wolf banner this day, and if it was to be their last battle, then they would go into it prepared to embrace death with their last breath.

Wilhelm's voice rose loud and clear above the battle cries. "Wolf's platoon!"

The men took up the shout.

"Wolf's platoon!"

"Wolf's platoon!"

Wolf beamed, his heart pounding and his blood hot for another fight. Invincibility pumped in his veins. If he could have dreamed a way to go to the next life, this was it: surrounded by his men, in a charge made for legends, swords soaked in the blood of enemies, pistol barrels red hot from spending every last bullet they had on them.

The Polish brothers bashed fists together. Van Horn called from the depths of his lungs. Nelson bellowed like a wounded bear. Each man shouted down any fear he had lurking inside him.

Wolf drove his horse in front of his men. "Forward trot!"

His men spurred their horses. Their gait sounded almost pleasant to their ears.

"Keep it tight now!" Wilhelm called down the line, the banner flapping in his hand. Their mounts held close to one another, the troopers preventing them from getting too far from the rest.

Payne saw this and pointed his sword in their direction. His men moved to a trot. A tit-for-tat command. He would match Wolf and then overpower them with superior numbers.

Wolf maneuvered his horse to the center of his men. He would be the point of the line. The tip of his unit's spear. He wouldn't have it any other way. Payne was his target, but he would slaughter every man before him to reach him.

The men urged their horses into formation, steering them to keep tight with a trooper on either side.

"Charge!" Wolf shouted at the top of his lungs. His horse churned out stride after stride. The wind whipped at his hair and beard, moving the brim of his hat upward. The field blurred past as they moved to full speed. Rain struck him, running down his face and neck. The men behind him unleashed their battle cry. Hooves ripped dirt and grass, flinging it airborne.

As the rebels closed, they whooped loud and high-pitched, but neither party would give beneath the psychological weight of a battle cry. Both sides were committed to mutual destruction.

Sabers were lifted high then lowered, curving over their mounts' heads as they galloped. Pistols were gripped in sweaty palms. Rough aim was taken, trying to hold steady on the mass of horsemen ahead of them. One of the rebels held a short shotgun over his forearm. When they closed within thirty yards, their revolvers puffed white smoke; one could hardly hear the shots as much as feel the zipping draft from the sailing bullets.

The faces of the Red Shirts grew clear. Crazed and violent. Men prepared to do unspeakable things to one another.

Everything quieted down as they got close. The hooves were muffled, the shouts muted, and the pistols half-popped. He stretched his arm further to gain extra inches on his adversaries before the units struck one another. Then the opposing riders collided.

With a smack, Wolf's sword pierced the man across from him. The rebel screamed with the blade's bite. He ripped his saber free, tucking his shoulder.

His line weaved through the rebels. Pistols cracked. Sabers slashed. Wolf ducked, a blade swooshing over the top of his head. He exchanged saber strikes with the second row of the Red Shirts, and they cut through his men.

The lines splintered in the chaos, drifting into individual fighting. Wolf's men were forced to fight two or three men at once. He broke through the mass of horsemen, wildly slashing, looking for Payne. Turning his horse, he waded back into the fray.

Van Horn took a pistol bullet to his chest, slumping him over his mount's mane. Bart traded saber blows with a rebel until he took a saber to the back. He growled in pain and leapt off his saddle atop the other man as if he were more animal than a man. Both men disappeared in the dust and smoke of battle.

Wolf deflected a saber strike with a diagonal defense and immediately slashed at the man's belly. Sarah took him away. He felt a bullet whizz past his head, and he ducked, turning to face another rebel. The rebel pointed his shotgun at Wolf with a nasty sneer.

"Ja!" Wolf screamed at him, trying to urge Sarah closer. Before he could close, a red hole appeared in the rebel's forehead. Blood released in a torrent down his face, his eyes rolling into the back of his head as he toppled from the saddle.

Wolf had no idea if the shot was meant for him or the other man. He supposed it didn't matter, but he suspected one of his sharpshooters could claim credit. The threat was dead, and he was alive with a vendetta.

He spied Roberts and Payne exchanging saber blows near the center of the fray. Urging his mount into the middle, a rebel pointed his gun at him. A tiny puff of smoke leaked from the hammer as it misfired. A moment later, a saber emerged through his mouth. It disappeared in a splash of blood. Adams smirked at Wolf and dodged a saber swipe from another man.

He turned back to Payne, who was now in a strict contest with Wilhelm. The sergeant used the wolf banner to deflect his dashing blows while trying to hook his saber into Payne's side.

"Payne!" Wolf shouted, kicking his horse.

His rival turned as he neared, snarling, "You will fall!"

The two men traded a series of saber jabs and thrusts, each man hungry for the other's blood. Another Red Shirt tried to intervene, and for a moment, Wolf thought he'd go down beneath both their blades, but Nelson used his saber like a spear to ram the man into the air then tossed him to the ground. He bent over and punched Payne in the side of his head with the hilt of his blade. Payne's head flew to the side and he almost fell from his horse.

"Fuck you!" Nelson growled. He lifted his arm to smite the captain from his horse and roared as a Red Shirt sliced his arm. He struck a hammer blow at his new opponent in a battle rage fit for a bear.

Payne shook his head and went on the offensive. He hacked and slashed at Wolf like a red-shirted demon. Hale screamed behind him as pitifully as a baby calf when he was cut down. Men called for help, and others gurgled and snarled as they breathed their last.

Only one thing drove Wolf onward and that was the death of his rival. He would have it. He must have it. His attacks grew stronger like snow turning into an avalanche of sharp metal. With each blow, Payne was slower and slower to respond. Wolf half-slashed across his chest and turned his sword for a piercing thrust. The point of the blade penetrated Payne's coat, shirt, and then the soft skin of his upper chest.

"Rarrr!" Wolf yelled from deep inside his lungs. Payne's eyes went wide with surprise. Wolf urged his horse closer, using his shoulder and back to force the sword even farther into his enemy's body.

Payne grimaced, twisting with every inch of blade as he fought it with every fiber in his body. The two opponents were close enough to reach out and grasp one another. Wolf could smell his sweat and rotten breath. He could almost feel his pain. His eyes couldn't leave his enemy's.

"You're a real cunt," Payne said, his mouth shaking. Then he spit in Wolf's face. The glob ran down his chin and he rammed the saber deeper into Payne and he let out a horrible scream.

Wolf was so vested in drinking in Payne's misery, he missed the fist sailing into his face. His head went back, and he released his grip on his sword hilt.

"Retreat!" Payne called to his men. In fits and starts, the Red Shirts disengaged.

Rotating his jaw, Wolf watched them ride. Pistol fire tailed the retreating men like nipping hounds of lead. "On me!" Wolf called out. His men maneuvered their horses around him.

"We must pursue," Wolf breathed, drawing his pistol. Wilhelm took his place on his right, Dan on his left. Hogan was there; blood ran down the center of his face. Nelson and Adams joined them but no one else.

Surely, others were coming. Wolf scanned the ground around him. Both his men and rebels lay strewn over the field. Men cried and moaned, cradling wound and injury alike. A horse screamed as it tried to stand but couldn't on its broken legs. More horses bolted across the field away from them, leaving their unhorsed riders.

The Red Shirts turned their horses around, and it looked like they were going to make another go of it. They stood, numbers reduced, momentarily watching Wolf's men. A few whoops came from their lips as they prepped themselves for another foray into the jaws of death. He could see Payne was bent in visible anguish, Wolf's sword still inside him.

"Sergeant, keep that flag held high," he said then gulped. They could not last another round.

"Yes, sir!" Wilhelm shouted. He lifted the banner higher into the air.

"Come and take it!" Wolf screamed across the field.

His men continued to toss out insults, their voices rising in feverish rebellion.

"I'll take your balls!" Nelson bellowed.

"And your wife!" Adams added.

With Payne at the forefront of the unit, the Red Shirts turned their mounts and departed. For the first time in what felt like hours, Wolf allowed himself to breathe.

The men around him cheered for a moment, battle fury burning bright inside their chests. Calls to the heavens for their deliverance. Yells of victory. Dan beat his chest with a fist. Adams and Nelson gripped forearms in a warrior's embrace. Wolf spun his horse, and the cheers died down in raw, dry throats. There were so few of them still mounted.

Chapter Thirty-Two

May 11, 1864
Near Yellow Tavern, Virginia

Rain clouds gathered above, seemingly dreading the battle unfolding on the land beneath them. In the distance, thunder rumbled from the heavens. Custer eyed the sky, wondering if it would hamper the rest of their fine little scrap they were having with Stuart's Cavalry Corps.

The weather could hinder their assault or give Stuart the opportunity to disengage and flee, something that would gnaw at the man if he hadn't reclaimed his wife. Stuart was in an unthinkable predicament devised from Custer's own fear of someone snatching Libbie from beneath him. Oh, how he would rage, and claw his own eyes out. He thanked God that he wasn't in that maddening position.

The ridge where Wickham had deployed his men and where Lomax had been driven presented a good position for defense. There was ample tree cover, and the ridge was elevated enough to provide an advantage.

His men would have to march through fields before reaching the wooded area in front of the ridge. Then there was Stuart's blasted artillery. That had given his troopers quite a fit in the morning hours. It would need to be dealt with.

A rider trotted through the woods, making his way as quickly as he possibly could. He reined his horse in front of Custer. "Sir!" The young lieutenant gave a snappy salute, knuckling his forehead.

"For Chrissake, man, do not salute me. We are close enough for a reb to get lucky." His mind quickly shifted to another mentor and friend who hadn't been so prudent, Major General John Sedgwick, only a couple of days past. The rumors were flying that he'd been sniped by a sharpshooter directly beneath the eye. An impeccable shot or an incredibly lucky one.

Just moments before his untimely demise, Sedgwick had ignored concerns from his aides that he was too close to the front, carrying on about how the rebels, "couldn't hit an elephant at this distance."

True words that garnered respect and also seemingly expedited his death, as the rebs truly could hit him from there. Within a minute, he had bled to death in the arms of his aide. It was a true tragedy, one that his corps and even the entirety of the Army of the Potomac felt deep within their hearts and souls.

The lieutenant let his hand fall, and his horse danced nervously beneath him. "My apologies, sir." He leaned from his mount and thrust a piece of paper into Custer's hand.

He grasped the note and waved the courier on his way. "Carry on!" Custer called at him and immediately unfolded it. As he read, a smile formed on his lips. He slapped the written orders with his other hand. "Finally, some orders we can rally behind."

His brigade staff had clustered nearby as the day moved to afternoon, both armies taking defensive postures toward one another, finding it prudent to toss artillery balls and shells at one another rather than participate in a pitched battle. That irritated Custer at his core. He understood the importance of ensuring all the divisions were in optimal placement for an assault, but direct expedient action could far outweigh a set-piece affair.

Colonel Alger glanced, raising his eyebrows. "Sir?"

"It's finally time to run these boys from the field."

"They have a solid position." Alger pointed out. "That battery is centering their line."

"Sitting like a pretty duck all day. Time to put an end to that. Good sir, that will be the center of our attack." He adjusted a glove tighter as he pointed. "Well, just to the right." Custer shoved the note into his black velvet jacket with gold trim.

"I'll need the 5th and 6th dismounted." He pointed again to the fields leading to the ridge that Telegraph Road split. "You'll engage those men on the ridge and your flank will pressure the battery. Don't worry about your left flank. The 1st Vermont will shadow you."

"Those boys want back in the old brigade, don't they?" Alger asked.

Custer smiled. "I'd take them back too if it wasn't for the conditions they'd force upon us." He referred to commanding under his rival Wilson. The 1st Vermont had to be given up in order for him to maintain his position. He knew those men had cried out in dismay, but those were the games officers played.

Lieutenant Colonel Stagg of the 1st Michigan stood nearby. "What about my men, sir? We would love a run at 'em."

"I haven't forgotten the brave 1st. There is a reason you're my favorite." He ran his hand along the outline of the road in the distance. "You boys are going to ride like the devil up that road there. Squadron by squadron. It'll take you right to the battery. I want Stuart's artillery."

Stagg gave a short grin. "And we'll get it for you."

"Is that those Maryland boys?" Custer said, trying to see the cannon. It boomed in the distance and sent a shell crashing through the trees like a wounded buck in a forest.

"I believe so, sir," Stagg said.

"Then let's remind them which side they should be fighting for."

His men laughed at that. It eased a bit of tension for the assault they were about to conduct. Custer had a way of doing that for his men. With either confidence or with a cool joke, he kept them confident under fire.

"Major Granger." Custer waved over another one of his officers. He considered Granger, an understudy and an upcoming soldier who had shown quality time and time again in this war, to have actually deserved his rise in station. "You're going to follow the 1st with the 7th Michigan. Fill in any gaps in their line. I want them to feel the shock of our assault. We won't be stopped."

There was only one of his regiments he hadn't dealt with: the 13th Michigan. He stared with distaste at Colonel Moore. He couldn't say if he'd ever seen a worse officer; the man lacked all quality aside from being agreeable to whomever was in charge. "I'll hold you in reserve."

Moore smiled beneath his chubby cheeks. "We will be ready at your beckoning call!"

Custer didn't bother to respond to him. "All right, men. Out to your commands. Hurry now, we want this over."

He studied the rebel position as his men organized and prepared for the offensive. His men had hustled to the front, every fourth man staying with the others mounts.

The 5th Michigan had their 7-shot repeating Spencer carbines. They'd been refitted before the campaign began trading in their Spencer rifles for carbines. In fact, his entire brigade, except for the 13th Michigan, had been outfitted with the carbines despite their differing designations earlier in the war.

The carbines were eight inches shorter and much lighter, making it easier for his men to wield on foot or horseback. Each man had been supplied with at least 200 metal cartridges in their pouches at the start of Sheridan's southward drive. He expected that they would be down to about 100 cartridges per man now. That would have to last until the wagon train reached them.

A man with a repeater could run through 100 cartridges in twenty minutes. Something that had held back much of the Army from receiving the guns earlier in the war. Didn't want to waste ammunition. Bodies in the rank-and-file were okay to feed to the meat grinder, but the ammunition was what stayed their hand.

The War Department had seen the Spencers' effectiveness in turning the tide against many foes and moved forward with the innovation. But his boys in the 5th and 6th Michigan had had their repeating Spencer rifles since Gettysburg, courtesy of Governor Blair, and were some of the most proficient handlers of the weapon in the whole army.

Dismounted troopers knelt around him, taking cover from an errant artillery shell. They checked cartridge boxes and held their Spencers with determination.

Alger joined him. "My men are ready, sir."

With a nod, Custer said, "You may commence the attack."

"Keep a good line for General Sheridan is watching us!" Alger shouted with a proud lift of his chin.

The bugler near Custer sounded the call for attack, and entire regiments followed by mounted squadrons marched forward with violent purpose.

Lightning crackled from the clouds above like angry flashing sabers of gold light. The ground vibrated beneath them, and it was hard to tell what caused the earth to tremble with such a fervor. It was as if a battle was being fought above in the heavens and had someway trickled to the earth below. Rain pattered down with curious indifference, slowly dampening the men as they marched.

His brigade's movement was as marvelous as it was precise. A fine body of men. It instilled pride in Custer. It wasn't long before the 5th and the 6th Michigan regiments engaged Wickham's regiments along the ridge.

Wickham's men had the advantage of better cover, but the beautiful Spencer carbines of Custer's troopers were fast and accurate, more than making up for any difference in position with deadly summation. White smoke rapidly enveloped the men as they fired into the trees.

Thunder boomed again, and he questioned whether or not a cannon ball sailed his way. It hadn't come from the skies nor the enemy, yet it shook the earth. The ground shuddered beneath the earthquake of a thousand hooves as if trembling before the face of God.

The 1st barreled down Telegraph Road. Each stride built even greater momentum. He was sure a castle wall couldn't stop them. Spanning some two hundred feet, they were a battering ram of man and flesh. The sheer number of tightly packed horsemen in the lead squadron made them formidable.

A yell overcame the thunder, hundreds of voices forming into one. It wasn't dissimilar to the rebel yell, but it was his men's very own battle cry. It was their call for blood and courage as they charged into the jaws of death.

Dirt and dust billowed around them, shielding them from view as if they were a blue windstorm racing for the rebels.

Custer mounted and pushed forward, trailing his dismounted men but far enough to the rear to send reserves in if needed. It irked him to be behind instead of leading from the front, but he had to be prepared to shift his forces at any given moment. Respect for Stuart's prowess demanded a level of prudence that he would entertain.

"Turn that cannon!" a rebel shouted. "Turn the cannon!" The artillerymen scrambled to reposition the two guns.

Gun smoke rose from the ridge where Lomax's men were hiding while peppering his charging horsemen. Ignoring the whipping bullets from the enemy until they could seize their prize, the 1st was forced to traverse through a stream and then a small rickety bridge.

His men pounced upon Stuart's artillery like a swarm of mountain lions on a pack of wounded dogs. The lead rider slammed his saber into the skull of a lieutenant with a damp thud. The young officer dropped like his legs had been cut from beneath him. Rebels raised their hands in surrender. The rammer swung his ramrod in circles over his head to keep the riders at bay, but he fell, pierced, as the riders passed.

With the threat of taking canister shot dissipating like a summer rain, his dismounted men pressed forward again. Did Wickham give way? He turned back toward the 1st. Their charge was waning despite the addition of Stagg's second squadron thundering home. Rebel horsemen had piecemeal attacked them, and although it was disorganized, it had slowed the power of the 1st Michigan's attack.

Time to apply more pressure. He pointed at Major Granger. He waved his hand rapidly toward the enemy like he was striking them with a tomahawk.

"Ya!" Granger shouted, and the 7th Michigan galloped after their mounted comrades. Lomax's men were falling back to a secondary ravine and ridge but still managing to batter the 1st Michigan's flanks.

Major Granger charged onward ahead of his men as if it were a race. They would hit Lomax's men before they had a chance to concentrate fire on the newcomers. *Ride, my boys*, he thought. The 7th had shaken off the mantle of their rookie status and was becoming a commendable unit.

At the lead, Granger closed on the rebels, his black hat waving over his head. The sight of such bravery made Custer warm inside.

A bugle call went out and almost the entirety of the attacking force wheeled to the right, galloping for safer ground. Granger and a few of his closest men carried onward; they were either too brazen or unaware of the danger ahead.

The cracks of a second volley struck home on the blue riders. Smoke obscured his vision. When they came back into view, saddles had been emptied of troopers, and Granger was nowhere to be seen. A horse screamed on the ground behind. More horses galloped away from the gunfire spooked.

"I do hope he has survived his charge," Custer said.

"Look!" his aide shouted, drawing his attention.

Brigadier General Wilson's men were adding their weight to Wickham's flank.

"Looks like the 3rd Indiana and a New York regiment." As much as he disliked the commander, he was happy to see them adding their weight to the fight.

The rebels teetered on the precipice of breaking. The 1st Michigan dueled with the 1st Virginia, but Stuart's battery was gone. The Confederate artillery was the linchpin of their line; without it, they would flounder and fold. Wickham's men were starting to fall back.

And almost as quickly as the attack had begun, it began to wind down. It was almost anticlimactic. Not that the victory was total or the contest weakly fought, but the speed to which the rebels had broken struck Custer as odd.

Usually they put up a much stouter resistance. *Perhaps we are on our way to ending this.* He forced that thought from his mind. He had some postwar ventures in the works, but war had always come easy to him. It was in his blood.

Not the classroom work or following all the rules and regulations. He'd barely passed and finished last in his class at West Point. But he'd seen men who had excelled in the classroom crumble in the face of the enemy. In all reality, he'd been saved by the Civil War. He'd been standing trial for court-martial when the war began, and the need for officers had granted him a favorable verdict. He was meant for the field not the classroom.

In the field, how an officer judged the terrain and positioned his men came easy to him. He could feel the time to apply pressure and when to hold back. The practicality of striking an opponent at precisely the right time, rushing his flank, encircling behind him. Or a daring charge. He'd aced all of these things in real time. It was as natural as eating and breathing to him.

Custer drove his horse in the direction of where the Maryland battery had once stood.

Stagg found him looking like a bloody butcher. Someone's blood had splattered his face. His hands were red as if he'd torn a man limb from limb. "Sent them running, General! Picked up a couple of guns and limber carriages." The Union army didn't need Confederate arms, but the Confederates needed them tenfold. "I have about eighty rebs prisoner."

"Treat them fairly. Any news on Major Granger? His attack seemed disjointed."

"We had a time with some rail fences and a bridge. I would assume they did as well." Stagg shook his head. "But I do not know his whereabouts."

Custer squinted over his shoulder. Horses screamed in pain, and nearby, a man held his face, crying. In the smoke and darkened sky, it was hard to tell which side he had fought for. Drizzle shrouded the entire area, making it difficult to see.

He spotted a man with an entourage galloping toward them. Flags billowed after him, whipping reds and whites and blues. Major General Sheridan.

"Sir," Custer said.

Sheridan beamed. "A resounding success! Ha! I'll have to send a telegram to Grant reiterating our victory here."

"Where are they retreating too?" Sheridan asked, eyeing the field of battle.

"Looks to be north and east," Stagg said.

"What's that way?"

A major with a long mustache spoke. "Toward the Chickahominy River."

"I would assume some would break for Richmond," Custer added.

"Assuredly, but now nothing stands between us and Richmond. Devin's boys already broke through both lines of defense earlier today. Ha!" Sheridan said, grinning. "We could make her ours before nightfall."

"I thought the objective was to destroy Stuart."

"And we have." Sheridan nodded as if he were about to receive the laurel wreath of a conquering hero. "His men are scattered like dust in the wind."

"They are, but surely they will regroup."

"Yes, but a great victory was achieved today."

Custer eyed the dead. Many of them were his. A noble sacrifice but a sacrifice nonetheless. He wondered about his men on the raid to capture Stuart's wife. He shook his head. They must know where the battle was being fought. They will find us when they are ready.

"Sir, I must let the men tend to their wounded and dead."

The grin faded on Sheridan's lips. "Of course. Well-deserved by all. Set out pickets. I don't want anyone sneaking up on us while we handle the business of the dead."

"Yes, sir."

Sheridan spurred his horse in the direction of a distant farmhouse, hooves tossing clumps of the wet earth.

Custer's insides were still ecstatic with victory, but the rain zapped his energy as its intensity grew. His men gave up a great cheer. They had driven the enemy away in chaos and dwindled Stuart's command with plenty of casualties and prisoners.

His brigade band took up the tune of "Yankee Doodle Dandy," and optimism flooded the Union ranks. They had fought a decisive battle against Stuart and won, the field in their hands. He wondered if it was his plan to draw Stuart out, or if it was fate, why they'd won here. Perhaps it was both. Perhaps everything was intertwined.

He raised a hand and waved at his men as they picked up the song. "Bloody good fight, lads."

Chapter Thirty-Three

May 11, 1864
Near Yellow Tavern, Virginia

The rain started in earnest now, capped by thunder and accented by lightning. Cold droplets slowly soaked the men. Wet men searched the dead, the water and blood mixing into the earth all the same. Wolf walked among the fallen, eyeing lifeless faces.

"Roberts?" Wolf said loudly, but his voice trailed away. He stepped through the tall grass. There were mounds of men and horses, but he didn't know which was friend or foe.

He stopped at a lanky body that wore Van Horn's pale face. The Dutch farmer finally looked at peace. His mouth even held a slight smile instead of his signature dour pout. Glassy eyes didn't blink as the raindrops struck him. Wolf bent down and closed his eyes.

"We found him," Wilhelm shouted.

Wolf hobbled toward the cluster of men. The wolf banner whipped in the wind as Wilhelm had planted his flag into the softening ground.

The men parted before Wolf, and he knelt onto both knees next to Roberts. Hogan's face was grave. Wilhelm slightly frowned.

"Bring me his canteen," Wolf said. Hogan disappeared. His eyes settled upon the broken form of his friend. "Hey, buddy. You okay?" His words rang hollow and false. Everything wasn't okay, but it helped the man to pretend they were.

Multiple saber wounds covered Roberts's body like a latticework of gashes. Gore-stained hands pressed on his own belly where a sword thrust had pierced him through. Blood squeezed out from around the wound, ignoring the hands stemming the red tide. His face was draining of all blood, becoming almost colorless. "Wolf," he said, his voice boyish and weak.

Wolf wrapped an arm around his friend, lifting him off the ground. Roberts winced and Wolf propped his head up on the crook of his arm. "You're going to be okay."

Hogan handed him the canteen. "Whiskey?"

"Aye."

He unscrewed the top and tipped it back into Roberts's mouth. In only a moment, the alcohol dribbled along the corners, and Wolf wiped it away with his sleeve.

Roberts gave him a smiling grimace. "Don't waste the good stuff on me."

"Nonsense." He dabbed the other side of Roberts's mouth. "We're going to get you back on a horse here. Send you to an old sawbones. Just like Gettysburg. Sort this all out."

The man's skin was too white. He was fading into a shade before Wolf's eyes. Wolf looked to Wilhelm for support. The seasoned sergeant had seen enough dying men to know a mortal wound, but one never thought their friend would die, not even in war. Or was it only friends that died?

Tears streamed down Dan's chubby cheeks from across the way. He held the body of his brother Bart in his arms. Sobs came from choked lips. Bart's arms lay limp in the air as Dan tried to squeeze life back into him.

Wolf let his eyes shut for a moment. *I tried to spare them this, yet they rode with me anyway.*

"Wolf," Roberts said with a gulp, drawing him back in. "Can I steal another nip? It's a bit cold out here."

It wasn't cold, not even with the rain. It was the fact men got cold before they died. "I got you." Wolf pulled him in tighter. His friend felt so small and frail in his arms. "I got you." He let the man take another swig of the whiskey. "I got you," he whispered. He rocked the man in his arms. He promised himself that he was beyond tears, but they came anyway.

They ran down his bristled face, blending with the rain into his beard. "I got you." He breathed hard through his nose. "I got you, brother."

His men slowly dispersed leaving him alone, his eyes vacantly soaking in the rain and the forest. He sat like this for some time, rocking his best friend like he was a newborn babe. Wilhelm's hand on his shoulder brought him back to the real world.

"Son." His voice held understanding and pain, shaking a bit at the end.

"What?" The rain forced Wolf to blink as he looked up at the sergeant. He wiped water from his face.

Wilhelm's eyes held grief, but he kept it together. "He's gone."

"No, he's just sleeping." Wolf half-smiled in pain.

Wilhelm squeezed his shoulder harder. "He's gone now." A moment passed before he spoke again. "You'll see him again."

Wolf looked down at Roberts. His face was at peace, life no longer residing in his earthly body. "I'm—"he started but couldn't finish.

"You did what you could. Now we must look out for those still in your command. The rebels could return with more men. We should find our lines as to not get caught."

"I tried to spare them this."

Wilhelm lifted his chin. "No one is blameless in war. It just happens. I led these men here as much as you. I cared for all of them too, but now we must move."

As much as it stung, he knew his sergeant was right. "Get the dead and wounded tied to their mounts." There would be time for mourning later, but he didn't know when. He hoisted Roberts's body on his horse. Sarah stamped her foot but didn't complain after Wolf mounted into the saddle.

The men walked their horses south. The bodies of Van Horn, Roberts, Shugart, Hale, Pratt, Bart, and James stayed silent and motionless. The remaining men were quiet. What had been gained paled in their eyes as to what they'd lost. But such is war.

Chapter Thirty-Four

Evening, May 11, 1864
North of the Chickahominy River, Virginia

They'd found the remnants of Fitzhugh Lee's Division regrouping north of the Chickahominy River. Pickets and sharpshooters manned the river's edge, and they'd dismantled part of a decaying bridge to discourage the Yankees from following, but none of the bluebellies had given any strong pursuit. His men made camp a half-mile from the river. Timid campfires surrounded them in the dying light.

Payne sat upright, leaning against a tree with a Model 1860 Light Cavalry Saber sticking through his upper chest and shoulder out his back.

He'd reported the wounding of General Stuart to some captain he didn't recognize, and his own men helped prop him against a nearby tree trunk. His men sat around a fire, their fervor for war matching the small flames. Their wounded lay in blanketed forms along the ground.

"Find me a damn surgeon!" he shouted at Fickles.

His lieutenant shied away from him. Payne was pretty sure he was the only man Fickles actually feared. And it was a legitimate fear. "Sir, I've sent for the surgeon twice now. There are just so many wounded."

Goddamn excuses. With his good arm, he grunted as he drew his pistol. He lined his bead sight on Fickles's head. "You'll return with a surgeon, or I'll shoot you dead."

Fickles paled beneath a mustache that lined his mouth all the way to his chin. "Yes, sir." The man stood and stumbled as he hurried to get away.

"You," Payne said to one of his privates, gesturing at him with his pistol. "Bring me whiskey."

The private's head bobbed. He was filthy and his hair ruffled. An air of exhaustion shrouded him, but he hustled all the same. He brought Payne the bottle and stopped short, offering it from a few feet away. He lifted his chin and set his revolver on his lap and snatched the bottle from his hand.

"Get out of here," Payne said. He tipped the bottle back and chugged the harsh liquor. It painfully seared his throat, bubbling like molten lava in his belly. It slightly dulled his senses, but his shoulder continued to throb. The blood had mostly stopped flowing, but Sergeant Turner had demanded he keep the blade in until they reached a surgeon. But as deep as the saber had bitten through his flesh and muscle, the real pain was the ongoing existence of Wolf and his little band of bandits.

He should have slain the crippled upstart in the duel, taken his scalp for his saddle, and been on his way. But before he could enjoy his kill, the Knight of the Golden Spurs decided to dash in and ruin everything. Then the brave bastard got himself shot too. Payne coughed to the side and brought the bottle back to his lips.

"Dumb ass," he spat. Stuart's wounding was mortal too. He could tell by the way the man was stricken. His body was rigid in pain like a piece of wood. His eyes held something in them too, the vacant stare of a man who knew his days were numbered.

His men started to stand at attention around the fire. They turned their backs to him. "Oh, thank God. Some smart bastard is going to remove this godforsaken sword out of me."

A man walked through them, his hand resting on his saber, wreathed stars on his collar. His general's coat was soiled and stained with someone's blood. His blackish beard was long and came to a point, laying over his heart. His hair had been brushed to the side, but loose strands fell in his eyes.

"Oh bloody hell," Payne muttered. He rose his voice and called at his men. "Get me the surgeon!"

Major General Fitzhugh Lee stood in front of Payne and was contemplative.

He addressed Payne like he was a common man, a mere pawn in the working class. "Captain Payne."

Payne looked at the evening sky shrouded by leaves above him wondering what he'd done to deserve such a prestigious visitor. The rain had been off and on over the day, mixing with his blood and making it a watery pink through his jacket. He put on a false smile. "Can you send me a surgeon, good General? I'll be bloody dead before the night's end at this rate."

"I will." Fitz eyed the sword hilt sticking out from Payne's chest. He gave him a slight grimace. His eyes held worry and grief but were hard too like he wanted someone to place his angst upon. "What happened to Jeb?"

"What do you think? Some dirty Yank got a lucky shot off. Went through the belly and out his hip. The wound was bad. I suspect mortal."

Fitz gulped, Payne's callous words reopening the wound of Stuart's unexpected demise. "Be careful, Captain. Do not bring such ill words down upon us."

He just didn't care anymore what these pompous blowhards thought. Without a war, they'd be glorified watchmen on the frontier dodging arrows trying to keep their scalp atop their heads. Then again, he would be a plantation owner with limited outlets for his tastes. War benefited them both in different ways. "I mean no disrespect, General. I only meant to convey the situation in clear words. My shoulder you see." He glanced down at the hilt of Wolf's sword with disgust.

Fitz crouched in front of Payne, shifting his saber out of the way. His eyes studied him. "How did it happen?"

"We were deceived by the Yankee bandits who had taken his wife. They ambushed us from the woods. Must have had sharpshooters among them. I lost a handful to the shooters alone."

Fitz studied the camp around him. "That's why he disappeared during the battle. When I rushed the 1st forward, he was nowhere to be found." His voice became more hushed. "I wasted many lives trying to find him. We thought he'd gone down near the battery."

"All in vain." Payne adjusted his back on the tree, sending shooting pains through his body.

Tears lined Fitz's eyes as he blinked them away, and his mouth curved in worry. "Where's Flora? She must be found."

"She escaped while we fought."

Fitz nodded and gulped, his throat jiggling. "I will make sure my men are on the lookout for her. She's a smart girl, I assume she would make for Richmond."

"Very smart." Payne grimaced. She could tarnish his reputation by repeating what he had uttered to her. But what could she really do to him? He was rich. His words were harsh yet true. Her husband was dying. Her recollection could be attributed to womanly grief at her husband's demise.

"Thank you for trying to save them." The general put his hand out and Payne gripped it. "Your country owes you a great debt. I will make sure Marse Robert knows of your sacrifice."

Payne squeezed harder and jerked him closer. Fitz tried to pull away, but Payne held him steady within inches of his face. Through gritted teeth he said, "Surgeon."

"Of course," Fitz said, nodding.

Payne released him. "Thank you, General. You are a lifesaver."

Fitz stood and eyed him with a touch of disdain. He turned and walked away.

Fickles rushed past the general. "Payne!" he called. "I have him."

A man in spectacles and a bloody apron, once white sleeves rolled to his elbows, trailed the lieutenant.

"Doctor, help this man. He is a true patriot," Fitz said.

The surgeon regarded the general for a moment, running his glasses up the bridge of his nose. "There are many more wounded I must see."

"You will stay with him until he is properly cared for."

The doctor raised his chin. "He is not the worst in my care. He can wait."

"I will carve out your eyes if you make me wait," Payne grunted.

The doctor eyed him warily along with Fitz. The general spoke. "You will fix him. That's an order."

"Yes, of course," the surgeon said.

"Very good," Fitz said. With a glance at Payne he took his leave.

"Get this goddamn thing out of me!" Payne shouted at the surgeon.

The surgeon ignored him, inspecting the wound while he drank more. "Can you move your arm?"

Payne lifted his hand and flexed his fingers, grinding his jaw through the pain. "Enough?"

"That's fine. I don't normally treat wounds to the torso. Usually you bleed out before you reach me." He eyed the wound. "Sabers are usually blunted, no?"

Payne grunted. "Does this look blunted?"

"We must do this fast and hope that a fever doesn't take you."

"I don't care. Just fix this."

The surgeon sighed. "This will not be comfortable." He opened a bag and removed a thin metal rod with an ebony wood handle. The head was rounded like a stirring instrument. He pointed at Fickles. "I need you to heat this until it glows."

"Ha." Payne took another swig of the harsh alcohol. "Do it."

"You won't be singing that same tune when we're through," the surgeon said.

"You know nothing," Payne hissed.

The doctor eyed him behind his spectacles. "Keep drinking. I don't have any chloroform."

It didn't take long until Fickles returned with an orange-glowing metal tool. It sizzled as rain fell upon it, little clouds of steam erupting off it.

"I will not be able to pull this out," the surgeon said to Fickles. "We need someone stronger."

Fickles looked nervous, taking a step back. His face was a shade greener at the thought. "I'd rather not."

"Do it, you coward," Payne slurred at him.

"I'll do it," said William Scott. The scout stood from the fire.

"You'd love to wouldn't you, Tiny Scott?"

"I won't say it wouldn't give me a bit of pleasure," he said. His gray-streaked black beard appeared even more feral with the weather.

"We all find pleasure in something. Even you, Scott."

"Hurry," the surgeon urged. "Strip him to the trousers."

Fickles cut his jacket from his back and then his shirt as gently as he could, but each movement tugged at the blade. The air felt cool on his skin as did the occasional drop of rain on his shoulders. Pinkish blood trickled down his chest.

The surgeon gave a nod, and Scott walked forward.

"Pull fast and true, Scott," Payne grunted with a fiery grin.

Scott put a boot on Payne's other shoulder, thrusting him into the tree as a brace. Payne growled with painful anger. The scout's hands wrapped around the sword's hilt, and he ripped it out like a lion snatching its prey.

The sword grated against bone as it was tugged from his body. He felt every inch of the cold metal inside him, grinding against his flesh's reluctant release. He found himself screaming from the excruciating pain, his eyes blackening.

Moments later his eyes came back into focus. His breath was sucked from his chest, and he heaved as he tried to breathe.

Scott held the dripping sword, staring at him.

"You pull like a cherry's first time," Payne said to him.

Warmness flowed from the wound, running down his breast and onto the ground. Blood pattered as it dripped onto the soil. It formed dark brown and grainy globs with the dirt.

"Iron," the surgeon said. Fickles handed it over. Payne's back was against the tree, and the surgeon didn't hesitate. The war had made them both hard to pain and suffering. He would be a liar if he claimed he didn't flinch when the metal got close to his damp cool skin.

The rod sizzled into his skin, sounding like bacon frying in a pan. It was the worst pain he'd ever endured: biting, life-sucking, and breath-taking. His flesh melded over the wound, puckering.

Exhausted men seated nearby around campfires gazed on, both concern and shame in their eyes. They'd heard him cry out in pain. They looked away.

"Turn him over."

"Mother of God!" Payne breathed. Strong hands flipped him. Payne tried to stand, he had to fight them. Once was enough. *No more. Not again.* But

Fickles and Scott held him down as easily as if he were newborn babe.

The ground was wet and smelled like freshly tilled soil. Soon the smell of his own flesh filled his nostrils as the wound on his back was sealed with burning fire. He screamed long and loud now. His men looked away, and he couldn't take his eyes from the flames.

The surgeon bent down again, apparently having missed a part. Payne screamed, only one word, long and painful: "Woooolllllffffff!"

Chapter Thirty-Five

Evening, May 11, 1864
Near Yellow Tavern, Virginia

A wet dusk approached, and Wolf's men were stopped by pickets from the 5th New York north of Yellow Tavern. The pickets stepped out from the woods, eyeing the wolf banner with suspicion.

Wolf held out a hand. "We're with Custer's Brigade."

A young private with a weak mustache grinned. "Oh really?"

"I ain't going to fight you. Get your commanding officer."

Wolf spoke with their lieutenant for almost twenty minutes before he left to find his captain.

The captain arrived with long-whiskered sideburns his eyes tired behind gold-rimmed glasses. He didn't think too highly of their story and left them under guard. It took a good deal of more convincing and name dropping until Wolf convinced him enough to send a rider to Custer's Brigade. An hour passed, and Wolf sat with his men under guard. Merciless exhaustion yoked them.

"I assure you Sheridan will want to speak with us," Wolf said.

"I second that. The longer you detain us the angrier he will be," Hogan added.

Their guards laughed. A particularly skinny private gave them a smirk. "Sure they will. I'm thinking that we'll get to execute you spies by dark."

Thumping hooves brought more riders from the interior of the camp. They bore the Cavalry Corps flag, a blue dovetailed guidon with white crossed sabers and a large red C in the center of the sabers. Next to that was Sheridan's personal guidon of red and white opposing stars on either half. Behind them flew Custer's personal guidon, the top portion blue and the bottom red, crossed sabers in the middle.

If the stars on his shoulders didn't give the major general away, surely his chunky little frame and wide-brimmed hat did. Next to him rode the athletic General Custer with his flowing golden locks and his hussar-style jacket that denoted him as a man of flamboyance, something that only a man of authority could pull off.

The captain hurried toward the riders.

Sheridan didn't even bother to let him speak. "Release these men goddammit. Can't you see they're with us?"

The captain opened and closed his mouth. "They're dressed like civilians." Hurriedly he continued blurting out, "Their banner wasn't standard regulation, sir."

"Don't preach to me about regulations. These are my men, you stinking buffoon of an ape. Release them immediately."

The captain lowered his head. "I apologize, sir."

"I'll make you sorry. You'll be damn sure to stay on guard duty for the rest of the war."

The captain hurried toward his men, waving his arms at them. "You heard the general! Release them!"

Wolf led his men and their mounts out of detainment. He walked his horse near Sheridan, looking up at him. "Sir, we have dead."

Sheridan eyed the bodies draped over saddles. "Put them with the rest." He pointed to a growing pile.

"We'll take them back to the camp," Wilhelm said to Wolf. "You tell them what we've done."

Custer nodded fiercely at the unit. "You men rejoin us when you're done caring for the dead." His tone conveyed sacred understanding of the need to care for their fallen brothers.

Wilhelm led the rest of the men into the interior of the Cavalry Corps bivouac.

Wolf mounted and accompanied the generals to a farmhouse they'd taken as headquarters. Everywhere there were Union cavalrymen. It was an intimidating and sprawling force. A few wore bandages around limbs, but most were excited by the small battle they'd recently fought. A battle which they were claiming as a victory.

The generals and aides dismounted, followed by a much slower Wolf. His injuries and exhaustion were finally rearing their ugly head. Being surrounded by fellow soldiers in the heart of his army's camp had begun to ease his wary nerves. In some ways it was a false sense of security, but it was much more secure than being in the field on your own with only a few reliable men by your side.

The ground met his feet, and the weight on his bad leg felt unstable. The gash over his ribs ached fiercely now. He eyed the cut and lifted his arm to run a finger along the length of it. It was sharp and tender, and his clothes stuck to the wound. Gingerly, he tugged his shirt and coat free of the crusting saber slice.

Custer eyed him over his horse. "Are you wounded, Lieutenant?"

"Not enough. I can get it looked at later."

"I'll send for the surgeon as soon as we are done here." Custer wrapped the reins of his horse around a tree. "I see you're missing your saber as well."

"Left it in a man."

Custer grinned beneath a wispy mustache. "No better place for it. You didn't take it back?"

"No, sir, he escaped with it."

"We'll get you another."

Wolf nodded somberly. "Thank you, sir."

They entered the house and Wolf's entire body felt shaken and weary. He ignored the desire to collapse and stood at attention as Sheridan pulled a cigar from his double-breasted frock coat before taking a seat in a creaking chair. He tossed his hat on the table, and with a grin, he lit the cigar then blew out a cloud of smoke.

"We had a nice fight today," Sheridan said.

"Good, sir," Wolf managed.

Sheridan puffed quickly, the tip flaring orange. "Well, what news of your mission man? Don't keep me in suspense. Were we lucky? Or did you succeed? I don't see his wife with you."

"I let her go."

Sheridan grinned around his cigar. "So you did snatch her." He glanced at Custer. "I told you he did. Did you see way they folded today? Ha!"

"We heard a rumor, Lieutenant," Custer said.

"What's that, sir?"

"That Stuart was wounded."

"I suspect he will die, sir."

Sheridan leaned his elbows on the table in anticipation. "Truly?"

"We did it, sir."

"Out with it, man. The story, I want a story for Chrissake. Are you dense?"

"One of my men, Sergeant Ira Roberts, shot him through his gut and out his hip. He was in immense pain, sir."

"That name's familiar." Sheridan glanced at Custer. "Why do I know that?"

"He was promoted with me, sir. We escaped Libby together." Roberts's record was much longer. *He enlisted with me. He fought with me at Gettysburg. We drank together. He loved a girl named Rosie. He fought Hampton and lived. He had no parents and the best eyes in the company.* But Sheridan would only understand his loss on the surface.

"So the bastard shot the Knight of the Golden Spurs." Sheridan leaned back in his chair. "Bring that fellow in. I'd love to meet him."

"He's dead, sir."

"How'd it happen? Don't spare a detail."

"Stuart was attempting to rescue her. He had a unit of men tracking us. Things went bad in the negotiations and a fight broke out." He left out the duel and Payne and the revenge. He left out that he was returning Stuart's wife to the worry-stricken general and the fact that Payne and Stuart were arguing about who was going to kill him when the shot was fired.

Sheridan shook his head. "He was a formidable opponent, but it could not last. Not with Little Phil on the chase. Did you lose many men?"

"Half my men."

"Half?" Sheridan nodded, tonguing his cigar.

"Yes, sir." Wolf kept his chin high. He was uncomfortable with the number of men he'd led to the slaughter. They followed him willingly, but ultimately, they died under his command.

"Those men did a great service. It was a fair trade to bag the pompous bastard."

Wolf stood silent. He would have traded all his men's lives back for Stuart's, goddamn the war effort. Someone else's men could be sacrificed.

Sheridan regarded him for a moment with a slight nod. He had expected Wolf to share in his joy, but then he realized that Wolf wasn't and became more somber. "War is loss." He pulled out a piece of paper and an inkwell. "I'm going to give you and your men a month's furlough for your exemplary service. All charges against you and Sergeant Roberts have been dropped and will be expunged from your records."

"Thank you, sir. I will offer it to them, but they won't take it."

Sheridan squinted at him. "What man doesn't want a furlough? Time to see his family? Rest and recuperate? Marry his lass."

"I will offer it, but we are the only family we have."

Sheridan grinned. "You sound like regulars to me. I will see that Grant knows of your sacrifice and service in my reports."

"Thank you, sir."

Sheridan shook his head. "If I had a company of men like you, I'd finish this war in a week." He turned toward Custer. "You're fortunate to have these men in your brigade."

"Yes, sir. They are a special group."

"Well then, Lieutenant." Sheridan took the cigar from his mouth and waved them away. "I release you to your men. Rest while you can because this war isn't over yet." A haughty grin took over his face. "I'm thinking a move on Richmond next. Really put a stranglehold on the bastards."

Wolf saluted both the generals, forcing a grimace onto his lips. They returned his gesture of respect. Their hands drifted down, and Wolf turned, leaving the room.

His boots thumped the wood floors as he departed. He passed other officers waiting for their commander. He went back to his horse and rubbed her nose while he unwound her reins from the tree, patting her flanks.

"You did good, Sarah," he said to her. Her eyes flicked open wider. "Have to get you fed here. You're looking thin."

"Lieutenant," came a voice.

Wolf turned. Custer walked his way to him. He held out a paper. "You should take this."

He took the paper in his hands. It was the furlough orders with Sheridan's signature scrawled across the bottom. "I don't want this."

Custer's eyes flashed. "I don't care what you want. You're still in this army? These are your orders."

It took a minute before Wolf could respond. "Yes, sir."

"Then take these orders. Your men need it. Your men deserve it."

Wolf folded the paper and placed it in his pocket. He gave his general a faint smile. "Thank you, sir." But his words came out flat.

Custer gave him a short grin. "You truly killed the fellow?"

"I suppose we did."

The general eyed the trees and the men resting about them trying to stay dry. "That's too bad. I would have liked to have met him sword to sword." The glory of a duel with such a legendary enemy glowed bright in his eyes.

"I am sure he would have been delighted by the prospect."

The trumpets of battle didn't fade in Custer's eyes. "What did he look like when he was wounded? Brave? Scared?"

Wolf reflected for a moment, recalling Stuart's face after the bullet had entered his belly. "I suppose he just looked surprised."

Custer blew air through his mustache. "As is any man who faces his own demise." Each man contemplated their own end in silence. "He would have been a good man to fight alongside."

"He would have."

"Today we dealt them a grievous blow. The more momentum we build, the stronger we become."

"We'll see it through until it's done."

Custer smiled at him. "Yes, we will. Carry on, Lieutenant."

"Where is our camp, sir?" Wolf said, mounting his horse.

"About a mile in that direction." Custer pointed.

"Thank you, sir."

"Get some rest, Lieutenant Wolf. It won't be long before I need you again."

Wolf walked his horse away in silence, his furlough orders burning in his pocket.

Chapter Thirty-Six

May 12, 1864
Richmond, Virginia

The rain came in a dreary drumbeat like a funeral procession. Throughout the night and day, it seemed the heavens mourned the loss of one of the greatest cavalrymen ever known. The horses clip-clopped in a slow and deliberate manner, mimicking their riders with drooping tired heads.

The quiet sobs of Flora leaked from the carriage behind him. The more he had tried to tune out her sorrows, the more they cut at him.

The woman had been through so much over the past few years. The split of her family. The death of her daughter. And now the unexpected dispatch of her beloved husband, a man she'd traded her former life for. Ostracized by her own blood now, where would she find a place to live and acceptance?

He'd given his favorite mount, Butler, a break from the fighting and riding, letting him walk unburdened behind. His backup mount, affectionately named Charles after his hometown of Charleston, South Carolina, was a gray gelding with a fine temperament, just not the same as old Butler. The coming rain caused his hip to ache. Each sway of the horse caused discomfort, but nothing could soothe the ache in his heart at the loss of his commander.

They passed the earthen walls surrounding the outskirts of Richmond. The guards got one glimpse at the stars on his collar and stood to attention. He didn't even bother to glance their way, focusing more on traversing this solemn path of grief. Then it would be back to war.

He was the next in line to lead the corps. However, he had never thought he would be in the position of taking command. He hadn't been given any orders from Lee yet to assume his new role. It would be soon. It had to be.

They couldn't afford to be leaderless in the face of the Union campaign. Not now when things were so close to the brink. His mind drifted to Fitzhugh Lee, Marse Robert's nephew. *He wouldn't give the corps to him, would he?* But then his mind wandered to his commander's other decisions as of late. He was no career soldier, an outsider, older than most of the rest. *No, I am the senior division commander. The orders will come soon. We don't have the luxury to tarry.*

Oh, how wars change things. He had gone from being a businessman and outdoorsman to a commander rising to lead his very own division. He would never be surprised that wasn't in his blood. He was a man who did the surprising. He was cool under Death's cruel watch. But he never thought he would be the senior major general in the Army of Northern Virginia Cavalry Corps. Fate was fickle and decisive, taking men before their time and watching others fade to dust.

They turned down Grace Street, which led to the house of Dr. Charles Brewer, Stuart's brother-in-law. The house reflected both wealth and respect. It was well-kept, having been recently scrubbed of all soot. The townhouses were all in a row, and a covered lamp flickered a flame on the street corner. They stopped and Hampton dismounted.

Stiffly, he walked to the covered carriage. He looked inside and Flora's face was between her hands. Her hair had a disheveled appearance and her eyes were rimmed with raw redness and tears. "We're here, ma'am."

She shook her head in slight nods. "I can't go in there."

He gazed down. He wasn't a man of great emotion, especially with the female folk. He found much greater comfort in the company of other men. Everything was easier, more linear, and straightforward.

"You should see him."

She glanced at him. "Why? He's already gone."

He peered down again, worried he'd caused her pain. "I know I would want my kin to say their goodbyes."

Her mouth twisted. "You were supposed to watch out for him."

"Ma'am, we are at war. It still rages north of here. I was not with him when he was injured. All I know is that as soon as he discovered you were taken, he wouldn't rest until you were found."

"Heathens! Every last one of them." She took a handkerchief and wiped her nose. "And your man was no better. He should be court-martialed." Her handkerchief moved to the corners of her eyes.

He sighed. "I am truly sorry for your loss."

"What would you know about loss?"

"My brother—"Frank's ghost was waiting for them on the porch of the Brewer home, pale and somber as if he grieved Stuart's death as much as the next man.

"I've lost my daughter and now my husband."

He held his tongue before he said something in anger. "They are all grievous. I do not pretend to know your pain." Rain dribbled off the brim of his hat. "However, I would like to step out of the rain."

She sighed audibly. She took out her umbrella and handed it to him. He slid it open, holding it high to ensure she didn't get wet. She offered him a hand, and he gracefully accepted before helping her down. Her boots sank into the mud with a squinch and he guided her from the muddy street.

Together they traversed the steps to the porch. A man with long muttonchops and a shaved chin awaited them there. He nervously wrung out his hands as they approached.

"Flora," he said. "I'm so sorry. We did all we could." He reached out to embrace her and she held out a hand. "Please, just take me to him."

"Of course, ma'am. General?" Charles said.

"Wade Hampton."

Charles lowered his head in respect. "I've heard of your brave exploits."

"Charles," Flora said.

"Yes." He pushed open the door and led her up a staircase.

Flora hiked her dress, forging her way up the stairs. There were other women and a cluster of Stuart's aides in the parlor. McClellan, Boteler, and Garnett. Everyone dried their eyes, watching Flora walk past.

Hampton nodded to the women but didn't say a word as was his way. *Frank would have made them smile, but now he was only a ghost along with the rest.* "Gentlemen."

The largest of the three aides, Henry McClellan, wiped his eye. "I apologize for our appearance. We are most distraught."

"No need, Henry. This is a most joyless time."

"He gave me his bay, General. A fine, beautiful animal. He said I should have him because he was bigger and would hold me better." He wiped his eyes again with a smile. "It is a mount fit for a king."

"If this country ever had royalty, he surely would have been," Hampton said.

"The finest."

"How can we go on?" Boteler said, his voice quavering. He nudged a finger beneath his glasses.

Hampton's brow creased, his voice growing in anger. "You have a responsibility to your country."

Boteler took a step back, and all the men appeared admonished with their honor called into question.

Lifting a hand, Hampton asked for forgiveness. "I apologize, we carry on because our nation needs us." He waited a moment, letting his words settle on them. "I must pay my respects."

The aides all nodded their understanding. The situation was gut-wrenching for them all.

The wooden steps complained as he made his way to the second floor. He was surprised by the man he met at the top of the stairs. He was tall and thin, and the goatee that hung from the tip of his chin reminded Hampton of a billy goat. His hair had a slight wave to it and stuck out around his ears. Sharp cheekbones accented his slender face. He held a top hat in one of his hands and wore a fine coat with a black bowtie.

"General, I didn't expect you," he said.

"Mr. President."

"These are grave times under which we meet. The heavens send their rain as the angels mourn."

"These have been hard days."

"I feel we will see more mourning rain before we are done."

"Aye, we will, but we will prevail. Even now Lee repositions to block Grant."

"I've heard. Do you think there is still a threat to the capital?"

"I do not, sir. They would never be able to hold it."

Davis blinked away his piercing stare. "Very good. I have full confidence in you, General."

"Thank you, sir."

"I am afraid I must keep this meeting brief. I must depart. There is much to do, and I like to have an eye on everything."

"Of course. Your presence here is an honor to us all."

"He was a dutiful patriot. If only all were so willing to give their lives for their new country." Davis walked down the steps, disappearing out the front door.

Many of Davis's friends held positions within the military as political appointments, something that should have gone to the side in favor of men with experience and proven leadership. He'd been heavy-handed with his control of the government, and Hampton's men still found themselves foraging and robbing the Yankees to stay fed. But he dismissed the man to pay his respects to a better man.

He turned toward the room. Crying could be heard from inside its confines. He gently pushed the door open. Flora lay across Stuart's chest, her arms covering her face. The general's face was pallid and lacking any of the lusters of life.

Stuart's beard laid limp, no longer bushy. His hair was damp and stuck to the side of his head. His appearance was almost peaceful.

A faint scent of death lingered in the room. Before the war, he would have turned away or covered his nose, but now it was second nature as he'd grown immune to it.

Silently, he stood observing. Time ticked by and his mind went numb.

Flora peered at him. "You can pay your respects."

He gave her a slight nod and joined her. He knelt to his knees one at a time. The floor was hard beneath him, and his kneecaps instantly complained. He folded his hands in front of him, and ignoring the smell, he began to pray.

Dear Lord, take this brave knight of the South into your heavenly Kingdom. He was always kind and just. His bravery knew no equal. He was a man but of the noblest kind. A warrior but more gallant. I pray that he finds peace in your gracious embrace. Help his family through this difficult time and ease their suffering. Help us fill his void on the field of battle. Carry your servants to victory. In Christ's name. "Amen."

Slowly, he got to his feet. He brushed off his knees to regain the feeling where they'd gone numb. Flora's red eyes were drenched with tears. "I just don't know if I can do this again."

He reached out and took her hand. "You can and you will."

"How do you know?"

"Is there any other way?"

She blinked rapidly and swallowed. "I will never love another man. I could never bear it."

He'd heard of widows never marrying again, but he had remarried after his wife had passed. It was all about companionship. A man could have more than one companion. He supposed a woman could as well in her life. But to take the dead's cold hand in yours and sleep in a cold dark bed for the rest of your life wasn't living; it was playing dead.

"You follow your heart, Mrs. Stuart."

She breathed through her mouth. "I am not mad at you, General."

"It's okay if you are, but I know you're not." Sometimes the anger made it easier to surpass the grief.

"But earlier."

"Do not concern yourself with that. This is the cruelest time on a person's soul." He'd been through it with Margaret, his first wife. Her affliction had come quick, and in twenty-four hours, she was gone. He supposed her situation wasn't that much different. A love taken before their time. His daughter, Sarah, reminded him of her every time he saw her; she looked just like her mother. Then his two beautiful boys, Wade and Preston. Each one like her in their own way.

"My behavior was shameful." She lifted her chin and dared him to counter her statement.

"If I could have saved him, I would have given my life."

Her mouth quivered, but she maintained her composure. "I know you would have. You are a noble warrior."

He felt blood rush to his cheeks. "You have my sympathy. I've never met a man with more zeal for life. He made men believe in the cause. Believe in their invincibility. We have a void to fill in our leadership and in our hearts."

"His loss will be felt for the rest of our lives." She picked up Stuart's sheathed sword that was leaning against a chair. "This is to go to our son. I have half a mind to give it away. War only brought this family suffering. Maybe it's best we never know it exists."

"Give the boy the sword."

"Why? So he can fall wielding it against another foe? Then a mother will be with only a daughter and nothing else."

"Give it to him so he has something to admire of his father. Something to remember him by."

"Would that he had a father to show him these things instead of a sharp piece of metal."

Hampton dipped his chin to chest, forcing his beard to fan outward. "One day he will want to know."

She studied the saber in her hands.

He didn't know what else to say, but the enemy still roamed free on his country's sacred ground. "I must take my leave for the Yankees do not rest." He turned to depart, and her voice stopped him in his tracks.

"General."

He regarded her from over his shoulder.

Her voice held the strictest conviction, as if she were a queen. "Whip those damn Yankees."

A short smile took his lips. "It'd be a pleasure, ma'am."

Chapter Thirty-Seven

May 12, 1864

Custer's Brigade bivouac, Near Yellow Tavern, Virginia

"Yellabelly," Hogan said with a smile. The Irishman shook hands with him, cocking his head as he spoke with sarcasm.

"You know I don't like that term," Wolf said with a smirk.

"Yet it is yours all the same."

"Not sure we could have done it without you and your men."

"Never a dull minute doing business with you." Hogan regarded the two sharpshooters behind him. "We sure as hell couldn't have done it without you and your men."

"Are you going to ride with us to take Richmond?"

Hogan shook his head. "Sheridan doesn't know it yet, but he isn't going to take Richmond."

"He isn't? We're so close. Stuart's command is leaderless and on the run."

"Leaderless, I think not. They have lost, yes, but other skilled commanders line their ranks, and at this point, what good would capturing Richmond do?"

"End the war?"

"No, no, no. This war will carry on past that now. Early in the war, yes. Now? Not so much. You'll be marching on past and rejoining Grant. I have a feeling we've been too long from him anyway."

"Really? We won't take Richmond."

"Not yet," Hogan said with a wink.

"George. Skinner," Wolf said with a nod.

"Pleasure riding with you boys," Skinner said.

George nodded with red-rimmed eyes yet a flat mouth. He had taken the loss of his friend very hard. Grief filled his eyes. He nodded to Wolf.

"I'm sure we will meet again," Hogan said. "You know if you ever get tired of this cavalry business, I might have a place for you over at the BMI."

"I heard they only took yellabellies."

"Ha. The very best yellabellies." Hogan stuck out his hand and they shook again. He then turned to mount his horse. "I know we will be seeing each other again."

"I'll look forward to it."

"Good luck, Lieutenant. If you can, stay in one piece."

"You as well."

Hogan waved as he steered his horse away. The BMI agent and the sharpshooters turned their horses, riding them through the campsites.

"Wily fellow, ain't he?" Wilhelm said.

"He is peculiar to say the least." He watched the men weave through the tents and fires until they disappeared.

Wolf wasn't sure if that was the path for him. The Bureau of Military Information always seemed to have a trick up their sleeves, dealing in the shadowy parts of a war. Perhaps he'd seen enough of this shadow war, always swirling around the rank-and-file conflict like a dangerous mist.

"Come, Lieutenant, let's pay our respects."

They gathered the remainders of the unit and they stood impatiently in a somber living line over the mounds of dead friends that now claimed permeant residence in Virginia soil. Dark dismal shadows cloaked the seven earthen mounds like funeral shrouds.

Other voices drifted from nearby campfires, but none were clear. They were only the voices of living men. The leaves rustled beneath the assault of raindrops. The graves containing the dead men were quiet, nothing stirring, and everything was still. Nelson adjusted his feet uncomfortably in the dirt causing it to crunch beneath his boot.

Dan's cheeks were rosy, and his chest shook as he quietly sobbed. The missing men gnawed at each and every man still standing, even Adams and Nelson.

Wilhelm and Wolf exchanged a glance. Shugart was the unit's resident holy man and he was dead and gone. Wolf's voice surprised him, words forming at his lips. They didn't hold the grace and faith of Shugart, but it was at least something. "These men know the true meaning of sacrifice. They came back for one of their own, knowing full well that safety lay in the other direction."

Dan continued to sob audibly, sniffling between cries.

"I know that these men will find Heaven. I know their cause, if only to protect their fellow man, was sound, and if God cannot see the nobleness in such actions then surely he knows their hearts better than me. For I saw men of valor and paying for that valor with blood. May they rest in peace."

A soft chorus of amens came from the short line of troopers.

"I've never led better men in battle than these. May God take their souls," Wilhelm added.

They stood silent.

Adams took his turn. "We didn't start the war out with you folk." He eyed Wilhelm who stood emotionless. "But we fought a war with you folk, and we fought well. They will be missed." He dipped his chin when he was done and nudged Nelson.

The big bear of a man eyed the rest of the unit. "It was a good fight. Sorry." He clasped his hands in front of him. His brief but kind words surprised Wolf, but he said nothing.

Dan waved a hand in front of him, shaking his head in grief. "No." The large Polish trooper walked away from the graves.

"You all will not be forgotten," Wolf said. He stood there for a moment, gazing at the ground.

Northern blood had been spilt, mixing with Southern blood and American soil as one. No one was absolved from it. The war had cut them deep, down to the very bones of their souls.

Stuart had fallen. Flora had suffered and would continue to only live with her husband's memory. Stuart's children would remember almost nothing of their dashing father, any moments mere renditions from their mother and family. His death was something his family would all have to live with. It was something that would haunt them for the rest of their lives. No man of flesh and bone to raise them, to teach them to ride, to walk his daughter down the aisle. Nothing more than fleeting memories.

Grant still battered Lee southward. Lee resisted with every bit of his might. They would continue watering the nation's fair ground with Southern and Northern blood alike. And when it was done, Wolf wouldn't be surprised if the nation was merely an island surrounded by the blood of those that resided there.

"It's not finished," Wolf said.

The men around him nodded. They filtered away from their friends and comrades one by one. Each man stared as if expecting their friends to rise from the dead or jump from the soil in some big hoax, but no dirt stirred in such a cruel jest.

Only Wilhelm stood with him now, minds wrestling between loss and vengeance.

"Do you think Payne still lives?" Wolf said. His voice was flat. He held disdain for the man and wanted revenge, but he was levelheaded. Wilhelm knew of the vendetta and shared Wolf's hate.

"If he yet lives, we will finish the game."

His words were twofold for he spoke about his own quest for vengeance as well. His crusade to avenge the death of his son at the hands of Wade Hampton.

Wilhelm's eyes still burned. It hid behind all the duty and honor and brave soldierly virtues. It was a smoldering fire that could only be quenched upon his or Hampton's death.

He was a man that Wolf wanted on his side. They were bound by a common cause. His time would come. Wolf didn't know when, but when it did, neither he nor Wilhelm would hesitate. Their fingers would be quick on triggers, their hands steadfast on swords, their minds cool and calm through the gun smoke, their wits quick so they would deal out death even quicker.

A violin sawed a lonely tune, and a few men picked up a song too faint for

Wolf to make out. But the words were sad and beautiful. It was the song that longed for a forgotten time faraway. He took out his furlough papers and tore them to pieces, letting them fall on the graves of the fallen.

Wilhelm silently nodded his head and turned away. He walked back to the campfire and took up his whetting stone. The soft sound of metal sharpening on stone could be heard scraping away before the burning fires of vengeance.

"Your death won't go unpunished," Wolf said to Roberts's grave. No response came from the oblong earthen mound, only silence.

It wasn't finished for Wolf. Not while Payne still breathed. It wasn't finished for Wilhelm. He supposed this war would never die in their minds. It just wouldn't finish. The divide was too great.

Still more blood would be needed to feed the American gods of war. Only when every last drop had been spilt would this nation rest. And he carried on because he still had more to give.

Historical and Personal Note

Thank you for reading the latest installment of the Northern Wolf series. I truly hope you enjoyed reading this novel as much as I enjoyed writing it.

Writing historical fiction is like walking a tightrope between fact and fiction. If you go too far toward history, you can fall into the doldrums of just a history book. If you swing too far toward fiction, you risk becoming too fantastical for your audience. In themselves, these aren't bad things. I am literally surrounded by history books as I write this, but if you are trying to write historical fiction, they are to be treaded carefully.

The bones of a good story remain the same no matter the genre: plot, characters, conflicts, and theme. But for a historical fiction novel, we need all these things and the history itself. Sometimes they walk hand in hand and the history practically writes the novel. At other times, the author must really massage his tale into the events. In any case, I think it is important to lay out the facts and fictions to facilitate a better understanding of the story.

The military actions surrounding the Overland or Wilderness Campaign is in fact a very difficult battle to study because of the almost continuous maneuvering by Grant/Meade and Lee. The campaign was spearheaded by the costly and inconclusive Battle of the Wilderness. It was a truly horrible affair where many wounded were burned alive in the fires surrounding the battle, and the Union did the unthinkable. They continued their campaign. This led to an almost ceaseless hit-and-run war between Grant's huge army as he attempted to out-position Lee and force him into a battle of his choosing.

There are many reasons why Grant's task was nearly impossible. The terrain, the varying capabilities of his commanders, the vastness of his army, and the expertise of his opponents are only a few of the reasons that this campaign was a struggle for Grant and the Army of the Potomac.

Grant's army sustained a number of tactical defeats, but ultimately the campaign was considered a strategic success as his goal was to pressure and destroy Lee's army and not merely sack Richmond. He mostly succeeded in exactly what he'd been sent east to do: grind the Army of Northern Virginia down and expedite the end of the war.

However, his victory was by no means total. Lee had won most of the tactical battles in the campaign and his army was not completely beaten, but much of their campaigning ability had diminished. The war most likely would have ended sooner had Petersburg been taken quickly instead of after a nine-month-long siege. The Overland Campaign marked the beginning of the end for the Southern Cause.

The casualties during the Overland Campaign were staggering and the bloodiest of the war—55,000 for the Union and 33,600 for the Confederacy. Historians tend to disagree on the number of casualties on both sides. But what they don't disagree on are the percentages of troops lost. While the Union suffered more casualties, it was a smaller percentage of their armies. Reinforcements were sent to replace the dead, so the impact to the Union war effort was less dramatic than it was to the Confederacy. With less manpower and fewer recruitment pools, the Confederacy struggled to replace their losses including those in leadership.

As this campaign was critical to the Union winning the war, along with Lincoln's 1864 election, there has been much study about the campaign as well as the individual battles that took place throughout it. I found the book *The Battles for Spotsylvania Court House and the Road to Yellow Tavern* by Gordon C. Rhea extremely valuable in making clear my understanding of the battles depicted in this book. I also found *Custer and His Wolverines* and *Gentleman and Soldier: A Biography of Wade Hampton III*, both by Edward G. Longacre, instrumental in grasping the men and the conflict they fought in.

I took much more liberty in this novel than in the two previous ones. While many of the main events did happen, some others did not. I wanted the reader to have a fully entertaining and exciting novel, and in order to do so, I had to bend historical fact in a few places and make it truly fiction. Let me break down some of the major liberties that were taken.

Elizabeth Van Lew or "Crazy Bet" was a Union spy and a member of Richmond's social elite. Her story is incredibly interesting. She feigned mental affliction throughout the war and is widely lauded as one of the best spies of either side. She located and retrieved Dahlgren's body after it had been taken from its display and buried in a shallow grave. She reburied his remains properly in a secret location, much to Jefferson Davis's chagrin when he sent for it to be returned North. Dahlgren's remains were delivered to his family after the war was over.

The relationship between Van Lew and Benjamin Butler was fictional as well, but they did communicate frequently on spy activities. In particular, they discussed the strength of the Confederate capital. It is important to note that Van Lew's intelligence assessment was largely ignored during Butler's planned raid. It was again ignored in the Kilpatrick-Dahlgren raid where she estimated a much larger force would be necessary to take Richmond than was sent on either raid. It can be speculated that her estimates were dismissed based on her gender and lack of military experience.

Erasmus Ross was a very real fixture at Libby Prison. Although he never ran the prison, he was a clerk who kept count and tabs on the prisoners. He probably wasn't as cruel as depicted and embodied traits ascribed to the prison's commandant Major Thomas Turner, who is sometimes confused with Richard Turner, a cruel jailor who was singled out for investigation after the war. The prisoners never suspected Ross was in fact a Union sympathizer, orchestrating and aiding the escape of Union prisoners and passing intelligence to leadership.

Many of the activities the prisoners participated in while held in Libby Prison were actual things they did to entertain themselves: riddles, chess, the *Libby Chronicle*(when it operated), debates, trials, even Spanish foreign language instruction by Federico Fernández Cavada, who went on to lead the Cuban fight for independence from Spain during the Ten Years' War.

We could probably have an endless debate over which prison was the worst, but understand that Libby Prison was one of the worst on either side. In my opinion, it was only overshadowed by Belle Isle and the deadliest prison, Andersonville. There were notoriously bad prisons in the North as well. Camp Douglas in Illinois and Elmira Prison in New York stand out. The only leg up the Northern prisons had on the Southern ones was access to more adequate supplies. An excellent book on the life of the prisoners is *Libby Prison Breakout: The Daring Escape from the Notorious Civil War Prison* by Joseph Wheelan.

No one was sent on a secret mission to kidnap J. E. B. Stuart's wife. This was a major liberty taken on my part, but I thought it made for an interesting premise for the Battle of Yellow Tavern. However, she did come close to capture at Beaver Dam which drove Stuart into a panic about her safety. She was staying at the nearby home of Confederate Colonel Edmund Fontaine when the Union went about destroying the rail station there.

Sheridan did set out on May 9, 1864, to destroy the Army of Northern Virginia's Cavalry Corps as a part of Grant's Overland Campaign. Scholars are split over the effectiveness of his efforts with most settling on how it would have been much more valuable for him to assist Grant instead of charging off on his own.

Grant did approve of his mission much to the indignation of Meade. It created a rift in Grant's command structure. The death of J. E. B. Stuart, the Knight of the Golden Spurs, Beau Sabreur, the beloved ostrich-plumed hat wearing and dashing gentleman cavalier haunted the Confederate war efforts for the duration of the conflict.

It was a major morale blow, and he was widely mourned by all, even his adversaries. It threw Lee's Cavalry Corps out of order for a time as succession was decided. I believe it was an interesting hesitation on Lee's part to not have a clear successor in such an important role. It seems in part his hesitation was due to the fact his son was a possible replacement since Hampton wasn't a Virginian, a professional soldier, and was older than most other commanders (the position required a great deal of energy and zeal).

For months Lee had his various individual cavalry division commanders report directly to him when operating apart from one another. This happened until command of the Cavalry Corps was given to Wade Hampton, who led them for the rest of the war with great skill and success despite the waning war effort. Surely giving the Cavalry Corps to Hampton earlier would have greatly aided Lee and freed him up to try and salvage what remained of his war effort. I do not think this would have changed the outcome of the war but would have perhaps lengthened it instead, again this is mere speculation.

The Battle of Yellow Tavern played out much the same way it was described in the novel. Although three of Sheridan's divisions took part in the raid, Custer's forces were at the center of most of the battle's fighting. The battle followed the initial redeployments of Lomax's Brigade as they were flanked by Devin and Gibbs. The battle lulled as Wickham took his place along a ridge. In the afternoon, Custer was the centerpiece for the battle's finale. With support of elements from Wilson's division on his left and Gibbs's Brigade on his right, Custer's Brigade marched forward, focusing on silencing Stuart's artillery. In the defense of Griffin's Baltimore Light Artillery, Stuart was mortally wounded as he tried to fill the hole in his line. The command passed to Fitz Lee and the rebels retreated.

Most historians attribute Stuart's mortal wounding to Private John A. Huff of the 5th Michigan, but it was largely disputed during and after the war who was responsible. I gave Sergeant Ira Roberts the credit, but he is a fictional character.

In reality, Private Huff was a forty-four-year-old former Berdan sharpshooter and was said to have shot Stuart with a .44 caliber pistol anywhere from 30 to over 400 yards away, but considering the weapon, it was probably from closer. There were others who claimed to have fired the shot that killed Stuart: Private Charles Dunn, Sergeant R. M. Bellinger, and even others from different regiments outside the Michigan Brigade. This is unlikely, however, due to the positioning of the regiments during the attack in relation to where Stuart fell. Mystery still clouds the facts today largely because Huff was killed a few weeks later and then Dunn a few weeks after that.

The introduction of the Native American sharpshooters (they were not citizens at the onset of the war) was a fictionalized account of fact. K Company of the 1st Michigan Sharpshooters was almost entirely composed of Anishinabek men made up of Ojibwe, Odawa, and Potawatomi tribes from northern Michigan. The Anishinabek made a public declaration against slavery and requested to fight on the Union's behalf despite public hostility toward arming indigenous peoples for national service. In 1863, losses from the war prompted the government to accept the indigenous peoples into their ranks. K Company served with distinction in Burnside and Parke's IX Corps during the Overland Campaign and the Siege of Petersburg, including the horrible Battle of the Crater.

George and James were not actual people and are entirely fictional. While there are some extraordinary individuals from this unit, I wanted to have more of a writer's license with their narrative. If you are interested in learning more of the actual unit, please check out *Deadly Aim: The Civil War Story of Michigan's Anishinaabe Sharpshooters* by Sally M. Walker, or for a more biographical account of the individuals, read *Warriors in Mr. Lincoln's Army: Native American Soldiers Who Fought in the Civil War* by Quita V. Shier.

Hampton did not attempt to visit Stuart on his deathbed. He stayed with Lee's army as they dueled with Grant. He knew very little in fact, just that Stuart went after Sheridan, and was surprised to find out on May 12, 1864, that his commander had been slain and his men routed near Richmond. Despite some differences, the men had an excellent working relationship and admired one another. Hampton issued a general order on May 16th that stated as much.

There were a few locations that stand out that I took liberty with: Shady Grove Methodist Church, Davidson Farmhouse, and Yellow Tavern.

The small church where Stuart met with his commanders before riding in pursuit of Sheridan was fictionalized. I gave credit to a nearby Shady Grove Methodist Church, but I was unable to locate the name of the actual church. The Davidson Farmhouse was completely fictional. Yellow Tavern was an actual abandoned establishment and no longer stands.

I sincerely hope that you enjoyed this novel as Wolf's story continues and our nation continues to bleed. If it isn't apparent yet, Wolf still has more of a tale to tell. Please be on the lookout for the next novel in the series.

Best,

Daniel Greene
March 31, 2020

Extras

Thanks for reading! The third novel of the Northern Wolf Series ended with blood. With every battle, the war becomes more a more personal conflict for those that survive. As you may have gathered, there are more books in the series coming your way. Pick up *Northern Dawn* **Book 4 of the Northern Wolf Series here!**

The Greene Army Newsletter: Want exclusive updates on new work, contests, patches, artwork, and events where you can meet up with Daniel? An elite few will get a chance to join **Greene's Recon Team**: a crack unit of talented readers ready and able to review advance copies of his books anytime, anywhere with killer precision. Sign up for spam-free Greene Army Newsletter here: http://www.danielgreenebooks.com/?page_id=7741

Reviews: If you have the time, please consider writing a review. Reviews are important tools that I use to hone my craft. If you do take the time to write a review, I would like to thank you personally for your feedback and support. Don't be afraid to reach out. I love meeting new readers!

You can find me anywhere below.

Facebook Fan Club: *The Greene Army - Daniel Greene Fan Club*
Facebook: *Daniel Greene Books*
Instagram: *Daniel Greene Instagram*

Website: *DanielGreeneBooks.com*
Email: *DanielGreeneBooks@gmail.com*

A special thanks to all those who've contributed to the creation of this novel. A novel is a huge feat and would remain as a file cluttering my desktop without the contributions of so many wonderfully supportive people. This includes my dedicated Alpha Readers, Greene's Recon Team, Greene Army, my editor Lisa, my cover artist Tim, Polgarus formatters, and especially my readers. Without readers, this is an unheard/unread tale. I can't wait to share more stories with you in the future.

About the Author

Daniel Greene is the award-winning author of the growing apocalyptic thriller series The End Time Saga and the historical fiction Northern Wolf series. He is an avid traveler and physical fitness enthusiast with a deep passion for history. He is inspired by the works of George R.R. Martin, Steven Pressfield, Bernard Cornwell, and George Romero. Although a Midwesterner for life, he's lived long enough in Virginia to call it home.

Books by Daniel Greene

The End Time Saga
End Time
The Breaking
The Rising
The Departing
The Holding
The Standing (Coming 2020)

The Gun (Origin Short Story)

Northern Wolf Series
Northern Wolf
Northern Hunt
Northern Blood
Northern Dawn

Made in the USA
Monee, IL
21 August 2022

12152226R00187